ONE

I stared at the blank canvas in front of me, incredibly frustrated. My preliminary sketches lay scattered on the floor at my feet. I'd painted over the lightly penciled lines I'd transferred onto the canvas from them twice already, unable to gain the same feeling from the larger version of the images that I'd had when I'd sketched them in my notebook.

I couldn't do this. I was a failure. I was a fool to ever think I could quit my day job. Just like I had been a fool to believe in lasting romantic love. Now, I had neither a job nor a husband, each taken by a woman who was younger and more attractive than me.

Over the years, I'd taken commissions for my art, and though I made a nice amount of pocket change, I'd never managed to make enough to support myself fully, relying on the shared income from my husband's and my day jobs to pay all the bills. After a brutal divorce, I'd convinced myself that now was the time of my life where I really needed to go for it and do a full show, encouraged by the dealer at my local gallery who loved the samples of my work that I'd brought in.

I was tired of managing a retail store. My husband had convinced me that was what I was meant for and that my art was only a hobby that would never support me. After signing the final papers severing our life together, I'd felt a sudden determination to prove him wrong. Seven months later, I'd proved nothing to myself but that rent and utilities and necessities like food could burn through my settlement money far too quickly, and if I didn't finish enough paintings, I wouldn't be having the show the dealer had offered to host.

At forty-two, I should already know what I wanted to be when I grow up, but I was deeply afraid that Mike was right all along, and that my art really was only a hobby. Now that I had to rely on it to support me, I despised this makeshift studio and the stench of oil paints. I hated the sight of those blank canvases mocking me, and worse, all the inspiration that had once filled me had fled the moment I'd determined this would be my future.

In pure frustration, I kicked over the easel, watching the canvas crash to the ground with a guilty feeling of satisfaction. It felt so good after months of struggle only to end up with less than a handful of finished pieces—none of which made me happy. I continued the destruction, flinging the cup of brushes across the room so the glass shattered against the wall, sending some of the most expensive brushes I owned flying.

As they clattered to the floor, the distinct sound of some of them snapping playing like music to my ears, I stomped on my collection of sketches, grinding my shoe into the paper and twisting the ball of my foot until the tearing sound made me laugh aloud.

I knew I was on the edge of hysterical, but I'd been pushed to my limit at this point. I had tried, damn it! I'd made my entire life about living up to everyone's expectations for me. I'd been an excellent student, a hard-working employee, and a

THE CLONE'S MATE

SUSAN TROMBLEY

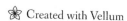 Created with Vellum

devoted and faithful wife. I'd never had the chance to be a mother because Mike hadn't wanted children, and since I was fool enough to think I loved him and wanted to spend the rest of my life with him, I'd convinced myself that I didn't want them either.

Now, I felt like I was too old to have them without risk, and he had a beautiful and pregnant wife who was only twenty-four. Apparently, it was only that Mike didn't want to have children with *me*. He'd had no objection to getting Melissa pregnant.

I left the sketches and made my way to the finished canvases propped against one wall of the second bedroom of the apartment I was renting. Picking up the topmost painting, I studied the dark and gritty alien landscape, rendered in sharply contrasted oranges and blues, broken up by vast expanses of many shades of gray and black. The desolate, volcano-riddled alien surface appeared empty and lifeless, but a small hint of hope existed in the slightest bit of green peeking up from a barely visible crack in the shadowy basalt.

I carried the painting I'd spent hours laboring over to the fallen easel, recalling my misery and struggle simply to mix the colors and then move the brush. Every stroke of that landscape had cost me dearly, sucking all the joy I'd once taken in creating art out of me.

With a triumphant cry, I smashed the canvas down over one wooden leg of the easel, and it pierced through the painting right at that tiny green sprig of a plant, completely destroying it.

I tossed the painting aside and turned my attention to the rest of the small pile, a slow grin spreading on my lips.

HOURS LATER, paint still spattering my clothing, I headed to the local hardware store, still breathing heavily as I bounced between elation and despair after a brief call to the art dealer that had ended with her disappointment but understanding.

I was done. Done with art that no longer inspired me. Done with my ex-husband and the heartache his infidelity had caused. Done with twisting myself like a pretzel to make everyone around me happy when I couldn't find my own contentment.

It was time to take my own future into my hands and grow up and stop daydreaming about being a great artist—or even one good enough to support herself with her work. Clearly, art wasn't my destiny. Equally clearly, I didn't have much of one, so it was time to make my own.

I just wish I knew what that would be as I strolled through the cleaning section of the hardware store while I waited for one of the employees to finish mixing the wall paint I'd ordered to repaint the bedroom after I'd ruined the existing paint with my cathartic destruction.

I'd seen an ad for an online college posted on the bulletin board near the registers, and I planned to study it a bit closer before leaving to see if any of the offered programs interested me. I only had a vague idea of what I'd like to do for a future career, since nothing had ever really appealed to me other than being creative, and there didn't seem to be many modern jobs that called for the kind of creativity I liked.

With a basket full of cleaning products and wall painting supplies, I returned to the paint counter, slowing my rush to grab my paint when I spotted the drop-dead gorgeous guy standing at the counter staring down at the finish samples.

"Satin is the best for the interior," I said impulsively, my heart thudding because I'd been so bold as to speak first to a total stranger. That wasn't my usual MO.

The man looked up from the samples, turning to regard me with eyes that were a striking and unusual purple color that looked unnatural, but coordinated well with dark brown hair tousled in a slightly long cut. His eyes had to be contacts, but the lush, long eyelashes that framed them were probably real, and I couldn't help feeling a little jealous of them.

He studied me briefly and I couldn't read the expression on his handsome face. There was no change in the elevation of his finely shaped eyebrows or movement in his chiseled jawline or tilt in his sensual lips.

"Is that so?" he asked in an oddly accented voice, glancing back at the paint samples. "You are an expert?" His gaze shifted to my basket of goods.

I couldn't place the accent, but it was subtle enough that I could easily understand him. What disturbed me more was his complete lack of expression and the almost disdainful tone that underlay his words. I already regretted speaking to a stranger. I should have gone with my introvert instincts and just grabbed up my paint from the counter without a word to him. This guy was way out of my league, and my already crushed self-esteem could not take a brutal brush-off after such an ugly divorce.

Still, now I couldn't avoid speaking to him again without making things even more awkward than they already were, so I shrugged, giving him a hesitant, sheepish smile. "Not of wall paint. I've just found from personal experience that satin gives a nice finish that doesn't show too much of the wall's flaws but it's still easy to wipe down."

He frowned, tapping long, elegant fingers on the counter. "I did not come here for paint," he said abruptly, just as the cute, young woman who did all the mixing returned to her station, her eyes lighting up when she spotted the man.

"Hello again, Jason!" she said with that tone in her voice

that told me I'd been a complete idiot to even think of flirting with the guy.

Obviously, he was interested in this other woman.

She was clearly more his type than I was, being a good fifteen years younger than me at least, and probably thirty pounds lighter, with not a single hint of gray in her long, thick, shiny hair.

Her name was Amy, according to her tag, and she had been unfailingly kind and polite while I'd ordered my paint. I couldn't hold the fact that she was younger and adorable and attractive to a man like this against her.

The man suddenly breathed in deeply, and his inhale was loud enough that I heard it. Then he glanced from Amy to me, nodding slightly. His gaze drifted from me to the aisle behind me, and I reflexively turned to look over my shoulder, seeing a woman standing there studying the rollers and drop sheets.

If Amy was cute, this woman was stunningly beautiful on a whole new level that belonged in Hollywood or on some Paris runway. I was surprised I hadn't seen her when I'd passed through that aisle, but I could hardly miss her now. Her eyes lifted to meet the man's and I could practically feel something between them crackling in the air as she also nodded slightly, a slow smile tilting her full, bee-stung lips. They looked naturally that large and shapely, rather than the odd duck-face look that sometimes happened with fillers. Her eyes were large and stunning, the deep purple color visible even from a dozen feet away.

Suddenly, the man turned to face me fully, completely ignoring poor Amy, whose face fell at being summarily dismissed by the hot guy that had to already be taken by the beautiful woman in the aisle.

"Will you join me for a drink?" he asked, his bizarre purple gaze fixed on me.

Even though he was looking right at me, I blinked at him in

confusion. It took a long, awkward silence before I realized he was addressing me, and it was only Amy's expression that cinched it in my head.

She looked shocked and then offended, her eyes hardening as her gaze raked up and down my form, taking in my slovenly clothing, mussed hair sprinkled with grays, and extra weight. The sweet, friendly employee was gone as she shoved my paint can across the counter, her eyes shifting back to the man, who still watched me as if she weren't there.

"Your paint is done," she snapped, "you can go now. I have other customers to deal with."

I huffed, taken aback by her rudeness. If I were her manager, I would have counseled her on her tone. Since I wasn't her manager, I took offense at her attitude, and I hate to admit it, but that was what made me tilt my head coquettishly and beam at the man with the most charming smile I could muster as I fluttered my pathetic excuse for lashes.

"I *am* getting thirsty. I suppose I could use a drink right now." I gestured with one hand towards the front of the store. "There's a coffee shop a couple stores down from here, if you'd like to meet there."

I shot a triumphant glance at Amy, who glared at me, even as she slapped a wooden stir stick onto the top of my paint can.

"I can walk with you to the coffee shop," the man said as he grabbed up my paint and the stick, then reached for my laden basket. "Please, allow me to help you with your burdens."

I couldn't remember the last time a man had offered to carry something heavy for me. Or hold open the door, or do anything chivalric, for that matter. I was pretty convinced such gestures were out of fashion now—much to my disappointment, as I'd always found them romantic.

Still, I was hesitant to allow him to take my basket, pulling it close to me and eyeing my gallon of paint in his hand with doubt. I shouldn't follow this complete stranger, even to a coffee shop that was public, without knowing more about him than his first name. It also almost felt like he was holding my paint hostage.

"Maybe it's better if I check out and load these things into my car before meeting you," I said, reaching one hand towards the can.

He shifted it away from my grasp, giving me a slow, devastating smile that bared perfect white teeth. "Your burdens look heavy. I'll carry them for you out to your vehicle. Then I will enjoy treating you to a... coffee." The way his lids narrowed around his eyes made that last offer sound like a promise of something far more delicious than a simple coffee.

Damn, he was so handsome he was almost beautiful. I didn't think I'd ever seen anyone so attractive in person. He looked more like an airbrushed photo of the hottest male model come to life. The only thing he was missing was the bit of scruff that was so popular with male models nowadays, though I personally liked that his flawless jawline was smooth shaven. Combined with the perfection of his skin, that smoothness seemed almost otherworldly, like he was some ethereal fae prince suddenly revealing himself to a mere mortal—and asking her out for coffee.

All in all, a pretty mundane offer, but one I couldn't refuse, because quite frankly, Amy was getting nice and pissed off that he didn't even glance her way again. I knew my satisfaction about that was petty, and perhaps it was a transfer of my rage about the woman who'd ended up with my husband—and the baby I'd never been allowed to have—that fueled my pettiness towards this young woman. I didn't like acknowledging that about myself, but hey, I'd just violently destroyed months of my own hard work. I wasn't exactly in a healthy emotional place to begin with.

I shrugged, giving in to the offer. How often did a girl get an offer like this? I'd be a fool not to see where it went. If nothing else, perhaps I could hook up with the hottest guy I'd ever seen. Sure, I wasn't likely to be able to keep him around for long, but even a brief affair would be a boost to my self-esteem at this point. He made Michael look like Quasimodo.

Still, although I lowered my free hand and even held out my basket for him to take it, I glanced with uncertainty towards the aisle where the beautiful woman had stood. She was no longer there, and I wondered where she'd gotten off to. Her appearance and the way she and this guy had looked at each other made me uneasy.

He seemed to sense the direction of my thoughts, perhaps because I was looking in the direction of where she'd been standing.

"My sister still has some shopping to do, I suspect," he said in a matter-of-fact tone, still overlaid by that subtle, unidentifiable accent. "She won't be joining us at any rate."

"Oh," I said, my eyes widening with my surprise, "she's your sister. Well," I regarded his ridiculously handsome face, thinking of the woman's stunning beauty, "your family has excellent genes."

He smirked and even that expression looked sexy on him. "Yes. Our genes are close to perfect."

That claim took me aback, but then I supposed I shouldn't be surprised the man was vain as all hell. Hot privilege and all. That kind of vanity could be insufferable in large doses, but then again, I was really only going along with this date to remind myself that I was still a woman, because after years of marriage to Michael—the last few without any real sexual interest from him—I'd forgotten that fact.

He walked alongside me as I made my way to the checkout, glancing nervously at him multiple times to make sure he didn't disappear. After all, maybe I had already passed the point of hysterical, and I was now hallucinating super-hot guys to cheer me up.

As we approached the entrance, I spotted his sister standing outside with two other men, both of whom looked from their side profiles to be as gorgeous as Jason. I felt a bit of shock along with my awe, and a tingle of awareness prickled along my spine. Something seemed off about this sudden influx of impossibly handsome people when I'd never seen their like before.

Even the cashier seemed awed, the young man's mouth gaping slightly as he stared at the man unpacking my basket onto the conveyor belt. Jason stood at least six feet tall, and his brothers—if that was who they were—looked even taller as they entered the store, leaving the young woman staring through the glass storefront at their backs.

Her gaze met mine and she smiled, lifting an elegant hand to wave slightly as she winked one large eye at me.

It was a bit awkward, honestly, but I waved back and gave her a cautious smile as the two new guys passed by our checkout without acknowledging Jason. They headed in the direction of the paint counter where Amy no doubt fumed in outrage at being passed over for a fluffy middle-aged woman in paint-stained sweats and an oversized T-shirt.

Jason wasn't much of a talker, which made things awkward for me, because I hated long silences when I was just meeting someone. I felt obligated to fill that empty air space, fearing that if I didn't, they'd realize I was a shy introvert uncomfortable in social situations. Instead, I grappled for topics, trying to ask as many questions as I could as I led him to my car where he stowed my purchases in my trunk.

He answered every question I asked about him abruptly, in ways that gave me almost no information, and discouraged any further queries in that direction. I quickly grew frustrated as I shut my trunk and turned to regard him, crossing my arms over my chest.

This would be a long and painful cup of coffee if he didn't start to demonstrate some conversational skills.

"Listen, uh, Jason," I said, shifting my weight from foot to foot out of nervous habit, "I don't think this is going to work out. I appreciate the offer of a drink and your help to my car, but I'm actually not really looking for dates right now."

His eyes narrowed and he frowned deeply as his dark brown brows drew together. I braced myself for the inevitable temper tantrum.

In my experience, good-looking men weren't accustomed to being rejected, and they tended to take it poorly—especially when they considered the woman beneath them anyway. And I was sure he did. I got the impression he was slumming with me, and my suspicions about why were growing enough to make me more cautious about this whole date thing.

Plus, he was as dull as dry toast. Seriously! The guy couldn't carry a conversation with the help of a cargo lift.

To my relief, his frown cleared away, returning his expression to a neutral one. He nodded briefly and smiled, though it was obviously forced. Then he reached out to pat me on my upper arm.

"I understand," he said calmly, "it's probably for the best."

As I glanced at his hand on my arm, he lifted his other hand, palm upwards in front of me.

I shifted my gaze to his palm and saw a strange powder in it, just as he pursed his lips to blow it into my face.

At first, I hacked and coughed, turning away from the source of that powder. Within moments, I felt an odd lassitude filling me.

"Come with me," he said in a hard tone. "Make no move that I don't tell you to make." He started to walk away.

I straightened into a stiff stance, then my feet moved against my will as I turned to follow him. I wanted to scream and shout for help, but I no longer had control over my own body. I also experienced a strange, almost disconnected feeling, as if I weren't even inside my body. It felt more like I was watching myself from a distance.

Jason ordered me to follow him to an alleyway near the hardware store, and as I passed the store, I saw one of his "brothers" walking out of it with Amy at his side. Her gaze looked distant, staring right past me, but her almost zombie-like movements matched my own.

The two men walked side by side into the alleyway, and Amy and I followed obediently, unable to even turn our heads to look at each other. Once we reached the alleyway, we saw the sister—although based on the passionate kiss she gave Jason and then the other man, I got the distinct impression they weren't related.

Or maybe they were. Who knew at this point? I sure as hell wasn't worrying about that as much as I worried about the fact that I had zero control over my own body.

Then I was glad I wasn't entirely in control of myself, because I probably would have crapped my pants when a small, sleek spaceship suddenly appeared in front of us as we reached the furthest depths of the alley. It became fully visible just as the last of the three "brothers" appeared with another young woman in tow, obviously as afflicted by the strange powder as Amy and me.

When Jason ordered me to climb into the vessel, my mind screamed in terror and panic, even as my body moved to obey.

I was being abducted. Now I knew why these people were so otherworldly beautiful. What I didn't know was why they

wanted three human women, none of whom looked particularly special in any significant way.

I never got the chance to ask why, because after entering
the narrow confines of the spaceship, Jason ordered me into a
coffin-like box and then told me to lose consciousness once I lay
inside it. I didn't even remain awake long enough to see the
other women climb into their enclosures.

TWO

I awakened to a silence so profound my ears rang from it. My eyes opened to complete darkness, and I lifted a hand to touch them to make sure my lids had really opened. In panic, I followed that up with a flailing of my arms, crying out with a trembling voice.

"Hello? Anyone?" My voice pierced the darkness, and my panicked breaths sawed over my nerves with nothing else to break up the sounds. "Is anyone there?"

I didn't feel like there were other people around. In fact, I felt totally alone, and the empty air around me confirmed that no one stood nearby. The temperature of wherever I'd found myself was just warm enough that it would have been uncomfortable if it weren't dry as an Arizona summer. It also would have been uncomfortable if I weren't fully nude.

I realized my lack of clothing as my full awareness returned, though I couldn't see myself, even as I frantically looked down and patted my body desperately. My hands passed over fully naked skin. I hadn't even been left with a bra for my slightly sagging breasts, when the girls needed all the extra support they could get at this stage in my life. If I had larger breasts, I probably would have been even more uncomfortable, but even with my tangerine-sized boobs, I felt their weight bouncing as I climbed to my feet slowly and unsteadily, my movements jerky.

I didn't feel any aftereffects of whatever drug I'd been given by the—and now my breaths grew even more panicked as I recalled everything—*aliens* that had abducted me. I supposed it was too much to hope that they might have some hot barbarian types around ready to whisk me away to their home world to make me the queen of their reverse harem. Hot guy Jason and his creepy sis and family were definitely not the type I'd want to find between the covers of a paranormal romance novel. Sure, they had the look, but the attitude was not doing it for me.

At this point, such thoughts were all that kept me sane as I distracted myself from the horrifying reality of my situation. I couldn't believe that only a short time ago, my biggest problem had been that I couldn't get the right mix of colors to make the exact blue I'd wanted for my painting. Granted, I was divorced and out of work, but those hadn't been "in the moment" kind of problems. One thing I *hadn't* been then was freakin' abducted by aliens.

That tended to change my perspective on things a bit. Now, all that other stuff I'd once stressed about escaped my mind and my lizard brain kicked in, my nostrils flaring as I tried to sense my surroundings without being able to see them.

The scent didn't give me much better information than my sight or sound. There was a clinical, sterilized smell to whatever place I'd found myself in, with an overlaying odor of a server room or computer bay. Something plastic and artificial, though the heat suggested it wasn't a room dedicated to electronics—

unless aliens had figured out a way to deal with overheating computers.

I also didn't hear the telltale hum of any kind of electronics. I didn't hear anything but my own heavy breathing, which suggested I was in a sound-proofed room of some sort.

No, I didn't like that thought *at* all. My brain had no problem imagining why that would be. I would rather find myself in the heart of some alien engine core than locked within a soundproof cell, though the best thing would be to find myself in my own bed, waking up out of a nightmare.

I wished I could believe that was all this was, but there was no mistaking the difference between dream and reality. Even the lack of sensory information was *enough* sensory information to convince me this was all terrifyingly real.

When it came to those senses, I was down to touch and taste since none of the others were telling me much. I felt the smooth, slightly cool surface of the floor beneath my feet, and could guess from that alone that the room was not a natural chamber but had been made—obviously not by man. I could also guess that Mr. Hot stuff Jason and his inbred family of creepy mannequin people didn't look entirely human in their true form either. Who knew what kind of ugly they were behind those human disguises?

"Alien-built" didn't give me any kind of comfort. The fact that I was in a room instead of a cave meant bad things as far as I was concerned.

Escape was clearly the order of the day. I didn't let my mind dwell on the likelihood that such a thing would be impossible. The fact that my clothes and shoes and even my hair tie had been taken from me did not give me a lot of confidence that I'd be able to pull off a prison break.

Sometimes, you just had to focus on doing something, even when you knew it was pointless, to keep from dwelling on what terrible thing might happen to you next. My steps were hesitant as I chose a direction and moved forward, sweeping my foot out in front of me along the floor before shifting my weight to it. I kept my hands out at arm's length, sweeping them back and forth in search of a wall, or even better, a door. Hopefully an unlocked one that opened onto a spaceship all gassed up and preset to take me back to Earth.

Yeah, I know it wouldn't make sense, but a girl can dream. I wasn't quite optimistic enough to hope for sexy barbarians of the alien variety or a buffet of "all you can eat" pastries that tasted the same as the ones I loved but had zero calories.

Hey, if they could send a spaceship to Earth, they should be able to make food that had no fattening qualities.

Yes, my mind dwelled on inanities. The lack of sensory information was close to driving me crazy, and without an imagination, I might have already been over that edge. If I didn't also have the attention span of a gnat, with my brain jumping onto tangent trains every other second, I didn't know if I would have survived even as long as I already had in this unknown, terrifying darkness.

I kept telling myself not to focus too hard on the fact that my hands weren't encountering anything in the direction I was going, and the smooth floor didn't change under the bare soles of my feet. I kept trying to focus on the thought of sweet, fresh-baked cookies instead of the unidentifiable odor that wasn't strong enough to either despise it or fear it. I feared, instead, the lack of information it gave me. The mind plays tricks when there's nothing for it to process. I could almost taste the sweetness of a forbidden and fattening dessert since the air carried no flavors to deposit on my tongue when I breathed in.

Even with all my mental tricks, I still almost gave in to despair when a dozen steps led me nowhere. In frustration, I turned ninety degrees, knowing that if I didn't do things methodically, I'd quickly grow disoriented. Hands out again, I walked several steps forward, keeping close count while humming just to have a sound other than my own breathing and thudding heartbeat and the eerie slide of my bare feet over the unknown surface of the floor.

Then my sweeping toes brushed against a wall and my shoulders sagged in relief as my humming cut off. I set my foot down with toes pressed against the surface that felt perpendicular to the floor, then cautiously rocked my weight forward, my outstretched palms encountering the smooth wall in front of me. Unlike the floor, it felt warm, but at least there wasn't any slime or dampness at all. Like the air itself, the wall felt dry.

It didn't vibrate or pulse or do anything at all weird beneath my fingertips. There was no way of knowing whether there was machinery on the other side of it, but I could guess that it was thick enough to keep sound out in both directions.

Still, it was a start—a way to orient myself. I kept my hands on the wall, sidestepping now in the direction I'd initially come from as I counted each step. I passed the number of steps I'd originally taken before turning, then went a half dozen steps further before encountering a corner.

I whooped as if I'd just won a contest. Then I remembered where I was, or more accurately, the fact that I had zero idea where I was, and the triumphant sound died down to a mere echo, quickly muffled by the oppressive silence.

I made my way around the wall, concentrating on counting steps and feeling for any irregularities on the smooth surface that would give me more information. I debated licking the wall because I was so desperate for more sensory input than what I was getting. I figured my tastebuds might be able to detect if it was metal or drywall or plaster or wood, though my palms told me it might not be any of those things.

Plastic had a very distinct taste too, as did Styrofoam soundproofing.

Don't ask how I know that.

I was certain I mangled the pop song I started humming again, but that wasn't why I ended up choking off that sound suddenly. It was the lights snapping on that silenced me, blinding me as a sudden squealing of metal sounded overhead.

The sensory overload of all this sent me collapsing to my knees with a scream, my arms crossing over my head protectively. I shuddered in fear as light after light flicked on, finally showing me the chamber in which I'd been measuring my blind progress.

It took a long moment after the terrible sound of screeching metal ended, the last echoes finally dying abruptly, before I dared to look to my side and saw the length of a tunnel, now illuminated, leading far into the distance before rounding a bend that put its ultimate destination out of sight.

The wall I knelt closest to appeared to be an endpoint of that tunnel, and I looked up to see metal grating above my head, with an access gate right there where I must have been deposited while I was unconscious.

In fact, the entire ceiling was made of metal grating, showing another tunnel above my head that had been revealed by a metal cover that had pulled back all along the tunnel's visible length.

Now, the acoustics gave me more information, though I suspected the tunnel above was also soundproofed. I debated trying to climb into the entry hatch, but the smooth white walls on this level showed no sign of places to grip and the grate was too high above my head to jump up and catch on to it.

The floor was white as well and as blank and uninformative as the walls. I saw nothing but my own well-lit tunnel, the dark tunnel above my head, and a floor between the two with another hatch near the bend.

My imagination didn't need to be active to recognize what this was, and my heart sank into my bare feet.

I was a rat in a maze, and I doubted the cheese would turn out to be a sexy alien mate. It might be my chance at surviving —or more likely, it might just mean another horrible way to die.

THREE

Even knowing that I was in an alien experimental maze didn't stop me from hoping for escape. There had to be hope, always, otherwise, why not just lay down and wait to die. I didn't have it in me to give up that easily. I would rather bash my head against the wall in an effort to put a hole through it before just fading away quietly.

I made my way cautiously down the tunnel, worried that some dangerous obstacle or trap would pop up in front of me. Instead, I just faced endless white walls dotted by bright lights and bare floors, with that strange dark tunnel above me.

When I rounded the bend, I spotted the first intersection of the maze, proving to me that I'd been correct in my assessment. The problem the rat always has is that they don't know why their captors want them to find the cheese. They just go blindly in the direction of that promised treat.

I wanted to put at least a bit more thought into my progress than a rat, though perhaps my captors expected that. Maybe they wanted to see exactly how creative I could get.

I liked puzzles, including mazes, but that was when I was

sitting on the couch in front of the television listening to a show playing as I drew my path over a paper maze. Now, that maze could kill me, or lead me to something worse than death. I had to think carefully about which way I wanted to proceed.

Deciding to do this very methodically, I chose to always take the right path, so that I could backtrack. Since I had nothing to mark my progress with, I was out of luck in that respect. I couldn't even scratch the walls with a fingernail. None of the paneling or flooring showed any kind of marring or irregularity that would serve as a landmark either. These bastards expected me to remember everything in my head. At least the rats had their nose to sniff out the cheese. All I smelled was my own body, which at the moment appeared to be clean, so my odor wasn't strong or offensive. It was, however, enough to cover the very faint scent of the plastic or sterile cleanser environmental odor. I still wasn't entirely sure which it was that was putting out that odor. Perhaps the walls themselves.

Or maybe they'd cleaned this maze with sterilizing cleanser that left behind that faint odor. If they'd cleaned the maze, my guess was that they'd used it before. Maybe it hadn't been simply animal or human waste they'd had to clean up—but rather blood.

Curse my overactive imagination! It can pop up like some twisted gremlin out of the blue, scaring the shit out of me. As if I needed it to now, but hey, why not add to my stress?

"They're just cleaning the waste," I whispered to myself.

Thinking of that, I felt a mild fullness of my bladder. If this maze went on too long, I might not have a choice but to cop a squat for a minute.

Yes, it did occur to me that if I could also poop, I might be able to overcome my childhood potty training to use it to mark my path.

Gross.

I wasn't at that point of desperation yet. Fortunately, for now, I had nothing knocking at the backdoor. I wasn't sure if that was because the aliens hadn't fed me in a long time, or if my body had been "cleansed" in an unpleasant way. If the second was the case, then I would be *so* glad I wasn't conscious for that.

I paused as I wondered if I'd been given an enema to keep me from pooping to mark my path, then wondered if the aliens could think that far ahead or even predict such behavior from a civilized human over the age of three.

I wish I knew exactly how prescient they were. Clearly, they were still experimenting on humans, so they didn't have us all figured out yet. Also clearly, humans were still experimenting on rats on Earth, and I was pretty sure we had them figured out for the most part.

So.... Yeah.

Taking all right-hand paths as the maze grew more complicated, presenting first two paths, then three, then four, I thought I could detect a pattern. Then the damned maze shifted on me, one opening sliding closed while another slid open.

Oh, these guys are total assholes!

"What do you want from me?" I shouted as I stared up at the dark tunnel above my head, clenching my fists in frustration as tears filled my eyes.

I'd just returned from a dead end to find my expected path blocked, forcing me to go another way.

That blank wall where there had been an opening just minutes before almost broke me, and since none of the bastards bothered to answer me, I shuffled onward, selecting the next right-hand path, though by this time, I realized that methodical choices wouldn't help me. Neither would marking my progress help me. Since they kept changing the maze, their intention wasn't clear.

How could they want me to find the end goal of it if they kept shifting it around?

I paused again, sniffling as I tried to bite back a helpless sob. Maybe they were changing things in a discernible pattern that I could predict. Maybe, if I figured out that pattern, I'd find the solution to the maze.

I should point out at this point that I'm not a damned genius, so if the aliens were hoping I'd figure this all out and skip merrily to my goal, they were out of luck. They should have abducted someone in MENSA.

Then it occurred to me that they *had* abducted other women.

If I could only find them, we might be able to put our minds together to figure this maze out. Now, I started calling out again, but not for the damned aliens.

"Amy?" I sped up my steps as I headed down a tunnel. "Are you around here, Amy? It's me, Rhonda. Uh... the paint-stained sweats lady from the hardware store."

I know she had to have seen me just as I spotted her being led by the creepy hot alien. I didn't know the name of the other woman who'd been brought along, but I still called out for her. "Hello, any human? Screw those alien bastards watching us! We can help each other get out of this."

My voice echoed a little bit, but there was a sound-deadening quality to the acoustics of this maze that made my cries die too quickly to travel far. I realized that if I had a better ear, I might have been able to use sound to help navigate the maze, but the alien bastards had apparently thought of that too.

Amy and the other woman could be right on the other side of any of these walls, and they probably wouldn't hear me even if I shouted my head off. I knew who *would* hear me though. I wondered if pleading would help.

"Please, whoever you are, let me go!" I sobbed again, feeling that hopelessness creeping back in like a damned sneak thief to steal my motivation to keep moving. "I don't know what information you're trying to learn from experimenting on me, but I'll bet I can answer your questions more accurately than my actions will."

I waited, biting back sniffles as I swiped impatiently at my wet face. No one answered me and after several more tries with the same lack of response, I gave up and screamed in frustration, lobbing every curse I could think of at the invisible watchers. Probably a bad move given I was completely at their mercy, but my emotions took over control of my mouth.

Like the other sounds I'd made, the echoes of my screams and insults died away quickly. Then another sound raised the hair on my neck as I slowly turned in the direction of it.

The wall had shut about ten feet behind me with a nearly silent snick, cutting off my escape, but what scared me more was that it was moving towards me, closing in on me.

I ran down the remainder of the tunnel and more doors shut in front of me as I reached a fork in the path, forcing me down another direction—then another. More of the walls slid towards me, and I realized that the maze was forcing me to take random paths, rather than allowing me to choose my own way.

Although perhaps the paths weren't so random. Nothing about the maze changed except for the scent.

I'd been sweating with fear and the warm temperature of the maze, but it wasn't enough to cause a lot of odor at this point. What I smelled as I was forced down one path then another was the increasing scent of something indefinable but unquestionably alien. The scent was strongest in the air around my head, though as I grew closer to its source, it had sunk down to fill the entire area, telling me it was likely coming from the dark tunnel above me.

I stared up at that darkness, barely able to see the ceiling of the above tunnel through the grating. I sniffed that scent, trying to identify it, to classify it.

It had a strong tinge of petrichor, but that wasn't the most significant note. There was nothing floral to it at all, nor fruity. Perhaps some kind of spice, but nothing I'd experienced before. It wasn't a grassy green smell, or any kind of weed. It was just... bizarre, and frightening because I couldn't categorize it, which told me it likely didn't originate anywhere near Earth.

It wasn't a bad smell, like strong body odor or waste or anything objectionable, but it still bothered me, chilling me to the bone. I didn't know what it was, and that meant it was potentially dangerous. And since the strength of that scent had increased, I was likely drawing too close to its source.

I frantically turned around to face the wall moving towards me, pushing me further towards the odd odor source, still unseen above me. Then I spotted a part of the wall slide open just before the other wall moved past it, forcing me to dive into the space as the other wall passed it, blocking my escape.

Still, now I was in a tunnel moving away from the odor, though it still hung heavy in the air. I felt a small sense of relief but knew that opening hadn't appeared by accident. Whatever game these creeps were playing had only just begun.

Then I heard a sound from the direction I'd just escaped that made me so cold with fear that the warm temperature of the maze wasn't enough to stop me from shivering.

The grating above me vibrated as something moved over it, but it was the purely alien shrieking and then horrifying chittering sound that emanated from far too close by that caused me to break into a run down the tunnel, desperately seeking a way to escape the source of that sound.

Overhead, new walls blocked the dark overhead tunnel, interfering with the path of whatever it was that moved towards me now, causing it to shriek again as it was forced—like me—to take a different path to its goal.

A goal I feared was me.

My gremlin brain decided to take that moment to provide a new scenario to my imagination. Perhaps I wasn't the experiment in this maze at all.

Maybe I was the fucking cheese!

FOUR

My thoughts were nothing but blank panic as I raced down one tunnel after another, hearing the creature in the tunnel overhead growing closer, then falling back with an enraged shrieking sound when something blocked its path while my remained clear.

I didn't have any doubt by this point that it was after me, and I also didn't have any doubt that the ones controlling this maze would probably let it catch me eventually. For now, they seemed to want to see how it solved the obstacle problem. I couldn't be certain, but I knew now that I wasn't the subject of this experiment.

I was definitely the prize. I felt sick to my stomach as I tried not to think too hard about the sterile odor, much less the alien one that increased and then waned as the creature came after me and then got held up by walls. The worst part was that I knew I was in a losing scenario. There was no way these monsters controlling the maze would let me escape, and since I was completely nude, I had nothing on me to help me. If I'd had shoes on, I might have been able to toss one into a door before it fully closed and use that path instead of the one they intended me to follow.

Ultimately, I think something like that would have only given me false hope though, since they could just make it easier for the creature to catch up to me.

Why did I keep running, even though I knew it was futile?

I was asking myself that as my breath grew labored and my breasts ached from bouncing and my legs trembled from exhaustion. There was simply no escape, but sheer terror kept me on my feet.

That sound, that alien scent, that knowledge that it would most definitely eat me once it caught me, kept me wending my way blindly along the path the captors wanted me to travel. I guess I preferred to die of a heart attack or simple exhaustion from running far beyond my capability than to be ripped apart and consumed like some horror movie victim.

If anything, maybe I'd run until I passed out, and then I wouldn't feel the agonizing pain of being captured and consumed.

Apparently, even an out of shape, forty-two-year-old can run for a considerable amount of time when something nightmarish was chasing them.

The enraged shrieks had stopped, but I could still hear the vibration of the grate over my head as the creature above remained in pursuit. Perhaps it realized that vocalizing got it nowhere with the controllers of the maze, just like I'd realized that. However, as terrifying as those shrieks were, the silence of the creature was even more so, since I had only the vibration of the grates to tell me it still pursued me, and that subtle sound and movement wasn't enough to tell me how far away it was.

Occasionally, the intensity of the alien's scent increased enough to tell me it was close, and my spine prickled like the creature's undoubtedly horrifying clawed hand was already dragging down it. Then I'd hear the slight sound of a wall snick shut above me.

My luck, or my captor's good will, ran out far too soon. Either that, or the creature outsmarted the maze controllers, because it somehow got ahead of me. As I ran down a tunnel, I saw it for the first time through the grate above, just in front of me, crouching and waiting for me to race beneath it.

I slid to a stop, my throbbing feet slipping a little on the slick tile, but I was too focused on what I could see of the nightmarish creature to care that I'd almost lost my balance.

The creature was some kind of insectoid, which might have explained the chittering sounds it had made initially. It had slick, huge insect-like eyes on front of its face and mandibles just beneath them. From its crouching position, it was difficult to make out much about its body, but I saw the hint of glasslike dragonfly wings flicking behind it with each terrifying staccato movement it made.

The creature appeared to be black as a beetle in the darkness of the above tunnel, but that could have been the lighting. Its carapace was so shiny that it glimmered in the light that escaped through the bottom of the grate to limn its horrific body, giving a suggestion of an oily purplish iridescence to its chitinous shell.

"Oh, hell no!" I shrieked and turned on my heel to race in the other direction. The hair on my entire body stood on end and goosebumps pebbled my flesh as I heard the bug monster's pursuit.

"Help!" I screamed desperately, over and over, my throat growing sore and my voice hoarse.

The bastards watching the show didn't do a damned thing to help me, and I didn't get too far before I heard a metallic crash behind me. I screamed mindlessly as the grate from the floor above fell with a loud clatter to the white tile on my own level.

The creature, on the other hand, dropped down silently, a dark, inky nightmare surrounded by the blinding white of the tunnel.

It only took a horrified glance back to see that thing before I hauled ass again. I knew I didn't have a chance in hell of escaping it now, but I couldn't stop and let it get me. I had to keep trying. Perhaps, the maze watchers would open another escape route for me and cut off the creature's route.

The monster pursued me on two legs, and another terrified glance over my shoulder showed that it had a humanoid form, though it also had four arms rather than two. The top set of arms had freaking pincers extended from them.

I was so dead.

Still, some part of my mind really thought I'd escape. Right up until the moment I felt a stinger impale the skin in the middle of my back, causing an agonized cry from me as I tried to speed up my steps. I realized that the creature had closed the distance enough to sting me, so I was probably already dead, and the venom just hadn't stopped my heart yet.

I felt a wave of heat filling me as my knees grew too weak to support me and I dropped to them. Strange sensations washed over my body, my skin at first flushing it until it felt like it was on fire, then it was so sensitive that I thought I could detect each individual molecule of air that brushed past it.

Then I felt bizarrely aroused, moaning as my nipples tight-ened and my core heated until it grew almost uncomfortable. My clit swelled and I groaned, falling back on my haunches to stare up at the grating overhead as I took panting breaths.

Each one carried an intense odor that had altered from the original scent of the insect creature, but it was still coming from the monster.

I couldn't think straight, and all my fear had dissipated until all I felt was lust. I collapsed onto my side, writhing on the floor as my hands slid down my body. I couldn't remember any time in my life where I'd ever felt this aroused—this in need of sexual satisfaction.

I was so needy that I turned onto my belly and crawled towards the monster's clawed, chitin covered feet, which had paused nearby. It did not move as I caught its ankles, pulling my way up its spiked calves, rubbing my naked skin against the cool surface of its leg plates.

I practically sighed in relief as I reached its groin, pulling my face level with the obvious erection that jutted from its body, poking out of an opening in the carapace at its groin. Unlike the rest of its body, this appendage appeared fleshy, with not a hint of chitin on it. Still, there was nothing human about that alien phallus. I only guessed what it was because it was long, thick, and phallic-shaped, but it had an oval tip instead of a mushroom head, and tiny hairs on the rounded end of it that glistened with fluid welling from a hole in the tip.

It reminded me a little of a phallic-shaped mushroom.

Not that I was spending much time ruminating on it. Instead, my mouth watered since the scent emanating from that fleshy appendage smelled heavenly and only seemed to increase my arousal. Nearly mindless with need and lust, I licked the swollen tip, and the fluid that welled from it made my tongue go numb.

Probably not the best idea, but I wanted more, and I went back for more.

The creature caught my shoulder in a lower hand to stop me, and with a hard grip, shoved me back onto my naked butt as it—I suppose "he"—crouched in front of me.

I lay back as he crawled over me, then writhed beneath him, spreading my thighs wide on either side of his so when he probed my soaking entrance with the head of that shaft, he had full access to settle his body between my legs and ram it home.

Which was what he did.

I cried out in pleasure, my thighs lifting to clamp around his waist. His lower hands grasped my legs just above my knees, holding them in place while his upper hands braced his weight on either side of my head. The pincers that had been extended when he'd dropped from the upper tunnel were now retracted, folded tight against his forearms, revealing that he had two functional hands on his upper arms as well.

My eyes widened as two stingers rose from his back and darted towards my naked body after he buried himself inside me.

Still, he felt so good filling me that I didn't scream when they both struck my body, the dagger long tips just barely puncturing the skin of my belly instead of penetrating it deep enough that the stingers alone could have killed me. I felt the heat of his venom injecting into me and spreading, with more of that wild need following in its wake until I rocked desperately on his shaft, driving myself towards an orgasm as it began to vibrate inside me.

In fact, his whole body seemed to vibrate, though he made no move to thrust, allowing me to set the pace, his insectoid head cocked slightly as his bulbous eyes regarded me unblinkingly on either side of an odd seam in the chitin of his upper face. As I moved on his shaft, the mandibles that sat tight against the lower half of his face shifted, splitting just enough that I saw there was something hidden beneath them, too darkened by shadow for me to make out more details. I suspected it was his mouth, and I only vaguely concerned myself that he would eat me. I was too excited and too out of my head with lust to care at that point.

Whatever aphrodisiacal venom he'd pumped into me was

working overtime. I didn't give a damn about looks. All I needed was for him to fill me like he was doing, and the vibration of his body drove me to an orgasm. As my sheath convulsed around his length, his head tilted. He lifted his body slightly to look downwards at where our bodies were joined, almost as if he was surprised by the feeling of my inner muscles gripping his flesh.

I was moaned and writhed, clutching at his second set of arms, my thighs tightening on his waist as I begged for more in a raspy, desperate voice. I felt terrified that he would pull out of me and leave this horrible need to drive me mad without fulfilling it. His stingers remained extended from his body, hovering near my naked skin, but not puncturing it again. His wings spread fully behind him, their span large enough for the rounded tips to bend against both sides of the tunnel.

When he lowered his head towards mine, I thought he was going to kiss me, which made no sense since he had no lips, only that hard set of mandibles. Still, I was reacting more than thinking, so when they came close enough to me, I peppered kisses across their chitinous surfaces. He tilted his head, then rubbed his mandibles along my lips, then nudged my jaw with them, and finally pressed them against my neck. It felt almost like he was sniffing my naked skin, but he had no nose, so that didn't make much sense either.

The whole time he did this, his shaft continued to vibrate inside me, and I had another orgasm, my body already primed from the first one. Again, this caused a reaction in him as he lifted his head and began to pull away from me.

I clung to his lower arms, the chitinous plates covering them slippery beneath my fingers, so when he pushed his body upwards, mine went with it.

"No!" I begged. "Don't stop! *Please*, don't stop now!"

His lower hands caught my waist and tugged my body

away from his enough for him to look down again at where we were connected. His extended wings flicked in a way that would have freaked me out in any other situation, since it was so reminiscent of an insect and so clearly inhuman.

Of course, now I was probably the creepy one, sticking to him like a tick, afraid not *of* him, but that he would pull out of me and leave me aching and empty and suffering from an intense need I'd never experienced before.

"This is your fault," I growled, then lifted my hands to his mandibles, tugging on his head until he raised it to regard me again with those blank, shiny black eyes. "You did *this* to me!" I said in a tone that I would normally have called whiny, but you could hardly blame me at that moment. "Don't you dare stop!"

I don't know what the aphrodisiac venom was that he'd injected me with, but it would make a fortune on Earth—or destroy mankind altogether if it wasn't diluted.

A lot.

The chitin beneath my palms vibrated almost as much as his shaft, making a humming sound. The creature himself made a quick chittering sound, mandibles shifting against his mouth again. He lowered them to my lips and bumped my face, pausing with his mandibles pressed against my mouth as if he were waiting for me to kiss him.

It didn't seem sexually motivated, but rather an act of curiosity, like nudging a lab rat that is lying still to see what it does next.

I didn't care about his motives. I kissed him a bunch of times on those mandibles, breathing deeply through my nose, because he smelled so damned good that I couldn't seem to get enough of his scent.

In fact, it only seemed to increase my desire, which wasn't waning at all, despite the two orgasms and another approaching rapidly as he continued to vibrate.

I arched my back as I climaxed for the third time, my eyes rolling back into my head and my entire body shuddering with my release. My inner muscles ached from the force of that climax, convulsing so hard around him that I knew I would feel sore later.

This time, he pulled completely out of me, and I screamed at him in frustration as he sat up, regarding my lower body with a cocked head, wings flicking.

"Damn you!" I shouted, then kicked his leg, the slick surface of his chitin hard against the bare sole of my foot.

Almost casually, one of his stingers stabbed my upper thigh. Again, it didn't penetrate deep enough to do much damage, but I felt the burn of his venom as the tip tore my flesh.

This time, it didn't increase my arousal. This time, I felt unconsciousness stealing over me as it pumped through my blood.

Just as the darkness claimed me, I felt his clawed fingers probing my entrance, then delving inside, like he was examining it.

FIVE

I woke up from an odd—and oddly arousing—dream that I had sex with a giant, humanoid bug. The weirdest part about the dream was that I could recall it had been the best sex of my life, which I suppose says something about what my life has been like up to this point.

I moaned at the recollection of powerful multiple orgasms, swallowing thickly as I turned my head and slowly cracked my eyelids open. I felt groggy, still tired, despite what must have been a long rest, because my body felt like it had been in one position for too long.

Then I realized more about the feelings in my body. Mainly, the feeling that I was restrained, except for my head, which could only rock from one side to the other. I couldn't lift it far, because everything below my neck was pinned by pressure that felt like a sheet that covered my body and had been pulled so tight that it was almost unbearable.

Panic chased away the grogginess as my vision sharpened and everything around me came into focus. I screamed as I turned my head from side to side, taking in all the machines surrounding me, and especially the one above me—the one that had far too many finger-looking probes with needles on the tips of them. Tubes and wires snaked all around, and there were vials that definitely looked like they contained samples of my blood hooked into a boxier machine near the one that haloed over my midsection with all the stabbies on it.

Other vials sat in the machine next to the blood vials, and these had fluids in them that ranged from white, to cloudy, to clear, with no markings on them that I could read. I searched frantically for any kind of marking on the machines, which fortunately weren't in motion, though I feared they could kick into gear at any time and start with the stabbing.

When I did find printing on one of the machines, it didn't look familiar. It appeared more runic, more ancient looking than anything I'd ever seen before. Or perhaps it was completely alien, which was the far greater likelihood.

Oh, I hadn't forgotten being abducted by Jason and his purple-eyed freak family. I knew that wasn't a dream. Now I had a bad feeling that the bug sex thing wasn't a dream either.

On the plus side, I wasn't eaten alive by the creature that had chased me through the maze. On the minus side, I wasn't likely to live long enough for a second date.

Not that I wanted one or anything. Now that I wasn't pumped to the brim with some bug-monster version of an aphrodisiac, I could recall my horror at the creature's appearance and movements quite vividly. That horror was trumped only by my terror now at being helpless beneath these mystery machines, with no idea what they would do to me once they started moving.

Okay, so I screamed. A little.

Maybe enough that I was hoarse, and my throat hurt. I mean, wouldn't anyone, in that situation? I think I lost my head, went a bit crazy as I struggled to move. I might have accidentally knocked myself silly by racking my head on the hard surface of the table the aliens had strapped me to.

The pain of that impact shocked me into silence so only the echo of my screams sounded in the chamber where I was imprisoned. To my relief, the machines didn't suddenly surge to life at any time. That relief was short lived when I heard the distinctive sound of a door sliding open.

I knew that sound well after being chased around a maze by moving doors and walls. I frantically turned my aching head this way and that, but the door that had opened was somewhere past the end of my feet so I couldn't see it, nor who came through it.

I didn't doubt that someone did come through it though. Or more accurately, some people, since they were engaged in a conversation with each other, though I couldn't understand a single word of what they said. Whatever it was, it didn't sound like any language I'd ever heard on Earth.

It also wasn't the kind of language I might expect from some monstrous alien creatures. It sounded like it came from humanoid-shaped throats and out of humanoid-style mouths. They made a series of sounds most humans could probably make.

I was guessing then that it wasn't my alien monster-bug returning to finish the job he'd so rudely interrupted with a shot of his knockout venom.

I wasn't sure if I should feel relieved or disappointed at this point. There were worse ways to die than orgasming to death. At least, I assumed there were. I sure as hell didn't want to find out, regardless. Some theories don't need to be proven, in my opinion.

The aliens approached my table, still chattering away in a very fluid sounding language that would have been musical, if they weren't evil monsters experimenting on people—and monster-bugs maybe? They both had deep voices that sounded male.

Then I caught my first sight of them, though they both wore masks covering their lower faces. They also wore white robes, and their skin was definitely inhuman despite the humanoid appearance of their eyes. One looked vibrant orange, the other a light pink shade—not the normal pink tone of some human skin, but an iridescent bubble-gum pink.

The orange one had startling blue eyes. The pink one had fuchsia eyes.

Their pointed ears extended just above heads covered with long hair that they had tied back. I had no idea precisely how long since I only saw them from the front. The colors of their hair appeared to coordinate with their alien skin tones.

Yup, they were space elves.

Evil space elves, by my estimation, seeing as I was unwillingly bound to an operating table of some sort.

"Hey, uh, maybe there's been a misunderstanding," I said in a hoarse whisper as the orange one came closer to my head. "I think you might have the wrong girl."

Blue eyes shifted to my face, and I couldn't read the expression in them as he studied me, but they looked as cold as their color. Then the orange alien reached towards my ear, and I flinched reflexively as his long, slender finger pressed something that had been attached to it.

And perhaps within it, since whatever he did, I felt a strange buzzing inside my head.

"Do you think it's a good idea to activate the human's translator?" the pink one asked as it joined the orange one near my head.

"I refuse to speak any of the ape-blood's ugly languages," the orange guy said to the pink one, before his cold gaze shifted back to me. "Human, I agree you are the '*wrong* girl,' but that is irrelevant at this point. You pose a mystery we intend to solve."

"Hey, I like mysteries," I said desperately, nodding my head. "I'll answer any questions you got and see if we can get to solving mine. No problem. Although," I wriggled my shoulders a bit, though they weren't moving far under the blanket thing, "I find it much easier to think when I'm not *strapped* to a fucking operating table!"

Okay, a little bit of a freak-out there. I mean, the surprised blinking of the orange guy at my sudden shout at the end of what I'd intended to be a very calm and convincing statement was almost worth it. But I realized I probably wasn't helping my case or convincing anyone to unbind me.

"Look," I said after a few deep breaths as both aliens' eyes narrowed on me, "I think we got off on the wrong foot, here."

"You do not appear to appreciate the position you're in, human," pink guy said in a tone that made me certain he had a smug, condescending smirk under that concealing breather mask.

I nodded again, craning my neck to focus my desperate eyes on him, trying to ignore the fuming orange dude who glared icicles at my head. "I assure you, the whole 'strapped to a table' thing is definitely sending a clear message." I glanced at Orange. "Not saying I 'appreciate it' per se, but I'm not doubting the position I'm in."

Orange made an impatient sound, lifting a hand to halt any further words from Pink. "*You* are not our focus, human, but Subject 34's response to you has raised questions—and concerns."

"Subject 34?" I swallowed through a lump in my throat, still feeling the rawness of it from screaming mindlessly earlier. "You mean the bug-guy?"

Despite the seriousness of my situation, I felt a blush burn my cheeks as I realized these bastards had watched the whole show. The last thing I needed to be feeling right now was embarrassment.

Mr. Pinky Pants huffed in what sounded like outrage. "That 'bug' is superior to you in every possible way, you primitive dullard."

Oh yeah, he was a real peach. I could already tell we were gonna be good friends.

"Really?" I asked, fluttering my eyelashes as I affected an innocent expression, because damned if his tone didn't bring out the worst in me. "That would make him *doubly* superior to you then, I'd say."

"Why are you engaging with the primate?" Orange asked Pinky Pants, impatience heavy in his tone. "Do not be drawn in by its games."

Look, I'm not saying I wasn't still scared enough to crap myself, though I didn't think there was anything left down in the old gut locker, but whenever I encounter uptight, arrogant asshats like these two, it's hard to keep my mouth shut. I'm an introvert, sure, but I'm not a masochist. I'll tell a creep off in a heartbeat if it will make them go away and stop fouling up my airspace with their sheer crappiness.

"Look here, elf boy, shouldn't you be back in the North Pole, finishing up those toys for Santa? Why don't you zip it and let the adults in the room have a conversation?" I glanced around in an exaggerated fashion, still struggling to lift my head off the table. "Oh, wait, looks like I'm the only adult in the room, so I guess I'll just have to have a conversation with myself. That way I won't need to dumb myself down to communicate with you two."

"Can we terminate her already?" Pink Bastard said, gesturing towards the boxy machine at my side as my blood froze. "We already have all the samples we need."

The fact that his tone held no emotion told me it was time to stop playing around with these two—and stop underestimating how deadly they were, just because they looked like escapees from a children's cartoon.

Much to my relief, Orange shook his head, holding up that staying hand again. "We don't know yet if 34 has imprinted. Killing her at this point would be counterproductive."

"We used the cure on him," Pinky Pie hissed, turning fully towards Orange. "He should no longer possess the imprinting genes."

Orange returned his chilly gaze to me, studying my face for a long, tense moment, before allowing his gaze to trail down my body.

Despite the presence of the blanket, I had a bad feeling he saw every naked inch of me, all squashed flat against the table. Not that I relished being naked even when gravity was the only thing pulling on me.

"If he didn't imprint, then we can't explain why he chose to mate with her instead of kill her like he did the others." His focus returned to my face, and by the tone in his voice, I suspected his lips would be pulled in disgust. "Why *else* would he show interest in mating with her?"

"Oh, that's a low blow, man," I said, bizarrely hurt, even though I didn't give a damn about the opinion of these two assholes.

I didn't need to travel across the freakin' galaxy to have my looks insulted. I could get plenty of that right at home. In fact, if I really wanted to be a masochist, I could just post a picture of myself online.

"You forgot to call me old, and remind me repeatedly that I've hit the wall," I growled.

"She does make a point," Pink Dick said, his tone thoughtful now. "She is not at her most fertile age. Her scent signature would make the lessening of her fertility clear to Subject 34."

Orange guy studied my body dispassionately again. "Kiari had this female's ovaries pumped with rejuv while in stasis to repair the deteriorated condition of her eggs and develop new ones. She planned to breed her on the Rim for more human slaves. Her hormone levels are nearly returned to her most fertile phase."

"Wait... who is Kiari?" Panic had returned to overwhelm my outrage and disgust with these two dickwads. "What the hell do you mean, with all the 'ovaries' and 'breed her' stuff?"

Orange chuckled as he regarded me with those hatefully dismissive eyes. "Kiari had plans for you and the other humans she'd harvested from Earth. Fortunately, we captured her and her harem and a nice collection of useful subjects. You," and here he glanced at my body again, "were not so useful to us, but we kept you around anyway, figuring we'd find a purpose for you eventually."

"I'm guessing that purpose won't be to bring peace between our people," I said bitterly, trying to wriggle my shoulders again.

"Well, look at that," Pinky said with sarcasm so clearly dripping from his tone that I was surprised the translator didn't just add "sarcasm" as a tag to the end of the words it spoke in my head. "The ape-blood is so clever."

"I have some questions for you, human." Orange picked up what appeared to be a smooth, flat tablet and held it in front of him, his gaze shifting from it to me, then back as he swiped his fingertips over it. "That is the only reason we are speaking right now. If you would prefer to end this interview, then stop wasting our time and answer them quickly and accurately."

"And what happens to me after that?" I demanded, my heart thudding as my skin broke out in a cold sweat.

It turned slippery against the blanket thing pinning me down, so I suspected that my restraint wasn't made of absorbent fabric.

"That depends," Orange said thoughtfully, now staring down at the tablet rather than looking at me. "If 34 has imprinted on you, we must destroy him, which makes you of even less use to us."

Pinky gasped, then turned a fuchsia glare on Orange. "We have years of work invested in 34! You can't just—"

"Do you recall the *last* time we allowed an imprinted athraxius hybrid to live?" Orange said to Pinky in a hard tone without even looking at him. "It's a pity, but it must be done. We cannot risk a repeat of the *Thrax incident*."

"We can try to use the cure again," Pinky said in a desperate tone, "we've heard that sometimes it requires reinoculation."

"Hm," Orange looked up from his tablet to meet Pink's eyes. "That is a possibility, I suppose, though we can't be entirely sure of the side effects. The 'cure' nearly killed him when it rewrote some of his genetic code. We still can't pinpoint exactly what it changed before it deactivated."

He returned his gaze to me as my own darted from one of them to the other like I was watching a tennis match, only in this case, I had a feeling my own fate depended on the outcome. I just wasn't sure who I needed to win, because I had no idea at all what the hell they were talking about.

"First, we should determine if 34 is even imprinted, and if so, why it happened, given he was supposed to be cured after artificial affliction. The flaw could be with the exposure process rather than the cure." He jerked his chin in my direction. "I will question the human female to see if we can gain any useful answers, though I don't have high hopes. Then we will put her back in with 34. If he can harm her, he is likely not imprinted on her."

"*What?*" I said, struggling fruitlessly again. "I don't know what the hell you're talking about, but if you doubt that bug thing can harm me, you should take a look at all the places it stung me!"

Both chuckled in a condescending way that almost made me forget how terrified I was with my outrage.

Orange tapped the surface of his tablet, his gaze fixed on it instead of me. "Subject 34 can create a venom that could kill you instantaneously and painlessly or draw out your death in the most agonizing way possible. I assure you, if he intended to harm you, you wouldn't be here to whine about it." He glanced up at me again, and the corners of his eyes crinkled slightly, which made me think the bastard was smirking. "Although 34's thought process lacks civilized nuance. He thinks in primal terms that our species long ago abandoned. What we consider 'harm' is far different from what *he* considers harm. He likely doesn't consider stinging you to pacify you harmful to you, so can still do it if he imprinted on you. Indeed, he could likely do far more to you than an imprinted Iriduan could even think of doing to their mate."

My breathing was labored at this point, and it didn't seem like I could drag in enough oxygen with my chest bound to the table so tightly. I felt lightheaded as more sweat made my naked skin slip and slide against the blanket.

"Look, I don't want to die, or be hurt, or even see the bug-uh—this Subject 34 again! So, maybe we can make some kind of deal, you know. I have money," I lied, "and precious works of art," I continued to lie. "Maybe we can do some kind of exchange for my freedom?"

Orange glanced at Pink, his eyes still crinkling in the corners. When his gaze returned to me, the crinkles had smoothed out. "I assure you, human, you have nothing. Even if we wanted your 'money'," Pink huffed in condescension at this, "or your 'art'," I could hear the sneer in Orange's tone, "your world is not the same one you left years ago. I sincerely doubt anything you owned there remains intact."

My eyes widened with my shock. "What do you mean, 'years ago?'" I rocked my head from side to side, moisture pooling in the corners of my eyes to drip down my temples. "How long," I swallowed thickly before I could continue speaking, "how long has it been since I was taken from Earth?"

Orange regarded me with his chilly eyes, and I just knew he was taking pleasure in my distress. "I would say approximately ten 'Earth' years have passed since Kiari harvested you. Much has changed for your world." This time, his tone sounded angry. "The *Akrellians* now control it." He spat out the unfamiliar word that didn't translate as if it tasted sour to him.

"Ten... *years?*"

I couldn't believe it. Didn't want to. The very idea that ten years of my life had simply vanished seemed almost worse than waking up on the operating table of my alien abductors. "Why... why don't I remember...?"

Pink sighed with impatience. "I thought you told me not to engage with the primate, Nirgal. She's clearly too ignorant to understand such simple concepts as 'stasis'. Why waste your time explaining?"

Nirgal seemed to agree with Pink at this point, his eyes sharpening as he regarded my devastated expression. "Tilhur is correct. I have wasted too much time speaking with you when there is much work to do. Subject 34 is supposed to be the pinnacle of our achievement here. With the cure we obtained at great cost and effort, he will be unstoppable and invulnerable to our enemies." He raked my body with a hard gaze. "But only if he *is* truly cured."

"The cure worked on Ilyan," Tilhur said defensively, clearly not wanting Subject 34 to be destroyed.

Nirgal made an odd hissing sound, raising one hand sharply to cut off any more words from Tilhur. "Ilyan is nothing but a fractured shell. The '*cure*' has only prolonged his suffering. Now, be silent. You are distracting me with discussions we can have later. I must interrogate this female so I can make a decision about what to do next."

Tilhur crossed his arms over his chest, shooting a glare my way before turning abruptly away from the table. "I'll run the samples then and check on 34. He is currently dormant, as you *insisted*."

"Activate his chip when you are done drawing samples from him, will you?" Nirgal said distractedly as Tilhur stalked out of my sight. "I don't want to waste time waiting for him to come around before we reintroduce the human to him."

Based on the sound of the door sliding open, then closed, Tilhur left the room. I wasn't sure whether it would have been better to be left with the pink bastard or this orange one, but I was certain I was screwed either way.

And not the kind of screwed that led to multiple powerful orgasms.

SIX

"Now, human," Nirgal said in a business-like tone, "tell me when you first detected Subject 34's presence. Was it the sound of him—or his scent—that let you know he was there?"

"Why should I answer any of your damned questions?" I ground out between teeth that wanted to chatter with my terror.

His eyes flicked up from the tablet, and the hardness of them made me shudder. "I think it would be in your best interests to cooperate."

"You're going to kill me anyway!" My voice shook and I hated myself for revealing my fear, but I figured he was already well aware of it.

"That isn't necessarily true. We held off on using you in our experiments because of your advanced age and general genetic unsuitability. We had much better subjects, but they all... perished when introduced to our hybrids." The corners of his eyes crinkled again, and I had no doubt he was amused by the death of all those others. "You, on the other hand, have managed to delay your demise, and we want to figure out why.

If you cooperate with us, perhaps you will earn a stay of execution."

"So... the others that were taken with me—Amy and the other woman—they're... they're *dead*?"

Now I felt like a total asshole for thinking Amy was a petty little witch. The poor woman! Both of them. I teared up again, blinking away tears that tickled as they slid down my face.

Nirgal waved a careless hand. "As if I paid attention to whatever names these creatures used to refer to themselves. I have no idea which ones you might have known." He studied my face for a long moment before adding, "if it makes you feel any better, Kiari had dropped off some of her slaves prior to our troops apprehending her. Those females might still be alive out there, though I *doubt* they are enjoying that life much."

"You're a real monster, aren't you?" I whispered, my throat bone dry.

"If you please," Nirgal said in a neutral tone, "let us continue with the questioning. How did you first detect Subject 34?"

I didn't answer for a long moment, glaring at him, wishing I had the power to kill him with my mind. Someday, if I ever escaped this nightmare, I would paint the bastard and add the horns that he should already have. Then I would burn the fucking painting.

He sighed with clear impatience and tapped something on the table out of my sight.

My muscles seized up in agony beneath the punishing pressure of the blanket as I was shocked by the table. It hurt so bad I couldn't suck in enough air to scream. The pain seemed to go on and on, every muscle in my body tensed and twitching from the current running through it.

Then it was over, and I sagged back against the table, struggling to breathe, my chest bruised from the blanket's pressure.

Tears dripped down the sides of my face, soaking my hair as I openly wept. All my bravado had disappeared. I couldn't "whistle in the dark" anymore and pretend everything was okay. I was so screwed and there was no humor to be found in my situation.

Hopelessness filled me as I mustered the breath to answer the question. "I smelled him first," I croaked out through an aching throat.

"Did the scent of him arouse you?" Nirgal asked in a very clinical way.

Still, the question caught me off guard and made me sick at the same time. I didn't think he was a pervert, given the tone he used, but at this point, I almost wished he was. I might have been able to seduce him in that case. I *was* certain he was a sadist, so I wasted no time in providing the answer.

"N-no. Not... at that time." When he raised his brows as if still expecting more from my response, I struggled to fill in details. "I only noted that it was different from anything I'd ever smelled before, and it unnerved me. I was... scared."

"Curious." His eyes narrowed. "Are you certain you felt no arousal whatsoever? Perhaps a hint of it beneath the fear?"

"I'm pretty damned sure I'd remember!" I cried out, then flinched as his gaze hardened and shifted down to the table. "I mean, I don't remember feeling any uh, *arousal*, until he stung me the first time."

"Hm." He seemed genuinely taken aback. "I wonder why he did not emit a mating pheromone to attract you immediately."

Since I was certain he was only speaking to himself, I didn't respond to that. Fortunately, I must have been right because he didn't proceed to shock me again at my lack of response.

"So, you didn't experience any heightened emotions other than fear until he stung you—and then...?"

I struggled to recall every detail of the encounter, because I had a feeling Nirgal would demand them. "Then, I felt an intense need. So intense that I crawled towards him, even though he's terrifying."

"And your arousal... did it cause you to produce lubricant at that time?"

"Lubricant?" It occurred to me what he was asking, but my fear was too great now to blush in embarrassment. "I was wet, yes. Wet enough to uh, lubricate things."

"But prior to him stinging you, you were not 'wet'?" Again, his tone was clinical and held no hint that he was turned on by this horrible line of questioning.

"I wasn't, no." I frowned, curious despite my fear. "Why is that so important, anyway?"

He tapped away on his tablet, not even looking up at me as he answered. "Arousal releases detectible scent signals that can alter the behavior of an imprinted male, particularly when the female is lubricated with it." He finally glanced at me. "However, it appears that you were not releasing any remarkable signals until he stung you. Yet, instead of venom, he injected you with a powerful aphrodisiac. One we have never seen him produce before."

"So, what does that mean?" I licked my lips because they were so dry they cracked when I tried to speak. "He was supposed to kill me, but he screwed me instead?"

"Precisely," Nirgal responded coolly, returning his attention to his tablet. "Even more interesting is how his prescience seemed to increase during this trial, with him foreseeing not only immediately incoming obstacles but also, apparently, your ultimate path, in time to intercept you while working around our efforts."

The fingers of one of his hands drummed on the edge of the table, making me very nervous.

"I wonder… I have always doubted the efficacy of the 'cure' we used on Subject 34, though it appeared to work on one of our other subjects. However, if it did work, that means he made the decision to mate you rather than consume you of his own will—which does not seem likely, given his nature."

"Maybe he just thought I was hot." I wasn't able to muster a joking tone, so the comment came out in a monotone that he must have taken seriously.

"Your temperature would not have been an attractant. There have been plenty of other targets that were just as warm, if not warmer, than you in the past."

I didn't bother to correct his misunderstanding. I was certain he would only use it to insult me if he understood what I'd actually been saying.

"If he is not imprinted, it is possible that he was just curious," Nirgal muttered. "Toying with his food perhaps, since he is so well fed he doesn't require constant consumption. In that case, his curiosity could make him even more dangerous than if he were imprinted."

Again, I figured he was talking more to himself than me, so I didn't make an effort to answer. I was having trouble breathing. Not from the relentless pressure of the blanket, but from my anxiety over what he would do to me next.

"I've observed the video feed of his mating with you, but it was difficult to interpret some of the actions both of you took." He tapped the tablet with the fingers holding it, not in a way that implied he was using it, but rather like a habit he had while thinking.

"Maybe because you've never had good sex before," I muttered.

He cocked his head as if he were able to pick up on my words, which scared the shit out of me. Or would have, if I had any left inside me. Then his eyes narrowed, and I realized he'd definitely picked up my words. I wondered if his translator was more advanced than mine, then realized that I was an idiot to even think it wasn't.

"I have not, but I am aware of the activities that take place during a mating. Still, it is useful to gain the perspective of the actual participants. Subject 34 is not communicative, despite the control chip we've installed in him, so we lack his perspective. You, on the other hand, do not seem capable of remaining silent."

I heard the warning in that tone, letting me know I should keep the insults in my head. Somehow, it didn't surprise me that the bastard was still a virgin though.

"I'm not sure exactly what you're asking for," I said, flinching as his hand lowered to the table again.

He returned his hand to the tablet's surface and swiped as if passing through several screens before turning it towards me to show an image of myself with lips pressed against the hard, chitinous mandibles of Subject 34.

"What are you doing here?" he demanded.

"It's called kissing," I said, a hint of sarcasm creeping into my shaking voice. "I'm not sure if your species knows what it is but it—"

He waved an impatient hand to cut me off. "We know what 'kissing' is, human. But Subject 34's mouth is not exposed at this point. What is the purpose of pressing your own to his mandibles? Were you aware that he has sensory receptors in them? Is that why you tried to increase his intake of your pheromone by doing this?"

My mouth gaped for a long moment as he glared down at me, still showing me that damning image. Wow, I looked really ecstatic in that still shot as I tried to meld my lips with Subject 34's mandibles. Despite my fear of Nirgal, my inner muscles clenched in recollection of how good 34 had felt inside me as I'd climaxed again and again.

"Answer me, human." Nirgal swiped a hand on the tablet, revealing another image of me kissing Subject 34 with obvious desperation.

Obvious to me, at least.

"I don't even know what all you're talking about with the pheromones and shit," I cried out as the lines between his frowning brows deepened. "I just felt like kissing him because I was really aroused. Kissing is a natural reaction to arousal for me!"

His frown lightened, though his glare still pinned me, clearly suspicious. Though how he believed I could possibly know anything about Subject 34 was a mystery.

He swiped over the tablet again, revealing another image. This time, 34's mandibles pressed against my neck as my head dropped back, a look of absolute bliss on my face that I'd never seen before. I had to admit, I looked almost... beautiful with that expression. I wasn't even aware I could look that enraptured.

I wanted to paint that image of myself, with my graying hair spilling behind me somehow looking far fuller and more voluminous than it was, my eyes half hooded with not a crow's foot in sight and my lips sensuously swollen and parted as I gasped with pleasure. I wish I could always see myself as that sexy. If I'd looked like that with Mike, maybe he wouldn't have moved on with a younger woman.

If Mike had inspired that kind of passion in me, maybe I would have looked like that with him.

"What is he doing here?" he asked, as if genuinely confused.

Dude needed to get laid, seriously. Although I pitied any woman who hooked up with him.

"I think he's nuzzling my neck," I answered distractedly, studying the image of 34 with genuine curiosity now that I wasn't running for my life in terror from him or needing him so bad my eyes crossed.

His head was humanoid shaped, the chitin plates formed like a helmet around it. In the close-up image of him, I could only partially see the hard ridges along his spine. The large, black eyes and the hard mandibles were a bit off-putting, but not so much that I didn't experience residual arousal from just the remembrance of what he had felt like against me and inside me.

"Why would he do this?" Nirgal asked.

I wasn't certain if this was a question aimed at me, or spoken to himself in confusion, but I answered just in case. I wasn't trying to get shocked again.

"I don't know, to be honest, but at the time, I thought it was like he was sniffing me, even though he doesn't have a nose."

Nirgal huffed. "He has a nose, but it is redundant given the sensitivity of his mandibles. Tilhur insisted we keep his facial features similar to our own, though I don't see the point of it. Still, he will look better on the promotional materials because of it."

"Promotio—" I shook my head, feeling the hard surface of the table against the back of it. "You know what, I don't care. That's weird, though. Not gonna lie."

His brows drew together again in a hard frown. "It's not pertinent to you anyway, human. Now, did Subject 34 make any sounds that might have been too low for our sensors to record?"

"He, uh, vibrated, and there were a couple of chittering sounds, I think." Nothing had stood out about the sounds he'd made. At least not that I think would be relevant to this guy.

"Honestly, I was being pretty noisy myself, so I wasn't necessarily paying attention to whatever sounds he made."

"That's hardly surprising," Nirgal said in a mocking tone.

Man, I really wanted to punch this guy!

"So, he didn't attempt to communicate with you in any recognizable way?" he continued without seeming to realize—or care—that I glared daggers at him, my lips now mutinously pressed together.

I shook my head, but when he remained silent, his frown deepening, I quickly gave a verbal response. I was pissed at him, yeah, but I'm not an idiot, nor a glutton for punishment. "No, he didn't try to talk to me."

Nirgal's hands clenched on the tablet. "How frustrating. He is quite stubborn. Why do they hate speaking?"

That last question he said in a rhetorical tone.

"Maybe they just don't like talking to *you*." I slammed my lips shut as I realized I'd said that aloud when he turned a fearsome glare on me, and his hand dropped to the table.

I tried to lift my body off the table without much success as I stuttered, trying to make up for speaking out of turn. "I think he wasn't interested in talking! He seemed to have only one thing on his mind."

This seemed to distract Nirgal. "And yet, he didn't ejaculate. That is another curiosity—and a disappointment, as we have yet to successfully harvest his sperm."

"Uh, eww."

He turned as if he were about to go, and I didn't dare hope I would get off the hook easily. "If it wasn't his intent to seed you, then why go through the motions? I do not understand his behavior, but we will put you in his enclosure this time and see how he responds. Hopefully, we'll gain a better understanding of his motives."

"Wait!" I struggled again, grunting as I writhed unsuccessfully under the blanket, my skin stinging from being dragged along the slick underside of it. "What if he kills me this time?"

Nirgal huffed as he stalked to the door. "That is the hope. If he can kill you, then he isn't imprinted, and we haven't wasted years of our time on yet another failure."

SEVEN

I had to lay on that uncomfortable table for what felt like forever, though I was also terrified of what would happen to me when they finally took me off it. Thus, I was a blubbering mess when two aliens finally appeared, dressed in full biohazard suits.

At least, I figured that was what the suits were, since they had that kind of appearance, though they were made of a shiny, vinyl-like material. The aliens' heads were completely covered, as was every other part of their body. Even their hands were gloved.

Curious that Nirgal and Tilhur hadn't been as concerned about being exposed to me. I hoped they hadn't discovered something that inspired this extra precaution when they ran the samples they'd taken from me.

What if I had some terrible alien virus? Or a flesh-eating bacteria? At the thought, my skin began to itch horribly, and I begged the silent aliens who unlocked the wheels on my table to put me under a hot shower and pump me full of antibiotics before my skin sheared off my body.

Naturally, they didn't respond to me, or do anything I pleaded with them to do. Fortunately, my skin stopped itching as they rolled me out of the room and along a long, white corridor, not much different from the maze they'd put me into earlier.

Bright, blinding lights passed overhead, forcing me to close my eyes as they took me down the corridor to some unknown destination.

No, I knew their destination. They were taking me to Subject 34, hoping he would kill me.

I was really hoping he wouldn't, and not because I wouldn't mind feeling the way I had the last time he had me in his clutches.

Who or whatever these aliens were, they didn't seem to be in complete control of their own experiment based on their frustrated questioning. Apparently, they couldn't make 34 talk, though they'd mentioned a control chip.

I would find that more curious if my mind wasn't racing with terror. The aliens seemed convinced 34 should have killed me, which meant that was his usual MO. The whole sex thing was the anomaly, and I wasn't sure it had been good enough for him to want to do it again.

I wasn't ready for my ride on the table to end when the aliens drew it to a halt. Only then did the pressure of the blanket disappear from my body. I sucked in a huge, grateful breath, my hands moving to reflexively scratch over the parts of my skin that had itched earlier. To my relief, my fingertips slid over smooth flesh. No sign of any rashes, bumps, or any other reason for the itching other than my own mind.

Without ceremony, the two aliens caught me by the shoulders as I sat up, then dragged me off the end of the table and shoved me towards a door. One look at the vault door that appeared solid enough to stop a tank made me struggle in their punishing grips, screaming as I flailed my arms, trying to land a wild punch on either side of me.

One of them took out a shock wand and jammed it into the naked skin of my side, my flesh jiggling as I convulsed, then dropped to the ground.

I'd bitten my tongue, though fortunately not hard enough to do any severe damage. Still, I felt the iron taste of blood in my mouth as they dragged me to my feet, the one with the wand still holding it at the ready in his other hand.

The other released me and stepped up to the door, entering something into the panel beside it that caused the vault door to unlock and swing slowly open.

As soon as the opening was wide enough to fit me, the one holding on to me shoved me into a small room with another door on the other side that was sealed closed.

I crossed my arms over my chest, shivering as my skin pebbled with goosebumps. I turned towards the outer door, which was now closing again, the biohazard-suited aliens standing on the other side of it. Once it clanged shut with an ominous echo, I turned to regard the room I stood in, noting that it contained no furniture at all and just looked like a large closet rather than some bug nest.

Meaning the nest was probably on the other side of that inner door.

The proof of this came when the inner door swung open towards the chamber beyond it. The smell hit me before the opening in the massive, heavy door parted enough for me to slip through it.

It was definitely the scent I recalled from the maze, only it smelled much stronger here. Like before, I noted that it wasn't unpleasant. Just... different. Alien. Something exotic and worrisome.

There was no reason I should feel aroused in that moment,

but I did, and I could only blame that on my recollection of my last encounter with the creature. Given nowhere else to go, I proceeded forward. I figured if it planned to kill me, there was nothing I could do to stop it, so there wasn't much point in delaying things by cowering in the anteroom near the outer door that I knew wouldn't open for me.

I crept into the large chamber, my feet sinking into sand as soon as I stepped past the boundary from the anteroom to the subject's enclosure. It was dark in the room, and the only light came from the smaller outer room that I had been thrust into by the aliens. That was just enough to limn the towering boulders and spiked plants that I saw within.

As I drew closer to one of the spiky plants that looked like an oversized version of a succulent, the ceiling overhead lit up with a series of stars and two moons. I stared upwards in awe at how realistic it looked, then recalled where I was and paid more attention to my immediate surroundings. The addition of the moonlight showed me the dangerous spines of the plants so that I didn't stumble into them. It also showed me the rock formations that I was certain weren't natural.

Light from the ceiling display also revealed the round curve of a skull nearly buried in the sand nearby, causing me to scream when I spotted it, and then stagger backwards, bringing myself to an abrupt halt before bumbling into another spiky plant.

My heart thudded as I regarded the sharp spines while slowly backing away from them. At this rate, I was more likely to impale myself to death on one of these stupid plants than get killed by the monster.

I had to be smart about this, except that I wasn't feeling very smart at the moment. I was terrified, and I also felt a sense of true hopelessness. No matter what Subject 34 decided to do to me, I wasn't escaping this nightmare any time soon.

I wasn't likely to escape it at all, and I had to accept that. Now, it was just a waiting game for death. I could stand at the entrance to this hellscape to wait for my demise, or explore a little further in.

Since I'm not a patient person and never did like standing around with nothing to do, I kept moving deeper into the chamber. I passed several rock formations until I reached one that appeared to form a crevice low to the ground.

There were more bones scattered around this dark entrance and many of them looked unmistakably human. Or humanoid.

My brief bout of courage disappeared as I gasped and peered frantically around me, slowly backing away from that horrific lair of a man-eater.

I spotted no sign of the creature, nor did it crawl out of that impenetrable darkness. My eyesight had adjusted to the much lower light now, and I could see further into the chamber. There wasn't much to settle my gaze upon. Just more of the same rocks and plants and sand, all faintly illuminated by semi bright alien moons.

No sign of Subject 34.

I could smell him though, and his scent was stronger near his crevice. He was probably in there, but I sure as hell wasn't going to get down on my hands and knees and check for him. Instead, I backed away, my ears ringing from the silence as I strained to hear any sound coming from that dark opening.

I finally moved until it was out of sight, turning my attention to the rest of the enclosure. I could climb the rocks, if I were willing to risk scraping my skin up on the rough, sandy surface of them, but there wouldn't be much point. The false sky told me the chamber was completely enclosed and the only escape was undoubtedly through that vault door I'd entered.

"Now what?" I muttered as I made a complete circle

around the enclosure in a far shorter time than I'd anticipated, only to discover that the vault door had shut on me and now I couldn't even escape into the antechamber.

I sighed and made to sit on the sand, before recalling that I wasn't wearing a stitch of clothing and sand had a bad habit of going into places it didn't belong. That left me leaning against a rock, my head in my hands, struggling not to weep with hopelessness and frustration.

My fear had faded, though it didn't completely abate, and depression replaced it. Maybe it would be better if 34 killed me and added my bones to his collection. Then I wouldn't have to face any more terrifying interviews while forced to lie on a shock table.

Then I wouldn't have to deal with the fact that I was never going home, and even if I managed to escape, ten years had passed on Earth. I had no idea what would happen if I suddenly reappeared there, but I knew that when I'd been abducted, I'd had nothing worth returning to. I wondered briefly what had happened to Mike and his new trophy wife. The kid they'd had would be around ten by now.

I also wished I'd asked more questions of Nirgal. Like who the hell the "Akrellians" were and what they were doing to my home world. I wanted to know how they'd even gained control. Didn't our government have all kinds of missiles and a space defense or something?

I vaguely recalled they'd had that when I was abducted. Of course, back then the idea of aliens had barely even occurred to me. I didn't spend much time dwelling on it. Like many others, I'd brushed off the increase in UFO sightings as simply human-made experimental aircraft that wasn't being disclosed to the public yet. I figured after about three decades, we'd learn all about those "UFOs" and discover they were just advanced military aircraft.

It wasn't that I lacked the imagination to believe in aliens. I just focused my thoughts on other things. Even my alien landscapes had been the product of surreal dreams rather than an attempt to envision other worlds that might really exist.

My thoughts had led me down a rabbit hole that allowed me to forget for a brief, blissful moment that I was on the brink of death. The chittering sound above my head quickly shattered that moment, causing me to scream and jump away from the rock, looking up to see Subject 34 crouching on top of it.

He was watching me with his expressionless domed eyes and mandibles that told me nothing about whether he was going to eat me... or do something far more enjoyable on my end.

He remained still, completely unmoving in an eerie and inhuman way. I trembled in terror, slowly backing away from him with my hands up in front of me as if I could stop him if he attacked me.

"Easy there, Subject 34," I whispered, figuring he wasn't likely to be able to understand me anyway, but unable to remain silent. "Don't eat me, okay. I'd be bad for your cholesterol."

He cocked his head, his mandibles twitching. I shuddered and took another step back. He crawled over the edge of the stone, the claws of his lower hands digging into it while his upper set of hands lifted, the pincers extending from his forearms over his hands, opening slightly as he regarded me.

His movements appeared swift and staccato, more insect-like than humanoid. His wings twitched behind him in brief flutters, creating a slight buzzing sound each time they moved.

"I'm serious," I said in a slightly louder voice when he didn't immediately attack. "I'm really bad for your health. Three out of four doctors agree that Rhonda-flesh raises your risk of heart disease."

As I babbled on, barely aware of the nonsense I was spouting, he crawled further down the rock. Then he dropped to the sand in front of it, causing me to shriek in fear.

Yet all he did was straighten to his full height, then stand there, as unmoving as he'd been when crouching on the rock.

"You know, you're not much of a conversationalist, are you?" I muttered, noting how much my hands shook as they remained in front of me. "I'm an introvert myself." I glanced in the direction of his crevice, which remained out of my view. "Of course, I don't make a habit of eating the people I don't feel like talking to."

I dipped my chin as I added, "not that I haven't been tempted to bash a few heads in on occasion, but I'm a civilized girl. I just painted pictures of those annoying people later and smashed the canvases."

Subject 34 watched me in silence, unmoving. I sniffed the air cautiously, wondering if he would release some kind of pheromone to tell me if he was DTF like before, or was more interested in chowing down on all my chewy bits.

So far, I smelled him with no problems, but I barely felt a tingling of arousal, and I'd had that from the moment I'd entered this place, so I didn't think he was emitting any additional "mating pheromone." He didn't smell bad though, even this close. In fact, he smelled surprisingly good. Good enough that I inhaled deeply, detecting a floral undertone to his musky, earthy scent that I hadn't picked up before.

Then I realized I'd picked up that teasing scent from the moment I'd entered the chamber. It only took a quick glance upwards to realize there were flowers on the tops of the spiky plants. That floral scent probably came mostly from them, but it did also seem to emanate from his direction, mixed in with his alien odor.

Nope, not aroused like I had been in the maze, but I did

want to get a little closer and press my nose against him and inhale, like I would sniff a shirt just out of the dryer. The longer he stood there staring at me, the stronger that desire to approach him grew.

I resisted it for as long as possible, continuing to babble inanities and nonsense without really listening to myself. My will was nearly broken as that scent washed over me, but apparently, he'd grown impatient with waiting for me to do something. He exploded into motion so quickly that I barely had a chance to suck in a breath for a scream before he caught me in his lower arms, his upper pincers spreading wide on either side of my head like he intended to snap it right off at my neck.

EIGHT

Apparently, I still had some fluid in me because I must admit, I peed a little when he grabbed me. I'm not proud of that, but hey, you try getting snatched up by a killer monster bug-man and see if you hold onto your bladder completely.

The fact that I didn't pass out or have a heart attack was a victory over common sense, in my opinion. I was certain I was about to die, but damned if it wasn't taking him way too long to strike the killing blow. I guess he liked playing with his food. I knew for sure that the asshole alien captors weren't going to rush to my rescue when he got all handsy like this.

"Whoa there!" I squeaked as one of his lower hands probed at my mound, the sharp ends of his claws scraping along my naked flesh to dive through the curls covering it.

The extended pincers on his upper hands snapped shut with an audible click, then retracted to fold back onto his forearms, leaving his upper hands exposed. One of them covered my mouth as his head cocked above me, his insectoid eyes staring down at me, unblinking.

"Uh," I said, my breath hot against his palm, "that's-hey! That's a little too friendly for a first greeting!"

Although, I guess technically, this wasn't our first greeting. I might have been a little too friendly myself saying hello to him last time by tonguing his dick. I wondered if he thought he was returning the favor as his clawed fingers felt me up in a way that had me both aroused and worried those sharp points would stab me.

He lifted his hand from my mouth, then turned his palm to study it like he'd never seen it before. Then he held it over my mouth again, barely hovering it in front of my lips, rather than covering them. At the same time, the hand questing through my curls and folds, teasing over my tender nub—unintentionally, I figured—paused before sliding down to my entrance. I could already feel my own slick making my inner thighs slippery.

"Okay," I whispered, "this is the strangest—"

He pulled his upper hand away from my mouth again and turned his palm to look at it a second time, then touched it with the claw tip of his other upper hand, tracing over the strange, small chitin plates that covered it.

Then his head lowered, and he moved his mandibles until they hovered right next to my lips without touching them.

My lips parted as I exhaled a breath, both nervous and turned on, despite how alien he looked—and was acting. His lower hand remained motionless on my mound, just resting there. It felt smooth and cooler than my body temperature, which in that area felt much hotter than the rest of my body.

I was certain by this time that he was pumping out some "mating pheromone" or whatever magic scent the jerky aliens thought he would be putting out before, because I was seriously turned on—in a situation where I shouldn't be.

He shifted to bump my lips with his mandibles. Not knowing exactly what he wanted, I pecked a kiss on the smooth chitin. Then another. I moved my hands towards him, but he caught my wrists with his upper hands, holding them away from his body.

I wondered if it was a defensive instinct, or if he really didn't want me to touch him. I figured if it were for the second reason, I couldn't explain why he seemed determine to make me desire him.

As if in answer to my question and doubt, he pulled one of my hands up to touch his palm, where my breath had brushed against it when he'd held it over my mouth. He lifted his head from mine and turned to study my hand against his.

I was much smaller than him. That was already obvious by the way he towered over me and was only reinforced by how tiny my hand looked in his. And he had four of those suckers!

I felt my need growing painfully strong as he seemed more inclined to investigate my body—the less interesting parts of it. I rocked my hips against the hand he still had settled on my mound, trying to send an unmistakable message that I was already ready to go.

He broke his gaze away from our hands and looked down, the hand over that part of me sliding further towards my entrance, delving between my generous thighs.

Normally, I'd be a lot more uncomfortable to be this naked in front of someone, but this time, I couldn't care less. I was way too aroused.

"I'm so down for this," I said on a breathless moan.

He moved his face closer to my lips. My moan grew louder when his claws slid through my slick as my legs parted.

He released my other wrist and lifted a hand to trace my lips with his claw tip. Then he made that weird chittering sound. His mandibles moved against his mouth as he tilted his head, nudging my lips again with them.

As I pressed another kiss to them, one of his fingers pushed inside me, claw and all. I tensed even as I sighed in pleasure against his mandibles, knowing that one wrong move would have that claw cutting into some extremely sensitive flesh.

Then he shocked me, even in my aroused state, when the lower half of his face just split open, his mandibles parting to reveal that he had lips and a nose under there, rather than the hideous mouthparts of an insect.

I gasped, noting very quickly how nice his lips looked, even if they were bisected by a line from just below his nose all the way down his chin. He also had two lines that looked like cuts, though they weren't bleeding or scabbed over, on his face on either side of his nose.

Then his eyes split open.

Well, the chitin around them separated, just like his mandibles, and I realized that they covered another set of eyes, like goggles.

Bug man had a handsome face under all that creepy stuff. It was actually more unnerving to look into the nearly human eyes of his exposed face than into those bug-like goggle eyes.

It wasn't that they weren't beautiful, though the irises were completely black, so there wasn't a differentiation between pupil and iris. He had nice, enviably long lashes too.

It was just that they looked cold as hell. I didn't see any sign of emotion in them, nor in the expression on his handsome, oddly scarred face. It was more like this face was the mask, rather than the goggle eyes and mandibles that had concealed it.

His expression was neutral, his gaze studying my face like a scientist rather than a lover. Still, when his finger probed deeper inside me, I gasped and then moaned with my arousal.

He put his lips against mine, just like he'd done with his mandibles. They were cool, firm, and that odd bisection in them felt obvious when they brushed over mine.

I didn't care. I wanted to kiss him, as alien as he felt against me. I pressed my lips more firmly against his, then moved them to caress his. He remained motionless, almost like he was waiting, as he'd done before. His stillness made me think of a predator preparing to ambush unsuspecting prey.

Frustrated by my inability to affect him the way he was affecting me, I sucked his bottom lip into my mouth, feeling it split at that bisection in a way that was alarming enough that I pulled my head back, breaking the kiss.

He made a chittering sound again, and I realized it came from somewhere in his throat, seeing the chitin at his neck shift now that I was this close to him. Then his lips moved as if he was trying to say something, but his expression screwed up into a scowl, his upper lip pulling back from his teeth like he was angry.

His teeth were perfectly straight and white and looked as normal as any human teeth behind those split lips. The lower lip pulled back together where I'd split it.

Anger isn't necessarily an expression I want to see on a man when he has a clawed finger deep in my lady bits, but at least it *was* an expression. It gave his face a more "alive" appearance, rather than some handsome wax figure. His shiny black eyebrows drew together, forming little frown lines between them that I felt a desire to smooth out with my finger.

He didn't react well to that, by the way.

I realized right at the time his stingers stabbed into my sides that I probably shouldn't touch the exposed parts of his face. As I sagged in his arms, feeling paralyzed by the venom that pumped rapidly through my blood stream, I berated myself mentally for forgetting I wasn't dealing with an ordinary man.

I couldn't move any longer, but he certainly had no problem moving. He gathered my lax form in his lower arms and darted towards his crevice.

And I mean *darted*—as in, he moved so fast my vision blurred. Also, I was struggling to breathe as the paralysis in my limbs spread to my lungs and throat.

Apparently, it was my time to die. The fact that I wasn't ready for that yet didn't seem to faze my killer, but I guess you don't touch deadly insects without expecting some negative reaction.

Like getting stung.

He crouched at his crevice, still carrying me as if it were easy for him to haul around such dead weight. I didn't want to think about that, nor about the fact that I still felt ridiculously aroused, given my imminent death.

It was just unnatural!

The inside of the crevice was black as pitch. I felt the sand beneath my back as he laid me down, and sensed his presence as he crawled over me, but couldn't see a thing. Now, my breathing became labored, stars appearing in my vision.

I barely felt the stings he gave me, but the rapid relief of my paralysis was amazing. I sucked in a deep breath, my chest rising so my breasts brushed against his chitinous breastplates. That let me know he was lying over me, no doubt supporting his weight above me with all four of his hands.

He hadn't killed me. At least not yet. But I was now his prisoner, hidden inside his crevice with him. I had no idea what he intended to do with me.

For the moment, it appeared he intended to keep touching me, because two of his hands returned to my naked skin. This time, they brushed over my breasts, without any obvious intent to arouse me, but my nipples still hardened at the feeling of his cool hands covering them.

This appeared to get his attention, and he focused on them. First, his fingers swept over them again, then I felt the brush of his mandibles against one hard peak, then the other.

I moaned, my back arching off the sand as my inner muscles clenched with need. He was barely touching me, had just nearly killed me, and had human bones all around his lair, and I still wanted him with a ferocity I had never felt before in my life.

"Please, don't make me wait any longer," I pleaded. "I need you inside me!"

I felt a hand cover my mouth, then lift, then a claw tip traced my lips. The chittering sound he made was loud in the cramped space of the crevice, letting me know it wasn't much bigger than the two of us. I inhaled his heady scent and my head spun from it, like it was a drug.

Or maybe it was all the venom he'd pumped into me.

He made an odd growling sound, then another loud chittering. Then he growled again, pushing his lips against mine. I felt them brush mine as he moved them. I wasn't sure if he was trying to kiss me like I had kissed him or trying to form words.

Whatever he was doing, it made his wings buzz, and I felt the breeze from them, wafting more of his scent into my nose. I sucked in another deep breath and fought the urge to grab him by the neck and pull his lips harder against mine.

Don't touch the insect, I'd learned.

Despite my hard-won lesson, I still rocked my lower body upwards, bumping my pelvis against his hips as I parted my knees to fall open on either side of him.

I didn't feel his erection at first and began to worry that I didn't arouse him the way he did me, but then his pelvis pinned mine to the sand, part of it pushing against my slit. With a suddenness that stole my breath, his phallus everted right into my sheath.

It was bigger than I remembered, though I'd been out of my head the first time. This time—though I was extremely aroused

—I still felt like I had more awareness than when he'd injected me with the aphrodisiac venom.

He filled me completely and stretched my inner muscles tight around his shaft. Given my state of arousal, he felt incredible. Especially when his body began to vibrate in that strange way that caused his plates to rustle and his wings to buzz—and his shaft to throb against my g-spot. With his pelvis pressed against my clit and his vibrating erection inside me, it didn't take long for me to climax.

He made another chittering sound, added a growl for good measure, then slowly shifted his still vibrating length inside me. It wasn't a thrust, exactly, more like he was reacting to my convulsions. I wondered if he considered them an attack of sorts, or what he was thinking about them. Whatever it was, he clearly didn't feel as threatened by my muscles gripping his shaft as he had when I'd tried to smooth the line between his brows.

Maybe it felt much better to him. It sure did for me. Especially when he started shifting within me. I figured I'd help him out a little and began to pump my hips. At first, when I rocked my pelvis back, his length pulling part of the way out of me, his lower hands caught my hips, tightening on my generous curves until his claws dug into my skin to hold me still. When I obeyed by not moving, he loosened his grip and I thrust my hips forward, driving him deep inside me.

This earned a chittering sound that I swore was startled. I pumped my hips backwards again, and this time, he didn't stop me. When I rocked them forward again, he had already figured out what I was trying to do and met my thrust with his own.

"Oh! Yes!" My eyes rolled back in my head as he drove so deep I felt him against my womb. "That's what I was looking for!"

I wasn't certain whether he'd imprinted on me or not, but

he wasn't killing me at the moment, so I figured I might as well enjoy myself, since he'd now figured out how to thrust, while still vibrating. It wasn't long before he drove me to another climax.

That's when I figured out that he probably liked the feeling of my internal convulsions, because after that second one, he seemed to make it his mission to cause more.

I had no idea how long he remained inside me before I finally succumbed to exhaustion and fell asleep in the arms of the scariest monster I'd ever seen before.

Would he eat me alive now? At this point, I couldn't find it in me to care.

There were worse last moments than this one.

NINE

An enraged and inhuman shriek woke me from a lovely dream of lying on a beach. If only the sand wasn't chafing my tender bits, it would be perfect. I didn't even smell the fishy brine of the sea. Just a delicious, indefinable scent that made me breathe deep with a longing for more.

That shriek was not the sound of the seagulls. Rather it made me think of horror movie monsters in dark, shadowy places.

The very pissed off kind of monsters.

I jerked awake to find that I still lay in complete darkness. My inner muscles ached but in a good way. Other than that, I felt surprisingly comfortable, given that I was naked and dusted with sand.

Sand sucks. You really understand that when you start moving after lying in it.

Given the horrible sound coming from just outside the crevice, I ended up moving fast as I jerked up into a sitting position, a startled cry on my lips.

Another enraged shriek came from just beyond the crevice

entrance, and I saw a flurry of sand moving to block the bright light pouring through that crack.

Then something else fully blocked the light. Some humanoid figure silhouetted for a just a moment before everything went dark.

Something grasped my ankle, which was closest to the opening, and with a hard tug, jerked me closer to the entrance.

I screamed as sand drove up my ass crack, but it wasn't the grainy enema I almost suffered that caused that panicked sound. It was terror, naturally, over whatever the hell was dragging me to my doom. I had no doubt that "hell" waited outside where Subject 34 was making infuriated sounds.

The thing that had my ankle in its grasp wasn't letting up, and I had two choices. Dig in deep and force it to drag me kicking and screaming or lift my ass off the sand and not end up with the mother of all butt rashes.

Did I mention that sand sucks? Naturally, I chose the second option. To my death I go, my friend. I'd already be weighing down my coffin with the extra sand weight I'd picked up so far.

I discovered that the "thing" that had me was some kind of robot made of pure white, shiny plastic with black, rubbery joints and neck. It had no face, just an oval head, like a stylized mannequin. Those were the kind that I hated. I'd rather have painted faces judging my fashion choices as they stared down at me than those blank heads.

The robot, being a robot, was a hell of a lot stronger than little ol' me. I couldn't break its grip on my ankle as it jerked me out of the crevice without ceremony—or consideration for the fact that I was made of squishy bits and connective tissue that didn't like being suddenly yanked in one direction.

I figured I'd pay for that later, but my attention ended up

focusing on my surroundings rather than myself as soon as the robot dragged me from Subject 34's crevice.

The creature in question knelt nearby, his lower claws digging into the sand, pincers extended and outspread on his upper arms. His wings flared behind him, and his armored face tilted upwards to stare at the alien standing surprisingly close to him.

"Subject 34 does not appreciate your removal from his crevice, but we still have no idea if he imprinted, so we will have to attempt another test."

Surprisingly, I recognized the voice behind that biohazard suit. It was Nirgal, who—despite having several robots at his disposal—had opted to personally oversee extracting me from the crevice.

What a dick!

I was under no illusions that he was there to rescue me even before he opened up his fat mouth to tell me exactly what his plans were, but his little monologue erased all doubts.

"He looks pretty ticked off," I said idly as the robot finally released me.

I rose painfully to my feet, sand pouring off my skin.

Nirgal shrugged one shoulder, barely glancing at the kneeling creature. "The control chip won't allow him to disobey my orders, but I have to admit, I'm surprised by how vocal he grew when he realized why we were here."

I glanced at 34, feeling bad for him, though I really should have been thinking of my own predicament. There was no doubt in my mind that these bastards were what made him such a killer monster. Then they treated him like a puppet to make the insult even worse.

"You'd better hope that chip never malfunctions," I noted as 34 turned his head so those goggle eyes fixed on me.

I yelped as the robot who'd so unceremoniously dragged me

out of the crevice grabbed my shoulder with a punishingly hard grip.

"Our technology is foolproof," Nirgal said huffily.

I raised my eyebrows at the alien. "If that's true, why do you care if he's imprinted? Can't you just make him do what you want anyway?"

Oh yeah, that pissed him off. I wouldn't have expected a scientist to growl like a bear, but he did as he gestured to the robot and it surged into motion, jerking me along in its wake as it headed towards the exit of the enclosure.

I was on to something there. I'd struck a nerve and Nirgal didn't appreciate it. I also wondered if I'd worried him, because he was hot on my heels as we left the enclosure. Apparently, he wasn't that confident about 34's control chip being foolproof.

Nothing is ever "fool proof." People don't realize how talented fools are at getting around proofs.

"So, this imprinting thing—"

An impatient cutting motion from Nirgal's hand silenced me as we waited in the anteroom for the inner door to close, then the outer door to open.

"The control chip will work, regardless," he said in a deceptively patient tone, like he was talking to an idiot, and he'd grown tired of it. "But if he's imprinted, it's still a waste. We'd have to keep his female around him, and we couldn't make him hurt her."

"*What* is your obsession with hurting people?" I shook my head as I stared at him.

"I have no obsession," Nirgal snapped. "This is for *science!*"

"Uh-huh," I said in a disbelieving tone. I left it at that though, because this guy was a sadist, and I wasn't trying to make my fate worse than it already would be.

"Did he ejaculate inside you?" Nirgal suddenly asked, his

helmet tilting downwards as he looked towards my naked crotch.

I quickly crossed my hands over it, realizing only now that I was still standing around naked. I guess you kind of get used to being so after a while. Only to be painfully reminded of it when evil aliens start eyeing your private bits.

"Hey!" I squealed. "Stop staring, pervert!" Weirdo!

"Just answer the question, human," his tone sounded not so much impatient as exasperated, and I wonder if I'd broken him.

I queried my body, as you do, and discovered that there wasn't any gush of fluid between my legs. Nothing to clean up, at least. I couldn't say if that meant 34 hadn't spilled a little semen inside me, but it certainly didn't feel like he'd pumped me full of it.

I slowly shook my head. "I doubt it, but I'm not entirely sure."

Nirgal's helmet fortunately shifted back upwards. "Very well. We will have to take samples."

"What?" I held up both hands, then realized I'd exposed myself again, then covered my crotch a second time. "What kind of samples? Wait! Don't strap me to the table again!"

"We would not have to bind you if you would lie still," he said in a snarky tone I didn't appreciate.

"Well, I wouldn't be moving around if you weren't freakin' poking and prodding me, now would I?"

"How should I know, human?" he snapped, then held up a hand, slowly shaking his head. "Why do I bother speaking to this creature?" he muttered.

Then he literally turned his back on me as the door to the outer corridor finally opened.

"Come along quietly and quickly." He stepped through that thick vault door and stalked out into the hall with two of the mechs behind him. "The mechs will make you suffer if you don't obey."

As if he'd given the command, the mech holding onto me squeezed my shoulder until I swore it fractured my bones as I yelped in pain. When it started towards the door, I made sure I hurried along with it.

Nirgal took me right back to the room where I'd been strapped to the table. It wasn't a long walk, but when a robot has a hold of you, every minute feels like an hour. Once inside the room, I obediently climbed onto the table, even though my guts felt like water and my entire body trembled.

"Now, if you attempt to move, I will seal you to the table to hold you in place," Nirgal said in a smug tone.

I laid as still as possible, only hesitating for a moment when he ordered me to put my ankles in the stirrups that extended from the end of the table.

I pretended I was at the gynecologist as the machine's probe entered me and collected whatever damned samples it needed. I also tried to ignore the feeling of needles piercing my arm, and something probing at the puncture marks where 34 had stung me.

"Why did you touch his exposed face?" Nirgal asked as if the sight of the needles prodding at those puncture marks made him recall that moment.

Which, of course the voyeuristic bastard had witnessed. He had probably hoped that paralyzing venom would mean my death. It almost had, but then 34 had taken me into the crevice.

It occurred to me belatedly that maybe 34 was well aware we were being observed and wanted to make the watchers think he was killing me. Then I dismissed that idea, finding it difficult to believe he was that prescient. I'm not even sure *I* would have been that calculating were I in his situation.

I was certain he was sentient, but given that he acted so

inhumanly, it was difficult not to consider his intelligence more primitive and animalistic.

If he was making plans like that, looking to outsmart his captors to keep a prize to himself, then Nirgal and his fellow scientists were pretty much fucked. They just didn't realize it yet.

"You didn't answer my question, human," Nirgal snapped, approaching the table with his damned tablet that I wanted so badly to smash over his head.

"I don't know, okay!" I winced as the needles finished digging into my skin and withdrew, feeling oddly as painful coming out as going in, along with the sample probe inside my sheath. "It was just... I always used to smooth out the frown lines between my husband's brows. It was a habit!"

Nirgal glanced towards the machine as it made several beeping sounds. "What strange behavior," he muttered, though his suit amplified his words so I heard them.

"Look, I'm not surprised you've never experienced affection before, but humans have this thing called 'concern for each other' that makes us want to comfort others and put them in a better mood. You all should try it sometime."

Nirgal snorted. "You humans act like you invented sapience. You are barely above animals, and you believe you should rule the galaxy." He glared at me, his eyes narrowing behind the shield of his biohazard helmet. "Your people know nothing about true mating and commitment."

"Okay." I nodded my head, lifting it off the table as I peered down at my naked, supine body, so vulnerable to this psycho. "You're right. Humans bad. We're all just a bunch of dumby dumb heads and your species is so super superior to ours."

"Exactly," he snarled, his tone indicating he was well aware of my sarcasm. He turned his attention to the machine. "Yet again, he fails to seed you! What is the point of mating with you then?"

"Maybe he—"

"Shut up, human! I wasn't speaking to you."

"Maybe you shouldn't speak aloud then," I muttered, lowering my head back to the table to stare up at the ceiling.

Hopelessness filled me as I pondered what my fate would be. This guy couldn't be reasoned with, and even if Subject 34 were strangely attached to me, he probably couldn't break free of his control chip to come to my rescue—assuming he would even choose to do so.

That was a big assumption when I recalled those cold, emotionless black eyes staring down at me with the same clinical detachment as Nirgal did.

"Will you be *silent?*" Nirgal said. "What *is* it with you, human? Why can you not keep your silence, no matter how much danger you're in?" He stepped closer to the machine, staring at something on it. "Is it a genetic defect?" he said more to himself than me as he studied whatever was printed on a screen I could barely see.

"I think I might need to shock you more," he ruminated, turning his cold gaze back towards me.

"No!" I held up both hands, shaking my head desperately. "I'll be silent. Promise! Pinky swear!" I held up a pinky.

He wasn't amused. He glared at that extended digit like he debated chopping it off. Then he tapped his tablet and spoke into some kind of communicator in his helmet. "Take the human to a holding cell. We'll begin separation protocol to see how 34 acts. We can evaluate his condition afterwards to see if he's suffered any deprivation effects."

Then he turned away, fortunately without touching the damned table to shock me. I laid perfectly still, barely daring to breathe for fear he'd change his mind and come back to torture me.

Man, I really needed to learn how to keep my mouth shut. Getting shocked would be so much worse than the detention I always got for talking back in school.

A robot entered the room as Nirgal left it. I slowly sat up as it approached me, glancing around for a handy surgical knife, or scissors, or something like what the protagonist always finds in the movies to strike out at their captors.

Yeah, that doesn't happen in real life, I guess. The room was empty of handy weapons. Just big machines and a couple more tables like the one I was now sitting on. I eyed one of the needles on the machine's finger-like extensions. It wasn't large enough to use as a weapon against the creepy robot. I was also certain that if I damaged the expensive machine, the least Nirgal would do to me was shock the crap out of me.

That realization left me with only one option. I climbed off the table as the robot came close enough to grab me. I sighed as it caught my shoulder and pushed me towards the door.

"Yeah, yeah, I'm going already. No need to get pushy."

TEN

I have come to the conclusion that soul searching sucks. Of course, when it's the only thing you have to do to kill the time, you end up doing a lot of it.

The aliens kept me in a small cube with nothing else to occupy me but studying my surroundings and thinking about the turn my life had taken. It wouldn't be so bad if the walls weren't clear so that my captors could observe me from every single angle at all hours of the day. It also unnerved me that I could observe other cube cells stacked like cargo crates in a huge warehouse.

Many of those other cells were occupied, but it looked like most contained animals. I didn't see a lot of evidence of sentient behavior. Of course, after meeting Subject 34, I probably shouldn't make assumptions about the other creatures. They might all be sapient alien species.

I didn't see any other humans, which made me uncertain whether I should be sad I was all alone, or grateful no other humans were suffering.

What I did see was a few other creatures that seemed like

the same species as Nirgal, given the strange coloring, long hair, and pointed ears. Those creatures had dragonfly-like wings similar to Subject 34's, and I wondered if Nirgal had them too and I'd somehow missed them. Maybe he'd kept them under his lab coat.

Those Nirgal-like aliens all looked to be in various stages of distress. Some were extremely gaunt, like they were starving to death, but when food was dropped into their cells—looking exactly like the grainy, tasteless food bars plunked into mine every so often—they ignored that food. Instead, they lay listlessly, staring at nothing. They didn't react at all when creatures in neighboring cells slammed against the clear walls to try to attack the colorful aliens.

The ones who weren't completely emaciated tended to shriek and bang on the walls with as much rage and frustration as I felt, though I'd discovered pretty quickly the futility of that. These aliens didn't seem to ever figure out that their efforts were pointless.

The cells appeared to be soundproof, so I couldn't hear their maddened cries any more than I could hear the other caged beasts, including a couple of terrifying giant black scorpions pacing back and forth in their clear enclosures, occasionally stinging the crap out of the impervious walls, their venom spattering the surface, only to be hosed down by machines that they also futilely stung.

Those things gave me nightmares! They also got fed raw meat rather than the protein bars the other aliens and I got, and I didn't watch them eat it.

Most of the Nirgal-type aliens didn't appear in the least bit interested in their fellow captives. I assumed they were male, given that they were nude and had flaccid penises hanging at their groin. They also had strange, segmented appendages at the base of their spines, curled up just above the curve of their buttocks. Occasionally, I'd see those appendages unfurl and scratch the walls with their clawed tips, but they were no more effective than the stingers of the giant scorpions.

I say "most" weren't interested in their fellow captives, because one did appear to be. He also just so happened to be my cell neighbor, but I didn't get warm fuzzies from him. Sometimes, he'd just stare at me with glass green eyes and an unreadable expression on a surprisingly handsome face. His eyes looked as cold as Subject 34's in those moments. At other times, he'd study me with an almost confused expression, his green brows drawing together over his eyes.

Like the other aliens, he was nude, but since he sat quietly in his cell most of the time, his bits weren't swinging around in what had to be an uncomfortable way. Usually, he had his knees drawn up and his hands folded over his lap to conceal his groin from me and perhaps any other watchers. I never saw his appendages unfurl, and his wings looked shriveled.

He had iridescent green skin and long green hair that was tangled like that of the others. Occasionally though, he made an attempt to groom it, running slender fingers through it, though it seemed hopelessly matted in some spots and would probably have to be cut off at the shoulder to get it completely smooth again.

He was lean but not completely emaciated like many of the others, and he ate every food bar put into his cell and drank the water from the machines that hosed us down as frequently as once a day. The excess water drained out of the bottom of the cells into clear pans beneath them, and a system of pipes drained the water away from the stacked cells.

My cell neighbor didn't do anything overtly threatening, but I still felt unnerved by his gaze, though I didn't get pervert vibes from it. Despite my nudity, I didn't get the impression that he found me desirable to look at. Most of the time, I felt like he was studying me out of curiosity. Other times, when his gaze grew colder than Nirgal's, I wondered if he was thinking about how fun it would be to kill me.

The handsomeness of his face also reminded me too clearly of my abductor, Jason, and his creepy bros, and I suspected they were of the same species as this guy and Nirgal. Though I detected marked differences in the arch of the brow, the coloring of skin, hair, and eyes, the precise shape of jaw and nose and eyes, they all seemed to possess a "sameness" to their features, as if they conformed to a very narrow beauty standard.

I had no idea why we were all kept in this warehouse of horrors, though I could certainly speculate all day long and scare the shit out of myself. A gigantic robotic claw would come in along ceiling tracks from time to time to snatch up a hapless captive, or in the case of the more dangerous captives, grab the entire cell from the stack. Where they went or what happened to them, I had no idea, but some didn't return. Others returned looking listless or extremely sick.

Creepy green guy's constant staring and occasional glaring weren't enough to keep my attention after the first few rounds of food bars. Despite everything I had available to look at, including the occasional robots and guards that walked the path between cell stacks, I grew bored and restless. Not bored in the sense of ennui from a comfortable life but bored in the sense that my body simply couldn't maintain the constant state of alertness and terror I'd been feeling up until my prolonged imprisonment.

That's when the soul searching started. It was also when I truly began to process everything that had happened to me since my abduction.

Looking back at my mindset when I'd gone into that hardware store, I almost chuckled at naïve self. Given my current predicament, my problems seemed almost petty back then. On the other hand, they'd caused plenty of emotional damage and heartache. The fact that I hadn't been physically in danger didn't mean I hadn't been badly hurt.

Michael might be distant figure, but my memory of his betrayal remained sharp. It shouldn't matter at this time, but I still felt the scar inside me. I'd put so much of my heart and my life into him, and I'd lost it all because of things outside of my control.

Now I had zero control over anything at all, and no outlet for the emotions ravaging through me in all this time I had to think.

Sadly, the best parts of my last year had probably been when Subject 34 had stung me with an aphrodisiac and made me feel passion and desire I'd never experienced on that level before. That hadn't even been my choice, but I couldn't deny that I would take that again in a heartbeat over sitting here ruminating in a prison complex alongside numerous other miserable and tormented creatures.

It was also difficult to accept that I would gladly relive my experiences with 34 over the divorce, the recriminations, the heartbreak of finding out the "other" woman was pregnant, and the loss of my artistic inspiration.

Ten years had passed on Earth, and given Nirgal's comments, I had no idea what had been left behind of human civilization or what state they were in. I didn't think the jerk would enlighten me if I tried to ask questions.

I acknowledged that it was a horrifying thought, and I hoped my home world was okay in the aftermath of their conquering by these "Akrellians," but I also had to acknowledge that I didn't want to go back there, regardless of what state the world was in.

I'd never been close to my parents or extended family, always feeling disconnected and misunderstood. I'd tried to cultivate the kind of relationship you'd always see in television shows, but it never felt natural to me. My parents had a certain image of what their child should be, and I didn't fit it. They'd loved that I'd had creative talent and had put me in all kinds of programs to nurture it, but the pressure to perform for them so they could show off all my "art" to their friends and neighbors made it difficult to remain inspired.

Convinced that I needed to grow up like an artist—whatever that even meant—they'd leaned heavily into the idea that I was unique and special and creative, to the point where I felt like they expected me to stand apart from my peers when I just wanted to fit in like any other kid. Still, being a child, I naturally tried to live up to their expectations and shoved myself fully into that role. I wore the right grungy clothes, took all the right classes, said all the proper subversive things, wore my hair in unusual styles, painted on bizarre makeup.

I hated it. The falsity of it all. If they had dressed me in pinafores and pigtails, I don't think I would have despised it more. It was a character for me. Later, I tried to fit into Michael's expectations for me, so grateful to abandon the "artistic" personality and style for something more mainstream and ordinary.

I'd been inspired and in love at that time, so I hadn't felt the same level of resentment I'd felt towards my parents for not nurturing who I was rather than who they wanted me to be. Still, when Michael grew more distant and I no longer had his influence constantly bolstering my new persona, that too began to fall apart.

I had never found myself. Not as a child, and certainly not as Michael's wife. My parents couldn't understand that and chalked it up to my "unique and original" personality and my artistic suffering. In fact, my mother had even told me with an almost gleeful tone that my heartache after the divorce would probably fuel my greatest "masterpiece," finally skyrocketing me to artistic success.

No pressure, Ma. Also, thanks a lot for the compassion and support.

That heartache had the opposite effect on my inspiration. I lost all my interest in art, though I suppose it would be more accurate to say it was buried, because now, it was surging back with the speed of a bullet train.

My fingers itched to sketch something, and my mind swirled with images of exactly what that something could be. I had so many ideas I was surprised they weren't pouring out my ears and nose. Sometimes, I muttered them aloud to myself because I felt such an urge to talk them out.

I wanted to paint Subject 34—to capture that shadowy creature on canvas, the way he'd been captured in my memory. I wanted to recreate the dark nightmare of him surrounded by a brilliant white background of the maze, and also, I wanted to paint the slight frown on a face too handsome to be human, with eyes too cold to be anything but insectoid.

I even wanted to paint my neighboring captive to recreate what almost seemed to be two distinct demeanors in his body language and facial expressions. One appeared almost thoughtful, if too clinical for my comfort. The other seemed as chilly and lacking in empathy as Nirgal. In fact, even Subject 34 had unnerved me less when I'd looked into his dark eyes for the first time.

I itched to paint Nirgal himself so I could then destroy the canvas with glee. Sometimes, I'd spend hours upon hours perfecting a painting of someone I despised just so their portrait was lifelike enough that I really felt satisfaction in destroying it.

Hey, everyone needs a hobby.

My inspiration had returned with a vengeance—in some

cases quite literally—and yet I had no way to make use of it. After half a year of struggling with blank canvases and a stack of paint tubes, now I had nothing but a ton of ideas and concepts and compositions in mind and only a clear, slippery surface where even the crumbs of my food bar wouldn't stick, especially not when the hose came along.

In addition to wanting to paint, I wanted to learn more about this new reality I'd found myself thrust into. I wanted to ask questions of the green guy, but our cells were soundproof, even if he felt so inclined to respond. Sometimes, I think he did.

Sometimes, I suspected his curiosity about me was as strong as my own about him.

I wanted to know what those other aliens were doing in their cells and why they were so distressed. Why they looked so sickly. I wanted to know what all the other beasts and creatures were, and what purpose they served in this experimental facility.

I *should* want nothing more than to return home. That would be the normal human reaction to such a situation as I found myself in.

I've spent my whole life thinking I "should" feel a certain way that I didn't feel, and it was starting to piss me off. It was about time I just allowed myself to be exactly what I wanted to be, not what I felt like others expected from me.

Hell no, I didn't want to go back to Earth! What did I have there?

Parents who wanted me to be something I wasn't—who would be horrified that I had destroyed some of my best work because they'd think it would have made me famous? An ex who didn't like who I'd become for his sake and discarded me like I was the empty packaging from a takeout meal he'd already consumed? A society that took one look at me and dismissed me as unimportant and past my prime because I was neither beautiful nor young?

Hell yes, I wanted to see Subject 34 again, because damned if that scary creature didn't also excite me, and not just when he aroused me. I've never felt more alive than I did when I was closest to my death. He'd reminded me of how much I wanted to live, when I'd sunk into a well of despair and ennui at a life where I'd only been waiting out the clock without much interest.

I knew that it wasn't normal to feel these things. I knew it was strange to want to remain in such a terrible place, with the hope that it could get better and maybe even more interesting, rather than returning to a more mundane, *safe* existence. I knew all this, just like I knew that I should feel about my parents the way the people in the television shows and movies felt about theirs. I knew that I should feel guilty for not being connected to them, in a way that they'd never been connected to the true me.

So, as I sat in my cell, searching my soul, now filled to the brim with inspiration, I acknowledged the truth. I wasn't normal, and that abnormality wasn't a quirky, artistic unique-ness that made me interesting. Then I allowed myself not to give a damn what other people would think about me and my oddness that wasn't odd enough.

I finally accepted that I'd been presenting one face to society depending on who I wanted to please and pretending that's how I really thought and felt, but underneath that face, I didn't fit into any box—no matter how oddly shaped.

It wasn't a realization that made me feel superior to other people, as if I'd figured out something deep and profound about the world that everyone around me was too blind to see. I'd simply accepted what I've always known about myself, and I suspected I wasn't the only one who'd come to this conclusion and decided to keep it hidden because societal pressure to conform is a bitch, no matter how happy you are with yourself.

And at the moment, epiphany notwithstanding, I hadn't gained a massive dose of self-esteem. I still had self-doubt, including about my current predicament. I felt like I should be doing more to escape, even if it would make me look as insane as those poor aliens slamming their fists desperately against their walls.

Green guy had apparently come to terms with his imprisonment, since he rarely ever moved from his protected position except to relieve himself or eat. Perhaps he was more like me, aware that he had limitations and that the challenges of this situation exceeded them. He certainly seemed more thoughtful than many of the others.

I don't think he was fully resigned to this fate though, since he still flinched whenever the claw would pass by, glancing up at it with dread sometimes, and sometimes with a calculating gleam in his green eyes.

One time when it passed, he met my eyes just afterwards, his own as sharp as the bottle green glass they resembled. A slow smirk tilted his lips.

Despite his thin frame, he looked dangerous, and I shivered, turning in my seated position to face the wall of my cell that looked outwards rather than continue meeting his eyes.

After that, I noted that he'd scooted closer to the side of his cell that abutted the side of mine. Eventually, a few meal bars later, he was leaning against that side.

Then he started tapping the wall of his cell near me. I didn't hear the sounds, but he made very deliberate movements. Slow, fast, fast, slow.

Over and over again.

He was trying to communicate. I really hoped he didn't expect me to understand whatever code he was going for, because that hadn't exactly been something we'd covered in any class I'd ever taken.

Since I couldn't explain my ignorance with words, I tried a shrug and a confused expression, shaking my head back and forth. He frowned, his shriveled wings twitching against the clear surface of the cell wall. I saw his coiled appendages at his spine unfurl slightly, then curl tight again.

Then I figured "what the hell?"

I had nothing better to do, so I tried some charades.

ELEVEN

I kept up the charades with green guy as time passed. The effort to understand what he was trying to say, while sending my own communication through gestures, kept me occupied at least some of that interminable time. I wouldn't say it sped up the crawling passage of days as I waited for whatever fate would ultimately befall me, but it gave me something to do besides navel gaze and daydream about having a studio full of blank canvases to paint.

Green guy was an interesting distraction. At times, he seemed almost friendly and definitely eager to communicate. I wondered how long he'd been in there, and I suspected he'd been a captive for a very long time. I think he tried to communicate how long by pointing at the mechanical claw whenever it passed and tapping his cell wall for a long count.

He didn't look thrilled that I'd had to shrug my shoulders and shake my head at that one. Still, despite my obtuseness, he continued to make the effort. As did I.

However, there were times when he refused to even look in my direction, unless he was sending me a furious glare. I didn't understand how he could be so eager one moment, and then suddenly shift into a glaring, scowling demeanor the next. His body language completely changed like his expression, growing stiffer, wings outspreading, fists clenching. Even his toes would extend like he was stretching them.

He remained seated in those times, but it seemed like he really wanted to get up and pace when he was agitated like that.

I could hardly blame him. The cells were small with low ceilings, which was fine for me, since I was only 5'4" but the rare times I'd seen him rise to his feet, he had to hunch and couldn't straighten to his full height.

I don't know how much time passed, but I was guessing by the amount of times I'd been fed that it was several weeks. If it weren't for green guy and the activities going on in the warehouse around me, I would have gone legitimately mad, just like some of those poor aliens still pounding away on their cell walls, some of them smearing blood from their destroyed fists onto the clear, slick surface.

Then one day, the claw came for me. It plucked my entire cell off the stack and green guy rose to his feet, pressing both palms against the clear walls of his cell as he stood and watched the claw carry me away. He was in the friendlier mood at that time, and we had been attempting to converse—unsuccessfully as per usual—when the claw came by. Once he'd noticed that it was attaching to my cell, he'd gotten an odd look on his face, then his body went slack, and his head bowed. When he lifted his head again, I saw the coldness in his eyes as they regarded me, a slight smirk tilting his lips as the claw pulled my cell away from his.

I felt those chilly eyes on me as the claw carried me down to the ground level, where another machine pulled one side of it off, allowing me to finally step out of the enclosure.

Right into the waiting arms of those creepy mannequin mechs. Two of them this time.

I followed them obediently, having noted previously that captives that were allowed the privilege of walking themselves to their fate did not do well if they attempted to escape their escort. I had no desire to be shocked to my knees or even killed.

The mechs led me past the room where I'd been previously and took me several doors down from it to another room. This one was as white on the floor, walls, and ceiling as the maze had been with only a table and two chairs in the room. One of the chairs had restraints on it.

I guessed that one was mine before the mech gestured to it. Other than the restraints, it didn't look remarkable. It didn't seem to have any signs of electronics that might send shocks through my body. Not that I had much of a choice but to sit in it.

I continued to behave as the mech activated the restraints, locking me into the chair at both my wrists and ankles. Then the two mechs took up positions against the wall behind me, and though they fell completely still and remained silent, I could sense them there. Just waiting for me to make a wrong move.

I tapped my fingers on the chair arm as I waited, humming another pop song under my breath. My mind raced with so many fears about what would happen to me next that I almost sagged in relief when good old Nirgal strode into the room, mask firmly in place, but no longer clothed in a biohazard suit.

This guy had nothing but ill will towards me, but at least he was familiar, and after staring blankly at a white wall for what was a good hour at least, I was desperate to see some color. He certainly made a splash of it as he sank into his seat on the other side of the table.

I'd noted as he'd moved into the room that I didn't see any

wings on him, but his white robe garment was voluminous enough to conceal them. Or maybe they were shriveled like green guy's wings.

I was now certain—looking at what I could see of Nirgal's face—that he was like green guy and the other traumatized aliens in the warehouse. Only he looked much healthier, though he was still pretty lean.

"Long time, no see, Nirgie. How you been?" I grinned at him as if I'd been relaxing on a beach for the last few weeks.

His eyes narrowed in a glare, raking my naked form with clear disdain before he spoke. "I can see that even time in a cage has not trained you to behave around your betters."

"Actually," I said in a conspiratorial tone as I leaned forward in my seat, "I've had an awesome time in the last, what, three weeks or so. I've navel-gazed so much I think I saw my spine through my belly. Also, I have a ton of ideas for some art pieces." I cocked my head at him. "I don't suppose you'd be interested in sitting for me, would you? I have the perfect place for a painting of you. You see, I'm planning on getting a cat when I get back to Earth, so I'll need a litterbox liner."

His eyes narrowed to slits, and I figured I'd pushed my luck as far as it would go. "You are infuriating," he growled, clenching his fingers around his cursed tablet.

Did that man go nowhere without it? I bet he slept with it still clutched in his hands. As much as that image of Nirgal lying in bed, cradling his tablet close to his chest, petting it and calling it his "precious" amused me, I kept the chuckle behind my lips.

He was already getting good and pissed.

"I won't allow you to derail this interaction, human," he said in a tone I knew came in a matched set with a snarl, even though I couldn't see his lips behind his mask.

I remained silent this time, because I had definitely pushed my luck as far as it would go.

He eyed me suspiciously for several tense minutes before he finally spoke again. "It would seem that Subject 34 has *not* imprinted on you. He shows no signs of deprivation from your absence." He raked my seated form again with a narrow-eyed glare. "I'm not in the least surprised he didn't miss *you*."

I actually felt a little stung, pun totally intended. I'd built up a bit of a fantasy around Subject 34 being imprinted on me, fated-mate style, and breaking free to come to my rescue, stinging the crap out of all these jerkoffs keeping me captive.

Still, I wouldn't let Nirgal smirk behind his mask from seeing me upset at the news. I shrugged it off, tossing my head to flip my uncombed, matted hair over my shoulder.

"That's fine by me. He was a bit too intense for my tastes anyway."

"In that case," Nirgal said, leaning forward in his own chair as he set the tablet down on the tabletop, "I would recommend you cease your attempts to communicate with Ilyan." He huffed in what I assumed was laughter, but it clearly held no amusement because he had the sense of humor of a potato.

Genuinely confused for a moment, I stared at him with wide eyes. "Ilyan?"

He didn't immediately respond, though he regarded me as if waiting for my brain to make the connections, which it did pretty quickly.

He didn't have to keep staring at me with that look that said I was an idiot.

"Oh, you mean *green* guy." I nodded. "Yeah, I was totally trying to talk to him. He's not that good at charades."

He didn't appreciate my name for my cell neighbor based on the outraged sound he made as he straightened. "Professor Ilyan was a brilliant scientist, until he was ruined by imprinting. I assure you, if you do not like Subject 34's *intensity*, you would do well to cease all communications with...," here he paused and when he spoke again, his voice dripped with contempt for me, "*green* guy."

"I don't know, he didn't seem that bad," I mused, mostly teasing, but also a little taken aback by Nirgal's warning.

The corners of Nirgal's eyes crinkled, and I just knew he was smirking again behind that mask. "Subject 34 kills his victims for food and self-defense. Ilyan's fractured side murders for fun. I would keep that in mind if you find yourself contemplating whether he would make a good ally for an escape attempt."

Okay, that sounded like a very good reason to give green guy a wide berth. In fact, now that old Nirgal told me that, I felt like I had a little bit of an explanation for the sudden shift in Ilyan's demeanor that I'd seen repeatedly in the weeks that had passed while I was stuck in the cell next to him.

Still, this guy had no room to talk.

"Is that a trait of your species or something?" I asked, narrowing my own eyes and raking him with a condescending look. "Killing people for fun? Like, what are you guys? Sadistic hell fairies from space?"

Nirgal slammed a fist onto the tabletop, startling me enough that I squeaked and jumped in my seat. "I am not a killer!" he shouted. "I do this for *science*!"

"Duuuude," I shook my head, "you really need to—"

He jumped up from his seat and leaned across the table to slap his hand over my mouth. "*Shut* up before I have you thrown into... the...."

His eyes widened and he quickly pulled his hand away from my face. "I am *not* a killer," he growled as he settled himself back into his seat.

"But, you kinda are, though?" I ventured, raising my tone at the end of the statement so it sounded like a less accusatory question.

He stiffened and his chilly blue glare grew even colder. He picked up that damned tablet and looked down at it in a dismissive fashion. "*If* you are done, I would finish this irritating meeting."

I exaggerated my actions as I looked around the room. "Oh, *that's* what this is." I shook my hands in the restraints. "I was a little confused for a moment. We weren't allowed to lock our employees into their chairs during the meetings I ran. In retrospect, it probably would have made them pay more attention. But then, the cops would have to get involved, and the lawyers, and it'd get messy, you know."

I watched his fingers tighten on the tablet until I was sure it would have cracked if it were one made by humans. I couldn't help grinning, even though I knew I was digging a bigger hole for myself. I was already doomed. Why not go out in style by pissing Nirgie off until he totally lost his shit?

I wonder what his superiors would do if he jumped up out of his seat and beat me to death with that tablet. Probably nothing, so I should quit messing with him.

"You are so... fortunate," he said in a tone that suggested he spoke between gritted teeth, "that we still require your presence to further our experiments."

I nodded. "I feel really fortunate, ya know. Like I just won the lottery."

He sighed and sat back in his seat, returning his cold glare to me. "Do you *ever* think before you speak?"

I shrugged with some difficulty, given the restraints. "Sometimes, but lately, I just figure why bother? You plan on killing me anyway, probably after tons of torture, so if I can get you pissed off enough to kill me quickly, yay for me."

"I don't arbitrarily kill subjects," he growled. "Everything I do is for—"

"Science." I nodded quickly, cutting him off. "Heard you the first fifty times. Now, what do you plan on doing to me next? Because me and green guy, we have a date for a game of charades, and I'd rather not miss it."

He stared at me in silence for a long time, meeting my eyes like a cat trying to assert dominance. I glared right back at him.

Damned if I'd be the first to turn away.

I almost crowed in victory when he finally returned his gaze to his tablet, conceding our little stare battle. "The fact that Subject 34 did not appear to imprint upon you makes his behavior towards you even more mystifying." He glanced up with a frown drawing his brows together.

Unlike when 34 had a couple lines between his brows, I didn't want to smooth Nirgal's with a gentle finger. I wanted to slap them flat with the palm of my hand. Hard.

He must have noted my gleeful expression as I thought about doing just that because his eyes narrowed in suspicion, and he darted a glance towards my restraints. "Though it is a relief that he isn't imprinted, we still can't be certain whether he must be destr— *What* are you staring at?"

His frown lines had deepened, and I studied them as if they held the secrets of the universe. My eyes almost crossed trying to focus completely on the space between his orange brows.

He lifted a hand to touch his face before he caught himself and quickly lowered it again. "Stop that!"

"Hm," I blinked as if coming out of a trance. "What was that you were saying?"

He drummed his long fingers on the table beside his tablet, and I could hear his heavy, angry breaths behind that bulky mask.

This was too fun. I really should stop before I pushed him too far.

"We are going to return you to Subject 34. If you can manage to *restrain* yourself around him, we want you to attempt to communicate with him."

"Hm," I said, glancing up at the corner of the room thoughtfully. "And... what do I get out of this, again?"

"You won't be tortured slowly and painfully," Nirgal said in a huffy tone. "That's what you get if you cooperate." His gaze took on a disdainful look. "And only if you can control your *baser* urges long enough for us to gain any real insight into Subject 34's thought processes."

"You know, Nirgie," I grinned when he stiffened at the nickname, "that would be a lot easier if I had some clothes to put between me and 34, because I gotta tell you, even then, it's gonna be pretty hard to resist all that sexy mojo he's putting out."

He remained silent for a long moment, and I wondered if he was speechless with rage right about now.

"Of course, if you just want to look at me naked, I suppose...."

"Gah!" He leapt to his feet, gesturing to the mechs with one hand while clutching his tablet in the other. "You'll get your clothes! Just do as you're told and flap your mouth at Subject 34 instead of us, you *irritating*, frustrating...grrr!"

He literally growled, then spun on his foot and stalked out of the room, clenching one hand into a fist as his other gripped that fucking tablet. I'm pretty sure it was his crutch. I imagined how he'd panic if it suddenly went missing, and I grinned again at the thought.

TWELVE

I have never been so happy to see my own panties in my life! At least my captors had cleaned them. They must have stored them at some point after I was abducted. It was just too bad they were granny panties, but I planned on wearing my paint-stained sweats and shirt into Subject 34's enclosure to cover them anyway.

I promised myself I wouldn't take them off because it was good to be dressed again. If a little binding now, after being naked for so long.

I hadn't been lying to Nirgal when I said 34 put out some serious sex vibes that were difficult to resist. Impossible, in fact. But maybe, with clothing on, there would be a delay that allowed my logical brain to regain control of my body before I threw myself at 34's feet and begged him to take me.

I also had to remember not to touch him in the heat of the moment. I reminded myself of that repeatedly as I followed my mechanical escorts to his enclosure vault after donning my clothing. I was thinking that maybe I should have wrapped my lady bits in duct tape, given the impact Subject 34 had on my libido the previous times I'd been around him.

Apparently, all I had to do was successfully communicate with an insectoid creature that could sting me to death in a second and made me want to crawl on my hands and knees and beg him for his dick.

Yeah, that should be a cake walk.

This time, I felt more sanguine as I waited in the anteroom between the outer door and the inner door for everything to be all locked up nice and tight. Don't get me wrong, I was still scared, but now that I knew a little more about what was happening to me, I could get a tighter grip on that fear.

Plus, I had clothes! Yay!

When I stepped out onto the sand of Subject 34's enclosure this time, I didn't get very far into the dimly illuminated habitat before he found me. He appeared seemingly out of nowhere and snatched me up so fast I made the mistake of struggling. Naturally, he stung me, the sharp tip of his stinger piercing my sweats to stab into my thigh.

"That's rude!" I snapped, then sighed contentedly as a nice, calm feeling settled over me.

Without any attempt at comment, he carried me towards his crevice, cradled in his second set of arms.

When we reached his lair, he grew agitated, making furious chittering sounds. He set me down on the sand, and I smiled as I leaned back against one of the stones circling the space in front of the crevice. I watched him slam angry fists into the barrier that blocked off his crevice.

I felt really good. Not necessarily sexual, at the moment, though I could totally go for that, but just relaxed. Mellow. Passive.

Definitely drugged.

He should stop doing that, I thought affectionately as he raged at the barrier keeping him from pulling me into his crevice. The thought was directed towards him always stinging me, but I also figured he was wasting his time trying to get back into his hole.

Our overlords had apparently decided they didn't want him hiding me away this time. They wanted to watch how he reacted to me, and I suspected that it would be much harder to do that from within that dark crevice, though I didn't doubt they had cameras in there somewhere secretly recording Subject 34's every move.

I should get on that whole communicating thing. Given that I felt pretty chill at the moment, I didn't see the big hurry. It was fun to watch Subject 34 move—inhumanly rapid and erratic as his motions were.

Not to mention violent. He was really clawing at that barrier. I wondered if he might actually succeed in getting it open at some point. It was difficult to concern myself as I lolled in the sand, feeling more relaxed than I ever have been before.

"Hey, 34," I said with a slur, patting the sand next to me. "Give it up and come over here. Cop a squat. I'm s'posed to chat wif you." I shook my head from side to side as 34 turned to face me, his pincers still extended and wings still flicking in agitation. "Wifth," I repeated, trying to enunciate that word that definitely came out wrong. "Wiffth."

I leaned my head back against the rock. "You know s'wat I mean."

I tried to point to myself and ended up poking myself in the chest, then my hand flopped onto my belly as I slumped further down against the stone.

"Chilllll, duuuude," I drawled, slapping my hand down to the sand again. "Sit." I giggled and patted the sand a few more times, then I petted it, enjoying the slide of the soft grains against my palm.

I was staring at sand pouring out from between my fingers after grabbing up a handful when Subject 34 seemed to appear right in front of me, startling me enough to snap me out of it, but only briefly.

I grinned up at him, blinking eyes that had grown accustomed now to the dim lighting of his enclosure. "Heeeey, you! How you been?" I pouted. "Missed you. Mean old Nirgie, keeping me 'way from you."

Subject 34 slowly knelt in front of me, cocking his head as if curious at my behavior, which was strange since it was his fault I was drugged to the teeth.

Being in that state meant caution completely went out the door. I patted the shoulder of his upper arm companionably as he sank into a full crouch right in front of me.

"Those guys are jerks. We know the deal." I nodded, feeling conspiratorial towards my fellow captive.

He tilted his head downwards as if studying my hand on his hard chitin. Fortunately, this touch didn't inspire him to sting me again.

"Whatcha been up to?" My head felt heavy as I rocked it towards him to get a better look at him. "Because I been having a blast these last few weeks."

I giggled again—a sound I hadn't made since I was in my teens. "I met a guy." This time I snickered. "Apparently, he's psychotic, which is sadly an upgrade from my usual dates. Last guy I agreed to go on a date with abducted me from Earth."

Subject 34 touched my lips with the claws of one of his lower hands. I kissed his claws, inhaling his scent. Even in my relaxed state, I felt the warmth of arousal increasing at his proximity.

He traced my lips with one claw, chittering softly. Then he

bumped his mandibles against them. I kissed them too. Beneath my lips, they separated. Then his actual lips pressed against mine.

I lifted one languid hand, palm sprinkled with sand grains, to touch his cheek.

He stung me.

This time, I barely felt the sting, but I did feel the sudden shot of energy and the immediate desire that had me wanting to pull all my hard-won clothes off again and splay myself out on the sand for him.

I shook my head, my lassitude and calm disappearing.

"Nope, not this time!" I turned my head when he tried to kiss me again. "I *can* resist!"

34 lifted his head, staring down at me through black eyes that were now revealed as the top of his facial chitin had split along with his mandibles. Those two lines I'd tried to smooth out earlier between his brows had returned, but I was a bit more aware of my position this time and resisted the urge to touch him again.

"I'm not going to let you keep drugging me, 34," I said in the severest tone I could manage, though my body ached now with the desire to strip and lay my body willingly beneath him. "You can't keep doing that stinging thing anytime you want something from me!"

To my relief, he didn't force the issue, though he wouldn't have had to push me very hard to get me to cave in this state. Instead, he seemed genuinely curious about my words, again cocking his head, his frown lines deepening as his lips pulled into a slight scowl. He studied my face, then lifted a lower hand to trace my eyebrows. Then he touched the same area between my brows where I had touched him.

His touch felt so good, even that tiny brush of a sharp claw tip against my skin had me all hot and bothered. To be fair, it was really whatever venom he'd pumped into me that put me in that state, but him touching me, and being so near to me with his huge, powerful body and bizarrely handsome face did not help cool me down.

I had enough sense to realize that if I kept talking, he might actually listen instead of getting sexual. It seemed like he was genuinely curious about my speech, perhaps even my expressions. Of course, it would be far more flattering if he wanted to get me on my back as soon as possible, but I got the idea that he was patient.

I also got the uncomfortable idea that the aphrodisiac venom itself was simply a result of more curiosity from him, rather than a genuine desire for me personally. It made me feel like I was as much of an experiment to him as he was to Nirgal and his ilk.

Still, something about me must have intrigued him enough for him to spare my life when he'd killed every other person he'd been given to hunt. I had to hold onto that and work out exactly what it was that he saw in me that made him so curious —so I could exploit the hell out of it.

If I could turn Subject 34 on his handlers, it would be a glorious bloodbath that I would revel in.

In theory.

I don't know how well I'd actually handle a bloodbath. Seemed a bit... gory. I wasn't much of a horror movie fan, though I loved me a good ghost story. I had a feeling my soft-hearted ass would end up feeling bad for his victims, even if they deserved everything they got.

I talk a good game, but I'm a total sucker.

While I pondered how I could turn 34 to my side, he continued to touch my face, exploring it with the concentration I might put into a painting. Every time one of my facial muscles moved to form an expression, it seemed to catch his eye and he'd trace that part of my face.

Then he'd touch his own face with his other lower hand. At the same time, his upper hands began to feel my hair, which was unfortunately very tangled after being hosed down every day for a few weeks with nary a comb in sight. Fingers just didn't do the job properly.

I felt bad for Subject 34 as I watched him draw his claws down his own face as if it were new to him and he was exploring it with as much curiosity as my own.

"It's a nice face," I said in reassurance, just in case he'd never actually seen his reflection. It didn't look like there were many mirrors lying around—or even still pools of water.

Not that he could understand me, but I figured it was worth a shot.

His wings flicked behind him when I spoke, and his claws returned to tracing my lips. His throat worked, a few chitters escaping him. Then his lips moved as if he struggled to shape words.

"Nnn-ice," he growled, his voice raspy and deep. "Nnn-ice faaay."

He touched his face, right below his cheek, drawing his claw over his cheek to then touch his chitinous mandibles tucked against the sides of his head. Then he traced the long scars on either side of his nose. His lips worked again.

Then the bisection of them split apart, and I realized with a gasp of horror that broke through the lust I still couldn't help feeling despite my determined self-control that his face wasn't exactly what it seemed.

His "mouth" split straight in half from below the nose to the chin, and those long scars were actually some kind of joining point that allowed the two sides of his face to spread wide open to display a true mouth hidden behind the mock mouth that had all the same elements as a human mouth.

Within his throat, now bared by that split lower face, two clawed appendages emerged from strange sheaths where a human's tonsils might be. Only these had much larger holes to fit the appendages.

"Holy shit!" I held up both hands in front of me, though I didn't dare to touch him. "What is that? What the heck!"

Within seconds, his face had pulled back together into the more human one, hiding all that scary horror monster crap behind a deceptively handsome façade. He blinked at me with those dark eyes, then lifted his claws to trace the lines bisecting his lips.

"Nnn-ice faaay."

"Uh... sure." I nodded reflexively, because you don't insult a giant bug man who just showed you his clawed throat appendages.

Seemed like a bad idea.

On the plus side, my arousal was fading, venom notwithstanding, so I didn't feel the same need to clamber all over his chitin covered body and impale myself on an erection he wasn't sporting at the moment anyway.

"I see you can speak," I said in a shaky voice that was a little too squeaky. "That's good. I mean, I don't know if you under-stand me, but—"

His claws cut me off and his mouth worked again, his lips moving several times without any sound coming out. He chit-tered in his throat, making me think of those scary clawed thin-gies that hid inside there.

"Sss-peak," he said after several attempts at making the sounds. "Unnnder-ssstand."

Now it was my turn to be curious. "I'm speaking English. You really understand me?"

Maybe he was only repeating what I said, like a parrot. Yet, I had a feeling he wasn't.

Did they seriously create something as dangerous as Subject 34 and then make it possible for him to learn this fast?

Of course, maybe he had a translator in his head like the one they'd put into mine.

Yeah, that was probably the case. Still, Nirgal had said Subject 34 never communicated, so I had to wonder why he'd decided to do so now.

He didn't answer my question, instead stroking my lips again, his upper hands tugging on my hair. When I winced as his claws got entangled, he paused. He blinked at me with that curious, coldly predatory gaze, then traced the muscles around my mouth.

I watched his face, noting the way his own muscles moved, scrunching up as if he weren't sure how they worked. His other lower hand touched his own face as he traced mine.

He was trying to learn how to make facial expressions. That much was clear. No doubt he'd noted the structure of his face, and I was willing to bet dollars to donuts—man, I missed donuts—that he wasn't born with that eerily attractive face. His false facial features had the look of the Nirgal aliens. Jawline too perfect, eyes slightly larger than human but nicely shaped, brows with perfect arches, straight nose and symmetrical high cheekbones. Not to mention those lovely lips even with the bisections, sexily plump, though not large.

His skin was a golden shade that wasn't human and had a similar iridescence to his chitin. All in all, the perfection of his face looked like a mask I now knew it to be.

"For the promotional material," Nirgal had said. They'd made Subject 34 look handsome to sell his existence to someone, it seemed. Clearly, his true form had not appealed to the beauty-obsessed aliens.

Great! Now I felt sad for him again. Even knowing what lay behind that eerie mask of his, I still felt empathy for the creature. Not only was he being controlled by the aliens, but he'd been fundamentally altered in a way that he was even now trying to adapt to. Maybe it was this alteration that made him so curious about me. Perhaps he'd only just discovered the contours of his face and wanted to study mine.

That didn't explain the whole sex thing when we'd first met though. If he weren't imprinted, I could only guess at why he'd decided to inject me with sex venom and do the deed. He hadn't really been studying my face then.

Or had he? Looking back, I realized I had no idea. This face of his had been hidden behind the hard chitinous outer shells of his protective goggle eyes and mandibles.

I let his hands explore me without protest because he didn't push my boundaries yet, which at this point had grown much smaller given the apparent wearing off of the aphrodisiac venom. Either the injection he'd given me had been much smaller than before, or I'd gained some immunity to it—or it didn't have as strong an effect if he wasn't doing something about my need.

I sure wished I could ask. I supposed I could, and maybe he'd even understand my question, but I wasn't certain he was capable of answering yet.

Nor was I certain he would. I had no illusions that I was in control here. He didn't behave like a regular person, despite his obvious intelligence. His actions seemed ruthless in the extreme—those of a cold predator who didn't consider his prey's feelings. He stung me without hesitation when I did anything he saw as a threat or an attempt to struggle.

I didn't sense any malice in his actions, but then again, I don't think most predators bear any malice towards their prey. That doesn't stop them from killing them, often brutally.

For the moment, 34 seemed more interested in inspecting me than eating me. As my emotions apparently played over my expression as I pondered the bizarre situation I was in, he continued to try to mimic them.

I missed that first dose of venom—the chill juice. I felt a lot calmer then than I did now, even if I had struggled to speak properly.

"So," I said after a long period had passed where he groped my face and his own and tugged painfully on my tangled mat of hair while touching the chitin on his own head, "this is a bit... weird. Can't say this is the strangest social interaction I've ever had, but it's definitely top ten, at least. Probably top five, to be honest."

He cocked his head, his gaze shifting to my lips, then lifting to meet my eyes. When he reached towards my eye with the claws that had been trailing along my jawline, I jerked backwards, cracking my skull on the rock at my back with a loud thud that left me wincing.

He made a chittering sound that had my clenched eyelids peeking open, my lips still pulled back in a grimace as I lifted a hand to rub the back of my head.

"No touching my eyeballs, k buddy." I tapped one finger well below my eye. "They're squishy and delicate. You start poking at them, you'll leave me blind."

The hand messing with my hair slid towards the bump that was now forming on my head. His fingers probed that tender part of my scalp, eliciting a pained moan from me that had him chittering softly in response.

"Yeah, that hurts a little, so be gentle, k."

"K-aaaayy." He stroked hard fingers over my head bump. "K-aaaayy buuud tee."

I didn't think he was answering me with a friendly response. In fact, crazy as it was, I thought I detected frustration in his growling, raspy tone as he struggled to form the words through lips he clearly didn't like using. I suspected those words didn't translate and that was why he repeated them. Perhaps he couldn't draw their meaning from context. Given his alien nature, that wasn't in the least bit surprising.

"I'll be honest," I said in a higher pitched tone than normal, "you're kind of hurting my head right now."

I probably should have allowed him to continue to probe that tender spot to his heart's content, because he suddenly caught me by the back of my neck with one lower hand and pulled me forward, his upper hands pushing my hair away from the swelling lump.

I felt his mandibles rub against the tender skin as I warned myself not to struggle, my face pressed against the hard chitin of his upper arm. Despite my determination not to piss him off with any movement, he still ended up stinging me. I felt the brief, sharp pierce of his stinger into my swollen scalp.

I cried out in terror, finally struggling for my life, but he held me in place with seemingly no effort at all, completely unfazed by my flailing arms and frightened screams.

I don't know how long it took for me to calm down and realize I wasn't dying in agony from his venom, but when he probed my scalp again with his fingers, I didn't feel any of the discomfort I'd felt from the bump before.

In fact, it felt nice and numb with not a hint of pain. Just in that one area, the scalp surrounding the bump as sensitive as ever to the scrape of his claws through my hair.

It was only after a thorough inspection of my scalp that Subject 34 finally released me, allowing me to lean back against the rock, staring up at him as he slowly rose from his crouch.

"Y-you did that to make me more comfortable," I said with surprise in my tone. "Why?"

He cocked his head to one side, his face now covered again

behind his chitinous mask. He made a chittering sound but didn't attempt to speak my language again.

I watched him turn his back on me with mouth agape, wondering where he planned to go as he spread his wings and leapt into the air.

THIRTEEN

"That didn't tell us much," a tinny voice said in my ear.

I shrieked and jerked upwards into a stiff sitting position, glancing around to make sure Subject 34 wasn't nearby.

"Damn it, Nirgie, what the hell are you doing inside my head?" I hissed as I lifted a hand to touch the translator. "You'd better not be reading my thoughts right now!"

"I am horrified at the very suggestion," Nirgal said in a stuffy tone. "I am not in your head, thank the Grand Spinner. I am speaking in your ear through the implant we installed there, you tangled twit."

I held up a hand like the jerk was right in front of me. "Listen here, buddy, you don't need to get nasty. I'm doing what you asked me to do."

"I suppose we can be thankful you managed to restrain yourself from mating with Subject 34. It spared us all an unpleasant scene. We *are* required to observe these interactions, after all."

"You know, you're starting to give me a complex, you dick,"

I snapped, pushing myself to my feet, then brushing off my sweatpants. "But I know the truth."

"The truth?" He sounded completely lost, much to my satisfaction.

"You don't have to keep up the pretense, Nirgie. I mean, it's pretty obvious."

"What nonsense are you yammering on about, human?"

I shrugged nonchalantly. "I'm just sayin'... you're not very slick about it."

"What is '*it*'?" he demanded, and I wondered if he was strangling his tablet at this moment.

I grinned at the thought that he'd probably need a new one by the time I was done with him.

"Aw, it's okay, Nirgie. I understand the real reason you're so mean to me. I won't take it personally."

"Would you just answer the blighted question, human?"

He was practically shouting in my ear now and I chuckled, taking a few hesitant steps near the rock I'd been sitting against just to make sure I wouldn't topple over. My legs felt rubbery and weak.

"What question is that, Nirgie?"

I looked around the enclosure surrounding the crevice area, quickly shifting my gaze away from the bones still littering the sand. I had no idea where the cameras were, but I didn't doubt there were many angles of me to choose from.

"What question? The... *damn* you, now I have no idea what in the Spinner's web we were talking about!"

"Where's Subject 34," I asked, relenting since I'd gotten a reaction out of him. It was so damned fun to push the jerk's buttons that I almost looked forward to talking to him.

He was silent for a long moment where I pictured him struggling to regain control of his temper. "We deposited food for him, and he has gone into the maze to hunt it."

I held up a hand, recalling now exactly how much of a monster Nirgal and his buddies were. I'd almost forgotten that. I supposed I should be thankful for the stark and sickening reminder.

"You son of a bitch!" I snarled, making my way around the rocks. "You had better not have dropped another person into that maze to be hunted by 34. If you did, I *will* find a way out of this enclosure, and I will hunt you down and take that fucking tablet of yours and bash your fucking head in with it!"

"We don't waste sapient subjects lightly," he said as if he had the nerve to be offended. "We've already ascertained Subject 34's ability to hunt with prescience. It has far surpassed our expectations."

"You are *such* a monster," I said, making my way towards the wall of the enclosure nearest the crevice. If this place had an outlet other than the vault door where I'd entered, it might be worth checking it out for a potential escape.

Even if it did lead back into the maze.

"We are *not* monsters! We are scientists." I could tell by his tone that he was growing agitated.

Good. Screw that bastard. I didn't even know how many poor, doomed people had raced around that maze trying to find an escape they'd never reach.

I hoped Nirgal suffered some day just as much as his victims had.

"In your case, it's apparently the same damned thing," I snapped, placing a hand on the wall, then shrieking and snatching it back to tuck it against my chest after receiving a painful shock.

"Subject 34 will not be occupied long, human," Nirgal said, changing the subject as he usually did when he had no defense for his atrocities. "I won't waste any more time being distracted from the purpose of this experiment. His actions were not entirely clear to us when he interacted with you, which is unfortunate."

"They weren't clear to *you* because you lack empathy, you bastard." Without touching the wall again, I started walking along it, pacing out the size of the enclosure.

"It is, of course, intriguing that he spoke." He ignored my criticism as usual. "Now I'm confident you can get him to say more. We've implanted the memory of our own language in his brain, and his translator will make it possible for him to understand yours. Thus, it's imperative that you communicate verbally as much as possible to increase the opportunities for him to reply. I suspect you'll have no trouble talking frequently. It's remaining silent that appears to give you difficulties."

I lifted a hand to rub my temple, sighing heavily as I continued my way around the large chamber. "I think you idiots are making a huge mistake with 34."

"What difference does it make what you think?" His tone dripped with condescension. "We are finally on the brink of a breakthrough with Subject 34. This experiment has far wider implications than you can imagine. Your thoughts on the topic are irrelevant."

"What is your ultimate goal, anyway?" I paused in my steps as I stared at the wall like he stood right on the other side of it. "Human scientists perform experiments to better the world and help people. That's why human experimentation has so many boundaries to it and so many ethical restraints. You guys, though, all you seem to do is create misery and pain and suffering. I've seen those poor people of yours in the warehouse. You don't even care about your *own* kind, much less any other creature!"

"The suffering of those males is not our doing," Nirgal said in a stiff tone. "They imprinted upon females that were not available to them. They would deteriorate and die no matter what we do to them. We are working on a cure that will save some of them—at the very least. A cure that was used on Subject 34 to protect him from imprinting."

I propped my hands on my hips, glaring at the wall, noting that it was made of large panels very tightly jointed together. Shocking panels, sadly, so there wasn't a likelihood of me being able to pry them apart.

"So that's supposed to convince me that what you're doing to them isn't wrong? You should see the way green guy stares with utter terror in his eyes at the 'claw' you bastards use to extract us. I know you're doing some fucked up crap to those poor people."

"Ilyan is a... special case that I have no intention of discussing, least of all with you. Nor do I intend to explain the purpose of this experiment. I don't need to justify my actions to you, human."

I regarded the wall with a smirk, hoping there was a camera around to capture my expression. "Oh, but I bet they bother *you*. Especially now, because someone is finally pointing out what a heinous creature you are." I waved my hand in the vague direction of 34's crevice. "That's why you're always shrieking 'it's for science!' whenever I mention the terrible things you do. As if that's an excuse to do whatever you want and screw anyone who has to suffer for it."

"You understand *nothing*!" Nirgal's voice shook with anger, and I suspected I'd really pushed a big red button now.

"Oh yeah." I tapped one foot, my hands still on my hips. "Then explain it to me, huh. I'm willing to bet you can't, because the minute you start thinking too hard about what you're doing here, you're going to have to see what you've become, and that's going to be a very ugly sight, Nirgal."

"Enough!"

I slammed my hand to my ear as he shouted into it, then

collapsed to my knees at the reverb sound that seemed to rock my skull. The vibration of sound reignited the dull ache in my scalp from the bump on my head.

After a long silence that rang in my ears, he spoke again in a deadly calm tone. "Subject 34 is returning to the enclosure now. You will meet him and attempt to get him to speak again. Do not speak to *me* again, human. I have nothing left to say to you."

"You can't escape your crimes, Nirgal," I said in a solemn voice. "They will always weigh on you. But you *could* lighten their burden by redeeming yourself." I stared at the wall with a pleading expression. "Let me go. *Stop* these horrible things you're doing! Save all those poor people in their cages!"

Nothing but silence met my plea, and I shook my head, my shoulders slumping. My worst fears were right. Nirgal was a heartless bastard, and I was wasting my time trying to reach him and open his eyes to how wrong he was. Apparently, he was a completely evil mad scientist-type with zero empathy—a sadist, responsible for such cruelties that there wasn't any coming back from them.

I was alone in my fight for survival.

Subject 34 appeared behind me so silently that I screamed when he grabbed my shoulder, completely unaware of his presence. I spun around, backing away from him. For once, he didn't sting me. I took that as a good sign.

Maybe I wasn't completely alone. In fact, perhaps I had the strongest possible ally in this hellhole.

FOURTEEN

"Okay, 34, now say, 'Nirgal is a used tampon.'"

Subject 34 studied me with an unreadable pair of dark eyes and an expressionless face, but at least his outer mandibles and chitin goggle eyes were retracted so I could see the more humanoid parts of him.

I'd been trying to teach 34 to speak for what felt like hours after he found me standing near the wall, glaring at it and wishing I could shoot lasers out of my eyes to disintegrate the jerk standing somewhere on the other side of it.

I was fairly sure at this point that 34 knew what I was trying to do when it came to getting him to communicate but he was being stubborn for some reason about making the same level of effort he'd seemed to make before.

Instead, he simply watched me in an unnerving fashion as I repeated phrases over and over again. At first, I'd tried to make them very simple, but when he didn't make the effort to speak in order to repeat them, I just made up the craziest things I could think of, and then it devolved into childish insults towards Nirgal.

I had to admit, by that time, I was good and hangry, so I blame my bad behavior on that. I really hoped I was pissing off the bastard though. I mean, he did say he had to observe everything going on in this enclosure.

My stomach growled in protest at the lack of sustenance. It was well past my usual protein bar time. Granted, my stomach had shrunk significantly since I'd been dragged out of cryosleep into a full-on living nightmare with the monster as my only friend, but my body still had needs.

Subject 34 stared down at the source of that soft noise with no shift in his expression, but with a tilt to his head and flicking of his wings as he crouched in front of me that I'd learned to equate with his curiosity.

Realizing things could go wrong if he misinterpreted those roiling sounds as aggressive, I quickly patted my stomach. "I haven't eaten anything lately, so my stomach is making sounds because I'm hungry."

If I'd expected a verbal response at this point, I would be disappointed. I wasn't certain what type of response I'd expected, since 34 could be so unpredictable. When he rose rapidly and gracefully to his feet, I jumped a little against the rock I was using as a seat back near his lair.

The way he towered over me unnerved me quite a bit, but it wouldn't have done me much good to take to my own feet, because he still stood significantly taller than me. I'd have to guesstimate he neared seven feet tall when standing straight.

He was a beast, in every sense of the word. Massive and armored and threatening, moving like quicksilver, fluid and fast. I didn't get the chance to ask him what was up before he spread his wings and leapt into the air. They blurred behind him as he flew away from me.

I called after him hesitantly, wondering what new idea had

popped into his head. It sure would be nice if he'd make the effort to explain himself to me, even a little bit.

I sat on the sand, leaning back against the rock, sagging with hopelessness and depression. I'd come to several conclusions in the last few hours.

One, Subject 34 did not desire me with the same level of arousal he inspired in me. At least, he'd made zero effort to "mate" with me since I'd told him I could resist his aphrodisiac-like venom. Maybe he was finally respecting my boundaries, but I found it difficult to believe he'd get things like that through his head that fast. Especially not if he really was into me like that. So, I was left with the only possible conclusion. Like my speech and facial expressions, 34 had been merely curious about my body and possibly his own, and he'd acted on that curiosity.

To say I was disappointed was an understatement. I'm not saying I wanted to fall all over him whenever I looked at him, but when I inhaled deep whiffs of his scent, I definitely felt a desire I couldn't completely ignore. He was still putting out some kind of mojo sexy juice. He just wasn't pumping it out to the degree that he had before.

Two, Subject 34 was a hell of a lot smarter than I think even his captors were giving him credit for. His failure to repeat the words I'd been saying to him had absolutely nothing to do with his inability to understand them. I could tell he did. Maybe some of my expressions confused him because there were the slightest variations in his expression—the most obvious being the lines forming between his brows—whenever I used human slang or metaphorical language. Still, he was getting the gist of it, far faster than I would have expected.

It killed me not to know what he was thinking behind those cold, dark eyes. I couldn't even see the wheels turning. No body language gave me a clear clue of his thought process. I'd learned to pick up a few hints like the flicking wings and cocked head, the occasional chittering that came from his throat, and a very subtle increase in the rare times he blinked.

Did his eyeballs never dry out?

I was so deep in thought that when he dropped down to the sand in front of me straight out of the air above, I screamed aloud and jerked away from him. Fortunately, I didn't hit my head this time. I wasn't sure I could handle any more of his "tender" nursing of my wound.

I screamed again when he dropped a bloody chunk of gore onto my lap. I flung it off me, shaking my hands as blood coated them, dark and coagulated. It dropped to the sand with a sickening thud, staining the pale, nearly white grains beneath it.

I couldn't identify what kind of flesh it was, or what part of whatever kind of body it came from, but I was only a little relieved to see that it had a patch of fur on it that didn't look in any way human. In fact, the vivid coloring of the fur was startling and seemed unnatural. Bright magentas and greens rather than any color that existed in animal fur on Earth.

Subject 34 bent to scoop up the gory thing and tried to hand it back to me with one clawed lower hand, gesturing to my noisy stomach with the other.

"Huuun-gry," he said in his growling voice. "Ssoundss huun-gry."

I swallowed the bile that rose in my throat, adamantly turning my face away from the offering. "No thank you, 34." I held up a hand like I could block that thing from getting any closer to me. "That's not the kind of food I was thinking of eating. I'm gonna give that a hard pass, k. I'll stick to fasting for a while."

He stared down at me, the gory chunk that was as big as my head dripping nasty blood onto my already bloodstained lap. I worried he'd force that thing on me given the intensity of his posture. It looked like he was about to insist I eat it. I don't know exactly how I knew that, but it could have been the way he was leaning slightly towards me, closing me in, wings spreading in agitation.

Or maybe it was the fact that his lips pulled into a true frown, which was a rare sight on his usually blank face.

I sighed in relief when he straightened and took a few steps away from me. Then I gulped and swallowed a bit harder when his face split open, and he lifted the grisly chunk of meat to it. Those clawed appendages darted out of his throat and started pulling off pieces of the raw flesh to masticate them before withdrawing them back into his gaping maw.

On the plus side, I no longer had an appetite. On the minus side, I was about to vomit all over this sand. I turned away, scooting my butt until I sat with my side against the rock instead of my back. I hummed loud enough to drown out the squishing sounds of him eating.

It didn't take long for him to consume the whole, massive chunk of meat. I wasn't sure what he'd do next, and I was hoping it didn't involve bringing more of that stuff to me—not even to eat it in front of me.

Then his lower hand fell upon my shoulder, causing me to stiffen in alarm.

He didn't touch me much, unless he was doing something to me that I probably shouldn't want, but definitely did. When he did make contact with my skin in any capacity, it was only because he had intent behind his touch.

Affectionate, he was not.

In this case, I figured it was to get my attention, and when I turned towards him, I saw that he must have grown aroused by his meal.

His alien phallus stood fully erect and jutting from a slit in his body, where a small plate of chitin over his groin had retracted away from the opening just like his facial armor and pincers retracted.

"Okay then," I said, my mouth instantly watering as the evidence of his arousal spurred my own, which had been slow boiling the entire time he'd crouched near me, sending his pheromones all over the place.

I pushed the image of him eating out of my head as I climbed to my knees, reaching to stroke his shaft with one hand that shook slightly.

Hey, he stings when he's touched, so I was a little nervous. Not nervous enough to leave it alone, because I really wanted it inside me. I wanted him vibrating in my body until I climaxed, slowly pumping in and out of me in a way that told me he wasn't really familiar with those motions.

He made a lot of sounds I couldn't interpret, but he didn't make a move to sting me when I circled my fingers around his thick girth. A drop of precum welled from the tip of his shaft as I slowly stroked from the base of it to the tip, moaning louder than the incomprehensible sounds he made.

Then one of his lower hands caught my chin, tightening on it until I gasped. As soon as my lips parted, he promptly probed them with the head of his dick.

Okay, I can do this. Hell, I even wanted to! It was a bit demanding on his part, but hey, we were still learning to communicate, and I kinda dug that dominating stuff—in small doses. I closed my lips around his oddly shaped tip, sucking it as deep as I could.

I was rewarded for my effort by a sudden burst of fluid into my mouth that had me choking and pulling back as I swallowed reflexively.

"Hey, I'm excited too, but next time, a little warning would be nice," I said, though without much heat as I swiped my lips.

"Fffoodd," he said with the effort he clearly put into

shaping the words with lips that I don't think he really knew how to use yet.

I blinked up at him in confusion, though I noted that he remained erect, my hand still circled around his shaft, the tip of it beaded now with drops of his ejaculate.

"Well, now things have gotten interesting," Nirgal said in my ear, causing me to yelp in surprise, then quickly release Subject 34's length.

I'd forgotten for a moment that we had watchers observing everything we did. I wasn't much of an exhibitionist, and I especially wasn't keen with having those creeps watching the show.

34 growled in a low, vibrating way that had his chest plates rattling, lowering his body into a crouch as he tilted his head near mine. His eyes had fixed on my ear, and I wondered if he could hear Nirgal's tinny voice emanating from it.

"Don't misinterpret his actions, human. He was not attempting to mate with you. He was trying to feed you."

"*What?*" My voice rose to a piercing pitch with that question.

Subject 34 growled again, pressing his head against my ear as if he wanted to feel the vibrations of sound coming from it.

"It is remarkable, isn't it? He can process nutrients within his body to produce a viable food source for others. It is one of many abilities he possesses when it comes to instinctively developing compounds for survival—many of which are not found in nature."

Oh, Subject 34 heard Nirgal alright!

I had no doubt of that now that he was prodding at my ear as I tried to pull away from him. I didn't think he liked what he was hearing either. I had no idea how much he could actually make out, but he was growling *and* chittering, and I took that as a bad sign.

34 held my head in place easily with one upper hand while he poked inside my ear with the other. His body dwarfed mine, his posture curling around me in an almost protective fashion while he sought the source of that sound. His lower hands penned me in against the rock while his upper hands were busy, so I couldn't escape him.

Not that I could anyway. I watched with wide eyes as his stingers rose on either side of him, the lethal tips hovering far too close to my skin for comfort.

"The implant is too deep for him to remove it," Nirgal said with serene confidence.

"Without piercing my skull, maybe," I muttered bitterly, yelping when 34's claw delved into my earhole.

"I don't believe at this point he will harm you," Nirgal replied thoughtfully even as Subject 34 lifted his head away from my face and withdrew his claw from my ear, staring down at me with a visible frown. "Something remarkable has happened. It appears he has *chosen* to claim you, because we have found no biological evidence that he's imprinted on you."

FIFTEEN

"Were you *feeding* me?" I asked 34, gesturing to his groin, the savory taste of the fluid he'd ejaculated still on my tongue. "With your-with... um... why use *that* particular body part?"

His erection had disappeared back behind the chitin codpiece that protected it, and his intent gaze still focused on my ear, his brows drawing together so closely now that the lines between them cut deep.

"Would you prefer he push food into your mouth with his chelicerae?" Nirgal said in a disdainful tone in my ear, causing Subject 34 to growl low in his throat in a way that seemed to blend with his angry chittering. "What other body part would he use? His stingers? Would you suck on those instead?"

"You know, dude," I said, regarding Subject 34's increasingly more intent glaring at that little speaker implant in my ear, "I don't think he likes you talking to me. Not one bit."

"Then tell him to speak directly to *us*, human. We would prefer to communicate with *him*, rather than through you."

"He's a used tampon," I reminded Subject 34. "You should tell him to go fuck himself. Cuz nobody else would want to."

"We sent you back into his enclosure to get him to communicate," Nirgal snapped in his snobby scientist voice. "Your current behavior is counterproductive."

"Seems like he has no problem communicating with me," I said with snark, grinning at Subject 34, who remained crouching over me, leaning his body over mine.

At least he no longer poked at my ear. I could understand him wanting to put an end to the annoying sound of Nirgal speaking, but not when it meant pain and possible deafness for me.

He shifted his dark gaze from my ear to my lips, then lifted a hand to touch my lower lip. I reflexively licked it, tasting some of the savory flavor from the "food" he'd given me in the most bizarre method of feeding someone ever.

He poked my tongue with his claw tip. Then he pried open my lips and teeth to my vocal protest. I finally just let him look inside my mouth because it was better than trying to fight him and likely end up stung in the process.

He prodded my gums, tapped my teeth, and then touched my tongue with obvious curiosity. When he finally released my mouth, he straightened so that he wasn't completely overshadowing me.

"Nnn-iiice ffaace." He followed up these words that clearly gave him some difficulty to form by touching his own lips, then mine again. "Ron-daa liiike."

I nodded, pleased to hear him forming words I could understand. Plus, it was the first time he'd said my name, though I'd repeated it many times when I was trying to get him to talk. "Yes, you have a very nice face, 34, and I like it."

He cocked his head, then lowered it to press his lips to mine. I responded by kissing him, even though I was still a bit wary of what hid behind those lips. They tasted of iron, and that flavor reminded me of the gory meat he'd consumed very recently. Still, they smelled delicious, like the rest of him, and I felt aroused again.

"Thirrr-teee fforrr liiike Ron-daa," he said after I broke the kiss—which was one-sided. He didn't really know what to do when he pressed his lips to mine.

"Aww!" I lifted a hand to touch his face, then froze before my fingers made contact with his skin, recalling what had happened when I'd tried that before. "I like you too, 34."

He caught my wrist when I went to lower my hand, then pulled it to his face. I flattened my hand as he pushed it against his golden skin, then drew my fingers over his cheekbone.

"This is truly remarkable," Nirgal said, completely ruining the moment.

I was so going to beat him with that tablet!

Subject 34 pulled away from me, shifting his focus back to my ear. "Thirr-tee forrr noot liiike Nirrgaall. Killl."

"Ha!" I said aloud, then slapped a hand over my mouth. I loudly cleared my throat as I lowered my hand, getting control over my broad grin. "Ahem. Well, you can't say I didn't warn you, Nirgal."

"He is still implanted with a control chip, human. I am not concerned. Besides, it is his nature to kill. The fact that he seems to have taken a liking to you and spared your life is the anomaly. One I'd dearly like to understand. At the moment, it is completely mystifying."

"Nirrgalll isss tammmponn," 34 growled, much to my hilarity.

If he hadn't been crouching so close to me, I would have collapsed to the sand and rolled all over it, laughing my ass off, especially when Nirgal started saying all these weird alien curses in my ear. I finally managed to recover the ability to speak around my howling laughter that had drowned out Nirgal's pissed off words.

I touched 34's face without thinking, cupping his cheek with real affection for the monstrous alien male. "I think I like you, 34! I think I like you a whole lot!"

I only realized what I'd done when his body stiffened, his head lifting away from my hand as he straightened in his crouch. He touched his cheek where my palm had been, tracing over his skin with the tips of his claws.

I eyed his waist nervously, but his stingers were nowhere in sight. "Sorry. I shouldn't have—"

He caught my wrist and tugged my hand back up to his cheek, nuzzling my palm like a cat. His skin was cooler to the touch than my own, perhaps even the same temperature as the enclosure we were in. I cautiously explored his features with delicate touches and slow movements, and this time, he let me draw my fingertip down the lines the formed between his brows. They remained creased as he studied me, watching my face intently as I explored his.

When I shifted my hand to touch one of his retracted mandibles, he sucked in a breath, turning his face so my hand came into full contact with his mandible. "Nnn-iiicee."

I smiled as I stroked my fingers along the chitin surface, noting that it wasn't completely smooth but had tiny, barely visible hairs poking from the surface that were so small that I hadn't noticed them until I felt them. "You like when I touch you here?"

"Liiikke."

I lifted a hand to one of the retracted lenses that covered his eyes when he was in full armored mode. He captured my hand before I could touch the slightly bulbous surface of it. "Nnnottt liiike."

"He's probably concerned about damage to those lenses. They do not regenerate with the same rapidity as his other chitin plates. No doubt due to the complexity of the—"

"Shut up, Nirgal," I muttered, returning my hand to 34's mandible.

He didn't release my hand, but I felt like it was because he enjoyed touching me, rather than that he feared I would damage some part of his body.

"I am quite proud of that adaptation, I'll have you know," Nirgal said as I sighed heavily and rolled my eyes. "I added it to his genome myself. It has improved this iteration of the athraxius hybrid, giving him an extra layer of protection the original subject did not possess."

Subject 34 stared at my eyes, then he looked up, his whole head moving rather than his eyes. I chuckled, ignoring anything Nirgal had to say at this point. I couldn't force him to shut up, but I wouldn't give him the satisfaction of responding to him.

"You just move your eyes to roll them, honey," I said with a grin to 34. "Not your whole head."

I demonstrated the eye roll for him, then chuckled again when his black eyes rolled upwards, making him look for a moment like a bored teenager who is so totally over it and literally can't even.

"You know, you're kind of adorable when you aren't being all sting-y and gore-chomping."

"He is a genetically engineered soldier!" Nirgal's tone sounded supremely outraged. "He is *not* adorable!"

"Are you afraid I'll make him soft?" I asked in a needling tone.

I leaned forward and pressed another kiss to 34's lips. They remained still, but he didn't pull away or sting me.

"You're gonna be a big ol' softy, aren't you, 34?" I said after making a loud kissing sound. "A real teddy bear. You'll never want to hurt anyone again after I'm all done with you." I smirked, just knowing our captor was watching our every expression.

I'll admit, I gained far too much entertainment from tormenting my tormentor.

"Waannt hurrt Nirgaall."

I laughed at the outraged sputtering in my ear, then my grin faded as I noted 34's cold, black eyes regarding it with an intensity that made even me nervous and would have caused Nirgal to poop his robe if he'd had an ounce of sense beneath all that blustery arrogance.

"The best way to hurt Nirgie is to ruin all his plans," I whispered, giving 34 another peck on the lips.

This time, he pushed them against mine, tilting his head and mimicking my earlier attempts to kiss him. I moaned and parted my own lips, drawing my tongue along his lower lip. The bisection of it felt odd to me at first, but his response was worth that strangeness. His entire body vibrated as his scent seemed to increase into a heady aroma I knew would be difficult for me to resist.

I was soon tugging on my shirt, pulling it up past my bra and wondering how I could get it off without breaking the kiss. When his lips parted, I delved my tongue inside his mouth, forgetting for the moment exactly what the true structure of that mouth was. My tongue stroked over his, tasting the savory flavor of him, and he met it with an unpracticed eagerness that turned me on even more.

As our tongues tangled, mine bumped against the split in his upper palate, reminding me again of the way his mouth actually looked, but by that time, I was already too far gone with my arousal to care.

His two lower hands roved over my body, claws tugging on the fabric that covered it, much to my frustration. I now regretted that I wasn't naked beneath his exploring palms. His upper hands cradled my face, not so much in a sweet, romantic way, but like he wasn't about to let me pull away.

He tore open my sweatpants at my groin, the thick material barely resisting his strong tug. I moaned into his mouth as his claws trailed over my seam, still concealed behind the thin material of my panty. His clawed finger traced my folds, and I bucked against it as it passed over my clit, moaning again.

To say this caught his attention was an understatement. Suddenly, his intent focus seemed to shift to that part of my body to the point that he even broke our kiss to bow his head, his gaze lowering to where his finger stroked me.

"Yes, 34, I like it when you rub me right there."

He cocked his head, pulling further away from me to my disappointment, but at least his hands remained on my body. Clearly, he had no intention of abandoning what we'd been up to. I realized he wanted a closer look when his upper hands dropped to the waistband of my pants. I thought he was going to tug them down my legs, but he gripped the sides of them and tore them in two like they were made of tissue paper.

I shrieked in surprise, then moaned in delight as he rubbed over my clit again, his dark gaze now fully fixed on my panty-clad mound. He dropped the two sides of my pants, his lower hands moving to my knees to push them apart so he could kneel between them.

I realized he was going to tear my panties a second too late. He shredded them with such a quick motion that my glistening wet seam was bared to him before I could suck in enough air to protest and show him how they could be properly removed.

It looked like I no longer owned a full set of clothing. Nirgal better hook me up with some new clothes after this! I didn't mind being naked around 34, but I'd had it with showing off my goods to everyone else and their mad-scientist brothers.

It did occur to me that we were still being observed, but I found it awfully hard to care when 34 turned his full focus to my clit. His two upper hands gripped my waist as I bucked my hips against his stroking finger, and he trailed the claws of his other lower hand through my curls to touch my arousal-swollen flesh.

"Ah, yes, 34! I *really* like it when you rub me there!"

He fingered my clit for a few more strokes, pinning my hips in place with his two upper hands as if he thought they were rocking to move away from his touch. Two fingers on his other hand parted my folds, exposing the nub of nerves he'd been rubbing, now throbbing from my excitement.

"Fooddd?" he said, causing my eyes to shoot open with alarm that pumped a burst of adrenaline through my blood, pushing back the lust long enough for sense to creep in.

"What? No!" I tried to cover my clit as he looked up to meet my eyes. "You're not supposed to *eat* me, 34! I thought we were friends!"

He straightened his upper body, shifting the hand that had been so nicely stroking me to his own groin. My gaze followed its movements, and I noted how the palm-sized, codpiece-shaped part of his chitin plating that covered his phallic slit retracted to sit just above it.

Then his shaft everted right into his hand, which encircled it. He stroked his thumb over the tip and drops of milky fluid welled from it. Then one of his upper hands lifted to my lips, his claws tracing them.

"Feeeding," he growled.

I slowly shook my head, licking my lips. "I can't do that, 34. My body doesn't make *food* like that." I realized perhaps the small nub of my clit had made him think it was akin to his shaft —not just a source of pleasure but also of nourishment.

This was the weirdest sexual relationship I'd ever had—not that I had much to compare it to. Michael had been an absolute bore in bed, but I'd been a dutiful and faithful wife.

"I mean, you *could* lick it," I said a little breathlessly as my gaze fixed on his erection hungrily. "And suck it, like I sucked on yours, but no fluid will come out. It will just feel *really* good for me!" My eyes closed as I moaned at the thought.

Then I thought of his mouth as it really was. Then I thought again about his completely functional tongue stroking over my clit, and I forgot what I was thinking before that.

My eyes shot open as he shifted. My slit already dripped from my arousal, but it grew soaked as he lowered his head towards my clit. Still, he was unpredictable and not exactly familiar with my body, so I felt a little nervousness creeping past the arousal.

"No biting!" My voice shook as I moved my hips back, reminded again of just how dangerous his mouth could be.

He pinned them in place again with his two upper hands. One lower hand still parted my folds, the other encircled his own shaft. Then his mouth lowered to my mound, and his tongue stroked over my clit, just like his finger had earlier.

"Oh god, yes!" My upper back arched against the rock, my hips unable to move as he tongued my clit.

My legs trembled on either side of his broad shoulders as intense pleasure flowed through me, enhanced by the pheromone he was putting out. His body began to vibrate again, his wings buzzing so much that they kicked up sand.

Then his lips closed over my clit and he suckled it. The vibration of the rest of his body resonated in his lips and through his tongue. The feeling of it combined with the intense stimulation caused me to climax almost immediately. He held my hips in place with his upper hands and caught my knees with his lower hands, keeping my lower body immobile as I cried out with my orgasm.

His mandible shifted against my inner thigh as my cum welled from my entrance and slicked my skin. He released my throbbing clit and then his tongue licked down my folds to my entrance.

I clutched the chitinous plates of his shoulders as it delved inside me, my inner muscles still convulsing around the thick length of it.

He ate me out like he loved what he tasted, the vibration of his body growing more intense, until all his plates rattled, and the buzzing of his wings whipped my hair around my face like a fan. He finally lifted his head to meet my eyes, his lips glistening from my slick. He tilted his head as he regarded my face, my breath rasping out of me in the aftermath of the intense climax.

One clawed finger traced my entrance, then delved inside it. His tongue stroked over his lower lip. "Fooodd herrree."

"Hm, I suppose he might gain some benefit from the biochemical components of your emissions," Nirgal said in my ear, snapping me out of that post-orgasm glow as I jerked up into a straight sitting position with a startled yelp. "I would not have considered it nutrient-rich enough to qualify as nourishment, but 34 can do more with less. He likely views this as an exchange of resources. Interesting."

"Dammit, Nirgal!" I shouted as Subject 34 growl-chittered, "*I'm* gonna be the one to kill you at this rate! You couldn't give me *five* minutes to enjoy the afterglow before you started yammering?"

"More time than that has passed since your apparent climax, therefore—"

"You just can't leave it alone, can you?" I asked, shaking my head as Subject 34 slowly rose to his feet, his gaze moving around the enclosure as if he searched for Nirgal.

"I fail to see why you are so upset," Nirgal said in a defensive tone. "You appeared to enjoy yourself and were not harmed in the process. You should be thanking me for reuniting you with Subject 34. It appears to be working out well for you."

Subject 34's erection had disappeared, concealed again behind the armor of his chitin. His face had also closed, leaving only that blank, insectoid stare and hard mandibles as he stalked towards the wall, his wings flicking.

I sighed, pulling my torn sweatpants back against my skin, realizing that fun time was over.

SIXTEEN

You know how it is when you can sit and talk to a man for a significant amount of time, and he seems to be listening intently to you and almost never interrupts so he can tell his own story without showing any clue that he heard anything you'd said at all.

Yeah, me neither.

At least, not until right now, while sitting with Subject 34. He had finally given up his investigation of the enclosure walls, after pausing for an extended time in front of one of them, his expression unreadable behind his chitinous facial coverings. Now he crouched in front of my makeshift seat on the sand. I still leaned with my back against the rock outside his blocked crevice.

"So, that's why humans don't actually feed each other like that." I finished my explanation about human eating habits, and hygiene—and *oral* habits, a blush still burning my cheeks.

Subject 34 had his face revealed again as he watched me like he actually cared what I had to say. It was such a strange feeling that I didn't realize I'd been pausing after every few sentences, expecting him to interrupt or cut me off or change the subject, until the silence stretched as he merely watched me with an expectant air, actually *waiting* for me to take a breath without jumping in with his own input.

Once I'd fallen silent long enough that he must have understood I had finished speaking, he responded, his lips forming the words with a little more ease than he'd had before. "Thirtee fore like feeeding."

Okay, I'm not gonna lie. I had liked it too. It was weird, and when I wasn't aroused to the point of crawling along the floor naked, it was a bit awkward to consider what was actually happening—an exchange of bodily fluids as food—but I wasn't exactly in Kansas anymore. Lots of things had been really weird in my life lately.

Not that I'd ever actually been to Kansas, but I figured it was as normal a place as you could find. Although, given what Nirgal had told me—if he could even be believed—Kansas might look totally different now than it had been when I'd been abducted from Earth.

My mind still boggled at the thought that I'd lost ten years and probably could never go home, even if I could escape. I wouldn't want to escape from these alien overlords only to find myself under the control of another.

I sighed, lifting a hand to trace the line of 34's cheek, framed by the chitin that covered his head and mandibles. "I think I could grow used to... uh... *feeding* the way you like." I narrowed my eyes and shifted my glare towards that wall that Subject 34 had stood at earlier like he was looking at something beyond that dull gray surface. "Seeing as Nirgal would leave me to starve in here!"

"I won't *not* have let you starve," he said in a defensive tone, speaking for the first time since he'd ruined the mood between me and Subject 34 earlier. "I merely delayed delivery of food you would find palatable to see if Subject 34 would behave as the first athraxius subject did and provide you nutrients from his own body. We have not observed this behavior in our subjects since that experiment went disastrously wrong. Even with the first subject, that observation had only been made from a distance with a maintenance drone rather than in a controlled environment."

"You're such a douche." I shook my head.

"Dooo shhh." 34 also turned his head to glare at the wall. Then he returned his intent gaze to me. "Whaattt is?"

I giggled, surprising myself at the girlish sound. I couldn't remember the last time I'd felt giddy enough to laugh like that. I guess the afterglow still remained to a certain extent. "I'm gonna save that explanation for another time, 34."

34 touched my ear, where Nirgal's annoying voice had fallen silent, thankfully. Then he traced my jawline, his claw poking gently beneath my chin to lift it. His lips lowered to mine and I kissed them eagerly.

He was learning, though he still had that awkwardness that I found strangely endearing. A sort of hesitance as my lips caressed his, like he wasn't certain how to fully mimic the movements. That awkwardness disappeared the longer I kissed him, and soon, he slanted his mouth over mine so that our lips pressed more fully together, deepening the kiss as mine parted. This time, it was his tongue that delved into my mouth, and I sucked it between my teeth, causing his body to vibrate as a low chitter-growl mixed sound emanated from him.

I don't know how far things would have gone, but my stomach chose to growl in hunger not long after he really started getting good at this kissing thing. I was already panting with desire, his body putting out that delicious scent again, when he lifted his head to break the kiss.

"Hun-gry," he said, and I swear I saw an anticipatory gleam

in those dark, enigmatic eyes. He traced my swollen lower lip. "Thirr-tee fore feed Ron-da."

I smirked, eyeing him with mock suspicion. "I'm starting to think you benefit from this whole 'feeding' thing, 34."

His lips spread in a grin that was a bit terrifying given how unfamiliar the expression clearly was for him, but hey, he tried. I gotta give him credit for that. I pecked a kiss on his lips, hoping to chase away that snarly looking grimace of a smile.

"Ron-da like?"

I wrapped my arms around his neck, kissing him again, much deeper before I pulled away to draw in a breath. "Oh yeah, Rhonda definitely likes!"

He straightened his upper body, still crouching in front of me in a way that looked like it would be uncomfortable after hours of doing it, but he seemed to be most comfortable like that. A glance at his groin showed me he had already everted his erection, and I licked my lips as I spotted the drop of fluid welling from the tip.

Strange the experience might be, but I was turned on like I'd never been before encountering Subject 34, and barely hesitated before I bent my head towards that stiff shaft. His plates were already rattling when my lips closed around the head of it. I sucked him as deep as I could, which wasn't all the way given the impressive length and girth of him.

Before, he'd ejaculated the fluid as soon as my lips closed over the tip, but this time, he let my mouth stroke over his shaft, my fingers curling around his girth beneath my lips to move in sync with them. He appeared to like what I was doing, since his claws delved into my tangled hair, scraping my scalp in a way that felt pleasant, rather than dangerous. His whole body vibrated, including the shaft in my mouth, making my teeth and tongue tingle.

This time, he seemed to control the flow of fluid from his

shaft, allowing me to suck it from him like I was drawing it in a stream out of a straw. If I wasn't so turned on that I was soaking wet, I might have balked at the oddness of all this, but at the moment, I didn't care how strange and almost forbidden it seemed.

I was giving an alien male a blow job and swallowing his ejaculate like it was a savory soup. It did actually taste that way. Savory without being too salty. It also wasn't thick and goopy but rather flowed nicely instead of sticking to the back of my throat so it would be a struggle to swallow it all. Though I was definitely aroused—and I was pretty certain he was too—I didn't think he was doing this particular act for sexual satisfaction.

I sucked him until his fingers tightened in my hair and tugged on my head, shifting his hips in his crouch to move his erection away from my lips. I had no idea how much fluid I'd swallowed, but I no longer felt any hunger. In fact, I felt sated without being stuffed to a point of discomfort.

I barely had a chance to sit up straight before 34 moved to part my legs. He tossed the two pieces of my sweatpants aside with his lower hands, baring my soaking seam to him. His upper hands caught my face, and he lowered his lips to mine, while his lower hands circled under my knees, pulling them further apart as he moved to align the head of his shaft with my slit.

He caught my moan with his hungry lips as he sank his length deep inside me, filling me in a way I'd never been filled before. He was larger than any man I'd ever been with, and I might have been intimidated by his size if he didn't make me so crazy with arousal. Each breath I sucked in through my nose as he claimed my mouth was filled with his scent as he thrust into me, his movements unpracticed—and unnecessary on his part, I suspected.

I think he moved like that because he knew I enjoyed the friction of it. His shaft vibrated inside me, the covering that normally protected his slit now bumping my clit with each thrust, also vibrating. The sensations were incredible, and I knew it wouldn't be long before I climaxed.

In the back of my mind, my awareness of my situation crouched like an unwelcome gremlin, waiting to skulk back into the forefront and remind me that 34 and I weren't alone as we engaged in this passionate act.

Nor were we free.

Both facts would disturb me if I weren't so overcome with passion and pleasure as he brought me to orgasm. He continued to pump inside me as my inner muscles convulsed around his length, driving me right back up the peak to a second shuddering climax that had me breaking our kiss to cry out, my arms lifting to clutch around his neck, holding on for dear life as I felt swept away by ecstasy.

34 caught me in his upper arms as I slumped against him in the aftermath of my third orgasm, my entire body trembling, a weak moan escaping my lips. He withdrew his shaft from my inner passage, much to my regret, and I barely had the energy to note that no fluid followed in its wake as it left my body. I figured he had again failed to come inside me.

I suspected he had his reasons, and given our situation, they were probably pretty good ones. I wondered how much pleasure he got from the mating act, since he didn't climax like I did. I was accustomed to being an afterthought in the bedroom, rather than the primary participant. I'd certainly never come three times in a row with Michael. I didn't even know that could happen until I'd experienced it with Subject 34.

Now, he arranged me on his lap, my legs parted over his thighs as he scooted closer to the rock, forming a kind of seat that was far less sandy than the one I'd been sitting on. I knew I would pay for that later with the chafing.

Ah, the chafing!

Subject 34 curled his body around mine, his arms forming a barrier on either side of me as he braced his palms against the rock. My head sat well below his own and he bent his forward to close mine in from above. As intimidating as it could be having all that sharpness and chitin and solid, immovable and unpredictable strength surrounding me, I realized what he was doing this time.

He was protecting me, forming a literal shield out of his body so that anyone who might want to take me from him would have to go through him first.

Aww, that is so cute!

Scary. But cute.

Now, I might have been able to convince him to let me chill on the sand without his guarding over me like a hungry wolf protecting its food, but since I actually felt pretty comfortable in the position I was in, I decided to snuggle up against his chest. The exhaustion I felt after all the fun times we'd had made me sleepy enough to doze off in his arms.

SEVENTEEN

Subject 34 really didn't like the "waterfall" that poured off one of the taller rocks, and he made his distaste for the sudden rush of water known in a very vocal fashion. I ignored his outraged chitters as I sighed in pleasure while standing beneath the water, rubbing the sand out of my hair and every other vulnerable—and chafed, damnitall—part of my body.

Nirgal had finally agreed to hose me off. Not that Subject 34 complained about my increasing body odor as time passed—don't ask me how much, because no one tells me anything—but I felt uncomfortable with it. After all, I still had to use the bathroom, and though I had a big sandbox at my disposal, I lacked toilet paper, so things were getting unpleasant for me.

I placed an order with Nirgal—as I put it—for a couple rolls of TP and a hose down, and he'd delivered on the second with an impatient grumbling, but I still had to wait and see if he'd provide the first. He was pretty stingy, and I mocked him for having a low budget on his research project. I gleefully implied that he couldn't get enough grant money, then regretted it because he decided to give me an exhaustive description of exactly how funding worked for these projects.

The dude really needed a hobby! Apparently, he didn't even get any mobile apps on his precious tablet. I mean, what the hell, right? No Sweet Smash? Really? How did the sadistic evil space fairies live like that?

Subject 34 occupied the majority of my time in the enclosure, so at least I didn't often get bored. In fact, the only time he wasn't nearby, giving me something to do—a lot of that something being very entertaining—was when he went into the maze to hunt for his meals. They wouldn't just toss some steaks into the enclosure for the poor guy. They made him chase down everything. Fortunately, I suspected Subject 34 enjoyed it.

Also fortunately, 34 seemed willing to listen to me when I insisted he not eat any more creatures that could talk. Since he dutifully nodded his agreement not to hunt sapient beings, I smirked towards the wall where I suspected Nirgal and his team watched us like we were animals in a zoo. I was getting used to it. I was even growing accustomed to Nirgal yapping in my ear.

None of the other evil scientists ever bothered to speak to me, so I figured Nirgie was the one running the show. Honestly, it was better that way. I wasn't fond of the Pinky Poo guy either. At least I'd gotten used to Nirgal, and he'd apparently grown accustomed to dealing with me.

"Add soap, and shampoo, and conditioner to my shopping list, Nirgie," I called aloud as I scrubbed at my body as best I could beneath the waterfall.

Under my feet, a grating had been revealed below the sand, sucking it down into a lower floor along with the water. The sand in this enclosure was often shifted by the opening and closing of grates beneath it, causing a kind of cycling effect that kept the detritus left by me and Subject 34 from building up and stinking the place up too much. The flowers on their lethal thorny plants also helped perfume the air and keep it fragrant.

Not that 34 ever needed any type of perfume. He always managed to smell yummy, despite clearly not being a fan of water. I did try to lure him beneath the waterfall, but even though he seemed intrigued by my exposed breasts and the nipples I tweaked as I fluttered my lashes at him, he only moved close enough to stand just beyond the spray, watching me patiently while in a low crouch.

I figured he was waiting for me to finish, and he proved me right, snatching me up in his arms as soon as I stepped out of the waterfall. I moaned as he explored my naked upper body, his clawed fingers curious as they moved over my skin. Then he lowered his head to rub his mandibles all along my torso. He dragged them over and over across my nipples, and despite the odd feeling of those hard parts of him, my nipples peaked, which brought them even more of his intent focus.

The water still dripping from my skin beaded on his chitin, sliding off like his plates had been coated to deter moisture. I told him I'd like it if he'd suck on my nipples like he did my clit, and I had to give the guy credit for being willing to try anything I suggested. Whether he enjoyed the act or not, my reaction to his bisected lips closing around one hard nipple seemed to please him enough that his plates hummed with vibration.

He slipped a clawed finger inside my already soaking slit, careful not to poke me with the sharp tip of it as he slowly fingered me. I clasped my legs around his thighs, below the silvery markings on the plates along the sides of his body that I'd learned caused his stingers to strike reflexively.

That would have been nice to know from the start. Much as I enjoyed the aftereffect of some of his stings, I wasn't keen to invite any more of them.

He held me easily against his body, standing with me as if my weight didn't strain him. Given the size of some of the prey he'd dragged out of the maze to finish off in the enclosure, since he didn't like being too far from me, I wasn't surprised he was so strong. Not that I was a behemoth or anything. In fact, my cage diet plan had drastically reduced my weight by the time I'd been thrust back into this enclosure. "Feeding" from Subject 34 had restored some of my lost pounds to me.

He sure didn't seem to mind my extra weight, and maybe even preferred me a little fluffier, since he wanted to feed me all the time. Of course, given the fact that he seemed to enjoy the process as much as I did, if not more, I guessed there were other reasons he was plumping me up too.

Nirgal never sent food I would eat, so I was guessing we were still in the "let's see if Subject 34 will keep providing for this chick" phase of the experiment. So far, it looked to be going well in that department. If anything, 34 seemed more attached to me with each day that passed—and if I was guessing the time correctly, quite a few days had passed.

I was all ready for 34 when he replaced his finger in my opening with his shaft, sliding it inside me with little resistance from my body, which was already craving more of him. It never took long to get me in the mood, especially since he pumped out so much of that sexy pheromone when he was excited that I was hot for him with just a few whiffs.

My thighs flexed as I began rocking on his shaft, but he quickly took over the rhythm, catching me by my waist with his upper hands as his lower hands cupped my buttocks. He pulled me down on his length, driving it deep before pushing me slowly off it, then pulling me back down again. His wings flared behind him as he pumped inside me, vibrating as much as his body did. He lifted one upper hand to circle the nape of my neck and tug my mouth towards his, kissing me with hunger and steadily increasing skill.

He still wasn't much for speaking, though he'd tried out a few more words. I guessed he wasn't fond of the language, or perhaps just the act of forming words with his lips. Or he was just a naturally reticent kind of guy. At any rate, he preferred making those chittering sounds in his throat and the occasional growling noise, and he did both as he brought me to climax, my back arching to push my upper body against his shivering plates. My nipples tingled as they brushed against the hard chitin of his chest.

My days often went like this while in the enclosure, and I wasn't complaining, now fully accustomed to the knowledge that we were constantly under observation. At first, Nirgal had expressed his frustration that Subject 34 still refused to communicate directly with any of the aliens and would only talk to me—and even then, he only ever spoke a handful of words.

As time passed, Nirgie seemed to chill out with all his bitching. Maybe, like me, he was finally learning to pick up on Subject 34's body language and he didn't need a constant stream of words from his test subject to realize what he was thinking.

So far, I'd detected quite a few emotions from Subject 34. The most obvious was anger, and he never directed that at me. It was always directed towards our captors. The others were more subtle, except for lust, which his vibrating gave away— though there were subtler signs before that started, like his scent, that told me he was in the mood.

His concern for me had also become clear, usually in the way he would surround me protectively when we slept, since he still couldn't take us back into his crevice. He showed his tenderness by mimicking my actions towards him, touching me the same way I would stroke him in a non-sexual way—okay, sometimes it was a sexual way, but still, I felt tender about him.

I couldn't say whether his feelings for me were as deep as love, and I wasn't sure whether that was the way I felt or not either, since my emotions towards Subject 34 were far more visceral and primal than I'd ever experienced before. He did appear to have affection towards me and showed it most when he would repeat my insults to Nirgal, one time even winking at me in a way that caught me off guard. I hadn't realized he'd picked up not only the gesture, but also the nuanced meaning behind it.

Needless to say, Nirgal wasn't entirely thrilled about our growing relationship, but he tried to mask his irritation now. I think many of my insults were starting to roll off his back. Perhaps I needed to take another tack to get under his skin.

Why I insisted on doing so, I couldn't say. To torment him, sure, but not speaking to him at all would probably drive him crazier in the long run. He basically pumped me for information daily, and much to my own confusion, I found myself chatting with Nirgal all the time, especially when Subject 34 was on the hunt. Though I never gave up anything I felt could be used against Subject 34, I did end up talking about the oddest stuff with Nirgal.

Random things like what my favorite stuffed animal had been when I was a child, or what painting I'd been picturing in my head for the last few days, or how I loved the smell of tire stores.

Like I said, weird shit, right? I blamed it on the strangeness of my circumstances and my almost crippling homesickness for Earth. Just like I'd spent hours gesturing in a pointless game of charades with green guy, now I was chattering away with my own captor, even as I found myself falling for my fellow captive.

It was difficult to tell sometimes what Nirgal was thinking about these conversations, but he did ask a lot of personal questions about me that I ended up answering, instead of evading them as I might have done at first. Within probably a week's time, I think he knew more about me than Michael had bothered to learn in twenty years.

The fact that he actually stretched his budget to provide the things I kept requesting from him probably had something to do with slightly improving my attitude towards him. Before long, I had a full range of hygiene supplies, including a brush and comb, a new set of clothing that I ended up not spending much time in, and even a soft mattress, with a blanket and a pillow. He dropped off all the items in the maze like they dropped off Subject 34's food.

Apparently, he drew the line at providing paints and canvas, but did surprise me with a sketchbook and a narrow box of sketching implements a few days after he started the daily waterfalls. I squealed with excitement when 34 returned carrying these items along with a few leftover chunks of gore that he'd fortunately kept from dripping on the sketchbook.

"Nirgie, you pumpkin-colored bastard, you keep giving me gifts like this, and I might actually stop hating you!"

"It's not a gift," he said huffily in my ear. "You have expressed that you have some skill with drawing. I insist you use these items to sketch Subject 34's body language and identify what all of it means. We could use those detailed views for our records. For science."

He hated being thanked, by the way, which was exactly why I did it every time. Honestly, it was probably a bad move, since his team might be wondering why he kept giving in to all the demands of a mere human, but I couldn't help needling him. He also always had an excuse like the rather lame one he'd offered for the sketchbook. I found his efforts to explain himself entertaining.

After taking a few minutes to truly admire the fine quality of the paper, and the fancy holder that kept the charcoals from staining my fingers, I immediately began sketching. The pencils, if they could be called that, drew far smoother over the expensive paper than I was accustomed to, but I quickly gained a feel for the drawing tools. Before long, I'd made a decent sketch of Subject 34, who watched my pencil move over the paper with his usual intense focus.

I was able to pick up on a new emotion from Subject 34 as his image grew clearer with each sweep of my pencil. He was excited to see his own sketch, creeping closer to me in his usual crouch and craning his neck to get a better view.

"It's not bad for a preliminary sketch," I said, though a little self-doubt tinged my voice.

Had I captured the tilt of his head well enough? Were the proportions of his broad shoulders and narrow waist a little off? And what the hell was wrong with the mouth? I'd always struggled with drawing mouths. Never could get those exactly right, and Subject 34's mouth was pretty special to me. I really wanted to capture it properly.

I'd probably hold off on asking him to show me his *true* mouth anytime soon to get a sketch of that.

"I suppose it is a passable effort," Nirgal said stiffly in a tone he used if he didn't want to give me credit for something when he knew I deserved it. "It is useful that you actually do possess the skill you claimed to have. This primitive medium has only recently regained popularity among our species, and it isn't easy to obtain such supplies. The investment must be worth the expense."

"Thirty-four like," Subject 34 said, shooting a glare towards the "Nirgal wall", as I now thought of it.

I handed the sketchbook to him so he could get a better look at it, since he was practically crawling into my lap to see it from the proper angle.

He studied it intently, tracing over some of the loose, sweeping strokes of the outline with his claws.

"You're so handsome," I said with a girlish giggle that would have had me rolling my eyes at myself not that long ago. I tapped the sketchbook. "Or, as we humans say, 'you're hot as... ahem... you're hot."

Nirgal had asked me to refrain from teaching Subject 34 human swear words, which apparently only translated as censored beeps in 34's head, but Subject 34 wouldn't be dissuaded by beeps without explanation. He'd demand to know what a word meant, and if he thought it would irritate Nirgal, he'd repeat it, and it would become one of the few words in his vocabulary that he actually deigned to speak.

Yeah, he'd picked up on that particularly bad habit of mine too. Since he couldn't just rip Nirgal to shreds like I know he wanted to, he helped me to torment the scientist with words.

"Thirty-four handsome?" He touched his face with the claws of one upper hand as a lower set of claws traced the lines I'd made for his lips. "Nice face?"

I'd been picking up what I worried might be some insecurity in 34, but I tried to dismiss it, thinking perhaps I was projecting my own insecurities on him. I had plenty of them!

In his case, I speculated that he worried about what hid behind that attractive façade and my previous reaction to it. In fact, he hadn't split his face open in front of me save for that first day, though he often brought meat back to snack on later.

When he ate now around me, he'd turn his back to me, and keep turning if I tried to move around to get a good look at his face. Something I'd only done once in an effort to inure myself to the sight of his true mouth. He didn't seem to want me to see it anymore, though he hadn't been shy about it at first.

"You have a very nice face, thirty-four," I insisted, tracing the bisections creasing his lips. "But I like you for a lot more than your pretty face, you know."

His lips spread in a crooked—still a little scary—grin. "Rhonda like feeding."

I crossed my arms over my chest, shaking my head at him. "Get your mind out of the gutter. Rhonda likes Subject 34 for being such a sweetheart to me." I shot a glare at the Nirgal wall. "*Some* people could learn from your example."

Then my gaze fell upon the sketchbook. I suppose maybe Nirgal was learning. At least he had finally realized that you could get more cooperation from your test subjects if you weren't a total dick to them.

EIGHTEEN

I sketched a lot in the following days, finding Subject 34 to be a fascinating model. There were so many complex lines to his body, what with the four arms, the wings, the many chitin plates that covered his body, and the rigid chitin plating that protected his head. It was challenging and thrilling to be able to replicate his image as close as I could.

He seemed to love my sketches and squirreled the loose ones away somewhere he wouldn't disclose, always glaring at the Nirgal wall after examining my drawings as if he knew Nirgal intended to retrieve the sketchbook once I'd filled it.

Nirgal also seemed to be satisfied with my drawings, apparently now convinced that I did have some skill. When I began sketching other things besides Subject 34—like the plants surrounding us—he didn't protest, much to my surprise, given his lame excuses for why he'd given me the book.

But he did speak up one day during Subject 34's hunt in the maze when he must have noticed me sketching green guy from memory.

"Why are you drawing Ilyan?" he demanded as soon as the

facial features became clear, his voice sounding harsh. "I insist you cease that."

I glanced up from my sketch, regarding the Nirgal wall only briefly before returning my focus to the drawing. I'd chosen to capture the less chilly look Ilyan had taken on during our time in the cages. The picture showed a wild, mussed, wide-eyed creature with a face too handsome to be human and eyes too haunted to be comforting.

"I kinda miss him," I said shortly, irritated that he'd decided to be a dick about my choice of subject now.

Things had been going so well between us. I even felt tolerant towards him now.

"You don't even know him."

I rolled my eyes, sighing heavily as I closed the sketchbook. "Duh, genius. I don't have to know everyone I draw. Besides, it's not my fault the cage you forced me to live in for weeks was soundproof."

"Ilyan is... *was* a friend," Nirgal said in a defensive tone. "He deserves better than to have his face sketched in that condition."

"He deserves better than to be cooped up in a cage like a fucking animal!" I shouted as I jumped to my feet, tossing the sketchbook and pencil on the sand. "Good god! If you treat your friends like that, I'd hate to see what you do to your enemies."

"Yes," Nirgal said slowly. "You would definitely hate to see it."

I pointed a finger at the Nirgal wall. "Is that a *threat*?"

"No, you aren't an enemy of the empire." Now he sounded almost weary, his tone taking me aback.

"Oh." Well, he'd just sucked the wind out of my rage sails for a moment. Then I recalled what we were talking about. I crossed my arms over my chest. "Well, you still shouldn't treat a friend like that."

"Ilyan is very sick," Nirgal said, again sounding weary. "He is also brilliant, which makes containing him in a more comfortable manner difficult. That 'cage' is the only way we've been able to keep him from escaping thus far. I assure you, we kept him in nicer conditions in the beginning of his *illness*."

"So, what exactly happened to him, anyway?" I lowered my arms to my sides and stepped closer to the wall. "Why's he so messed up?"

"He is fractured," he said the word in a barely audible tone, like someone might use when speaking of a serious, terminal illness. "He imprinted on an enemy female, leading to the inevitable deprivation without access to her pheromones. When he contacted me after escaping the purge of his research facility, I did my best to keep him comfortable. It was my mistake to hold off putting him in cryo to slow his deterioration. I thought we were closer to a viable cure at that time than we were, and we needed him to help us restart his important research."

"So you let him suffer, for *science*, huh? How *not* surprising, Nirgie."

"Yes. I did. I hadn't expected him to fracture. It is a rare condition. One I never would have thought him capable of experiencing. I regret my shortsightedness. Now, even though we have cured his affliction, we cannot heal his fracture. Nothing can."

I realized that Nirgal was wracked with guilt and was confessing to me like I was a priest. It made me feel sorry for him, then irritated at myself for letting him get under my skin. I shouldn't care one damned bit if guilt was eating him up inside. But damn it, I am nothing if not a softie. The story was getting to me, I had to admit it.

"What exactly does it mean when you say he's fractured?"

"That is far more complicated than I'd expect you to understand. Suffice it to say, his consciousness has split into two distinct identities, and only one of them retains the friend I remember. The other is extremely dangerous and completely without empathy. Without even the *capacity* for empathy. He kills without remorse, and still possesses the brilliance of Ilyan's mind, so the potential for destruction that his escape could unleash upon this galaxy can't be overstated."

"You know, I've gotta be honest, Nirgal. I haven't seen a whole lot of empathy coming from any of you guys. Seems to me like green guy is just as bad as the rest of you, if what you're saying is true."

He didn't respond for a long moment, and my ear practically rang with that prolonged silence. "Perhaps you have a point. Yet the rest of us do not redirect asteroids to obliterate colonies for no other reason than because someone residing there offended us."

I gasped, shaking my head in disbelief. "Please tell me you're exaggerating!"

"I wish I was," he said, and again I heard the weariness. "Fortunately, we were able to destroy the asteroid before impact and recapture Ilyan, but it became obvious that we couldn't risk him escaping again."

"So your empire, they don't execute criminals like that?" The idea of what Ilyan had attempted to do, the mass murder he'd tried to commit, shook me to the core.

Sure, he'd seemed a little... cold sometimes. But what Nirgal was saying was far worse than what I'd imagined he was capable of doing.

"When they are fractured, we study them. It would be a waste to destroy a useful subject who can hopefully help us learn how to undo the damage."

I didn't like the lack of ethics these aliens had when it came to their scientific endeavors, but if Ilyan's condition was as bad as Nirgal said it was, then I could understand why they would want to find a cure for it. I honestly couldn't really blame them.

"And are you all any closer to a cure for this 'fracturing' thing?"

"We have cured the imprinting affliction—in some of our subjects, though there are caveats even to that, I'm afraid. With that cure, we might be able to identify what process the mind undergoes to cause a fracturing, but that must be monitored during deprivation. The cure works too quickly to prolong deprivation enough to cause a fracture. In order to break a male before the cure is complete, he would have to endure extreme torture in addition to deprivation. We would not do that to a subject unless we know he can even suffer a fracture. Like I said, it is a rare condition."

I held up a hand. "Hold up a second! Did you just say you would *torture* one of your own people just to cause this horrible condition—that you have no fucking *cure* for?"

"Not unless we knew they would—"

"Nirgal!" I planted my hands on my hips. "Don't you dare give me this 'it's for science' bullshit! I don't care how important the cure is that you're trying to find, you don't torture human subjects."

"We are *not* humans!" Nirgal snapped with irritation. "Nor could we even use humans for such experiments. This condition is unique to our species. What other way would *you* suggest we find a cure for it? Or would you rather we simply execute anyone unfortunate enough to suffer it? Do not hold us in suspense, oh wise Rhonda! Clearly, you humans have all the answers when it comes to proper scientific research. What fools we Iriduans are not to follow the example of the scrabbling ape-bloods splitting atoms and dropping their bombs on each other or sewing human fetal tissue to rodents for experiments or cloning humans without any concept of how dangerous such technology can be."

My mouth hung open at his rant, his voice rising until it was almost a shout in my ear. I clapped a hand to it as if that could mute him, but obviously, it did little to shut him up, given the speaker inside my ear.

This time, I didn't feel such a sense of victory at setting Nirgal off. He was really pissed, and he got snarly and sarcastic with his anger, his tone dripping with condescension with every bitter word he bit out. I had definitely poked a sore spot with this conversation, and as much as I hated to admit he was right about anything, I supposed he had a point about me mouthing off about how wrong he and his people were with their science, while being ignorant of any other solutions to solve their unique problems.

I realized that sometimes, people had no options that weren't horrible in some way, other than to do nothing at all, and that would lead to yet another horrible outcome. I couldn't give him an answer for how to treat a terrible condition that had destroyed someone he'd considered a friend. I couldn't even suggest a more humane and ethical compromise for how to research such a thing. I was just as ignorant as he implied with his insulting comments.

"Look, I'm sorry, Nirgal," I said holding up both hands in surrender. "I'm not trying to suggest I know better than you."

"Spare me your apology, human. I neither need it, nor care to have it. You are nothing but a test subject to me. Do what you're in there to do and stop irritating me."

He didn't say another word to me after that, and I wandered listlessly around the enclosure, wondering if I was experiencing Stockholm Syndrome, because I actually felt depressed that he was mad at me, even as I paced the confines of the cage he kept me in.

Subject 34 seemed taken aback when I rushed to hug him as soon as he crawled out of the hatch that led to his part of the tunnel maze. I'd been waiting for him and though it probably hadn't been more than a half hour since my argument with Nirgal, it felt like it took him forever to return.

Despite his surprise, he hugged me back immediately with his lower arms, dangling the large hunk of gory meat he had in one upper pincer out and away from me, so it didn't drip blood onto my head. He stroked my hair with the other upper hand, that pincer retracted back onto his forearm.

"What wrong?" he asked, then I felt his body stiffen in my arms. "Nirgal," he growled in a deadly voice. "I kill soon."

I sighed against his chest, squeezing my arms tighter around his waist, careful not to bump the silvery marks. "It's okay, Thirty-four. I'm okay. He didn't do anything to me. I'm just...."

I shrugged, then released him and stepped back. "How was your hunt?" I said in a falsely bright tone to change the subject, glancing at the meat before quickly looking away as I swallowed my gorge. "I take it you caught all your prey?"

"Not speak," he promised, gesturing to the meat.

"Good," I grinned, though I still didn't look too closely at the meat. "I'm glad you're taking that into consideration now, Thirty-four."

"Still kill Nirgal," he said, glancing towards the wall, which was currently out of view from this angle, though I had no doubt there were plenty of cameras giving the scientist a full view of our conversation. "Not eat." He lowered his gaze to me. "Nirgal taste bad."

"Yeah," I chuckled, though it lacked much humor, "he probably does."

NINETEEN

Nirgal didn't speak to me again. Not that day, nor the next, nor the next. No matter how long I sat in waiting silence while Subject 34 hunted in the maze, I heard nary a peep from him.

I suppose there wasn't much he needed to say to me, but that hadn't stopped him from yammering constantly before. After probably a week had passed when I realized I had actually begun to miss his voice, I started up with very deliberate needling, in the hopes that I could anger him into speaking to me.

My efforts were met with more silence. He also didn't send anything else to me through the maze, nor comment on my sketches, which had almost filled the book by this time. I'd drawn Ilyan several more times, quite openly, hoping he would make a comment, even if it were a mean one. I'd even drawn the darker side of Ilyan's expressions—the coldest and most unnerving one.

The stare of a man who would murder countless innocents over an insult.

The very idea made me shiver, and it also made me regret

my hasty words to Nirgal. As horrible as it was to imagine torturing some poor male until he cracked just to learn why it happened in the hopes of curing the resulting condition, was it worse than allowing the condition to persist, when it could lead to the creation of such monsters? The kind capable of killing tens of thousands, maybe even millions, without batting an eye?

The old question of sacrificing one life to save many was one I'd never been able to ponder for too long. I hated that moral quandary and figured better people than me should be the ones to make such decisions.

Not that I thought Nirgal and his fellow scientists were better than me, morally. Far from it. I had no doubt Subject 34 hadn't been created with peaceful intentions. He was clearly designed to be a killer. Perhaps his unique biochemistry could provide some benefits to others, but I doubted the Iriduan empire cared about doing so. At least not in a meaningful way that countermanded the destruction they would make Subject 34 cause.

I didn't know the whole story of why they felt they needed him. Nirgal had never responded to those kinds of questions, not that I'd asked a whole lot of useful questions of him. In fact, he'd been the one interrogating me most of them time. He knew my favorite foods and I didn't even know his last name.

Or if he had one.

Or if his species used them.

Hell, I didn't know much at all about the Iriduans. I only knew they were called that from our last conversation. I'd shown zero interest in them. That probably worked to his benefit, leaving me in the dark about what I was up against, but in retrospect, it had been shortsighted of me to blabber on and on about myself and not even ask a few questions in return.

I'll admit, I felt a little sheepish for being so self-focused. It's difficult to consider anything other than yourself when your life is always potentially in danger. Not from Subject 34. I didn't feel any fear about him. I did, however, fear the scientists keeping us captive. Clearly, they didn't have ethical limits, if they could even consider torturing a victim without dismissing the idea outright.

Also clearly, they seemed desperate enough to try drastic measures if they thought they would work, which explained why I was even in this enclosure with Subject 34. I couldn't see any other reason why getting him so attached to me would benefit them unless they'd needed information about him so badly that allowing him to bond with a fellow test subject had been worth the risk.

Thirty-four sensed my growing depression and correctly guessed the cause of it. He glared at the Nirgal wall frequently now, and even paced in front of it several times in agitation.

"Nirgal speak," he'd demanded on more than one occasion.

Even that had gotten no response from Nirgal, who'd been so determined to get Subject 34 to speak directly to him. Now, he'd apparently changed his mind, and even Thirty-four didn't like this prolonged silence from our captor.

Though we still made love frequently, with me growing ever closer to him, definitely feeling as if I might just be in love with the monster guy, a pall settled over our days as Nirgal failed to communicate at all.

I loved being with Subject 34, and I enjoyed sketching him, and I loved talking to him, though he rarely had much to say in return.

Okay, I loved him.

There wasn't much question about that. I knew it was foolish to let myself get so attached to him, particularly in our circumstances. There was no way our captors, Nirgal included, would let us live "happily ever after" spending every moment of the rest of our lives in this enclosure. The Iriduans had a plan for Subject 34, and I was pretty certain I wasn't to be a permanent part of it.

If Nirgal would just talk to me, I might have been able to coax some information out of him that could prepare me for the inevitable, but as it was, weeks passed without another word from the guy.

Then the day arrived that the scientists and their mechs came for me.

They were ready to separate us. Apparently, they'd gained all the information they wanted to gain from their observations of us together. What they planned to do with me, I didn't know, but I had no doubt it wouldn't be good when a bio-suited alien entered the enclosure through the anteroom vault door, escorted by a squad of mechs.

They'd tried to lure Subject 34 away with a hunt in the maze, but he wasn't having it that day, and it was almost like he'd sensed they would come for me. He burst into motion the minute the vault door opened, charging towards the alien entering like he would tear him to shreds.

Then he shrieked in agony, which sent me running to his side as he jerked to a stop, then fell to the sand, writhing in pain. His upper claws clutched at his head as his back arched up off the ground. His clawed toes curled downwards, his stingers whipping angrily from his back. His wings kicked up sand as he continued to spin and writhe, chittering and shrieking in agony.

"Stop it!" I screamed, lunging at the alien, who stood with a hand pressed to a device on his wrist that I knew was causing 34 so much pain.

The alien thrust me aside, knocking me to the ground. I struck the sand with a muffled "oof." Then the alien turned his cold, fuchsia gaze towards me.

"Tilhur! Where is Nirgal?" I demanded, jumping back to my feet as I brushed sand off my mended sweatpants.

I flinched with every scream from Subject 34, but kept my focus on the Iriduan, knowing that I had to convince him to stop this, since neither 34 nor I could attack him effectively.

To my relief, he shifted his finger on the device, and whatever was causing Subject 34 so much pain ended, but quickly resumed when 34 tried to move towards him again.

Tilhur took a quick step backwards at 34's lunge, and I noted that his fingers shook as he reactivated whatever device caused the agonizing pain, sending 34 back to the sand with another shriek.

"Do not attempt your wiles on me, human," Tilhur said in a shaken voice, splitting his attention between me and 34. "I will not be swayed like Subject 34 and Nirgal."

My brows lifted as I eyed him. "Nirgal? Where is he?"

Tilhur's chuckle sounded so cold that the hairs on my nape rose. "He's serving science in another way now, since it appears he has lost his reason."

"What are you talking about?" I said breathlessly, a terrible feeling in my already sinking stomach. "What did you do to Nirgal?"

Tilhur jerked his head towards 34 and the mechs surrounded him, blocking me from seeing him. "Nirgal attempted to betray his people because of you and your constant blathering. For that crime, he has become part of an experiment. He might fracture. He might not. There's no way to tell beforehand, so we'll just torture him until he does—or dies. Honestly, I don't care, either way. He has always been an obstacle to my advancement."

I shook my head, both shocked and appalled at his words. I actually feared for Nirgal now. "Are any of you Iriduans ever *good*? Or are you truly evil space fairies?"

Tilhur huffed in indignation. "Don't bother trying to play on my sense of guilt like you did with Professor Nirgal. I have a stronger will than he did. I will not be convinced by your ignorant ramblings about 'good' and 'evil.' Our research will improve the lives of the Iriduan people. Nothing else matters but that."

Had I actually gotten through to Nirgal? And if I had, it seemed that I'd doomed him to a horrible fate. One probably far worse than the one even I faced.

Tilhur didn't leave me in suspense about my own fate. As he fiddled with his wrist device and the mechs surrounded an enraged Subject 34 he continued to speak.

"Subject 34 must be reprogrammed now because of Professor Nirgal's ill-advised efforts to better understand his attachment to you. However, I believe we can speed along that reprogramming by forcing him to eliminate you. Once you are out of the way, this obsession he appears to have for you will fade as fast as the taste of your blood in his mouth. Then we can get back to the important work we've been doing with him."

"He would never hurt me!" I shouted at the cold-blooded bastard.

His laugh raised the hairs on my neck as he tapped away at his wrist thing. Subject 34 suddenly lurched to his feet, chittering mournfully. I could tell each halting step he took towards me was a battle for him, but there was no question he was advancing at Tilhur's will rather than his own.

"We have always had control over him," Tilhur said in a smug tone. "He *will* kill you. He may not like doing it, but eventually, he'll recover—or we'll do a flash of his memory using the chip. He'll get over you either way, though I'd rather avoid the memory flash, since he did advance his communication ability after spending this time with you."

I held up both hands as Subject 34 moved closer, shifting

my attention between him and Tilhur's wrist device. "Thirty-four, fight this bastard! I know you can!"

"Thirty-four fight," he said in a mournful tone, and for a moment, I had some hope as he tried to turn his body towards one of the mechs trailing him.

"We aren't having a repeat of Thrax," Tilhur muttered as his fingers flew over the wrist device.

I shifted closer to the evil alien as I backed away from Subject 34, my heart breaking as I saw how much he struggled against the control of the chip.

Control he ultimately couldn't break.

He turned back towards me with a moan of agony, his stingers coiling at his sides, their tips dripping with venom.

When I turned towards the vault door, Tilhur chuckled. "Where will you run to, human? There are an army of mechs just beyond that door. You won't get anywhere. Accept your fate. If you truly care about Subject 34, make this easier on him. Each time he resists the control of the chip, it causes him intense pain."

The last thing I wanted was to cause Subject 34 pain. It crushed me to see him so tormented as each of his steps dragged through the sand in his slow advance towards me. I knew how fast Subject 34 could move. If he weren't fighting the chip, I would already be dead. I might not have even had a chance to blink before he killed me in that case.

But he *was* fighting, for all he was worth, which gave me time, though it still left me little options. Tilhur was right. Running wouldn't do me any good. One of those creepy mechs would just catch me and hold me in place until Tilhur forced Subject 34 to kill me and then eat my corpse.

I tried not to think about the fact that I would soon be in the stomach of my lover. Would they have to flash his memory to make him forget the horrifying act of eating me? Or would his insectoid nature end up drowning out the sweet, loving person I'd seen take shape in these last weeks in my company?

What would all of this do to Subject 34 in the end? No matter what, he'd remain a slave to bastards like Tilhur, and someday, those bastards would send him out to kill other people.

Innocent people, probably.

And all the while, the one Iriduan I'd apparently convinced to reconsider his actions would be tortured until he either fractured or died. Nirgal could be no help to me here, and I tried not to think about what nightmare he now endured. Perhaps he deserved some of it for what he'd put so many others through, myself included, but I was a strong believer in redemption. If he'd tried to undo some of the damage he'd done, then he wasn't completely lost to the darkness that a creature like Tilhur seemed to embrace gleefully.

I had wanted Nirgal to find a conscience, and it seemed like I might have guided him to it. Yet, my efforts led to his own downfall. Just like humanizing Subject 34 might have been the worst thing I could have done to him, because I knew he would suffer for having to destroy me.

I moved a few steps closer to the door, Subject 34 mere steps away from me now.

Tilhur chuckled, clearly enjoying my fear and indecisiveness. And here I'd thought Nirgal was the sadistic one. I could tell I wouldn't be getting through to Tilhur at all. I'd seen the signs of emotion in Nirgal from the start, which was why I'd been able to get under his skin in the first place, but Tilhur—he was a cold bastard through and through. There was nothing I could touch inside him, no heart the most impassioned plea could move.

So I didn't feel a lick of remorse when I lunged at him,

throwing all my weight behind my charge as I slammed into him.

He was tall and lean, like Nirgal, and apparently delicate because he crashed to the sand like a fallen tree, yelping upon impact. Then he cried out in pain as my full weight came down on top of him. Granted, he hadn't been bracing himself, clearly not expecting me to attack him instead of trying to run for my life.

What an idiot! That's what you get for underestimating the intelligence of an "ape-blood." Give me no other choice but to attack or die, and I'm attacking like a battering ram.

I smashed my fist into his helmet, then winced as it rocked back from the hard surface that definitely wasn't as vulnerable as it looked. I pinned his body to the sand though, and his feeble struggles were almost laughable. Clearly, he'd been skipping the gym. I wasn't exactly a gym rat myself, but I had a significant number of pounds on him, and he was—quite frankly—a total wuss.

I kneed him in the groin, hoping that would help incapacitate him as he struggled to reach his wrist device with his other hand. He grunted in pain as I drove my knee up into his groin once, then a second time, causing him to buckle with a low moan, his eyes slamming shut. He gagged, the sound amplified by the speaker in his helmet.

Still, he tried to touch the wrist device, which had apparently paused Subject 34, because my lover stood frozen in place, all the mechs also on pause around him. I had to guess they'd been brought in here to guard against 34 attacking Tilhur, and the dumbass hadn't even considered little ol' me turning the tables on him.

Still, I knew it wouldn't be long before whoever was observing all this from beyond the enclosure got over their surprise and reactivated 34, so I swiped my own fingers across the wrist device.

"Don't fight it, 34!" I shouted. "Strike me dead!" I looked up into his blank, outer eyes. "Trust me, baby! Because I trust you."

He still moved slow enough that I could act as he charged me and Tilhur, both of us struggling on the sand. Bracing my back foot on the ground, I buried my knee in Tilhur's stomach and with a heave that took all my strength, I rolled us over until he was on top of me. In that same moment, Subject 34's stinger struck, burying fully into Tilhur's back.

The Iriduan sagged on top of me as Subject 34 struck a second time, my vulnerable self covered by Tilhur's surprisingly heavy corpse. I frantically swiped on the wrist device to shut off the "kill" command.

My efforts brought up a series of symbols that I didn't have any hope of reading. I also didn't dare trying any of them, lest I force something worse than a kill code on Subject 34.

Like causing him pain again.

What I did see, much to my surprise, was a shutdown code. I recognized it because it matched the one that had been on the machine used to draw samples from my body. I'd seen it flash when the machine was complete. Like a "power off" button, it had a distinctive and recognizable design that no doubt existed on every electronic device these aliens used.

I worried that I'd cause something terrible to happen to Subject 34 by pushing it, but right now, he was paused again, and I heard sounds of alarm echoing from within Tilhur's helmet that told me someone somewhere intended to act. I pushed the button, and the device stopped glowing, all the symbols disappearing.

Suddenly, I heard the deafening sounds of machines being torn apart, along with a victorious shriek from Subject 34.

Then Tilhur's body lifted off me, and Subject 34 dropped him unceremoniously at his feet before bending to take my hand in his lower hand to pull me back onto my feet.

"Rhonda safe?"

I nodded, swallowing thickly. Adrenaline was pumping. I would break down later, I supposed, but for the moment, I was still in peril. We'd escaped Tilhur, and a glance around showed me that Subject 34 had made quick work of the mechs.

Like, *really* quick work. It was a bit intimidating how rapidly he'd dismantled the robots. To my surprise, he bent again to snatch the wrist device off Tilhur's arm. I grabbed his lower hand when he lifted it to touch the screen of the wrist device.

"No, 34! We don't know what those symbols mean. You could end up hurting yourself if you turn it back on!"

He cupped my cheek with one of his upper hands. Then he touched the screen, bringing the symbols back up. His body tensed as the device activated, but his claws moved rapidly over the symbols.

"They taught you to read their language!" I slowly shook my head. "For brilliant scientists, they aren't that smart."

His fingers scratched over the device, bringing up symbols so rapidly that they blurred before my eyes. Then he brought up something that looked like a map of some sort. He seemed to study it for several long moments as I anxiously bounced on the balls of my feet, my gaze returning to the vault door again and again as I waited to be swarmed.

It had probably only been a few minutes since we'd overcome Tilhur, and Subject 34 was moving fast, but I knew the other scientists had to have a remote control for 34. They weren't the most cunning folks, but they couldn't have been stupid enough to send the only control device into the enclosure without making sure they had a backup.

Whatever the case might be, 34 clearly had his own thoughts about it.

Suddenly, part of his head chitin fell off. I freaked out about it. I'll admit. What seemed to be a part of his skull just popped right off his head.

Then I saw pulsing brain matter exposed where that chitin had been and I screamed, rushing to snatch up the chitin to press it back into his hands. One of his pincers extended as he lifted his upper hand, and I shouted in alarm when he used the tips of it to prod at his brain.

"What the fuck, 34! Stop that! You're going to hurt yourself!"

He held me off with his other upper hand, his lower hands busy with the wrist device. His pincer delved deeper into his squishy, gory looking brain matter, then he withdrew something shiny, blinking, and trailing little wires.

"Oh my god, I'm gonna faint!" I said with a horrified gasp. "Did you just perform brain surgery on yourself to remove the control chip?"

Yeah. Yeah, he did.

He tossed aside the chip and I spared only a quick glance at where the bloody thing fell in the sand before I insistently pressed the piece of head chitin back into his hands.

"How do you know you won't get an infection?" I didn't bother to hide the worry in my voice.

"They come," he said without answering my question as he pushed the head chitin back over his exposed brain.

It made a clicking sound, then seemed to fuse to the other plates covering his head, the seams formed by its separation rapidly disappearing, even as I heard the approach of reinforcements on the other side of the vault doors.

TWENTY

I suspected that our captors had wildly underestimated Subject 34, and they would eventually pay for it, but for the moment, even he knew we were better off escaping the squad of mechs entering the enclosure. He led me to the maze hatch, and quickly broke it open with a few hard slams of his upper fists.

Once he'd jerked the cover off the hatch, he swept me off my feet with his lower hands, then unceremoniously shoved me through the hatch. Pumped with adrenaline, I was still moving fast, though my entire body trembled as reaction began to set in. I quickly crawled through the hatch until the tunnel opened up to a point where I could stand.

Subject 34 was right behind me when I rose to my feet, his movements as he climbed up into the shaft barely making a sound compared to my noisy crawling. He picked me up in his lower arms again—to my protest—then raced down the dark tunnel. For a few moments, I felt blind in the darkness, but then I saw the lights from the lower tunnel as the sound of his steps changed when he crossed the grating. I shuddered at my recollection of being in that place now below us.

Walls were already shifting into place as 34 ran much faster than I would have been able to keep up. He seemed to anticipate them as we moved through the maze above the other maze. He had some destination in mind, but had to take a roundabout route, because our captors were trying to cut off our escape.

Mind you, I didn't think there would be a full escape from this maze. At least, I hadn't found one, but it turned out that I was dead wrong. Try as they might, they couldn't completely block 34's path, since each time a wall moved to block one opening, it exposed another.

That's what you get when you had a budget. You couldn't put unlimited walls in your death maze.

They did try though, and several times, I thought they would succeed in cutting us off so the noisy squad of mechs chasing us would catch up and kill us.

Well, they'd probably kill me. Maybe they'd do some damage to 34 before he destroyed them. I knew it was me they wanted dead. They probably figured once I was, they could regain control of Subject 34.

Then something more ominous occurred that left me certain we would die—or at least I would.

The maze began to fill with gas. Subject 34 chitter-growled in rage, then sped up his steps when I didn't think he could possibly move any faster, his wings twitching so rapidly behind him that they buzzed. I kept my silence, clinging to his chitin as my heart thudded and fear-sweat soaked my shirt and pants.

I trusted 34 to keep me safe to the best of his ability, and that ability was great. I just wasn't sure we could escape our captors when they'd had the upper hand for so long.

But they no longer had control of 34, and I don't think they saw that one coming.

He broke through a hatch and dropped down into the lower

tunnel to escape the gas. There was more of it in this tunnel, but not in such a thick cloud that it left me choking. I'd begun to grow groggy, and my breathing became difficult, so when 34 stung me, I barely felt it.

I did, however, feel the burn of some kind of stimulant rushing through my blood from the place he'd stung me, and I jerked into alertness in his arms. My head rushed with blood, my nostrils flaring as I sucked in air free from the gas while he moved further away from the vents spilling it into the lower maze.

Then we reached a dead end, with no sign of moving doors or walls. This didn't stop 34 though. He extended his pincers and jabbed them at a panel in the ceiling. It was clear that this part of the lower maze wasn't below 34's portion of the maze. Instead, the panel broke away after several hard strikes from 34, to reveal an opening leading to some new chamber.

Grasping the sides of the square hole with his upper pincers, he hauled us upwards, his lower arms shifting me so that I was held against him with my legs dangling against his. Even with this shift in position, we barely fit through the hole because of the size of him and the rigidity of his chitin.

On the other side of the hole lay a staging area for his prey, with a few of the clear cages I'd become far too familiar with, several machines that looked like the one that had taken samples from me, and a variety of sealed crates and shelves. It was about the size of a large garage, and even had a garage type door, though the top of the door had a cut-out to fit around a huge track that also looked familiar.

It was the track for the giant claw that led into the warehouse where all the clear cages were kept. I had no doubt the other side of that garage door would be that warehouse, though I didn't hear any sounds coming from that other side. Not surprising given the fact that those cages were soundproof.

"There will be guards out there," I whispered to 34.

He nodded in a staccato motion, then set me on my feet. I stepped away from him as I glanced back at the open hatch, thinking about all the doomed prey that had been dropped through it into the maze.

Was I to be doomed as well? I turned my attention back to Subject 34, who was now pacing in front of the garage door in an inhuman fashion, his wings flicking.

I loved him—this monstrous alien creature. I wanted him to be free from this horrible life of imprisonment and enslavement. I didn't know what kind of life awaited him beyond the confines of the warehouse, and I wasn't certain it was even an environment I could survive, but I suspected there wasn't much in the way of environment that he couldn't handle.

I couldn't give up hope of at least Subject 34 escaping these Iriduans alive.

Then I thought of all the other victims, trapped in their clear cages, helpless, desperate, despairing. Always watching the claw passing overhead, fearing they would be the next to be plucked from their perches and dropped into a nightmare. Granted, some of them, like poor Ilyan, were too dangerous to roam free, but there were likely others who deserved at least a chance to find a better life.

Then I thought of Nirgal, my tormentor whom I had grown oddly fond of, and now, his own people tortured him to see if he would become like Ilyan.

"Thirty-four," I said in a hesitant voice, unsure whether I should even voice the direction of my thoughts.

He turned from the large door to face me, his body language showing that I had his full attention, though I suspected he always remained aware of his surroundings on another level perhaps a human couldn't understand.

"Can you read these symbols?" I asked, pointing to the

various markings along the wall and on the machines and the crates.

He nodded immediately, without turning his head to scan the room. I'd already guessed that the little, black half bubbles found at several points on his head chitin were also eyes, allowing him to see with a far greater periphery than any human.

"Do you see anything in this room that might help us free the captives in the room beyond this?"

Subject 34 could probably sneak us past the mechs, but I couldn't just leave this place without trying to help others escape.

He turned his head this time, regarding everything closely. I returned to the hole that led to the maze, my ears straining for sounds of pursuit. If they figured out where we were, they wouldn't necessarily have to come at us from below. They could already be amassing on the other side of that door.

Then 34 chittered in a sound I took to be pleased as he strode to one of the machines. He pushed some buttons, brought up a screen, then started swiping and tapping away.

The door descended into a slit in the ground rather than upwards like a normal garage door. Then the giant claw entered the room on its overhead track, having apparently been stowed just outside the door.

As I feared, there were mechs on the other side of that garage door too, along with some floating drones. Voices shouted from the drones, demanding our immediate surrender, but Subject 34 quickly dispatched the mechs that charged at us as I ducked behind some crates.

Whatever they were using to shoot him with seemed to be ineffective. Maybe it wasn't lethal projectiles but rather some type of stunning round, but they were outmatched. He quickly disposed of the threat, including the drones, then chittered for me to follow him as he leapt onto the claw.

He held me close with one lower arm as his upper hand moved over controls on the claw. Suddenly we were moving. I clung to one of the arms of the claw as it moved out of the storage room and then over the rows of cages. When we passed over the first stack of them, Subject 34 did something on the claw's control panel that caused the cages below us to open.

The mechs that amassed in the walkways between the cage stacks suddenly found themselves under attack from creatures crawling out of—or flying out of—their many different cages as 34 opened one after another. There were so many creatures, and I had no idea how many were deadly to us as well as the mechs and guards below, but we didn't really have time to take an inventory first.

Armed drones flew towards us, but before they could fire upon us, they were swarmed by a variety of winged creatures, including some of the Iriduan males who were apparently in better shape than the ones barely able to crawl out of their cages.

I wasn't certain whether the escaped creatures were deliberately helping us, or just enraged at their captors and getting some of their own back. I supposed it didn't matter.

We passed over Ilyan's cage, and I had a moment of doubt, but Subject 34 freed him before I could warn him not to. On the one hand, I knew what the bad side of Ilyan was capable of, and I feared him for it. On the other hand, I'd seen how much captivity was destroying him, and I wondered if being forced to live out the rest of your life in a tiny, clear cage was the answer for curing such a horrible illness as being fractured.

He'd been watching our advance. I felt his eyes upon us, though I wasn't close enough to see whether they were cold or simply calculating, so I had no idea which part of him was in charge now. His wings were shriveled, so he couldn't fly out of his enclosure, but he wasted no time leaving it, leaping lithely down the stack of cages, easily dodging angry critters darting out of their own prisons.

I felt torn, wondering if we should follow him and keep an eye on him so he didn't escape this place to go redirecting asteroids or something equally as destructive. Still, if he brought hell down upon our captors, it might be very useful for us. Given the way he moved as if he was driven by some purpose, it was clear he wasn't leaving without taking some of them down.

The rush of captives escaping preoccupied the mechs and guards so much that they couldn't get a bead on us, but I didn't feel relieved yet. We still didn't know what kind of defenses guarded the outside of this warehouse. Granted, we had a whole army of pissed off captives now working towards dismantling the very walls of the place, but I didn't know what kind of army would meet us when we succeeded.

We reached the end of the row of cages, then passed down the other side of the warehouse to free all those creatures, only adding to the mayhem. At the end of the track, Subject 34 caught me up in both lower arms and jumped off the claw. We landed lightly on a cage on one of the bottom stacks thanks to his wings slowing our fall.

Then he immediately shoved me aside, shrieking in challenge as something struck at him.

TWENTY-ONE

The giant scorpion fighting Subject 34 took up most of his attention, which meant I had to leapt to the next cage to avoid the second one that crawled towards us.

I didn't want to disturb 34 during a deadly battle that I felt almost certain he would win easily, yet a bit of doubt was enough to scare me. I skirted the edge of the clear cage, now empty, though smears on it showed that it had been recently occupied. The second monster scorpion tested the sides of the outer cage walls to see if it could scale them, and at first, I figured I might be safe because its legs didn't seem to gain any purchase on the slippery surface, but then it managed to pull itself upwards, tail lifting towards me.

"Oh shit," I cried out, wishing I had something like a ginormous tennis shoe to smash it with. Although that shoe would have to be the size of an SUV to do much damage to the thing.

Subject 34 had to catch the thing's stinger in one of his pincers while fighting off the pincers of the other scorpion, both his stingers slamming home in its cluster of eyes.

Don't think I didn't note the resemblance between that eye

cluster and the little eyes on 34's head. I'd already made the connection weeks ago. I could guess that Subject 34 was fighting his own kind at this moment. Maybe even his own clones. Sadly, these more insectoid versions of him were not so inclined to like me as he was. Fortunately, they weren't nearly as agile as he was.

*Un*fortunately, they were a hell of a lot more agile and faster than *I* was.

Subject 34 found himself hard pressed, even with four arms and two stingers to hold off both of them, and one of them seemed to decide I was a much better—as in easier—target. It managed to break away from 34, losing the tip of its stinger in the process, and come after me again.

Tail splattering venom from the hole where its stinger had been, it skittered towards me so fast that I could barely get away from it even with a head start. I hopped up on the stack of cages like Q*bert, screaming the whole way.

A pincer caught my foot, causing me to cry out in pain. Then the creature shrieked as a blast from some kind of weapon struck it in the eye cluster. It released my ankle and shied away as another blast came from behind me. I spared a glance over my shoulder, spotted a naked and flaccid green penis at eye level to me, and quickly turned back to face the scorpion as Ilyan blasted it a few more times with a weapon that looked like it had been yanked right off the body of one of the security mechs.

"I owe you one," I said breathlessly as the scorpion shrieked in a final death knell, its body curling inwards as it toppled off the cage stack.

Apparently, the mechs did have lethal ammunition. They just hadn't been using it on Thirty-four. Thank god they were idiots!

"Consider this my repayment for opening my cage," he said

in cultured voice that was at odds with his nudity and ragged appearance.

"Gotcha," I replied, holding up a hand to block my eyes as I nodded, not wanting to gawk at the man's junk when he stepped up to the edge of the cage we were on and looked over it at the fallen scorpion below.

Then Subject 34 leapt onto the cage, his pincers catching Ilyan up and jerking him off his feet.

"No!" I cried, jumping up to insinuate myself between Ilyan and 34. "He just saved my ass!"

Ilyan already sagged in 34's grip, the weapon slipping from his hands, and I realized that 34 had stung him. I shook Ilyan's arm, yelling in panic at Subject 34. "Don't kill him, damnit! He saved me!"

Subject 34 stung Ilyan a second time, and the Iriduan jerked in his grip, his green eyes suddenly popping open as he sucked in a gasp. His faced twisted with agony, his body arching in Subject 34's hold. His voice came out choked, his lungs rasping as he drew in desperate breaths.

"Thirty-four, what did you do to him?" I demanded, shooting a glare at my lover.

"Kill," he said. "Revive."

I returned my attention to Ilyan, sighing in relief as his body seemed to relax somewhat, though his face still crumpled in pain. "Is he gonna be okay now?"

"Alive now."

Thirty-four still hadn't mastered the nonchalant tone, but I got the gist of his mood as he tossed Ilyan's unresisting form over his shoulder, holding him around the waist with his upper arm as he caught me with the lower arm on the other side of his body.

The Iriduan seemed to be unconscious, which I think he'd be grateful for at this point. His wings curled against his narrow back, shriveled up until they barely resembled wings at all. I hoped there was a way we could heal them, then shook my head mentally at my concern for him.

The guy was seriously sick in the head, and neither me nor Subject 34 were qualified to help him. We were in the process of helping a very dangerous alien escape this prison. Yet, I couldn't accept telling 34 to dump Ilyan back in one of the cells and leave him behind as we made our way of the cage stacks and down to the paths below.

Maybe it was better that we kept an eye on him. Subject 34 could kill him quickly if he switched from scientist to murderer while around us. After all, he'd apparently already killed him once. The ability my monstrous lover possessed to produce lethal venom—and an antidote—at will was something else. Perhaps, in helping Subject 34 escape, I'd already released something even more dangerous than poor, broken Ilyan.

Still, I felt not an ounce of guilt about it. Subject 34 was mine, and I would never leave him behind. Not even if I'd been granted the chance to stroll out of here without him by the Iriduans themselves. I would always fight to have him with me.

I felt bizarrely protective of Ilyan too, despite never having actually spoken to him. He'd kept me company in our odd charades fashion during the weeks of time I'd spent in the clear cages. His story made me sad for him, and I'd always been a sucker for a sob story. He was like a little stray kitten mewing at my feet for somewhere warm and safe to stay—a cute, murder-y stray kitten... who could wield a blaster-type weapon to kill a giant scorpion to save my ass.

A stray tiger, maybe.

The crowd of escapees had broken through the barricaded doors leading out of the warehouse on both sides of the building. We could have followed many of them that escaped into what appeared to be warm sunlight. In fact, Subject 34 started heading in that direction. He paused when I asked him to, as if it didn't even occur to him to ignore me and keep going, since there wasn't anything I could physically do to stop him.

I loved this monster so much! The fact that he actually paid attention to me and what I wanted was so refreshing after twenty years of kowtowing to Michael's wishes!

He stared down at me, his eyes hidden behind his outer eye lenses, his body language patient, despite the deadly chaos flowing around us. I jerked my chin towards the other door—the one leading back into the rest of the facility, where mechs poured through only to find themselves beleaguered by the creatures and captives that appeared hellbent on getting vengeance on some researchers, rather than escaping into the great outdoors.

"I want to see if we can find Nirgal," I said, glancing at Ilyan's unconscious form slung over Subject 34's shoulder.

I worried that I was asking too much. Maybe I was overburdening 34 when we should be focused on escaping this place. The worst thing I could do was get him recaptured again because I was slowing him down rescuing people who probably didn't even deserve to be rescued.

Still, I'd managed to get through to Nirgal, if Tilhur was to be believed, which meant there was still hope for him.

Subject 34 nodded, to my relief. Then he sucked all that relief out of me with his words. "Yes. Find Nirgal. Kill."

"Uh... honey, I was thinking more along the lines of um, saving him."

His wings buzzing was the only sign of his confusion and agitation.

I stroked his chest chitin, a hesitant smile on my lips. "I know he's been mean to us, but he tried to do something good in the end, and I think that effort earns him a second chance. Don't you?"

"No," he said simply, but then he turned and headed towards the battle taking place between freed captives and outmatched mechs.

Fortunately, the captives had pushed the mechs back into the corridor beyond the warehouse entrance, so when Subject 34 charged bodily through the mass of writhing combatants, scattering both mechs and captives like bowling pins, we were able to pass through with minimal fighting on our part. Not that Subject 34 didn't snap a mech head off and slam an overeager captive against the wall to help clear our path, but neither I nor Ilyan took any damage in the crowd before we broke through.

We weren't the only freed captives to take advantage of the open corridor beyond the struggle. A dozen other captives raced past us, some of them flying, some spitting venom, many shrieking or growling, some yelling obscenities that translated— so much for that beeping bullshit. I guess the Iriduans had no problem translating their curses into English, they just didn't care to do it the other way around.

Automated gun turrets fired on some of the escapees, but the winged ones managed to get ahold of them and tear them apart, allowing the rest of the ragtag rebellion to pass with only minimal casualties.

Other than those automated defenses, the corridors stood mostly empty, save for the occasional mech that the captives quickly swarmed and dispatched. More creatures raced up behind us, catching up to us as we made our way through the facility. The flashing lights and blaring klaxon of alarm added to the chaos that spilled from the warehouse into the once calm hallways of this scientific hell.

Some of the researchers tried to bar themselves behind laboratory doors locked down tight. Apparently, they didn't take into account the strength and determination of their captives, because the mass of powerful—even if weakened by their ordeal—creatures and Iriduan test subjects broke through those doors. I flinched and turned my head away as squishy scientists screamed in a blood-curdling fashion not long after their labs were breached.

I swallowed my gorge, my eyes tearing up when I saw some of the creatures dragging out pieces of the scientists, leaving behind a smeared trail of blood as they gobbled up the gory flesh.

Subject 34 carried me along without pausing to take part in any of the door breaking. In fact, he didn't hesitate in his rush through the corridors until Ilyan regained consciousness and started struggling on his shoulder, apparently tired of being bounced around like a sack of grain. A quick sting from Subject 34 sent him back under, and we were on our way again.

I shook my head in commiseration with the unconscious Iriduan. I'd so been there! I loved Subject 34, but he really had to learn not to sting everyone without so much as a "how do you do?"

Still, Ilyan's struggle probably would have been a hindrance at this time, and I wasn't confident that he would accept remaining in our company without a little time to persuade him that he was better off with us than dead. We didn't have that time, so 34's more expedient method had to suffice for now.

"All of these rooms look like labs," I said to 34 as he carried me on past one door after another. "They're probably keeping Nirgal in one of them."

"I find," 34 growled, passing another door without pausing, as if he knew exactly where he was going.

Maybe he did. Now wasn't the time for explanations. Especially since he treated talking like I treated eating my vegetables. It was a necessity, but I did it as little as possible.

Finally, he paused at a door that had yet to be broken down by the mob of freed subjects now starting to crowd the corridor.

Subject 34 set me on my feet and then unceremoniously dumped Ilyan onto the tiled floor with a thud that had me wincing. I rushed to prop the unconscious Iriduan up against the wall, wincing at the smell coming off him. The poor guy hadn't been bathed properly in who knew how long, and it was obvious in the odor coming from him as well as the matted hair and dull green skin. His slender body had barely any muscle tone, and his cheeks were gaunt, though he still possessed the strong, perfect jaw of a Hollywood actor in his prime. The alien would be very attractive if he wasn't an absolute mess.

I pushed that idle thought away. Okay, it wasn't entirely idle. I reminded myself that I wasn't attracted to the insane alien who was in dire straits, even if he did save my ass recently. I already had an alien I was in love with, and this girl didn't get greedy when she'd already been so blessed.

Subject 34 used all four of his limbs to smash at the door, and the power behind his blows would be terrifying if he weren't on my side. The door panel shuddered beneath the strength of his strikes, vibrating in its track. Still, it held after a half dozen hits, and I began to fear we wouldn't get it open, despite the deep dents Subject 34 left in it. Then several Iriduan males joined us at the door. Not all of them were emaciated, and they added their own kicks and punches to the metal panel. Finally, with a great squealing sound of tormented metal, the door buckled in its frame, breaking the seal and leaving a hole where Subject 34 could grip it and yank it out of its track with a mighty heave.

"That was so hot!" I said aloud, then blushed when some of the naked Iriduans glanced in my direction.

I turned my burning face away from them, watching 34 toss the door panel aside like it weighed nothing. Then he shoved them out of the way as they crowded the now open doorway like they hesitated to charge inside. It seemed strange that they would pause here, when so many of them had rushed into the other rooms in search of scientists to kill.

I could tell they feared this room just by their body language. I didn't need to hear their soft whimpers as they shied away from entering it, their wings tucked and their bodies curling in on themselves as if regretting even opening that gateway to what was probably their version of hell.

"Ronda not look," Subject 34 said from just inside the room, his body blocking my view. "34 get Nirgal."

I gulped, keeping my eyes turned away from the interior. It had to be bad if 34 was warning me not to peek. It had to be really awful. The kind of thing he'd know I hated, just like I hated the gory chunks of meat he'd once offered me.

I waited with my heart pounding, wondering if Nirgal was even still alive. I also kind of feared that 34 would kill him but pushed that worry aside. He knew I wanted to save Nirgal, and he'd always been on my side before, so there wasn't a reason to assume he'd go against what I wanted in this one thing.

Except that he hated Nirgal as much as I once had. Maybe even more so. Nirgal had been his creator and his tormentor for even longer than he'd had me as his captive.

Some of the Iriduans clustering around the open doorway finally entered it, their chins lifted with determination. The others watched from the hall as the Iriduans within began destroying things. I didn't hear the screams of any scientists, and given the expressions on the faces of these freed captives, there would definitely be screams if they'd found any of them hiding in there.

Then Subject 34 appeared at the door again, carrying something that I glanced at only once before turning away to vomit what little remained in my stomach from the last time 34 had "fed" me.

I hated blood and gore, but it was so much worse when it

was all that remained of someone you kind of knew, even if you didn't like them. I wasn't the kind of person to want to get back at someone by doing worse to them than what they'd done to me. Nirgal had held me captive, scared the hell out of me on numerous occasions, treated me like an animal, and made me miserable.

But he hadn't left me in the state he was now in.

"Is he alive?" I asked, keeping my head turned as my gorge remained in my throat.

"Is. Barely. Kill Nirgal more merciful."

Tears filled my eyes as I nodded slowly. Subject 34 was right. Given what little I'd seen of the blood-soaked naked body of my captor, a quick death would be the kindest fate for him.

"So 34 let live."

I blinked in surprise, glancing at 34 again, then quickly away as my stomach threatened to rebel again. "You want to let him live now?"

"He suffers."

Okay, my lover had a vindictive streak. I supposed that shouldn't entirely surprise me. I wondered guiltily if he'd actually gotten it from me. He'd seemed far more pragmatic and unemotional when he'd first encountered me than he did now.

Just in case, I made it clear where I stood. "I don't want to make anyone suffer, 34. I don't hate Nirgal anymore."

"Ronda want Nirgal. 34 keep him alive."

"I don't *want* him!" I crossed my arms over my chest, eyeing the Iriduans now coming back out of the horror room, some of them also burdened by other, tormented Iriduans, most unconscious, though one of them moaned in agony as the Iriduan carrying him passed us. "I just didn't want him to have to stay here and be tortured!" I held up a hand, still avoiding looking directly at Subject 34's burden. "Don't get my interest in him wrong, 34. I love *you*, not him. He still pisses me off."

"We should get out of here," a weak voice said, causing me to glance over at Ilyan, who had apparently regained consciousness as he lay propped against the wall. His eyelids hung low over his eyes, which looked lucid and not ice cold, much to my relief. He was still out of it, based on the way his voice slurred, but he seemed to be aware enough of what was going on around him to understand the danger we were still in.

"They will purge the facility," he mumbled, his head falling forward when he tried to move it.

"Purge?" That didn't sound good. That sounded like dropping a nuke on a zombie outbreak kind of bad. "With bombs?"

Ilyan made a muffled sound that I think was supposed to be a yes, then slumped down until his body lay in a heap against the smooth wall.

I glanced at Subject 34, my gaze skimming over Nirgal's unconscious and bloody body. "They're gonna blow this place! We gotta get out of here!"

TWENTY-TWO

Ilyan shot to his feet like a rocket when Subject 34 stung him, his eyes wide, his shriveled wings flickering, a shout on his lips.

He gripped the wall with one hand to steady himself as he turned an angry glare on 34. "Stop doing that!"

To my relief, his eyes, though a little wild from what was probably some kind of adrenaline shot, didn't look cold and remote. I took that to mean the scientist was in charge, not the killer.

Then Ilyan's gaze fell upon 34's burden. He sucked in a pained breath, his features pulling into a scowl.

"Is that Nirgal?" he said in a low voice, as if he wasn't sure he wanted the answer.

"I think they were trying to fracture him," I said, drawing his gaze to me.

He made a low growling sound in his throat as he glanced back at Nirgal. "Curse the Spinner and all her threads," he said in a voice shaking with fury. "Such a thing is monstrous!"

"I'm glad we can agree on that."

He eyed me again, his gaze sweeping me from head to foot.

Fortunately, he kept any critical comments he might have had to himself, and I couldn't read anything in his expression, but he didn't exactly have much room to talk. At least I had clothes on. I had to keep my eyes well above his waist, and it was difficult not to accidentally catch a glimpse.

"We will have to see if they were successful in their efforts," he muttered, shaking his head slowly as his gaze returned to the mess in Subject 34's arms.

A mess I still refused to examine too closely. I worried that Nirgal was too still, barely a sound coming from him, and even that was only labored breaths that seemed far too weak to sustain any living creature.

"We have to find a doctor or something!" I insisted, turning my full attention to Ilyan. "I had 34 revive you because you're the same species as the people running this place. I was hoping you could tell us how to get out of here before they purge the joint."

"They'll have shuttles," he murmured, one hand stroking his chin, which—despite his dishevelment—was free from any kind of stubble. "Some of them were likely deployed as soon as the alarm went up, but there might be a few available." He glanced at Nirgal, his lips pulling into a deep frown that also creased his verdant brows. "They should have a healing tank on board. I can only hope it will be enough to help him in the state he's in."

"He said you were a friend of his." My tone held sympathy. I couldn't even look at Nirgal right now, and I was still technically his enemy.

I couldn't imagine what it would be like to care about him and have to see him in this state.

Okay, so maybe I could kinda imagine what it felt like, but I wasn't dwelling on that kind of stuff right now. We still needed to escape this place.

Ilyan huffed but didn't comment, instead turning to face the corridor where the activity around the room had died down. Apparently, the other Iriduans had collected or destroyed everything they'd wanted to in that lab, because they had moved on to other doors down the way.

"I can probably override a shuttle's lockout," he said as he began moving in a direction away from the warehouse.

Subject 34 made a grumbling sound that I hadn't heard from him before, and it looked like he debated tossing Nirgal over his shoulder the way he had Ilyan in order to pick me up again to carry me. I held up both hands to stop him from putting that thought into action.

"I can move pretty fast when I'm motivated, 34." I started after Ilyan, calling over my shoulder, "and I'm definitely motivated right now!"

Fortunately, both Ilyan and Subject 34 could read the symbols on the signs as we passed through the corridors, because I was totally lost. The place was almost as much of a maze as the one they put their test subjects in. I followed both males as they raced to our destination, which I really hoped still had at least one shuttle sitting around, gassed and ready to go.

Given the amount of death around every corner in this facility, I got the feeling not many of the Iriduan scientists had a chance to escape.

"How long until they purge this facility?" I said between gasps for breath as I raced on Ilyan's heels.

I struggled to keep my eyes fixed on his shriveled wings and not the weird appendages below them that coiled right above a very nice, naked green ass. I would not check out the hot alien while we were running for our lives. Especially not since I loved another alien altogether.

I had no idea what was wrong with me. I've always been a one-man kind of girl, with eyes for no one else when I was in love. That probably explained why Michael was able to hurt me so badly. He took my devotion and unfailing loyalty for granted and left me with nothing but heartbreak.

I chalked up this weird attraction to Ilyan to an affection I'd gained for him during our captivity. He'd literally kept me sane while I was trapped in that little box, which was kind of ironic given his own state of mind.

They found the shuttle bay and Ilyan managed to hack into the door control panel with ease, which had my brows lifting in surprise. Nirgal had said Ilyan could escape almost any kind of prison, which had led to him ending up in that little and uncomfortable cage next to me. Still, I would have thought an advanced alien species would have better security.

It occurred to me as we entered the shuttle bay that Ilyan hadn't answered my question about the bombs about to drop on our head. I parted my lips to ask again how long we had, then my jaw dropped as I took in the shuttles.

They were far nicer than I had expected for a mere research facility. I'd thought they'd be boxy and utilitarian. Instead, they were sleek, sideways teardrops that shimmered in the bright lighting of the bay.

There were only two of them, but we only needed one, so we were golden. The ceiling above us had been retracted already and the bay had a few more empty slots, which probably meant at least some others had escaped.

Ilyan didn't hesitate to rush towards the nearest shuttle. Subject 34 sent me a questioning glance, and I nodded for him to follow, then remained close on his heels, avoiding any close looks at what he carried.

I feared that Nirgal couldn't take much more of this. I'd never seen anyone in such a terrible condition before. He literally wasn't recognizable, and flesh had been flayed from his body in multiple places in addition to all kinds of terrible and chilling lacerations and bruising that spoke of unimaginable suffering. I had no idea how Ilyan had recognized him. Perhaps it had something to do with his coloring, or the black markings on his limbs, face, and torso that looked like tiger stripes.

Markings neither Ilyan nor the other captive Iriduans had on their bodies, making Nirgal's distinctive.

"Do we need to worry about any kind of security on this ship?" I asked to distract myself from thinking about Nirgal as Ilyan messed around with a panel on the sleek side of the shuttle.

The hull of it towered over us. The thing was the size of a small passenger airplane, if it was smooshed into a teardrop shape with a lotta of junk in the trunk and a short, pointy nose.

"If we don't give the right codes, the security satellites will shoot us out of the sky," he answered with calmness I definitely didn't think was warranted given his words.

"Uh, maybe it would be better if we went out into the wilderness instead." I glanced around at the bay, noting that none of the other escapees had made it this far yet.

Or maybe they were aware that they needed a special code phrase to get past the killer satellites.

"If we do that, we might not outrun the blast, and Nirgal will surely die without immediate treatment," Ilyan snapped, clearly finally feeling the pressure.

Maybe Subject 34's adrenaline shot was wearing off. I glanced up at the shielded eyes of my lover. He looked supremely calm, not in the least bit shaken by our escape.

The monster-man had literally just performed brain surgery on himself, so I had no idea why I thought he'd be losing it at this point. Still, his serene demeanor reassured me as Ilyan managed to get the shuttle to manifest a doorway in what I'd thought was a smooth hull. The opening was so tightly sealed that I couldn't see the seams until the door slid open.

A ramp of steps unfurled from the shuttle and Ilyan raced up them, gesturing with one hand for us to follow. Subject 34 waited for me to enter, then his heavy steps bent the ramp as he followed me.

Nirgal started moaning just as we entered the shuttle and I took my first look around the interior. I glanced over my shoulder just as Subject 34 stung him and his body sagged in 34's lower arms again.

"He's still alive, at least," I said without trying to conceal my worry.

"Not for long if we don't get him in the tank." Ilyan gestured for us to follow him as he headed down a narrow corridor of the disappointingly utilitarian interior of the pretty teardrop shuttle.

It was the size of a small plane and looked like one on the inside. Still, there was some kind of healing tank that looked a bit like an iron-lung. Nirgal fit completely inside it, head and all.

Ilyan muttered something to Subject 34 before leaving the tank room, which I guess was a med bay, though it was so tiny that I couldn't even fit into it until Ilyan left because the tank itself and 34 took up all the available space.

The Iriduan headed towards the control room of the shuttle, telling us over his shoulder to sit tight and keep an eye on Nirgal.

"What about the code to get past the satellites?" I asked nervously.

"I'll figure something out." He waved away my concerns flippantly.

"Uh, Ilyan...."

He paused in the corridor just outside what I took to be the door into the control room of the shuttle. When he turned to regard me with lifted brows, his expression questioning, I bit my lip, debating whether I should speak my concerns aloud.

Time was ticking away. We really didn't have the luxury of doubts about our allies. Still....

"Are you gonna be... okay?" I asked, meeting his eyes and hoping I didn't see them suddenly shift into that cold, hard gaze.

"You're worried I'll lose control to my fracture?" he asked mildly.

I felt relief that he seemed unoffended by the concern, nodding without a verbal answer.

"I believe he will remain dormant during this escape," Ilyan said with a confident tone.

Then he turned his back on me, slapping his palm to the door panel. As I turned back to the tank, I heard him say something else that raised the hair on the nape of my neck.

"Yes, I don't think Ilyan will reawaken anytime soon."

I jerked my head around to look at him, but he disappeared into the control room, the door sliding closed behind him. He smirked as he turned to face me, just before the door cut off my view of him.

TWENTY-THREE

"We might die," I said to Subject 34, proud of myself for keeping the absolute terror I felt from choking off my voice.

34 cupped my face with one of his lower hands, but he didn't offer any verbal reassurance. In a way, I appreciated that. He wouldn't lie to me. He wouldn't pretend we weren't in dire straits.

"Even if those satellites don't shoot us down," I said in a whisper, "I think Ilyan's fracture is in control of him. He will probably kill us."

Subject 34 chittered in a way I'd come to recognize as his version of a chuckle. My lover wasn't often amused enough to show it, but he apparently found this funny. His other lower hand wrapped around my waist, tugging me against his hard body even though it was a tight fit in this small med bay.

"I'm serious, 34!" I hugged him around his waist, keeping my arms away from his silver marks. "I'm scared!"

We'd already taken off, so it was too late to escape now. The shuttle engines barely made a sound as they vibrated the floor beneath my feet. I had waited in breathless silence while we ascended in what I assumed to be a rapid enough pace to create some g-forces, but I felt nothing in the way of inertia. The only way I knew we were accelerating was by the increase of vibration coming through the floor. The technology left me impressed, I had to admit.

"34 protect Ronda." One of his upper hands stroked my hair soothingly, while the other smoothed over my back.

"I don't think even you can protect me from a satellite missile." I sighed heavily and leaned my cheek against the hard chitin plates of his chest. "I hope whoever Ilyan is right now, he can manage to get us through that obstacle. I really don't want to blow up today. Come to think of it, there isn't any day where I want to blow up. It's kind of a quirk of mine that I'd rather remain in one piece."

"Ronda trust green guy. 34 trust Ronda."

I snuggled into his arms, enjoying the cool, smooth feel of his chitin beneath my cheek. "I love you, 34. You make me feel safe, even when we're probably going to be smithereens in a few minutes."

"Love?" Given the confusion I sensed in his tone, I thought back over our time together and realized I hadn't told him I loved him yet.

I lifted my head to look up into his face, smiling when I saw that his faceted eye shields had retracted to show me his beautiful dark eyes. "Yeah. I love you, 34. If we have to die today, then there's no place I'd rather do it than in your arms."

He stroked his claws through my hair. "What love mean?"

I cocked my head, pondering the best way to explain it. "There's no, uh, translation for it in that head of yours?"

His mandibles retracted to show his lips in their usual firm and impassive line, but his brows drew together in thought as his eyes grew distant. He was clearly searching for the meaning his translator gave to the word.

"Means mating?" he asked, his frown of confusion deepening.

"Ugh!" I rolled my eyes. "Of course, these Iriduans probably don't think of love the way we humans do." I patted his chest, where a human heart would be, but come to think of it, I'd never actually heard his heartbeat, so I had no idea what was under all that natural armor plating that covered his body.

Well, I knew what was under one part of it, but now was not the best time to think about that. I wasn't feeling sexy, nor hungry.

"Love for a human is like...." The words didn't come for me, at least not easily. I had to really strain to find them, because explaining love was difficult even to another human.

I knew Subject 34 felt some affection for me. He was protective of me. He seemed to want to spend all his time in my company. He listened to me as if he found what I had to say interesting. He showed me respect and didn't condescend to me, even when he was so much stronger and more capable of dealing with our circumstances than I was. And each moment I spent with him seemed to change him until he evolved from cold and ruthless to caring and thoughtful.

"Love is inspiration, and devotion, and dedication. Love is caring more about someone else's happiness than your own. Love is sometimes sacrifice and pain, but it also makes you feel like you can stand atop the world and reach for the moon and stars. Love is... everything. It is the real purpose and meaning in life." I stared up at him, still struggling to explain what most humans just knew instinctively. "You can love many people in your life, in different ways. It's not all just 'mating'. Parents love their children," I sighed, "and sometimes they know how to show it, and children love their parents. And brothers love their brothers, and sisters love their sisters, and friends love each other. It's just... the whole point of everything. To find love. To cultivate it. To hold onto it. To cherish it."

I finally had to shrug, unable to think of another way to explain it. "Love is what makes life worth living, 34."

"Love is Ronda." He stroked my hair away from my face, lowering his lips to mine.

His kiss took my breath away and distracted me enough that I forgot the danger we faced, the possibility of blowing up within minutes.

Did this alien male of mine just say I made his life worth living?

I sank into his embrace, allowing him to keep me occupied so I also forgot the uncertainty of our ally. I was even able to push aside my concern for the Iriduan laying in the healing tank next to us, the extent of his injuries shielded from my eyes, but not from my memory.

"You will be happy to know that we are still alive," Ilyan said wryly, his voice startlingly loud as it blared from a hidden speaker overhead. "If you manage to detach yourself from the test subject long enough to look at an outer view screen, you'll see that we've passed the defensive satellite array."

At the sound of Ilyan's voice I broke away from 34's kiss, sucking in a deep breath, my head spinning from the headiness of his aroused pheromones. If there had been more room in this med-bay, I probably would have climbed him like a tree and begged him to strip me naked and bury himself inside me. Healing tank notwithstanding. Sure, I would have felt bad about it later, but it was difficult to think straight when 34 got his mojo juice flowing.

"His name is 34," I said, licking my swollen lips as I watched the minor flash of irritation cross Subject 34's face.

He was definitely learning how to use his facial muscles.

"His name is irrelevant to me," Ilyan snapped over the

speaker. "What I need to know is where, exactly, you plan to go now?"

I blinked, startled at the question. And then even more startled at the realization that I couldn't think of where to go now that we'd actually managed to escape. "Uh... why is it up to me, again?"

The speaker crackled like someone smacked it. Or probably hit the microphone on the other side of it. Maybe while in the midst of lifting their hands to rub their temples. I could just picture Ilyan rubbing his head as if it ached.

"We are all outlaws, or targets of the Iriduan empire," Ilyan finally said with a long-suffering sigh, "and the only thing currently unifying us is you. So, *you* decide where we go now."

This revelation bought another couple of rapid blinks from me. I shifted my gaze from Subject 34's now impassive face to the speaker. "Wait, *I'm* unifying us?" I shook my head. "Don't make *me* the leader! I don't want that kind of responsibility!"

A bitter chuckle rose from the speaker. "You're the queen. You decide where we go. It's a male's job to follow his queen, or have you learned nothing about our species in all your time being our captive."

"Whoa, whoa!" I held up both hands, glancing quickly at Subject 34 before returning my attention to the speaker I couldn't actually see. Perhaps I should be looking towards the door to the corridor outside the med-bay. "What's with this 'queen' crap? You're not *my* 'males'!"

I quickly hugged Subject 34's waist as I amended that. "Except for 34, of course!"

"Then you will abandon Nirgal and I?" Ilyan asked with a tone to his voice that I couldn't interpret.

I wasn't sure anymore who controlled Ilyan's body at the moment. Him or his fracture. He'd seemed to imply that his fracture was the one in charge with his parting words to me earlier, but at the same time, there hadn't been that telltale coldness in his eyes before he'd turned away from me to enter the control room of the shuttle.

"No!" I glanced at the healing tank. "Of course not. I'm not saying I'm going to leave any of you behind. I'm just saying that neither of you belong to me. I mean," I spun my hand as I searched for the words to explain myself, "you know, like, as a lover or mate or boyfriend or anything romantic."

I suddenly worried that I was misinterpreting his words and maybe reading too much into what he was saying. Maybe he hadn't been talking about that kind of thing at all, and now I'd made things really awkward by assuming that.

He didn't respond to that, and his prolonged silence made me babble nervously. "I mean, I know about the whole 'imprinting' thing, sorta."

I still didn't really get it. Like how it all worked, or what exactly happened when a male imprinted on a female, but I could tell even when Nirgal talked about it that it was pretty intense and life-altering for Iriduans.

"But I thought you were cured of that, like Subject 34."

The door to the med bay slid open, and I jumped a little in 34's embrace when I saw Ilyan standing on the other side of it. He had found a jumpsuit somewhere in that control room because he was now dressed, but he still looked like he'd been dragged by his hair and starved and beaten.

34's stingers extended, hovering between me and Ilyan, and he shifted his body so he blocked me if Ilyan chose to attack.

"I am cured of my affliction," Ilyan said, his green gaze intent on me, not cold and remote but also not kind or affectionate. "But apparently, I am still prone to the *influence* of a female."

"Oh," I slowly nodded, understanding now. "You know,

that's a common thing to happen when people go through tough times together. They tend to form a bond, but once we're out of danger, you'll meet some nice... uh... space fairy woman and fall in love—"

He scowled, looking less than friendly, but again, not cold or cruel or murder-y. "Your ignorance of my species shows in almost everything you say."

"Well, that's not a very nice thing to say," I snapped as Subject 34 chittered angrily at Ilyan. "Listen, if this is your way of flirting with me, you need some serious practice."

"And how, *exactly*, would I get that?" Ilyan asked with bitterness sharpening his tone. "I wasn't trained to be a mate to a queen. I was trained to be a scientist." He gestured to Subject 34. "And yet again, I find myself bound to a human female who has chosen a *test* subject over me!"

"34 isn't just some test subject!" I said angrily, though I also felt a guilty thrill that Ilyan was confirming he had some romantic interest in me. I knew I shouldn't feel that way, but I couldn't help it.

I'd bet green guy cleaned up nice. I hugged Subject 34 a little closer, reminding myself firmly that he was the only alien I needed in my life.

"If he's not a just a test subject," Ilyan said with a sneer as his gaze raked Subject 34 from head to toe, much to 34's complete disinterest in his regard, "then why doesn't he have a name?"

I lifted my chin. "He likes the name 34. So he *does* have a name!"

"He took the name you gave him because he doesn't care," Ilyan shouted, causing Subject 34's stingers to dart in his direction so he took several steps away, ending up standing out in the corridor. "You are the one *creating* his personality! He thought of nothing but hunting and killing before you. Any loyalty or compassion or devotion he shows you reflects what you've shown him. Don't you *see* that?" He glared at Subject 34. "He was not intended to claim a mate!"

"And you weren't trained to be very nice to women, apparently!" I snapped, patting 34's chest chitin reassuringly, though he seemed unfazed by Ilyan's rudeness. "But at least Subject 34 can learn how to love! What about you, huh?"

"Give me a chance and I'll show you," he said in a low voice, his eyes unreadable now, but not carrying that hard, ruthless look I'd come to associate with the bad side of him.

I shivered a little at the promise underlying his tone, and it wasn't with fear. I sucked in a ragged breath, turning my face so I wasn't looking at him any longer. I stared instead at 34's chitin plates, stroking my fingers over them.

"I'm already in love with someone, Ilyan. I'm sorry, but I'm sure once we get things figured out—"

"Athraxius," Ilyan said in a hard tone, "do you care if your woman takes other mates in the custom of the Iriduans?"

When Subject 34 chittered at me I glanced up at his face in surprise. There was a questioning tone in that sound.

"Want what Ronda want," he said when Ilyan and I waited in silence for his response.

Ilyan gestured to him with a triumphant wave of his hand. "Do you see, woman? He only wants your happiness because it is all that gives him meaning and purpose. Given that evidence, it seems that Nirgal and his team failed, yet again, to strip the worst traits from our genome before splicing them into Subject 34."

I shook my head, denying his words even while taking great comfort from them and no small amount of pleasure at the idea that Subject 34 was so devoted to me. After what Michael did to me, I was left believing no one would want an aging, never-been artist-slash-store manager. Now, I had two alien males who wanted to be with me, and even though I knew that something in their biology made them feel that way, rather than my own desirability, it was a heady experience.

"I thought both of you were cured," I insisted, still unable to trust that Ilyan—who had cheekbones and a jawline to die for and the sensual lips of a male model—was interested in not only taking me as his mate but would be willing to share me with another male.

It was so strange and felt so forbidden to even consider such a relationship. I knew there were some humans who engaged in that kind of lifestyle, but it had been so far out of my experience that I'd never dreamed it would happen to me.

Or that I would choose it. I hadn't even been able to keep one man happy until "death do us part". What was I thinking by even considering juggling two of them?

Ilyan responded to my comment by stepping cautiously back into the med-bay, eyeing Subject 34's extended stingers. He paused just inside the door, since there really wasn't room for him to step any further into the room. Then he tapped the healing tank.

That action brought up a holographic panel that appeared solid even though it floated in the air above the tank, rather than flickering and translucent like those kinds of things always were in the sci fi movies.

"The *cure*," he said, his gaze scanning the screen, "removes the biological requirement for a specific female based on her scent signature." He tapped on the holographic display, his finger passing through it.

A new "window" opened on the screen, showing a strange fractal looking crystal thing, flashing lights along all its spears.

"Nirgal was injected with the nanites recently," Ilyan said. "Some are still active, but I suspect their work will be complete soon, despite his current condition." He shook his head. "It is a pity they deactivate and dissolve after rewriting the affected genetic code of an imprinted male. I doubt I would be able to draw a stable sample to study them. More's the pity."

I held up a hand like I was in biology class, knowing I had a test coming up but completely clueless about what the hell the teacher was talking about. "So you're *not* imprinted on me?"

His eyes shifted back to me, then lifted to meet Subject 34's steady stare, his handsome features pulling into an irritated scowl. He returned his gaze to me.

"I am not *biologically* imprinted on you." He studied me as if he were seeing me for the first time, despite having been in the cage beside me for weeks. "However, it appears I have emotionally imprinted on you, because I do not like the idea of being separated from you." He shot another glance at Subject 34. "Nor do I like the idea of losing you to another male." He curled his hands into fists, stepping back into the corridor as he glared at me like all this was my fault.

"I do not like this feeling," he growled.

Then his body stiffened, his eyes closing briefly.

Subject 34 also stiffened, chitter-growling as he moved me further behind him until I was wedged between him and the tank, the bulk of his body blocking mine from Ilyan's view. I peered around 34's massive body and met the eyes of the green male.

"Shit," I muttered eloquently. "What did you do to Ilyan?"

The fractured part of the Iriduan chuckled darkly, a smirk tilting his shapely lips. I hated to admit that he still looked damned attractive like that. In fact, maybe that mocking expression made him a little more attractive. Edgy. Dangerous.

I'd never expected to find that type appealing.

"Ilyan's mind is very strong," the fracture said. "It is a struggle to take control, and I must admit that I rarely succeed.

It is only when he *wants* to retreat into the shadows that I have free reign."

"Well, that's just rude," I snapped, hiding my fear of the fracture behind my sharp tone. "We were in the middle of a conversation! How's he just gonna duck out like that?"

Ilyan's fracture made a hmph sound that dripped with arrogance as his chin lifted. His chilly gaze left me to regard Subject 34 thoughtfully, shifting from his face, which was now covered, telling me 34 was on guard, to his extended stingers that hovered in the air between the two males.

"I wouldn't try anything foolish," I said smugly, stroking my fingers along the length of one of 34's extended stingers.

He rewarded me with a chittering sound, but his stinger didn't waver.

The fracture chuckled again. "Does he know how to pilot a shuttle?" He cocked his head, returning his scathing gaze to me. "Do you?"

Ooh, he got me there. "Well, I'd rather one of us try than have you pilot us into a colony. Or an asteroid."

Great comeback, me! Ha! More like potentially pushing button—or was I giving him ideas?

His mocking expression disappeared, his face going completely impassive, his lips a tight verdant line in a face that had eerily perfect male features. "I have reasons for everything I do."

"Yeah, sure. Don't we all." I glanced at the healing tank, thinking about Nirgal and his constant insistence that all the terrible things he did were "for science!" "The question is whether your reasons are actually good enough to commit such terrible acts."

"Who are you to decide that, Rhon-da?" He drew out my name sarcastically, condescension in his tone. "Or do you consider yourself the arbiter of morality? A human?" He scowled. "Don't make me laugh at the painful irony."

"Dude, you guys need to get over this human hate." I tried to prop my hands on my hips, but it wasn't happening in my wedged position. Instead, I cracked my elbows painfully on the wall penning me in close to 34 and the tank.

Evil Ilyan waved away my words. "This isn't about humans. It's about power, and the fact that every sapient species desires it, and we all will do anything we can to gain it. Humans are only one of many species always vying for more than what they already have. What makes your species so irritating is your smug sense of self-righteousness. It is rather hypocritical, don't you think?"

"All right, we're gonna have to agree to disagree on this one, Ilyan—or whatever you call yourself."

"What makes you think I don't go by the same name?" he asked in a neutral tone. "Do you think I am so far gone that I've lost my identity?"

I sighed. "Look, I don't want to be at odds with you. This is a small ship. I'm super tired, and Subject 34 had to perform brain surgery on himself, so I doubt he's feeling chipper at the moment either. Can we table this whole philosophical discussion for another time? Like maybe never?" I narrowed my eyes on Evil Ilyan. "Just, you know, don't kill us, and I think we can all get along until we decide what to do with our lives."

"You are a very odd human," Evil Ilyan said with short laugh that I suspected held more exasperation than amusement.

I stroked my fingers along Subject 34's stinger again, smiling up at my dangerous mate, his face concealed behind his chitin eye shields and mandibles. "Yeah. I have my moments."

TWENTY-FOUR

I had no idea how much time passed before I finally awoke from an exhausted, dreamless slumber. You would think I'd have had nightmares after all I'd been through, but I couldn't remember a single thing other than falling asleep on the tiny cot in a tiny cabin with Subject 34 wedged right next to me, taking up all the floor space.

He'd insisted in his wordless way that he would guard over me while I slept. While I didn't like that he might be uncomfortable, I also wasn't sure he was. He liked tight crevices and spaces, and he didn't need a soft mattress to lay on with all that chitin protecting him. He also had no problem sleeping in almost any position, though I wasn't sure how much he'd actually slept during my rest.

Evil Ilyan didn't murder us in our sleep—a courtesy I couldn't help but appreciate. Granted, getting past Subject 34 would be tough for anyone, least of all an underweight, half-starved, exhausted evil space fairy. Maybe he was just waiting for the murdering until he got his strength back up.

Or, maybe he wasn't as homicidal as Nirgal seemed to think. Granted, I couldn't ignore Nirgal's story of the whole asteroid thing, but since Evil Ilyan refused to give his own side of that tale, I wasn't entirely certain Nirgal's story was accurate.

Speaking of Nirgal, I should probably get around to checking on him at some point. The anxiety I felt about his condition constantly nagged at me, though I tried to keep it pushed to the back of my mind.

I crawled off my cot once Subject 34 cleared some floor space, yawning hugely and feeling like I'd played chicken with a semi-truck and lost. My whole body ached, and I still felt wiped out. By the time I finished rubbing the sleep out of my eyes and opened them, I came face to face with a familiar erection.

Honestly, I should have been used to this by now, and to a certain extent, I was. I didn't hesitate to close my lips around Subject 34's girth and suck hungrily, my hand curling around his shaft beneath my lips. That part wasn't necessary for me, or him, but he liked it, and I liked the way it made his whole body vibrate with pleasure. I also liked how it made him pump arousal pheromones into the air, so my head spun with them, and my core ached to have him inside me.

Making love to him would be tricky in this tight space. After all, he was standing partly in the corridor in order to allow me space to sit up on the cot to suck him. In fact, as much as I wanted to, I doubted we could complete the act while in these tight quarters.

So, I made the most of stroking my lips over his length, my cheeks hollowing as my head bobbed. I licked his shaft and the head of his erection in teasing flicks, and he rewarded me with a flow of his delicious ejaculate. He'd somehow altered the taste of it over time, asking me in single word questions what flavors I liked and managing to replicate the basics, like sweet and savory, with more complex flavors of spices increasing with each iteration.

I don't think he'd expected that feeding me like this would be so pleasurable for him when he'd first done it, but based on his reactions, I knew that he enjoyed it as much as I did. Each time we did it, the process ended up lasting longer, as he slowed the flow of his fluid so that I had to tease and suck it out of him. I would say he was making me work for it, if I didn't enjoy doing it so much.

When he finally sated me, it was my turn, and I had to admit I was grateful I'd had the chance to take a shower in this shuttle, though the confines of the "cleansing closet" had been tight for me. To be fair, they would be tight for a twelve-year-old, so it wasn't a size issue. Especially since my unusual diet had thinned my body a bit, though Subject 34 seemed to prefer me at a fluffier weight. I think he worried when I grew much thinner than I had been when he'd first seen me. Whatever was in that fluid he created, it had plenty of calories.

I doubted my own "fluid" reciprocated. I wasn't even sure it contained anything of value for him, yet he seemed to savor making me come, then licking it from inside me. I wasn't about to complain. Again, he had to take up most of the corridor to work his head between my thighs after divesting me of the jumpsuit I'd found in a drawer filled with them.

Though the suit was a tight and awkward fit that was made for a lean, male body, it came off pretty easily, though Subject 34 left it crumpled around my calves as he feasted on my slit. All four of his hands caressed my naked body while I writhed in pleasure, approaching a powerful orgasm.

I shuddered with a series of soft cries as I climaxed, my inner muscles convulsing as 34 delved his tongue inside me, licking eagerly at my cum. My lower back arched, but he kept my hips pinned in place with his upper hands so he could feed. His lower hands slid over my trembling thighs, his claws teasingly scraping my sensitive skin.

Now, *this* was the breakfast of champions! I had never been a morning person before this, but I gotta say, waking up was now the second-best part of my day. Dinnertime was the first. Actually, both were pretty damned good. As were the occasional snack times.

This "exchange of resources," as nerdy Nirgal would say, put a whole new meaning into the words, "I love to eat."

Not only did I finish "breakfast" feeling sated, but also incredibly relaxed and pumped with feel-good hormones.

It made facing my current situation a little easier as Subject 34 finally let me up and helped me pull my jumpsuit back on.

As good as I felt, I still had to sigh heavily as I squared my shoulders, my brain kicking into gear and out of post-coital mode. "So, we have to deal with Evil Ilyan somehow," I muttered to 34, "and check on Nirgal." I chewed my bottom lip, feeling an uncomfortable clutch of worry in my stomach.

I still felt sick recalling poor Nirgal's condition. I really hoped that healing tank worked miracles, because I wasn't sure an ICU in a hospital could handle what had been done to him.

"34 protect Ronda," he said with supreme confidence in his tone.

Actually, I wasn't sure if that was what his tone said. He didn't have much tonal variation when he spoke aloud. Most of the emotion in his sounds came from his chitters and growls, where there was plenty of variation. I just assumed confidence in this case because Subject 34 was unflappable most of the time. If he were upset—like truly, genuinely upset—he would shriek like a horror movie monster and then tear something apart. Fortunately, I doubted that something would ever be me.

"What should I do about Ilyan?" I whispered, cautiously peeking out into the corridor where Subject 34 now stood, blocking the path.

I assumed if anyone was out there eavesdropping or had been enjoying the previous show, he would have let me know. It looked all clear, but there were probably cameras or open intercoms or something in this shuttle. I should probably be careful what I said about the current pilot of this vessel.

"Ronda want?" Subject 34 asked, with no inflection in his voice.

If he were a human male, I would be searching for a hint of jealousy or unhappiness in his tone, but I honestly doubted I'd be able to detect it even if he felt it. So, I had to outright ask, even while wondering if Ilyan—and his evil other half—was someone I could handle. I mean, I'd worried that he would murder me in my sleep. That kind of thing doesn't make for a good, trusting, stable relationship. He was broken, and I didn't know that anyone could fix him, least of all, me.

"I don't know if it's safe to even consider taking him on as a lover," I said, still in quiet voice.

34 cocked his head, his dark eyes regarding me with a curious expression pulling his brows together. "34 safe?"

I chuckled since his question made him sound almost offended. I patted his chitin-covered chest reassuringly. "Only for me, babe. You're only safe for me."

He slowly nodded his head as if still unsure of the gesture. He'd made the effort to mimic my movements as he came to understand their meanings, but he was still learning, and not entirely thrilled with them, if I read his reluctance correctly.

"Ilyan safe for Ronda."

That wasn't a question, but it certainly raised plenty of them in me. "How do you know?"

"Otherwise, 34 kill. Ilyan smart. Not want to die. Not hurt Ronda."

My mouth fell open as I absorbed his words. I probably shouldn't have been hoping for 34 to claim that Ilyan loved me madly and could never bring himself to hurt me. My monster lover was far too pragmatic for that, and likely hadn't even considered it. After all, I'd had to explain the concept of love to him, and I wasn't sure I'd done a very good job.

"I don't know what I should do, 34!" If he had said that he didn't want me to take Ilyan as a lover, then the question would be easily resolved, full stop.

I might have felt a bit of disappointment. Maybe more than a bit, because I had to admit to my own shame that the green guy did put some butterflies in my stomach when I should have been wholly focused on Subject 34. Regardless of how he might make me feel, I had always placed my fidelity above all else.

Yet, this situation was far different from any I might have encountered before. For one thing, the Iriduans apparently had a polyamorous culture that meant they were accustomed to a female having multiple partners. For another thing, Subject 34 genuinely didn't seem that concerned about losing my affection if I took Ilyan as another lover.

Not that he needed to be. I loved him and would do anything for him, but even with that kind of reassurance many human men would feel jealous and insecure, and I couldn't honestly say I'd blame them, as I would never want to share Subject 34 with another woman. I'd been deeply scarred when Michael had left me for another woman, and I hadn't felt the intensity of emotion for him that I felt for 34.

In truth, I feared that I wouldn't be able to spread my love around without diminishing it, as I'd never been in love with more than one person at a time before. The last thing I wanted was to have a partner who felt neglected or less loved than my other partner.

I had no idea how the Iriduan females dealt with such a challenge. Making multiple lovers happy seemed daunting. Especially when one of them had some serious mental issues that I would also have to navigate with absolutely zero training or any true understanding of his condition. I had a feeling it differed significantly from anything I would have encountered with a human, and it wasn't like I knew what to do when it came to human psychology either.

The only person who could probably best explain Ilyan's fracture to me—other than Ilyan himself, and I didn't want to force him to speak frankly about it—was currently in a healing tank. I wasn't even sure if Nirgal now had a fracture of his own. If he did, maybe he wouldn't want to talk about it either.

34 brushed his claws through my hair, smoothing the strands that were nice and clean after my shower, though a little tangled from sleep. "Ronda take. Don't like, then kill."

"What?" I shook my head sharply. "No, 34! That's *not* okay!" I sighed in exasperation, but hugged him around the waist, avoiding his stinger marks. "You can't just use people like that and then toss them aside if you grow tired of them. You especially can't just *kill* them if you don't want them anymore!"

I rested my chin on his chest, staring up at him. "If I took Ilyan as a lover, then it would be a forever thing for me. Just like it's a forever thing for me when it comes to you. I couldn't accept anything less for myself, and I'd never expect anyone else to accept less than forever."

Subject 34's shrug was one thing he'd gotten very good at, it being the one human gesture he appeared to relish. "Ronda choose. 34 not kill what belongs to Ronda."

He was a menace. For real! Still, I couldn't help but love the monster. It was pretty heady that he had so much devotion to me. His pragmatic simplicity was also oddly charming in comparison to the way I'd always overthink everything, second-guessing myself constantly—like I was doing in this situation. I found Ilyan more than attractive. I'd sort of bonded with him while we were in captivity, and according to his own words, he'd ended up bonding to me. Subject 34 seemed to be perfectly fine with me taking him as a lover, and Ilyan seemed to accept me having another lover.

I wouldn't dwell on the fact that Ilyan had mentioned Nirgal as if he also was mine. We had no idea what condition Nirgal would be in, if he even survived, but I doubted it would involve being bonded to me. Besides, I still had some bones to pick with him. I wasn't sure if I could ever picture myself even kissing the guy, much less making love to him.

Even if he had kind of grown on me. I had never understood how someone could end up feeling any kind of affection or attachment to their captor, until it happened to me.

Nirgal was a problem I didn't need to deal with at the moment. I needed to decide what to do about Ilyan, and how to handle Evil Ilyan.

And then, there was still the question of where we should go now. I was guessing Earth was out of the question, given it had apparently been taken over by aliens. I supposed I could point to some distant star and say, sure, head there. Why not?

But what I wanted was to find somewhere that I could be with Subject 34 without us being constantly monitored and studied like lab rats. I wanted to find a place where we could build some kind of home and live a life that was peaceful-ish—I mean, I couldn't expect 34 to turn into a tame pet, and I wouldn't want that anyway, so complete peace probably wasn't in the cards if I stayed with him.

If I kept Ilyan with me—if I took him as a mate the way he seemed to want—then I would have to contend with the less than peaceful Evil Ilyan as well, which meant more challenges to my daydream of peace and quiet and white picket fences and cookouts with the neighbors.

The two dangerous males were more likely to kill our neighbors than host a BBQ for them.

TWENTY-FIVE

I sought out Ilyan, briefly exploring the shuttle, which wasn't very large at all. There was a captain's cabin, I guess, though Ilyan hadn't used it. Based on the condition of the cockpit—or bridge, or whatever the heck it was officially called—he'd slept in there, the shuttle on autopilot while he no doubt waited for me to make a decision about where to go.

I entered the control room with 34 on my heels, his body strong like an iron giant behind me, ready to sting the hell out of Ilyan if he caused me any problems. Honestly, sometimes his protectiveness made me nervous for other people rather than myself. After all, 34 had already technically killed Ilyan once.

Maybe he was right that even Evil Ilyan wasn't crazy enough to risk Subject 34's anger again.

Speaking of Evil Ilyan, he appeared to still be in control, based on the chilly glare he leveled on me as he turned in his captain's chair to regard me.

"I want to speak to Ilyan," I said without ceremony, crossing my arms over my chest to hide their shaking.

Subject 34's lower hands slipped around my waist, holding

onto me as if he was supporting me. I felt a rush of gratitude and warmth towards him. I'd discussed this whole thing with him for probably far longer than I needed to, before coming into this cockpit, but I'd been talking it out for myself, since Subject 34's only responses were for me to do whatever I chose. He just wanted me to be happy.

"He isn't interested in resurfacing," Evil Ilyan said in an annoyed tone.

"Let him out!" I snapped, nervousness rather than impatience sharpening my tone.

"I wish I could!" he suddenly snarled, leaning forward in his seat, then freezing as 34's stingers rose on either side of me in a threatening display.

He slowly sank back against the seat, and I noticed with surprise that his shriveled wings had grown and smoothed out until they looked to be back to their full length. They extended on either side of the thin seat back, gleaming in the bright lighting like glass sculptures of dragonfly wings.

"I told you he had a stronger will than I do," he said sullenly, his cold glare never leaving my face though he was clearly well aware of the danger of those hovering stingers. "He doesn't let me just drag him out of dormancy whenever I'm tired of dealing with this miserable existence."

I lowered my arms to my sides, feeling an unexpected rush of sympathy for Evil Ilyan. "I'm sorry. I just assumed...."

"That I was the bad guy?" he asked in a wry tone. "I suppose in a narrow-minded binary view of morality, I would be considered that, but much to my own frustration, the 'good guy' is far stronger than I am. He keeps winning, regardless of what battles we fight."

"Why won't he come out of hiding?" I slipped out of Subject 34's hold and settled in the smaller seat next to Evil Ilyan.

The green guy sneered, his upper lip pulling back from beautiful, perfectly straight teeth that showed none of the ravages of his captivity and depravation that remained evident in his gaunt face and too thin body. "He is a coward. Why else?"

I blinked in surprise at the vitriol in his tone. "You hate him, don't you?"

Evil Ilyan shrugged. "He could have killed us when he had the chance. He could have ended us both so we never fractured. Instead, he changed his mind, still thinking he had a chance to salvage something out of his ruined life." He made a low growling sound, his sneer turning into a full, dark scowl that cast shadows in his gem-like eyes. "I think some part of him believed he could find a way to make that woman accept him as a mate, if only he was clever enough."

I'll admit, I felt a little jealous. I had no right to, and clearly, things had not worked out for Ilyan in that department. Still, I felt the little bite from the green-eyed monster—who was not the one sitting beside me.

"Was she that amazing, then?"

He looked at me like I'd suddenly grown two heads. Two really disgusting heads covered with pus-filled pimples. "She meant nothing to him until the moment he imprinted on her. Make no mistake about how our biology usually works, woman. If he hadn't caught her scent and felt the affliction take hold, he would not have felt any attraction to her at all."

"But he's cured from that, right? Why does he feel attraction to me?" The more I learned about this "imprinting" stuff, the more confused I felt.

I mean, I'd read my fair share of paranormal romances. I knew a lot of them had heroes who imprinted on their fated mates. I loved that kind of thing, but in the romances, it always worked out great. The heroines always ended up with the heroes in a lovely "happily ever after," which I couldn't get enough of in my fiction.

It didn't seem to always work that way for the Iriduans, and I realized that things could get really messy for them if the heroines didn't imprint the same way on them and ended up moving on with someone else. Yikes! When I really thought it over, I realized it could be terrible. Maybe terrible enough to tear a man's soul in two.

Evil Ilyan waved a languid hand as if my words were an annoying insect. "Ilyan seems to think the cure itself does not change the strength of our emotional bond to our queens. If something attracts us to a female, be it a scent, or something else about her, we'll develop a strong emotional attachment that is comparable to the physical imprinting. In essence, our brains are hard-wired for imprinting, no doubt to complement our body's biological requirement for the female that afflicted us."

I leaned forward in my own seat, my mind racing as I thought about his words. "But you said Ilyan had already imprinted on another woman. If his emotional attachment to her was so strong, why would he want to be with me?"

"Because he never emotionally bonded with that other female," Evil Ilyan said as if the answer was obvious. "The cure would probably fail to be completely effective for a male who had already formed an emotional attachment to his queen. He would no longer die from deprivation, but he would crave her for the remainder of his life. Mind you, all of this is Ilyan's supposition, not my own. He spent a lot of time in captivity pondering this but did not have the luxury of studying it personally, since he was a test subject rather than a researcher when he was exposed to the cure."

"Okay, if that's what Ilyan thinks, what do *you* think?"

He seemed surprised that I cared about his opinion. His

eyes widened and his mouth dropped open as he sat back in his seat. Then his brows lowered again, his scowl reforming.

"I think," he said in a sarcastic tone, "that Iriduans put too much emphasis on imprinting to explain their strong emotions for their queens. My species has forgotten that we also feel affection and love just as our 'cousins' do. Not everything is a result of our biological imperative."

The tone he used was combative, even condescending, but after pondering his words, I suspected it was intended to distract me from what he was actually saying.

Evil Ilyan believed in *love*, while "Good" Ilyan thought everything he felt was a result of a genetic imperative. "You think Ilyan fell in *love* with me?"

"Don't get it twisted, human," Evil Ilyan snarled, waving a hand in front of him as if slapping away my question. "Even if he did, it won't be like all your human fantasies. We are *not* like humans, though our two species share a common ancestor. The emotions we feel manifest differently. Some of us would say more *intensely* than those of most humans we've studied."

I sat back in my chair, crossing my arms again. I shot a quick glance at Subject 34, who had moved out of the doorway, allowing it to slide closed and now stood close to me, though his stingers were tucked away again.

"As human as I am, I feel love *very* intensely, thank you very much!" I said, returning my gaze to Evil Ilyan. "I love Subject 34 on a visceral level that I've never felt before. I would do anything to be with him."

"How lucky for him." Evil Ilyan's voice dripped with sarcasm, his eyes narrow, his scowl deepening.

I leaned forward in my seat again, my hands resting flat on my knees. "You can shove your sarcastic remarks where the sun doesn't shine, Evil Ilyan, because I happen to care a lot about Ilyan too!" I poked a finger in the direction of the door leading out into the corridor. "And I'm sick with worry about that damned scientist lying in the healing tank who I risked my own freedom and 34's to rescue, so don't you give me that tone and act as if your species is somehow *so* superior to my own when it comes to love!"

I didn't quite realize my words as they spilled out of my mouth until Evil Ilyan's eyes widened, then he tensed. His lids closed tight, his expression shifting to one of complete impassivity. I watched with a feeling of morbid curiosity as different emotions flicked across his handsome face. His tense body sagged a handful of seconds later, but the transformation of his features was so profound and unnerving that I felt like it had taken much longer.

"That's eerie," I admitted aloud when Ilyan opened his eyes again.

They weren't much softer than Evil Ilyan's, to be entirely honest. For the "good guy," I got the feeling Ilyan wasn't exactly the knight-in-shining-armor type. I would say "calculating and superior" rather than "virtuous and honorable." I began to wonder if there was a truly "good" version of Ilyan.

Of course, there wasn't a truly "good" version of Subject 34 either, and I still loved the hell out of him. I chuckled at the thought. Maybe in a way, I *was* loving the "hell" out of him. After all, he was less inclined to kill when I asked him not to, and he did that because he was devoted to me.

I pondered Ilyan speculatively, wondering if I could do the same to him, even as my nervousness ratcheted up more in his presence.

There was a definite, noticeable difference between him and his fracture. I'd picked up on it before, but now, it was much more obvious without the walls of our cages between us. It was almost like his scent itself changed along with his body language and demeanor.

"You needn't stare at me like that," Ilyan snapped, his brows pulling together in irritation at what he must have seen on my expression. "It's impolite."

"Do you... *remember* anything we just talked about?" I asked carefully.

Ilyan's chin lifted, and I noted that he had a more arrogant demeanor than his fracture. "Of course not! A fracture is a serious nuisance. I have no recollection of what it does or says when it is in control. Fortunately, it rarely is."

I smirked even though his condescending tone rubbed over my nerves. Maybe I felt like I needed to take him down a peg or two. "Rarely... except when you duck into hiding like a coward."

That one stung him, and I didn't need his pained gasp or reflexive flinch to recognize it. The expression that flicked over his features made me feel like a total asshole.

He could have killed us when he had the chance....

I should have considered my thoughtless words before I let my irritation speak for me. No doubt he already felt like he was a coward, and I only rubbed salt in the wound. His fracture certainly felt that way about him.

This whole conversation wasn't going well.

I raised both hands. "I'm sorry, Ilyan. I shouldn't have said that. I don't think that you're—"

"I am," he said in a dull voice. "I continue to fail because I *am* a coward."

"Hey!" I said, leaving my seat to kneel in front of his. "Don't say stuff like that!"

He shied back when I leaned towards him, a panicked expression on his face as I rested my hands on his knees without thinking.

They were covered by the fabric of his sleek jumpsuit, but I still felt the warmth of his skin beneath my palms. I gasped and pulled my hands behind my back, my cheeks burning with a blush.

"Sorry! I shouldn't have touched you. I didn't mean anything by it." My words babbled out of me in my embarrassment.

"It meant nothing then?" he asked, and I couldn't tell what he felt from his neutral tone, though his eyes still looked a little wild.

"I mean," I stammered over the words, "I actually came in here to tell you that I would like... that I want...."

I glanced over at Subject 34 for support. He stood immobile and impassive by my chair, though his expression appeared watchful and alert for any threats from Ilyan.

When I turned my head back to face Ilyan, he lowered his head and kissed me, catching me by surprise at his fast movement.

I had no thought other than that his lips were warm and firm, and he smelled really good. Not mind-altering, Subject 34-aroused-pheromone good, but still, he smelled like delicious-man kind of good. The kind you just wanted to bury your nose in and inhale deep. The kind of scent that clung to a man's shirt and made you want to use it for your pillowcase so you always had sweet—and sexy—dreams.

His kiss was clumsy, and I wondered if it was his first. There was something charming about that thought that made me catch him by the nape when he made to pull away. I deepened the kiss, my lips parting so my tongue slid along the seam of his mouth.

He gasped in surprise, and I delved my tongue past his parted lips, enjoying the moan that escaped him. He tasted as good as he looked, and at first his tongue was hesitant with his uncertainty, but he learned quickly, soon mimicking my movements, his head tilting to deepen our kiss.

It felt surreal to be in this position. I remained aware of Subject 34 still being in the room, my love for him as strong as ever, yet I was also swept up in the feeling and scent of this other alien male, feeling the bond between us strengthen with each hungry tangle of our tongues.

The guilt and shame I'd worried I'd feel with kissing another male didn't manifest. Instead, I felt the rush of arousal dampening my core, making my jumpsuit wet between my legs as I thought about his tongue stroking other parts of me the way it was now stroking inside my mouth. The more confident he grew with his kissing, the more demanding he became. His hands slid over my arms, tugging me up out of my kneeling crouch.

I climbed onto his lap, my mound bumping the erection that bulged at his groin. He moaned into my mouth, his hands clutching my arms as he rocked his hips upward to drag his length over my sensitive clit.

This tore an answering moan from me that had him burying his fingers in my hair and pulling me more firmly down on his lap. I rocked my pelvis so my clit rubbed against that firm ridge until both of us were shivering on the brink of a climax. The fact that we remained fully clothed was the only irritation I felt in that moment. I wanted him inside me so badly.

Apparently, he felt the same because he released the fistfuls of my hair that he'd grabbed to pull apart the front seam of his jumpsuit. As soon as I realized what he was doing, my hands shifted from the nape of his neck to slide down his bared chest, skating over the thin pectorals and almost concave abdominals.

His lower back arched as my fingers curled around the smooth length of his shaft, the warmth of it so intense that it almost felt like it burned my palm as I slowly stroked it. As I teased his erection, wrapping both hands around the sizable length of it, his hands worked on parting the seam of my jumpsuit.

He broke our kiss to lower his head to my nipple as soon as he freed my breasts from the fabric of the jumpsuit. I moaned in pleasure, each suckle on my hard bead pulling like it was directly attached to my eager core.

His hand cupped my other breast, while his free hand trailed down my stomach to delve between my folds. I bucked when he brushed his fingers over my clit, and he focused on that spot, allowing me to rock my hips to set the rhythm that had me coming far too soon.

He jerked the jumpsuit off my shoulders and halfway down my arms until there was enough slack in the material for him to free my soaking slit. I felt bound by the strong material, my upper arms pinned to my sides as he lifted my thighs, parting them a little further over his lap. His head lifted from my swollen, throbbing nipple as he stared down at our laps.

I stroked my fingers through his long, silky hair, tracing the pointed line of his ear as he encircled his hand around his own shaft and positioned the head of it at my slippery entrance. His other hand caught a generous handful of my buttock and pulled me closer to him as he penetrated me. The feeling of him sliding deep, thrusting into me made me cry out in pleasure.

He groaned, his head falling back on the seat of his chair, his eyes closed, his perfect jaw tight, a muscle ticking against the verdant skin of his jawline. When his eyes opened to look into mine, his pupils had dilated until only a thin halo of green surrounded them.

He buried his hand in my hair again, tugging my lips to his as he slowly drove deeper inside me until he was fully seated. As his mouth claimed mine, he used his free hand on my hip to urge me to ride his shaft.

A part of me remained aware of Subject 34 nearby, watching everything with no sounds that might have given me pause or made me feel uncomfortable. It was more like he was guarding me but letting me do this thing with another male. Again, where I'd expected to feel guilt or shame, I only felt gratitude towards him. Despite being in the room, he wasn't making things weird or awkward for my first time with Ilyan.

I wasn't sure if this was Ilyan's first time with anyone. Based on his kiss, I'd thought it might be, but he certainly seemed to know how to use his body—and how to touch mine to bring me pleasure.

Still, for all his apparent knowledge, his excitement drove him to pump up into me hard even as I rode his lap, his thick length impaling me deep with each movement. His mouth consumed me, capturing every moan and soft cry that left my lips, even as his sounds of pleasure teased mine.

Then I felt something brushing my clit that wasn't either of his hands. I made to lift my head from his lips to see what it was, but he held me firm by his fist in my hair. Whatever it was that brushed my clit pushed more firmly against it, then began to vibrate.

I rocked my hips forward with him deep inside me, the vibration against my clit and the feeling of his shaft rubbing against my g-spot sending me quickly to my peak. When my inner muscles convulsed around him as I toppled over it, he pumped harder into me. It wasn't long before the hot burst of his seed bathed my womb, his shaft jumping with each pump as it shot inside me.

I slumped against his body in the aftermath, feeling his ejaculate slip out of me as he slowly withdrew. His hands stroked my naked back in a soothing manner that I suspected was uncharacteristic of him. His body sat languid against mine, his muscles relaxed in his seat.

"That was—"

He made a muffled sound of outrage as I clapped my hand over his mouth, lifting my head to meet his glittering green eyes.

"Don't talk, Ilyan," I said gently, shifting my palm off his mouth to trace his lips, which were pulled into an irritated scowl. "I'm not sure what you were intending to say, but I got a bad feeling about it, so I'd like this nice afterglow to last."

His brows pulled together in anger, and I couldn't resist. At least he didn't sting me when I used my fingertip to smooth the lines between them, but his scowl only deepened.

"You don't know what I was going to say," Ilyan snapped, gripping me by the wrist and pulling my hand away from his face. "You're making assumptions about me based on little evidence."

I sighed, pulling away from him to slide off his lap, straightening my jumpsuit as I went. "Okay, you're right. What were you going to say?"

He straightened in his seat, his hard green gaze narrowing. "I was about to say, 'that was a disappointment'," he snarled, then spun his chair around so that its back faced me.

TWENTY-SIX

Okay, maybe I deserved that. I mean, I had assumed he would say something to ruin the mood without giving him a chance to prove that he wasn't a total asshole. Maybe he didn't plan to say something so hurtful, but I hurt him first, and so he struck back at me with something he knew would cause pain.

Yeah, I was gonna go with that because Subject 34 was looking a bit homicidal as he glared at the back of Ilyan's chair after my recoil and gasp of shock.

Now was probably the time to retreat for a bit and think about things, because I was pretty sure it might be my fault this whole experience ended up going bad. After all, everything had been really, really good until I decided that Ilyan was going to screw it all up with a few words and reacted a bit hastily.

Michael would do that to me all the time. We'd have sex. I'd be basking in the afterglow, and then he'd make a comment that would destroy the mood. Usually, it was something about my weight. I suppose I'd decided that Ilyan could be as cutting and cruel as Michael—perhaps even more so, given his obvious sense of superiority—and I'd been on the defensive.

It was possible that he would have said exactly what he ended up saying, cutting me deep, just like he ended up doing. I mean, I had a thing for the guy, but I wasn't under many illusions when it came to his personality. His arrogance was evident in every line of his body—when Ilyan was in charge of it.

The interesting thing was that "Evil Ilyan" didn't carry himself the same way, with that same superior confidence. I found that curious even as my ego was stung as I turned to leave the cockpit, insisting Subject 34 just leave it alone when he looked like he wanted to drag Ilyan out of his seat and beat on him for a while.

Or just kill him, because Subject 34 was pretty efficient, and didn't usually bother with warnings.

Since I still felt this was mostly my fault, I didn't want anything to happen to Ilyan. I had to process too many emotions about what had just happened and sticking around to play mediator between the two alien males in my life would be too much for me to handle right now.

As I approached the door, Ilyan spoke without turning around in his chair. "You still haven't decided where we plan to go." His tone was hard and cold, without any hint of affection or even uncertainty.

Oh yeah, he was pissed. "Uh... do you have any suggestions? I mean, I'm guessing Earth is out of the question."

His condescending snort raised my hackles, but I pushed aside my irritation, reminding myself that his attitude might very well be my own fault.

"Returning to Earth with your *test* subject would be suicide. In fact, going almost anywhere with that creature will be difficult. If you want a suggestion, you'll have to tell me what, exactly, you intend to do for the foreseeable future."

He still wouldn't turn around in his chair, so I couldn't see his expression or body language, but his tone made it clear he wasn't pleased at all with me.

"I want to find somewhere that we could make a home together," I said, realizing how unlikely it would be that such a place existed.

Finally, Ilyan turned in his chair and I noted that he'd righted his jumpsuit, just as I'd quickly fixed mine to cover all the evidence of what had happened between us. Well, all the evidence save for what was soaking the crotch of my jumpsuit— the slippery reminder of our combined orgasms.

He leaned forward, his gaze as cold and hard as bottle glass. Again, I wondered which one of his fractures was the "evil" one. I might have been getting things wrong from the start.

"The only places where you would be able to safely live with," he shot a disdainful glare at Subject 34, who growled in response, "*that*, is an uninhabited world." He leaned back against his seat again, his wings flaring behind him. He rested his elbows on the seat arms and steepled his long fingers in front of him. "Or the CivilRim, I suppose. If you aren't concerned about routine violence."

"That doesn't sound promising."

Ilyan shrugged one shoulder, still holding his evil villain pose. His handsome face looked so chilly and remote that I was kicking myself for possibly screwing up whatever was between us before it could even begin. "The '*Civilized*' Rim is a misnomer, if there ever was one. It is the shore where every outlaw, outcaste, and dreg of polite society washes up." He huffed, his brows lowering to cast his eyes in shadow. "So it could be the perfect place for us."

Well, he still said "us" so maybe I hadn't completely screwed things up with him. He didn't look very interested in continuing what we'd started.

"Is there somewhere specific on this CivilRim that you were thinking of?"

"There's a black-market world I've heard of, though I've never personally been there."

The way his gaze shifted to one of uncertainty made me suspect he might have actually been there, although perhaps he hadn't been the one in the driver's seat at the time.

"Sounds dangerous," I said with my own uncertainty.

"34 protect Ronda," my beloved Subject 34 responded before Ilyan could.

Ilyan shot another irritated glare at 34, who flicked his wings, chittering sharply at the Iriduan.

"It is true that Subject 34 will prove useful in such an environment." Ilyan lowered his steepled fingers, using one hand to gesture to 34 in a dismissive manner. "Even his appearance won't be questioned. There are many species not recognized by the Syndicate that have found their way to the CivilRim, most through the slave trade."

"You're not putting a slave collar on me, so don't even suggest it." I crossed my arms over my chest, shaking my head firmly.

"As intriguing as that thought is," he muttered as some emotion flickered in his eyes that had my core clenching in response, "It isn't likely to be necessary. You'll have him," he jerked his chin at 34, "for protection, and Nirgal and I to handle the details of life on the Rim. All you'll have to do is sit back and look pretty as your males serve you." He scowled and I had no problem detecting the bitterness in his tone. "It's what will be expected when those who understand my species see two Iriduans with a female."

"That's not what I want from you, Ilyan." I sighed, running a hand through my hair, recalling how good it had felt to have him clenching his fingers in it. "Or... uh... Nirgal." I felt a blush rising to my cheeks that made no sense, unless I acknowledged that I did have some feelings towards Nirgal that I shouldn't have.

I glanced quickly at Subject 34. "I don't want you to serve me, either, 34. I want us to be equal partners in our relationship."

"We aren't human males," Ilyan snapped, slamming his fist down on the arm of his chair. "Stop treating us like we are."

I blinked in surprise, taken aback by his tone. He sounded genuinely upset, not just arrogantly offended that I would compare him to a human.

His eyes met mine and they weren't as cold as they had been. In fact, they almost seemed to burn with some emotion I didn't know if I should acknowledge.

"We are not *casual* about our women or the devotion we give to them," he ground out, his cultured voice turning ragged with frustration and anger.

And maybe hurt.

"If we say we are bound to you," he continued, still in that harsh tone, "then we *mean* it, and you are more precious to us than life itself. We will never grow tired of you or bored of being with you. We won't cast you aside for some other, younger female. We will *always* see you as the most beautiful creature in creation, and nothing else will matter to us but making you happy."

My mouth gaped open as I stared at him—this incredibly handsome alien male whom I'd insulted because I'd been too afraid he would say some cruel or cutting remark after I had sex with him. There was no question in my mind that Ilyan suffered from a superiority complex, but he was as good as saying that—when it came to me—he felt entirely different.

"Ilyan, I'm sorry about—"

He waved away my attempt at an apology impatiently, his

scowl deepening as he turned his chair so its back faced me again. "I will enter the coordinates for that world I spoke of, as well as some other possible worlds primitive enough that we can disappear into the wilderness. You decide what you want to do and let me know. Don't take too long. We don't have many resources on this shuttle."

I accepted the dismissal because I felt confused and off-kilter. I left the control room with Subject 34 on my heels, taciturn as always. I appreciated his silence in this moment because it gave me time to process my racing thoughts.

From what Ilyan said, he appeared to know at least some of my insecurities. Given how little chance I'd had to have a conversation with him, that seemed impossible. Unless he'd actually understood a lot of my charades back when we were in our cages.

I'd pretty much assumed that he remained as clueless as I did about our wordless conversations. Because I'd felt safe in the knowledge that there was no way I would ever have to discuss with him the things I'd said with gestures and motions rather than words, I'd gone into deep detail about anything that occurred to me during my weeks of imprisonment.

Many of those things had been about my personal failures at life. My failure to keep Michael happy. My failure to make something out of my passion for art. My failure to be the success my parents had hoped I'd be.

I'd also explained with complicated gestures how Michael had cast me aside. I couldn't even remember how I'd used charades to explain that he'd left me for a younger woman, though I might have formed a cradle with my arms. I know I used a lot of exaggerated facial expressions during that time.

If Ilyan had understood only a fraction of what I'd tried to tell him through exaggerated gestures and expressions and maybe even lip reading, then he would know about some very personal things I'd never shared with anyone else—other than Subject 34—and Nirgal, ironically. That was unnerving given how little I actually knew about him. The things he'd tried to tell me in return hadn't gotten through, and near the end of my time in that cage, he'd pretty much given up trying to pass on any information and had simply watched me wildly pantomiming most of the time.

It had mostly been a game for me to pass the seemingly endless time stuck in that miserable little cage. I'd never imagined that Ilyan was getting far more information about me from that game than I was about him. Knowing that he was aware of my insecurities wasn't even the most startling part of all of this.

What stunned me the most was the sudden understanding of why he'd bonded to me. I'd thought he'd just enjoyed the company during his imprisonment, but if he'd understood some of what I'd been trying to say, then he'd learned about me, maybe even knowing me better than most of the people who had ever been in my life. As crazy as it seemed to me, he appeared to like what he'd learned. Or at least, he'd felt some kind of connection to me because of it.

And now I'd gravely insulted him. The worst part about my hasty action had been that it could have ruined his first time with a woman. I still wasn't entirely certain about that, but from what little I knew of his species, the males took one mate, and mated for life. He'd essentially said so himself. Whether they could engage in casual sex outside of that wasn't clear to me. Whatever the case might be on that, what had happened between us wasn't casual for him. I couldn't possibly doubt that now.

As I stopped at the cleansing closet to shower and grab a clean jumpsuit, I pondered my situation and what I would do next. I discussed the idea of going to this "CivilRim" place with Subject 34, who didn't have much input to offer, being as clueless about it as I was. Poor 34 had spent his entire life in a lab. He had no idea what was out there in the great beyond.

At least that made two of us. I was glad that Ilyan seemed to know something about where we might be able to go.

There might be one other source of information, and the time to check on Nirgal felt long overdue to me. I'd wanted to check on him before going to visit Ilyan, but I'd ended up so twisted up with nerves inside about what I'd planned to do that I'd needed to take care of that first.

Boy, how I'd taken care of it! And then totally blew it!

Even though I still felt twisted up inside, I was better able to focus this time and made my way to the med-bay. It seemed like such a grand description for a tight little cabin with a healing tank as the sole furnishing.

That tight bay seemed a lot tighter when I walked in on Nirgal climbing out of the tank, buck-naked. He glanced up as the door slid open so he met my wide eyes, his own eyes widening.

TWENTY-SEVEN

"You!" Nirgal said in an accusatory tone.

"Nirgie!" I cried out, throwing my arms out like I wanted a hug.

The urge to pester and irritate him rushed to the fore even as I felt a wave of relief to see him looking... well...*alive* was pretty much all I could say at the moment.

"I *despise* that name," he growled, glaring daggers at me.

He had no hair, his orange dome completely bald, though I saw the shadow of hair that would eventually grow back. He'd had strands of blood soaked and matted hair when we'd rescued him so the healing tank must have removed it all. Probably to deal with the multiple lacerations and wounds on his skull.

Those wounds, flaying, and lacerations were healing well from what I could see, though his whole face and body remained puffy from swelling tissue.

Unlike Ilyan, Nirgal's body was covered with black stripes, looking stark against his orange skin. I'd thought they were only on his face, crossing his currently crooked and healing nose and sweeping up both cheeks, but lines also striped his lower face and trailed down his neck. Even more lines striped his chest, arms, and legs. A black chevron marked his lower torso from his ribs to his groin, terminating in a point right above his penis, like an arrow marking the sweet spot. He wasn't quite marked like a tiger, but the coloration definitely reminded me of one.

My brows lifted as I stared rudely, trying to avoid looking too long at his groin as he hopped out of the tank, his flaccid but sizable penis bouncing then swaying with his movement.

"Where are we, human?" he snapped, drawing my gaze back up to his brilliant blue eyes.

I shrugged, swallowing around a lump in my throat before I could answer. My stomach filled with butterflies, and I wondered what the hell was wrong with me that I could possibly feel this way about him—of all the aliens in the galaxy!

"You'd have to ask Ilyan that," I said with a heavy sigh as Subject 34 stepped in close behind me, drawing Nirgal's full attention.

The scientist paled to a peach tone, shying back against the tank. "I created you!" he said in a quavering voice as Subject 34 nudged me to move me aside. "I gave you life. You would be nothing without me!"

I placed a staying hand on 34's chest, shaking my head as I met his dark eyes. "No, we don't kill Nirgie unless he refuses to behave."

A long, tense silence passed before Subject 34 relented and took a step back. Nirgal sighed in visible relief, his shoulders sagging.

Then he shifted his attention back to me, though he continued to cast uncertain glances in 34's direction. "Did you say 'Ilyan'?" His eyes widened so much that the whites fully surrounded his irises. "By the Spinner's silk, is *he* on this shuttle too?"

I nodded, unable to completely quell my grin at his alarm. I couldn't help it. This guy brought out the worst instincts in me. "Yep." I popped my lips on the word, my grin widening.

"Are you suicidal, human?" He stared at me like I was the one who'd lost my mind.

I crossed my arms over my chest. "Well, let's see. I did insist we rescue you, at great personal risk to myself and my beloved 34, so maybe I am."

His brow furrowed, making my fingers itch to smooth the lines between them. "Why would you do that?" He shook his head, his confusion evident. "If you already escaped the facility," he gestured with one hand to the med-bay, "and I can only assume you did, since you're roaming free on this shuttle, what possible purpose could keeping me hostage serve for you?"

His eyes widened again as he glanced nervously towards the corridor behind me. "Was this the fracture's idea? What are his plans for me? Ransom? The empire will never pay it. Not for *me*," he said with a bitter tone.

I sighed, actually feeling a bit sorry for Nirgal. It never even occurred to him that I'd wanted to help him when I rescued him. I suppose it was natural for him to assume I had nefarious intentions. The evil me—who fortunately wasn't free of my control at any time—seriously debated letting him believe we were keeping him hostage. But all I had to do to silence that petty part of me was take one look at his ravaged body. He might have healed enough to regain consciousness and make his own way out of the tank, but he clearly wasn't well. And he'd suffered greatly.

Maybe I had decided he'd suffered enough.

"Ilyan is in control of his fracture," I said in a reassuring tone, "and we're working together right now to find a safe place to go. You're not our hostage. We'd like you to join us. But I'm sure we can work out something different for you, if you want us to drop you off somewhere." I shrugged like it didn't matter to me, but I felt anxious about the thought that he might ask us to do just that.

Ilyan hadn't made that suggestion, so I had no idea if he would even agree to it. He seemed to assume Nirgal would remain with us as if that was a foregone conclusion. I wondered how close of friends they were. Nirgal was obviously afraid of Ilyan's fracture, but he'd referred to Ilyan before as if he'd cared about him.

Nirgal expression shifted to one of alarm again. "Drop me off?" He shook his head quickly, the light of the med-bay reflecting off his bald dome. "There's no where I could possibly go, given my betrayal of the empire." His eyes narrowed as he glared at me. "This is all your fault, curse the silk! I shouldn't have listened to all your nonsense about 'morals and ethics'! What does a human know about our important mission?"

I ignored his accusation, sighing with relief. "Well, I guess you're stuck with us then. I'm sure Ilyan will be happy to hear that."

Nirgal huffed. "I doubt that." He crossed his arms over his lean chest, which didn't boast much muscle but wasn't as thin as Ilyan's underweight body. "Ilyan and I had a falling out. I'm surprised he hasn't killed me yet."

He glanced at the healing tank, then at me, then shot a quick and nervous glance at Subject 34. "Unless you're the one in command here." His expression took on a curious cast. "If so, how are you controlling him?" He lifted a hand to his neck as if he expected to feel something on it. "Did you collar him? You haven't done so to me." He scowled. "I'm not certain if I should be happy about that or offended that you see me as unthreatening."

"Uh...." I debated how to explain the situation to the guy.

It was all a little awkward what with him standing there completely nude. As distracting as his markings were, my gaze still wanted to hone in on that no-no part of him that decent folks covered up.

Not that I was a decent folk or anything, which was pretty much why I struggled not to stare.

"So, Ilyan and I are, um...."

What were we, exactly? Nirgal stared at me, waiting for me to continue, his gaze still curious.

"We're together," I finished lamely, unsure what the exact term would be for the Iriduans.

Calling Ilyan my "boyfriend" seemed as inaccurate and weak as calling Subject 34 that. Neither of them were boys, and my feelings towards them far surpassed "friendly."

Nirgal waved an impatient hand. "Of course you're together. You already made it clear he was here on the ship. Are there any other escapees from the facility on this shuttle?"

"I mean, we're *together*, Nirgal." I tried a meaningful look, but he still appeared clueless. "You know, to-*geth*-er!"

"Are you suggesting that you're his *queen*?" Nirgal asked after a long, silent moment passed where I watched his confused expression shift to one of comprehension, then complete disbelief. His tone confirmed that he highly doubted my words.

"That's the word." I pointed at him. "That right there. Pretty sure that's what I am to him."

"That's not possible!" Nirgal shook his head, bracing one palm on the healing tank as if he needed the support to keep from collapsing. "He was cured! Besides, he didn't imprint on *you!*"

I shrugged my shoulders, casting a glance over one of them to meet Subject 34's impassive gaze. His lips tilted in a slight smile as we both turned back to watch Nirgal struggle with what I'd told him. "He says that he wants me as his mate, and I've accepted his offer."

Oh, how I had accepted! I really regretted how things had ended, and I figured I'd need to make it up to him soon. Especially now that Nirgal was up and around. I needed Ilyan firmly on my side in case Nirgal tried anything funny. The fact that I also *wanted* to make it up to him was a given.

"You know, you said Subject 34 was cured too, Nirgie." I grinned as he glared at me. Then I lifted my hand behind me to rub 34's chitin covered chest. "Funny how that doesn't seem to matter sometimes."

I regarded Nirgal's face thoughtfully, keeping my attention above his neck with a struggle. "Ilyan said that you had been given the 'cure' too."

Nirgal's lips, which were rather nice and shapely, pulled back in a scowl. "They wanted to fracture *me*! After all I've done for the empire! They used a *bioweapon* to force me to imprint. A weapon I wasn't even aware we possessed!" He shook his head, his cold eyes narrowing in anger, though at least I could tell it wasn't directed at me.

"So...." I watched him carefully, paying close attention to his eyes. They still looked very Nirgal-like, which meant they were already cold as hell. "Did they... uh... succeed in fracturing you?"

Nirgal huffed as if offended. Then he waved away my question with one imperious hand. "Obviously not. I feel fine."

My eyes were crossing in my fight to keep them fixed on his face. "Um, Nirgie, you think you could put on some clothes?"

He drew in a startled breath, then covered his groin with both hands, glaring icicles at me.

Fighting a smile, I scanned the cabin, spotting the seam of a cabinet door in the wall. I didn't even have to move to stretch my hand to tap it on the square by the edge of the seam.

It popped open, revealing a stack of folded fabric.

"Yay! Jumpsuits." I finally unleashed my grin, tugging one of the folded suits out of the supply cabinet to toss it to Nirgal.

He caught it with one hand, turning his back on me. "You needn't sound so thrilled that I will be covered, human," he muttered. "I wouldn't force my attentions on you."

I eyed his iridescent wings, still slightly shriveled but looking much better than they had when we'd rescued him. Below them were the odd appendages that coiled at the base of his spine, black stripes encircling the iridescent orange chitinous segments.

I'd felt Ilyan's appendages on me in a very intimate way, and just the memory of that made me blush and hastily lift my eyes before even admiring his naked backside.

"Yeah, yeah," I said, pretending nonchalance as I noted that the stripes on the front of him continued on the back. "I'm an inferior human. I get it. No need to reiterate it."

He stepped into the jumpsuit, then pulled it up his legs with jerky motions. "If the sight of my body bothers you so much, you could always turn around and look away," he growled as he pulled the jumpsuit onto each arm. "There's no need to stare at the freak."

I blinked in surprise at his words as I watched his wings twitch and bend in a surprisingly flexible way until they poked through the holes in the back of his jumpsuit. They slid out of it as he fitted it onto his shoulders.

"What do you mean, *freak?*" Again, I felt sympathy for him that I wondered if I should feel.

His tone had been bitter when he'd called himself that, so clearly it bothered him. I just didn't know exactly what *it* was that bothered him. He looked fine to me.

Very fine. He had the eerie, almost too handsome chiseled jaw and high cheekbones of his species, with very kissable looking lips and eyes a shade of blue that looked inhumanly striking. His nose had been broken during his ordeal and it seemed that the healing tank hadn't bothered to set it straight for some reason, but that slight crookedness gave his face character.

He turned sharply as he closed the seam on the front of his jumpsuit, a scowl on his face. "You're not blind, human. My markings are obvious to anyone with sight."

"The tiger stripes? You... does that make you a... um, *different* from other Iriduans?"

He crossed his arms over his lean chest, lifting his chin so he looked down his crooked nose at me, though he was already tall enough to look down upon me, so he didn't really need to take that extra step.

These Iriduans, I swear! They must breed for arrogance and smug superiority. This was precisely why Nirgal brought out the worst in me, I think. I wanted to knock him down a few pegs. Or maybe flat on his back.

And then crawl on top of him and…. Well, that part wasn't important. I pushed the thought away, seeing as Nirgal did not appear to have any attachment to me whatsoever. I had no idea why Ilyan seemed so certain Nirgal would want to remain with us.

"*Tiger* stripes?" His lips came together in a tight line, his sun-kissed brows tugging together until the flesh between them was so creased they practically met in the center. "I think that might be even more insulting than the usual comments leveled at me."

I held up both hands. "I'm sorry, Nirgal. I wasn't trying to be offensive. I'm just really confused. I think your stripes are beautiful."

He blinked, his brows lifting and the lines between them smoothing out on their own. "You think... you really think so?" His jaw gaped as if I'd said something shocking.

I nodded, oddly charmed by the uncertainty in his question. It appeared that I'd found an insecurity of his, and for once, I didn't have the desire to mock him or tease him about it.

"I do. Your stripes are very striking against your orange skin. Besides, a tiger is a gorgeous and powerful predator on Earth. One of the most beautiful creatures in the entire world, in my opinion. You could do a lot worse than be reminiscent of one."

"*Nirgal*, a predator?" Subject 34 said, startling me with the reminder that he stood right behind me, stoically watching everything. He made a chittering sound of amusement that Nirgal pointedly ignored.

I hid my grin, concerned that it might undermine my compliment. I wasn't amused at Nirgal's markings, but at Subject 34's sudden comment and his version of laughter. He was so reserved usually that those little comments and hints of his personality were all the more welcome and enjoyable to hear.

Nirgal regarded me for a long moment, his brows lowering back into their normal dour position. "A tiger, hm?" He lifted a hand to stroke his chin thoughtfully. "I'm not familiar with 'Earth' animals. I shall have to seek an image of this creature."

"Do your people not normally have body markings?" I asked, unable to contain my curiosity even though I feared it might give offense.

Hey, he'd asked me all kinds of personal questions while I'd been a captive. I figured it was my turn to ask a few of my own.

He frowned, those mobile brows pulling together again. I really, *really* wanted to smooth them out. Then maybe kiss away that frown.

"I did not shed my juvenile markings during Meta. The fact that they reformed with my body while I was in my cocoon implied that I still clung to the memory of the creche. To retain these marks is considered a mental weakness. An inability to adapt to change."

He gestured to his face. "I could have had them removed, but my file—like my body—was already marked with my failure, so there wasn't much point, even if I wanted to hide them." He straightened his back, his wings splaying out, though they couldn't spread far behind him. "But I choose to wear them openly, because I am no juvenile, nor do I care to return to the creche. I always found them beautiful in my reflection in the pond, so I carried them into my adulthood."

His wings folded tight to his back, his eyes no longer looking as cold as they studied me. "I still find them beautiful, and I'm not ashamed of them, but no one else has ever said they agree with me on that before."

"Maybe you've just been hanging out with the wrong people, Nirgie." I grinned as he scowled at the nickname.

Then his expression shifted to one of reluctant amusement. His smile transformed his severe features, making him breathtaking, even with the damage still evident on his body.

"You are a very frustrating female," he said in a tone that almost sounded admiring, even as his smile widened. "You drive me insane sometimes." He slowly shook his head, his smile fading as his gaze shifted to Subject 34 then quickly returned to me, his stance stiffening as if he was wary. "I know you're doing it on purpose. At first, I just assumed you were angry at me—in retrospect, rightly so—but now, I'm not so sure."

It was my turn to cross my arms as I regarded him. "At least you can now acknowledge that what you did to me was wrong."

He nodded immediately, surprising me with his quick capitulation. "I learned the hard way how terrible our actions—my actions—were. I am sorry, hu—Rhonda." He sighed heavily, his shoulders sagging as his wings flickered behind him, still wrinkled and shriveled. "I wanted to believe that our cause was important enough to justify any measures we took. My people are in trouble. Besieged on all sides by those who would see us eradicated from the galaxy altogether. Other species have grown envious of our power and influence," he lowered his head, his gaze falling from mine, "and my empire has grown bloated and rotten from within, too hungry for that power and influence to care what it costs."

I glanced over my shoulder at 34, who stood as calmly as ever, still as stone. The perfect predator, capable of hunting down prey, or patiently lying in wait to ambush it. When I turned my head back to Nirgal, his blue eyes had fixed on me again, no longer glittering with a remote chill that I began to suspect was defensiveness.

"What exactly was the purpose of your experiments?" I could tell that 34 had been made to be the perfect killer, but there was only one of him. Surely, he couldn't take on an army of enemy troops.

Although, I might be underestimating him.

Nirgal sighed, then shrugged his shoulders. "I suppose it doesn't matter now how much you know about my work." He nodded his chin at Subject 34. "He is capable of naturally creating the very type of bioweapon that was used to forcibly imprint me or any other male Iriduan, in addition to any other substance we could possibly require. Ilyan originally created him to mimic Menops queens to infiltrate their colonies and assassinate them, rendering their troops useless. However, our leadership realized that he could also mimic the odor print of a female Iriduan. My initial intention was to use that ability to aid those males who were suffering deprivation."

He shrugged. "It wasn't long before that intention expanded to include creating a weapon to gain control over rebel groups that have been tearing our empire apart from within. And of course, there's no question he would be price-less on a battlefield, given his significant skills beyond his chemical compound creation."

"So you intended to use the same—or a similar—bioweapon on other Iriduans that Tilhur ended up using on you?"

Nirgal clenched his fists, his scowl returning to harden his gaze. "The bioweapon they used on me wasn't from Subject 34, which means they already had access to it, likely even before his iteration. I was never informed of this, and I suspect it was because they had other uses in mind for Subject 34 all along. I was merely an ignorant tool for them."

"Is that why you tried to betray them?"

Nirgal stared down at the healing tank instead of meeting my eyes. "I *betrayed* them because I listened to you. You made me think about the ethical questions I'd never dared to ask before. We are not... *trained* that way—to consider ethics when planning or carrying out our experiments. The pursuit of scientific advancement is paramount for the Iriduans. Nothing must stand in the way of that goal. Our rivals, like the Lusians, do not bother with ethics, which is why they've become the most advanced species in the galaxy. Our ancestors also didn't concern themselves with ethical restraints, and they achieved wonders in ancient times that even the Lusians have not managed to this day. We can't possibly compete unless we follow their example."

"You say that, but you still listened to me." I felt flattered that I'd managed to break through to Nirgal. No, it was more than flattered that I was feeling towards him.

It was pointless to keep denying it.

This time, when he met my eyes, his didn't look at all cold. "You make me feel... strange, Rhonda. I'm still not sure I like how I feel when I'm around you. My stomach knots and my skin gets too warm when I think of you." His eyes widened in alarm as he looked downwards, his wings flaring as far as they could behind him.

My own gaze followed his and I caught sight of the bulge in his jumpsuit just before he covered it with both hands.

"I am cured," he whispered, the light bouncing off his head as he shook it. The look in his eyes when he met mine was panicked. "Why do I still feel this way about you?"

TWENTY-EIGHT

"She gets under your skin, doesn't she, old friend?" a voice said from behind us. "Burrows into your brain until there's no hope of getting the thought of her out of it."

I spun around, bumping into Subject 34 as he stepped out into the corridor, revealing Ilyan standing behind us. The green male leaned against the corridor wall, regarding me with a slight smile. That smirk didn't reach his intense eyes, the pupils slightly dilated.

Nirgal gasped, then stepped closer to me so he could look out into the corridor. I inhaled his scent, picking up something delicious and male beneath the antiseptic that coated his skin.

"Ilyan?" Nirgal's tone suggested he wasn't entirely sure who would respond.

I could totally understand his hesitation.

Ilyan nodded slightly, his gaze meeting Nirgal's. "Accept that she's our queen now, my friend." Ilyan's smirk widened. "There's no escaping it. I tried to hide from the way she makes me feel, but she dragged me out into the light, refusing to let my fracture remain in control."

"That is probably for the best," Nirgal said warily, his gaze searching as he studied Ilyan. "He has not served you well since your sundering."

Ilyan shrugged one shoulder as he straightened from the wall. "And what excuse do you have, Nirgal? After all, you destroyed your own life by turning against the empire, even without the presence of a fracture. When I discovered you'd tried to betray your mission at her urging," he grinned at Nirgal, "I realized that she'd already gotten to you too. Nothing else could possibly convince *you* to alter your plans."

Nirgal stiffened, standing so close to me that I felt his body heat radiating off him. If I leaned just slightly backwards, I'd bump into him.

"I don't understand." His voice sounded tight, and just as stiff as his body behind me. "I didn't imprint on her. I was careful not to risk exposure."

Ilyan shrugged again. "And yet your body responds to her now that you're cured. Perhaps if you'd imprinted on another female and weren't cured, you would have been able to get her out of your system." He chuckled as his gaze shifted to meet mine. "Although I doubt it, even then. She's special." The caressing way he said those words made my body flush with heat and my heart thunder in my chest.

Every woman wants to hear she's special to the man she loves. I'd just never thought there would be three of them at the same time. It was a bit overwhelming, to be honest. The fantasy of a reverse harem seemed to go a lot smoother in my head than it was going in reality.

Nirgal still seemed hesitant, despite his body's response to me. Ilyan still seemed offended, even though he was clearly in seduction mode. Only Subject 34 was unfazed by any of this. I already knew that little fazed him—unless it posed a threat to me.

"You do realize that your fracture still poses a danger to us all," Nirgal said to Ilyan.

I jumped a little in surprise when his hands came to rest on my shoulders. It seemed almost natural to sway backwards to lean into his body. Although a part of me still felt strange about the whole "three lovers" thing, I enjoyed the feeling of his warmth against my back and shivered in pleasure as his hands slid down my arms, then slipped to my waist. He might be distracted by his concern over Evil Ilyan making a reappearance, but that didn't soften the hard ridge at his groin that pressed into my lower back as he pulled me closer against him.

To say this entire situation left me conflicted would be an understatement.

My feelings for Subject 34 were visceral—primal in a way I've never felt before. It was like terror turned to fascination the moment Subject 34 first captured me, and that grew into something deeper in that lizard part of my brain that didn't recognize the civilized concept of love. Instead of such a meek and mild idea, I felt something deeper—a need in my bones to be with Subject 34.

My feelings for Ilyan had grown during our shared captivity, where he'd become an odd sort of confidante, both of us communicating only through gestures. His presence and attention had kept me sane, and my gratitude for both had blossomed into something stronger, until I realized that someone I'd never even spoken to meant more to me than Michael ever had.

Nirgal was a different story altogether from the other two. I'd hated him at first, with good reason. I'd also feared him, with good reason. Yet even in the beginning—even when he'd had me strapped down on a table for his experiments—I'd felt a bizarre and unwarranted attraction to him. My defensive response had been to needle him in the hopes of pushing him to pass some point of no return in his treatment of me where I would no longer feel anything but hatred for him. Yet no matter what I'd said to him, he'd never gone too far for me to forgive him. Instead of ending up hating him, I'd been left feeling panic at the thought of losing him.

Could this unfamiliar relationship really work for the four of us?

I didn't realize I'd asked that aloud until Ilyan and Nirgal fell silent. I'd been so deep in my thoughts that I'd missed what they said to each other. No doubt Ilyan was reassuring Nirgal that Evil Ilyan wouldn't kill us all in our sleep. I was mostly confident he was right by this point, though Ilyan's fracture was a wild card. Fortunately, my green guy appeared to have control over it.

Nirgal's arms encircled my waist, embracing me from behind. "You aren't the only one who finds this unfamiliar." His voice sounded strained, and I guessed that part of the reason for that was what pressed into my lower back. "Neither Ilyan nor I were trained to be mated. We are scientists, not lovers."

"Most people don't have to be trained to be in love," I said with a weak chuckle, lifting my hands to run my palms over Nirgal's forearms.

The fabric of his jumpsuit was loose on him, his wrists narrower than I remembered from when I first met him. Like Ilyan, he'd been deprived of proper nutrition during his captivity.

"Trained males know how to please their queens." Ilyan's bottle green gaze rarely softened, even when he studied me like he was now, but his expression was stark with a desire I didn't waste any more time denying.

I couldn't wholly understand what miracle had taken place to bind not one, but three, alien males to me, but I also couldn't complain. Well, I certainly *wouldn't* complain!

"I'm already pleased with all three of you." I stroked my fingers over one of Nirgal's long, lean hands, enjoying the smooth feel of his skin beneath them. "I want this to work. It's just not what I'm accustomed to."

Nirgal's embrace tightened at my caressing touch, grinding his erection into my lower back and the top of my ass. He groaned softly, the hand I wasn't touching sliding down my waist to grip my hip.

Ilyan eyed Nirgal's hands on me, his lips tightening as his eyes narrowed.

"I'm worried," I licked my lips nervously at Ilyan's expression, "that one of you might become jealous."

"At least two of us," Nirgal growled and a glance up at his face showed that he regarded Ilyan like a snake facing down a mongoose.

Subject 34 shifted his curious gaze from Ilyan to Nirgal and back, crossing his upper arms over his chest and his lower arms over his stomach plates as he regarded the scene. He seemed relaxed, so I doubted there would be any physical violence anytime soon, but the tension was definitely growing, and the very thing that had worried me the most about this unconventional—for me—relationship appeared to be happening.

"I thought your people normally mated this way," I said uncertainly, attempting to step forward to put a little distance between me and Nirgal because Ilyan's expression grew more forbidding.

What would I do if they couldn't reconcile their antagonism over this arrangement? Would I have to choose one of them over the other? I couldn't even imagine making that choice at this point. I already loved them both.

The big L-word when applied to them shook me to the core, even acknowledging it in my head rather than aloud. I didn't have time to process my own admission because Nirgal wasn't keen on releasing me, even to put a slight gap between us, and Ilyan looked like he was about to turn the show over to the more dangerous side of himself.

"Hello?" I waved my hands in front of Ilyan's face as a muscle ticked in his jaw. "You said yourself that your people mated this way, Ilyan. So what's with the angry expression now?"

"Nirgal and I have been rivals since we left our cocoons," Ilyan finally said after a long, silent glare at Nirgal. "I had not intended to share a queen with him." He shrugged one lean shoulder. "Of course, I had not intended to *have* a queen either." His gaze shifted to Nirgal's arms possessively wrapped around my waist again. "I didn't anticipate how much I would dislike seeing him touching what belongs to me."

Okay, I was going to let that slide, because I felt like they all belonged to me in return so I could sort of understand where the sentiment came from, even if the phrasing of it raised some red flags. Ilyan was technically one big red flag anyway.

Come to think of it, so were Nirgal and Subject 34. They were each a field-sized, bright crimson flag snapping openly in the breeze. I shouldn't be under any illusions that my life juggling the three of them would ever be peaceful.

"You have some nerve, Ilyan!" Nirgal growled. "Don't act like you have never taken something that belonged to me before. You *stole* the original athraxius project from me."

Nirgal shifted his body so he moved me further into the med bay, while nudging his own way out of it. I realized he was placing himself between me and Ilyan.

"You think I don't know that you tricked me so you could get close to the Knowledge Director to ingratiate yourself so you would be selected over me?" Nirgal said in an angry tone.

"I labored for years as a mere *assistant* researcher after you betrayed our friendship!"

Ilyan's gaze had hardened, and I would bet Nirgal's eyes looked like icebergs at this point as they glared at each other. Ilyan glanced at Subject 34, then returned his glare to Nirgal. "It seems you made up for lost time, didn't you? You promised me you would help me to avoid deprivation, and instead kept me out of cryo until I suffered so much that I fractured, just so you could use my knowledge for your own success."

I held up both hands hoping to silence them as Nirgal shifted me further behind him, his arms now leaving my waist as he faced off Ilyan.

"Hold up, both of you!"

A pair of cold blue eyes and another of hard green eyes fell upon me, and I sighed in dismay at the tension and angry scowls on both their faces. "Clearly your antagonism towards each other isn't about me."

I actually felt relieved about that. If we could clear up their issues with each other, we might manage to have a harmonious relationship.

"Of course it's about you," Nirgal said in his irritating condescending tone.

I missed his tablet, because if he held it right now, I would snatch it out of his hands and smack him upside the head with it.

"34 not like either of you. Would kill both. Ronda say no." My monster mate shrugged his shoulders as if this was all no big deal. "34 put up with you. Both put up with each other."

I shoved past Nirgal to make my way to 34's side and wrapped my arm around his waist. His lower arm fell over my shoulder, holding me close against him.

I regarded both males, who stared at me and 34 with equal scowls. "Listen, I already have my doubts about all of this. I'm sure I've made that clear." I met Nirgal's eyes, then Ilyan's. "But I love you both as much as I love 34. I want to make this work, but we can't do that if the two of you are always at each other's throats."

I gestured to each of them. "Obviously, you were friends once. You have some bad history. I get it." Then I waved towards the cockpit. "But we're all in a pretty big mess right now, and we need to be a cohesive team to get through it and find a safe place to rest, so I'd say let's put the past behind us."

I fluttered my lashes at Nirgal, who didn't look like he was softening to my argument. "After all, Nirgal, I'm forgiving you for what you've done to me. I think you need to forgive Ilyan."

I then turned my gaze on Ilyan. "You've also done some pretty unforgivable things, Ilyan, but I won't hold that against you, because I love you. I love Nirgal too, so I think it's time you forgive him. If you won't do it for his sake, do it for mine."

Ilyan was the first to relax, his shoulders rounding as he leaned against the corridor wall again, barely shooting a glance at Nirgal before returning his gaze to my face. "Rhonda, we still haven't discussed what happened between us."

"*What* happened between you?" Nirgal demanded, and I could hear the tinge of jealousy in his tone as he stiffened even further, his fists clenching at his sides.

I sighed and rubbed my forehead where a headache had begun to throb. I slipped my other hand into Subject 34's upper hand. "These two wear me out, honey. You want to return to my cabin?"

"34 feed Rhonda?" he asked hopefully.

I chuckled and nodded my head, feeling my core tighten in anticipation. "Definitely."

Ilyan and Nirgal both protested as I walked away arm-in-arm with Subject 34. I waved a hand over my head.

"You two discuss your problems and get your shit together,

and then we'll talk about the future." I paused, 34 immediately stopping beside me so he didn't drag me down the corridor. I turned halfway around to look at them both, then pointed at Ilyan. "If you bring out Evil Ilyan to harm Nirgal, I will never forgive either of you. Are we clear?"

Ilyan huffed in outrage. "*Evil* Ilyan? By the Spinner, is that what he calls himself? How uninspired."

"I suspect that's what our queen calls him," Nirgal said in a dry tone. "Expect many nicknames from now on. Most of them will be insulting, if she holds true to form."

I smiled sweetly at them, then blew them a kiss. "See you two later. Love you."

For once, both their hard gazes softened at those words.

TWENTY-NINE

Despite a very pleasurable meal, I couldn't relax as I normally would. I spent the whole time worrying about how Ilyan and Nirgal were getting along without a mediator to keep them from killing each other.

Or keep Evil Ilyan from killing Nirgal, more likely.

This concern left me too distracted to make the most of my intimacy with Subject 34, but to my great relief, he didn't comment on it. Nor did he make me feel guilty for not giving him my full focus. Subject 34 was my rock when my worry over the other two threatened to sweep me away and possibly drown me.

It was ironic that the most dangerous of my new "mates"—I guess I'd call them, since "boyfriends" wasn't working for me— was also the most stable and calm of the three.

I'd dropped the L-word now, so my own feelings about them were out there for them to see. I had to trust that they really did feel the way they appeared to feel because if this all a game for them, then they would know they'd managed to hurt me.

Fortunately, I didn't think they were playing around when it came to their feelings for me. I also felt the connection when I was near them. The chemistry sparking between us nearly set me on fire and certainly made me hot. Plus, Nirgal seemed as baffled and disconcerted by his body's reaction to me as I had been when I'd realized I had an attraction to him. I doubted he was that good of an actor. If I'd learned anything during my recent experiences, it was how to read body language. The bodies of both Iriduans said they desired me as much as I desired them.

To go from a discarded ex-wife to a "queen" of three alien males, all of whom were incredibly sexy in their own way, took some mental adjustments. Perhaps it was for the best that they didn't give me much time to dwell on my own circumstances.

After Subject 34 and I made the most of my cramped cabin, I was unable to rest, despite being satiated and post-orgasm. I needed to check on the other two. Besides, we still had to come up with a plan. By now, I'd decided we should check out the CivilRim world Ilyan had mentioned, but I wanted Nirgal's input.

I would always want the input of my mates before making decisions that would affect all of us. I found being solely responsible for their health, happiness, and welfare disconcerting. At the same time, I probably cared more about them than anyone else in the galaxy, so perhaps there wasn't anyone better suited to the task.

We found Nirgal and Ilyan sitting at the sole table in the shuttle's cramped version of a cafeteria. The tiny closet of a breakroom at my old retail store was bigger than this sorry excuse for a dining chamber. I sighed in relief to see that they both looked alive and unharmed, but then my stomach dipped to see them still glaring at each other. Muscles ticked in both their jaws as they stared each other down.

At least the food wrappers in front of both of them were empty. They must have been ravenous to eat together when the antagonism clearly remained.

"You two still haven't worked out your issues?" I asked as they broke their staring match to look at me standing in the doorway with Subject 34 at my back.

"It's not that simple." Ilyan crumpled up a wrapper in one fist, leaning on his forearm as he glanced at Nirgal again, before returning his gaze to me.

"It's very simple," Nirgal snapped, his long fingers moving to snatch up one of his wrappers to fold it neatly into a small, compact square even as his gaze remained on me. "You are my future, and Ilyan has a bad habit of stealing my future from me."

His blue eyes never looked so warm when they'd fallen on me as they did now. My heart lifted at his words, but I also sighed in exasperation at them.

"I said I love you *both*," I reiterated as I walked to the table.

I paused in front of it, standing between the two seated males. Lifting both hands at the same time, I caressed their faces, stroking my fingers down their high cheekbones to trace their phenomenal jawlines.

"No one is stealing me from anyone." I met Nirgal's eyes, then turned to look at Ilyan. "Is that clear?"

Ilyan smirked, shooting a glance at Nirgal. "She already sounds like a queen speaking to her harem."

I felt the blush burn my cheeks even as Nirgal's stiff shoulders relaxed and a slight smile quirked his lips. "I suppose she does. I haven't had any contact with females in this capacity, so I'm not sure what to expect."

He captured my wrist when I made to lower my hand, tugging me closer to his side of the table, his blue gaze intent on me.

"No poaching," Ilyan growled, capturing my other wrist to pull me away from Nirgal.

Subject 34 chitter-growled angrily as he stepped closer to us, and my two evil space fairies released me.

I sat down at the table between them, propping my elbows on the top and steepling my fingers. "Okay, I think we need to have a discussion about a lot of things, since it's clear the two of you have been wasting your time glaring at each other."

I turned to Nirgal and took his hand, tracing my finger over the black stripe that wrapped around his wrist. "Nirgal, Ilyan came with us to save you. Clearly, he still cares about you."

"He probably intended to kill me," Nirgal said with a narrow-eyed glare at Ilyan.

"Probably," Ilyan replied with a superior tone that made me roll my eyes.

"Would you two just put your dicks away for a minute and let me talk!"

They stared at me with wide eyes, their jaws gaping with twin expressions of shock. Then Nirgal glanced down at his lap, his free hand lowering as if to check that his jumpsuit was sealed at his groin.

I couldn't help it. I burst into laughter. They watched me with incomprehension, shooting glances at Subject 34 as if he could explain what was going on with me.

I finally got control of my laughter, though a few giggles continued to escape. Honestly, I was a little bit on the edge of hysteria at this point as I realized the stress I'd face trying to reconcile these two. They were both stubborn, arrogant, and adamantly convinced that they were in the right.

"I wasn't speaking literally." I grinned at Nirgal, releasing his hand to stroke his thigh. "The two of you are so busy competing with each other that you won't listen to me when I say you don't have to compete! If you truly want me as your 'queen'," that was still such a strange term for me, "then you already have me. You don't have to measure yourself against each other to win me over."

I lowered my other hand to Ilyan's knee, giving it a reassuring squeeze before stroking my palm higher on his leg. He responded by shifting closer to me, his eyelids falling to half-mast as a pleased smile touched his lips.

"Please stop fighting with each other." I shared my glance between them. "We all have to let go of the past—and believe me when I say I have a lot of my own baggage to dump out the airlock!"

I turned my full gaze on Ilyan. "Like the baggage that had me ruining the moment after we made love for the first time. I was afraid of what you were going to say to me because I've been hurt by cruel remarks in the past."

Ilyan had the grace to look guilty as he lifted a hand to stroke my hair away from my face. "You have to know I didn't mean what I said." His eyes darkened as his pupils dilated. "You are the first and only woman I've ever mated with, and the experience was far from disappointing."

"I wouldn't know what that's like," Nirgal said stiffly, clearly feeling left out, even though my hand still caressed his thigh.

I melted at Ilyan's words, and his confirmation that he hadn't been with any woman before me. Granted, there had been the woman he'd imprinted on, and that was a story I'd still love to hear, even if I might feel a bit jealous. But in the end, I was the one he bonded to even after he was cured. I was the one he shared his first experience with.

Even as I felt like a pool of mush, Ilyan's gaze hardened as he shot an irritated glare at Nirgal. "You weren't exactly in any condition to mate your queen at the time so stop buzzing like a juvenile's wings. The sound of your complaining is annoying."

"I can't recall why I ever befriended you in the first place, Ilyan Tironus!" Nirgal's tension resonated in the leg muscle beneath my palm. "Your creche might be noble, but *you* are an off-breed."

Ilyan smirked. "Your petty insults don't please our queen, Nirgal of commoner creche Mashda. Maybe someday you will learn to read her—hopefully not after you make her despise you as much as I do."

"Stop. It!" I slapped both my palms on the tabletop, shooting an infuriated glare at them. "Seriously! What do I have to do to make the two of you get along so we can pick a fucking planet to settle on before we run out of food and Subject 34 decides to eat you both?"

My beloved monster punctuated my point by extending his upper arms and spreading his pincers wide. "34 feeling hungry," he said in his deep, growling voice.

Inwardly, I smiled, but I kept my expression deadly serious as I waved a hand towards him. "These little rations you two are eating won't be enough for 34. We need to find a place with a reliable and plentiful source of food." I regarded them both in turn, softening when I saw the hurt beneath their stubbornly stiff expressions. "Can we just *try* to put our pasts aside and focus on the future?"

They both nodded in unison, the movement just as stiff and reluctant as their tight expressions. They continued to glare at each other as Nirgal crossed his arms over his chest and Ilyan leaned insouciantly back in his seat.

I sighed, rubbing the throbbing muscle at my temple. "So where to, boys?"

They shifted their gazes to me, their eyes softening from the stone-cold stares they'd given each other.

"You want our input?" Nirgal sounded surprised that I would ask for it.

"Of course," I returned my hand to his thigh. "I want us all to agree on our next course of action, because it will affect us all."

His hand rested on mine over his leg as if he wanted to make certain that, this time, I kept it there. "Ilyan mentioned the suggestions he made." An expression crossed his face that told me he was fighting back an insult towards my green guy.

I knew where some of his antagonism came from. I could recognize that it was defensive. Nirgal's guilt at letting Ilyan get into his current condition of being fractured made him push the other male away with insults and anger at past wrongs he believed Ilyan had committed against him. My evil space tiger fairy didn't like acknowledging his own guilt and asking for forgiveness, even as it ate him up inside.

I knew he would come around eventually, and it had taken a while for me to convince him to listen to me before, but when he finally did accept his guilt and seek to make amends, he went all in, regardless of the consequences. He was worth redeeming.

"There is another option Ilyan failed to suggest that would be safer than a primitive world, or the CivilRim."

Ilyan looked startled at this, then his green eyes narrowed on Nirgal. "You had better not say what I think you're about to say."

Nirgal's jaw ticked even as he returned his gaze to Ilyan. "The empire will know we survived. They will have footage of our escape. There is only one option that offers the best chance of evading their hunters." He gestured to Subject 34. "We must disappear the same way the first athraxius experiment disappeared."

"That first experiment believes I am dead!" Ilyan pointed his finger at his temple like it was a gun. "I'd rather not risk the chance that he discovers otherwise." He lifted his chin as his hand lowered back to the table for his fingers to drum on the top of it. "Besides, what you're suggesting means treason."

Nirgal ran a hand over his bald head, his palm rasping over the stubble that had already begun to shadow his scalp. "We're well beyond worrying about that label, Ilyan. If the empire finds us, we'll be lucky to be immediately executed. A likelier fate would be years in an oubliette before we're granted the mercy of death."

Ilyan closed his eyes, leaning back in his chair. "They didn't kill me after my first failure, nor after the actions of my fracture." He bowed his head, his eyes opening to reveal that his pupils were now mere pinpoints as he stared at the table.

"You know that's only because they had a use for you." Nirgal's tone was almost gentle this time.

Where I really saw his sympathy for Ilyan was in his expression, which Ilyan missed because he was staring at his fingers tapping the tabletop, clearly a sign of nervous energy.

"We have no guarantee that the Akrellians won't blow us to space dust if we transmit our location to them."

Ilyan's tone told me he was wavering, even as I stared back and forth between them in confusion. I wanted a full explanation of what we were talking about here, but at the same time, they were finally communicating without open antagonism. I was reluctant to interrupt. I could get answers afterwards, before we made our final decision.

"They might be our enemies, but they aren't fools." Nirgal shot a glance at Subject 34. "They welcomed the first athraxius, no doubt realizing his potential value to their people. I doubt they would destroy another one who reaches out to them for sanctuary."

"That first athraxius is my primary concern," Ilyan insisted, straightening in his chair and leaning forward as he rested his forearms on the table.

Even though I felt a little like they'd forgotten my presence, despite Nirgal still holding his hand over mine on his thigh, I kept my silence, curious about what they were discussing. I still had so much to learn about my new mates that it felt almost overwhelming.

Nirgal rubbed his chin thoughtfully with his free hand. "Perhaps we can request that Thrax is not informed of our existence."

Ilyan huffed in skepticism. "If the Akrellians discover another one like him, they are likely to inform him. Besides, where exactly do you think they'd resettle us?" He gestured again to Subject 34, who suddenly looked extremely interested in the conversation. "They would put us where they put the other athraxius. That likely means we would encounter Thrax —and Claire." He ground out the last name like he could barely stand speaking it.

"Who Thrax?" Subject 34 asked, shifting closer to stand behind Ilyan, looking very intimidating. "One like 34? Want meet. Maybe kill. Prove 34 stronger."

Since Ilyan had already been killed by Subject 34 once, it wasn't surprising he felt intimidated as he leaned his body away from the hulking male behind him.

I had to interject, even though I wasn't entirely certain who these people were, though I could guess at what Claire meant to Ilyan. I shoved away the sting of jealousy, reminding myself that he was mine now. "No killing, 34. Not even another male like yourself!"

Ilyan regarded 34 with narrowed, suspicious eyes before returning his attention to Nirgal and I, his gaze pointedly meeting mine. "Do you see how this option would be a disaster, my queen?"

I did, honestly. I had to admit I was still leaning towards the CivilRim idea as I turned my gaze to Nirgal. I flipped my hand beneath his, so I could lace our fingers together. "Do you really think this would be a wise choice, Nirgie?"

His sigh might have been at my nickname for him, but he didn't pull his hand away, his gaze intent on mine. "The CivilRim is a dangerous place even without imperial hunters and enforcers always grasping for our wings. I don't want to put you in that kind of danger." He shot another glance at Subject 34. "Even my finest creation can't keep you safe every moment of your life, and I can't stand the thought of losing you."

That kind of sentiment went a long way towards convincing me to consider Nirgal's side. If I didn't know better, I'd suspect him of saying it just to manipulate me. After all, Nirgal had spent a lot of time learning my weaknesses along with my entire life story during my time in 34's enclosure. He knew I was a sucker for romance, especially grand romantic declarations.

On the other hand, I believed he meant what he said. His tone was too fervent to be false, and he'd never struck me as particularly skilled at acting.

"What about a primitive world where the imperials won't think to look for us?" I didn't feel a whole lot of hope on this option, since I wasn't exactly a survivalist.

Nirgal captured my other hand, linking his fingers with mine, ignoring Ilyan's growl of annoyance. "The kinds of worlds we could find outside the influence of Syndicate species would be just as dangerous in their own way as the CivilRim. I also wouldn't be able to provide the life my queen deserves in such a primitive place. I fear you would be unhappy there." His wry smile didn't hold much amusement. "There wouldn't be any paints or canvas for you there, Rhonda. No expensive art supplies. No soft mattress or pile of pillows. No comfortable clothing."

Okay, he definitely knew my weaknesses. Given the fact that he'd supplied all those things for me while I was his captive, it wasn't surprising he could guess that I preferred those luxuries I could only get on a civilized world.

I *could* live on a primitive planet, if there was no other option, and I know that if these three were with me, I could find happiness there, despite the dearth of amenities I'd grown up enjoying. Still, Nirgal had some excellent points. A glance at Ilyan showed that he realized it too.

"Maybe the Akrellians will have mercy on us," I said uncertainly, shrugging one shoulder.

"34 want meet Thrax."

Well, the Akrellians already had Subject 34's vote, though I would prefer that they keep our existence a secret from this "Thrax" and "Claire." Especially Claire. I feared that once Ilyan saw her, his cure would revert, and he'd suddenly be madly in love with her or something along those lines. I mean, I didn't really know how it all worked, and from what Nirgal had said, the cure itself was unprecedented and experimental.

What if it failed and he ended up obsessed with another woman, forgetting all about me?

Or worse, what if Thrax killed my Ilyan, because that seemed to be what concerned Ilyan. Obviously, his former test subject didn't hold kind feelings towards him. Though Subject 34 had proven that the right motivation could convince him to forgive his creator. If this Thrax was born from the same genes, maybe he could also be reasoned with to forgive his.

Nirgal's eyes remained on me, ignoring the other two. "This decision rests on you, my queen. I believe we can convince the Akrellians to give us sanctuary if we offer them knowledge in return, but Ilyan's reservations aren't without warrant. It's possible that our pasts will condemn us in their eyes—or the eyes of the other athraxius."

I hated that this ultimately came down to me. Seeking sanctuary with the Akrellians had two votes. The CivilRim one. But I knew that they considered their desires irrelevant. They would go wherever I voted. I could already tell.

Thus, the burden was on me to make the right choice.

THIRTY

I had to make an impossible decision, and I dreaded it for hours before finally coming to a conclusion. After a long time in the cleansing closet—honestly sort of hiding out while I debated—I gathered up my mates in the mess hall again and gave them my vote.

As I suspected, my vote was the only one that mattered. They immediately agreed to my plan, even though I wanted someone to talk me out of it. I knew that regardless of what decision I'd made, there were innumerable dangers and unknowns. I'd tried to consider everyone in this choice.

I really hoped it was the right one!

Ilyan retired to the cockpit to pilot the ship. Subject 34 stayed in the cafeteria, raiding the ration storage cabinet, and Nirgal, who was clearly exhausted and still recovering from his ordeal, retired to the sleeping bay after our family meeting.

The shuttle, while appearing large on the outside, had very cramped quarters, which I supposed was to be expected. In fact, my tiny cabin was the one designated for the captain of the small vessel. Ilyan explained that it was really only intended for short journeys. That was yet another reason we couldn't delay making our decision, though I would have preferred to get a whole lot more information about all our options.

The sleeping bay provided the only other sleeping area in the shuttle, and while the room was much larger than my cabin, that was only because sleep pods packed it full, which weren't much different from the healing tank in their design. There were fifteen of them, though I couldn't even imagine cramming sixteen people on this shuttle.

I found Nirgal inside one of the pods, his face gaunt, his swelling flesh looking much better than it had when he'd first crawled out of the healing tank. I had intended to speak to him privately, but it was obvious he needed his rest, so after checking his vitals, which were displayed on the side of the pod, I turned to leave the bay.

As I reached the door, I heard the pod's lid open. When I spun around to face it, Nirgal was sitting up, leaning his forearm on one edge of the pod opening. His beautiful blue eyes regarded me warily, his expression equally as uncertain.

He still looked tired. I wanted to apologize for waking him and urge him to return to sleep, but instead, I returned to the pod. I stroked my fingers over the top of his head, feeling the stubble of hair that covered it.

"I don't understand why you make me feel this way," Nirgal said, lifting his hand to draw his fingers along my forearm. He captured my hand in his as I trailed my fingers down his face.

His lips felt warm and soft against my skin as he kissed the back of my hand, inhaling deeply as if my scent pleased him.

"You know, Nirgie, I had the same confusion when I realized I was attracted to you." I moved closer to the pod, my belly pressing against the hard metal hull of it as I lifted my free hand to curl around the nape of his neck.

His eyes were solemn as they met mine. "The things I've done to you are unforgivable, Rhonda."

I shrugged one shoulder, a smile tilting my lips. "Yeah, probably. Lucky for you, I'm a very forgiving person."

I bent to press my lips to his, inhaling his scent as hungrily as he'd inhaled mine. He smelled like he was fresh from the cleansing closet, his unique and exotic woodsy odor subtle, though it increased in intensity as my lips caressed his.

Nirgal's kiss was the most hesitant I'd experienced from any of my alien mates, though his hand captured my nape when I made to pull away, uncertain if he was ready for kissing in his current condition.

"I won't be good at this," his breath warmed my tingling lips. "I have no experience with such things and only observations of you and Subject 34 to go on. Watching you kiss is far different from feeling your lips on mine."

The chemistry I felt with Nirgal meant he could clumsily maul me with his mouth, and I'd still feel my core heat with arousal. I grew wet at the thought of teaching him not only how to kiss, but how to make love.

I had never been with a virgin before being abducted. The few men I'd slept with before Michael had all been experienced lovers. They'd had other women they could compare me to, and I'd always felt self-conscious that they would find me wanting in those comparisons. Had those women been more beautiful, better kissers, more skilled with using their mouths in other ways?

Now, I had three mates who were all mine. Not one of them had been with any other woman but me. There was something very appealing and exciting about that thought.

Not to mention reassuring.

Nirgal's lips softened the longer I kissed him, tilting my head to press our lips more fully together. My tongue slipped from between my lips to tease along the seam of his. He made a surprised sound, then his lips parted. His tongue met mine and I drew it between my teeth, sucking it in a way that made him moan.

I couldn't wait to show him how good it would feel to have my mouth on other parts of him. I knew he was well aware of oral sex, since he'd observed me and Subject 34 all this time. I hoped he was anticipating it as much as I was. I did want to take things slow, even though the hunger inside me to climb into the pod and onto his lap was great. He was still recovering, and even if he had been in perfect health, this was all new to him.

Well, he'd *seen* more than enough, but he'd never done anything like this.

My good intentions evaporated as he tugged open the collar of my suit. His kiss grew more demanding as he parted the front of my suit and slipped his warm hands inside to cup my breasts. It was my turn to moan against his mouth as he caressed my naked and sensitive flesh, teasing the stiff beads of my nipples with his fingers.

"I want to touch you everywhere," he said between kisses, his breath rasping against my swollen lips, his voice gravelly with his desire. "I want to make you cry out in pleasure and climax as I lick you."

I never would have expected Nirgal to whisper dirty desires to me, but I wasn't about to complain. His words and the hunger in his voice had me soaked with my excitement, and I knew he'd figure that out soon as his hand slipped down my stomach beneath the fabric of my jumpsuit, further parting the opening as it sought my mound.

"You naughty space fairy," I said with a moan as his fingers stroked over my folds, rubbing my clit with unerring accuracy.

He might be a virgin, but he knew what I liked. He'd had

plenty of opportunity to observe what brought me pleasure. That should weird me out or make this whole relationship awkward, but my life had long ago past the point of strange, rocketed right through bizarre, and was now on the brink of freaky. I was all for jumping into the freak zone!

"Mm, Rhonda," he growled when his fingers slid to my entrance, feeling the wetness of my slick. "You've been driving me crazy since they pulled you out of cryo!"

His thumb continued to rub my sensitive nub as he slipped a long finger inside me. He didn't go nearly deep enough for my satisfaction. I wanted him buried inside me, not just his fingers but that beautiful tiger striped dick he had hidden under his jumpsuit.

His mouth consumed me, his kiss growing less uncertain and more skillful as he gained confidence in my responses. I could still tell he wasn't experienced at it, but I could also tell he was feeling the same sparking chemistry that I did as his lips caressed mine demandingly.

I unhooked the collar of his jumpsuit and pulled it open, then trailed my fingers down his chest, passing them gently over his still healing skin. The fabric of his suit, like mine, parted easily when I drew my hands lower.

He slipped another finger inside me, sliding both of them deeper as his other hand replaced his thumb on my clit.

The size of his shaft surprised me when I circled my hand around it. He was far larger than I'd expected, though even flaccid, his penis had looked sizable. Now I understood why, my fingers not even close to meeting around his girth as he rocked his hips upward into my slow stroke.

He was larger in that area than my other two mates—not that such things mattered to me. Somehow, I hadn't expected Nerdy Nirgal to be the one with the largest dick of the three.

Not only in girth but in length. He would stuff me full, and my inner muscles clenched in anticipation.

"Rhonda," he said, his voice harsh as I teased the sensitive skin of his shaft. His hand caught my wrist, tugging mine away from him.

I pulled away from him in surprise, worry creeping in that I'd pushed too far, touched him too intimately. Then I met his eyes, and they were nearly black with his arousal. He gripped the side of the sleeping pod and vaulted out of it, proving that he was more agile than I'd expected, despite the torture he'd endured.

He had a predatory look in his eyes that caused me to back away, even as my core clenched in anticipation as his feet landed on the metal paneled floor beside the pod. They were bare, the striping that marked his body extending even to the tops of his feet. I didn't have much time to examine them, nor the impressive, bobbing erection at his groin before he caught me around the waist and drew me closer to him, his hold firm so I couldn't escape him.

Now that we were both standing, he was much taller than me, bringing me eye level with the intriguing view of his chest and the stripes that marked it. I lifted a hand to trace one of them, my tongue swiping over my swollen lower lip, already missing his kiss.

"Strip naked for me, human," he growled as he lowered his head to speak in my ear. "Before I do it for you."

I shivered at the promise in his voice as I shrugged the jumpsuit off my shoulders. My hands shook with anticipation and nervousness. There was something about Nirgal that put me on a different kind of edge than my other two mates. With each of them, some dynamic existed between us that made our connection unique. In Nirgal's case, there definitely remained a captive/captor feeling of vulnerability in me when I was around him, even as I eagerly removed my jumpsuit, and he made no move to divest himself of his.

I might have been self-conscious about my body, with all its normal human marks, freckles, moles, stretchmarks, cellulite, and pretty much everything that separated me from the airbrushed models that far too many people believed were really that perfect. The visual evidence of Nirgal's desire for my body chased away any self-doubts. Besides, this male knew very well what I looked like nude. He hadn't always been complimentary about my appearance either, so I was glad I could see what I was doing to him now.

His erection jutted from the opening of his suit, and my mouth watered when I glanced down at it. Either he was reading my mind, or he had his own ideas that ran parallel to mine, because he ordered me in a gruff voice to kneel in front of him.

I knew exactly what he wanted from me, and I wanted it too. After falling to my knees, barely noticing the hardness of the floor, I circled my fingers around his shaft. Even though he'd slipped into a role of commanding me, his body trembled, and I felt it radiate through the hard but silky flesh in my hand. When I licked the precum welling from the tip of his shaft, he moaned, his hands bracing him against the side of the sleeping pod.

Then I closed my lips around the head of it and sucked, drawing more of his length inside my mouth, my tongue trailing along the edge of his cockhead. My jaw stretched wide to accommodate his girth, but I was too excited to care, enjoying the sounds of him gasping and moaning as he clutched the side of the pod.

I took him in my mouth as deep as possible, using my hand to stroke his shaft in unison with my mouth pulling on the sensitive tip and what little more of him I could fit in my hungry mouth.

He tasted savory, his precum closer to a human male's than Subject 34's in flavor and consistency, but that wasn't really what this was about. I wasn't feeding from Nirgal, any more than I would from Ilyan. I wanted to give him pleasure, and based on the sounds he made, I was succeeding.

As I knelt naked on the floor in front of him, my thighs grew even more slippery from the slick that soaked my entrance. I was so aroused that I rubbed my own clit as I sucked on Nirgal, loving the way his hips rocked in tune to the strokes of my mouth on him. The clawed appendages that were normally coiled at the base of his spine extended from the opening in his suit, their tips trailing over my naked shoulders. The segmented lengths moved farther downwards, exploring my body as I pleasured Nirgal with my mouth.

When his hand fisted in my hair as he cried out a guttural command to stop, the claws of his appendages dented the soft flesh of my breasts.

"You do that too well," he said breathlessly, his grip still firm in my hair as I slowly dragged my lips from his length, giving him one last lick on the head of his shaft. "I feel like I'm on the edge of a climax, and I want to be inside you when I come for the first time."

It registered for me that he'd never even had an orgasm before, as crazy as that seemed. It reminded me that my mates weren't human, as if the tiger-striped iridescent orange skin, clawed appendages, and glass-like dragonfly wings weren't enough.

I rose to my feet without needing him to tell me to, and he freed my hair and slid his hands down my body. He caressed my curves as if he couldn't get enough of them, grabbing a good handful of generous flesh on both my buttocks to pull me against him, rubbing my belly against his hard length pinned between us. The clawed appendages snaked over my body, vibrating like crazy, the barbs extending and scraping my soft, naked flesh roughly. Instead of hurting me, the feeling stimulated me, my nipples hardening until they were almost painfully tight.

Nirgal didn't explore my naked body long before he suddenly turned us around so I was leaning against the sleeping pod. I realized very quickly that I would need the support, because he kissed his way down my body, pausing only briefly to suckle each of my aching nipples before trailing his mouth lower. When his lips closed around my clit, my knees grew so weak that I practically laid on the side of the pod to support myself.

Two of his fingers slid inside my slick entrance and he fingered me as his tongue swiped over my throbbing clit, dragging slowly and teasingly at first, then speeding up as my cries and pleas grew more desperate. When I came, I had to clutch his shoulders, my entire body shuddering with the force of my orgasm. He made a satisfied sound as my inner muscles clenched around his fingers, lifting his head from my mound as he licked his lips. His dark, nearly black eyes met mine as he rose to his feet.

I clutched his shoulders as he withdrew his fingers from me to encircle his girth. He positioned it at my entrance, then slowly pushed it in, my inner muscles still squeezing in the last convulsions of my orgasm.

He was so large that at first my body tightened around him, resisting his penetration as I had a sudden moment of panic. All of my mates were larger than anyone I had ever been with before, but Nirgal was the biggest, and I suddenly worried I couldn't handle all of him.

Then I saw the rapturous expression on his face, his eyes so dilated that only a mere sliver of a blue halo remained. The tightness in his jaw, the near grimace on his lips as he tried to hold back his own orgasm, and the tension in his body as he drove himself deeper inside me turned me on so much that I let go of any fear that held him at bay.

Suddenly, he slipped fully inside me, stretching me wide and settling so deep and close to my womb that I could feel the tip of him brushing it almost uncomfortably.

Even in a standing position, he filled me completely when he was buried to the hilt. My eyes rolled back in my head when he began to pump his hips, rapidly picking up the pace as if he'd lost the last of his control.

He pulled me close to his chest, burying his nose in my hair as he thrust into me, driving my legs wider and wider apart as he pushed as deep as he could go without me tensing up and pulling back when he struck a little too deep. The sleeping pod supported me from the back, and he held me close from the front, pinning me to it as he claimed me completely.

It didn't take long for him to come at the rate he was going, and his whole body stiffened as he climaxed. A loud moan left him as his hot seed shot into me, bathing my womb. As he thrust into me a few more times while his shaft throbbed inside me with each spurt, I had a brief moment of panic about pregnancy, then brushed it aside, too wrapped up in the moment to worry.

After all, Nirgal was a scientist. Surely, he would be more cautious if he hadn't made certain he couldn't get me pregnant.

Could an alien even get a human woman pregnant? It didn't seem likely, and I had already decided that they couldn't after Ilyan had spent inside me. Because, again, they're scientists. They wouldn't risk getting a human woman pregnant when she was in her forties and lost in space.

All those kinds of concerns slipped away from me as he

cradled me close, slowly pulling out of me, his seed leaking from me to drip down my thighs.

"One of these days, I'm going to have sex in a bed." I snuggled into Nirgal's chest, smoothing my hands over the bare skin I could touch through the gap in his jumpsuit.

"I imagined what this would be like," he murmured, his breath hot against my scalp. "To be inside you, claiming you as my queen. Sometimes, I would even be envious of Subject 34 when I was supposed to be observing you both from a clinical perspective."

His body tensed against me, and I tried to lift my head, but he clearly wasn't ready to release me, so I relaxed in his embrace again.

"I didn't understand why those thoughts would even occur to me, especially as you made every effort to infuriate me." His tone sounded wry, though I still detected the gruffness of his arousal tinging it. "I know what a 'douche' is now, by the way. I could have gone my whole life without knowing that bit of information. Even a powerful craving for knowledge has its limits."

I grinned against his chest, planting a kiss on the naked striped skin peeking from the gap in his jumpsuit. "Did it work? Did I make you mad enough to break your tablet?"

He chuckled. "I only snapped one, and I had a backup. But it wasn't your insults that caused me to do so."

I lifted my head to meet his eyes. They weren't dilated any longer, but they were still darker than the brilliant and icy blue I'd grown familiar with. Now they were a sparkling sapphire that was stunning against his orange skin tone.

"What made you break your precious tablet?" I grinned again, thinking about how much I'd wanted to snatch it from him, just to see him freak out.

Apparently, he could live without it though, so maybe it

didn't mean all that much to him. Or maybe he'd just abandoned that part of his life completely and no longer needed the object that had leashed him to his former masters.

His slight smile faded, and a dark scowl replaced it, driving his brows together and pulling his lips back. Even as I watched, his beautiful eyes took on an icier blue cast. "I broke it when Tilhur told me they planned to force Subject 34 to kill you and consume you just to see how he would react when the deed was done."

I gasped and pulled away from him, not because I was angry at him, but simply out of horror. "They *what?*"

That had been exactly what Tilhur had intended to do to me when he and his robots had entered the enclosure, so I shouldn't have been surprised by this revelation. It still shook me, reminding me how much I was at their mercy when it was easy to forget that fact now that I felt safe in the arms of my three mates.

Nirgal regarded me with a stark expression, the anger still present in his tight features and the tension in his body. "The suggestion shocked and enraged me, though I should have expected it. Tilhur claimed that I was losing perspective, and he was right. I could no longer ignore the atrocities we'd committed."

His scowl deepened into a frightful expression, his eyes glittering with a coldness I remembered well. "I would not condone another one." His gaze softened as he stroked his fingers over my swollen lips. "Least of all, such an atrocity against you, Rhonda."

"I'm glad you tried to stop them, Nirgal."

His lips twisted bitterly. "Tried. But I failed. Tilhur realized I would betray the empire after his suggestion and had me watched so that they detained me the moment I made a move against our mission." He pushed my hair away from my face with both hands, cradling it as if I were precious to him—far more so than that stupid tablet had been. "I think he made the suggestion because he knew it would force me to act against them."

"I'm sorry you got captured and tortured for my sake." I kissed him softly.

"For *your* sake, I'd endure it all again without hesitation," he whispered against my lips.

THIRTY-ONE

I was still enjoying a post-coital buzz after a trip to the cleansing closet, humming softly to myself as I checked on Subject 34, who rested in my cabin, on the floor beside my bed instead of in it. I'd urged him to get as comfortable as he could, and apparently, he found the floor more comfortable than the admittedly cramped bed.

He'd awakened as soon as I approached the cabin, so he was already alert when I popped my head in, but I waved for him to remain on the floor, not wanting to disturb his rest any further. He expressed a desire to accompany me as I further explored the shuttle, but I asked him to remain to "guard" my cabin. It was the only way to convince him to return to sleep.

Even though my mates seemed to want to please me and cater to me, I felt guilty accepting all their efforts. Especially when I worried that they were depriving themselves of something necessary. Like sleep or food.

I probably shouldn't have made love with Nirgal so soon after he left the healing tank. He had been drained even before

I went into the sleeping bay. He'd also been determined to remain on his feet as long as I stood in it after our time together. By the time I convinced him to get back into the pod and rest up, he sagged with exhaustion.

Now, he was comfortably asleep, getting the rest he needed, and Subject 34 was also getting rest. I was a little tired myself, but I knew I wouldn't be able to sleep. My mind raced with thoughts and concerns over what our future held. I worried about the three alien males I'd come to love and feared what would happen to them if my decision was the wrong one. I also worried that they would wear themselves out trying to please me when all I wanted was for them to be happy in their life with me. I also wanted to please them, and hoped they'd let me. I liked to spoil my man with attention, and even though having three of them was a bit overwhelming, I still possessed the same urge to show them I loved them with my every action and word.

Even after my time with Nirgal, this whole arrangement still felt a little surreal to me. I couldn't believe that I had three sexy males who called me their queen and treated me accordingly. I wondered what Michael would think about that, a smirk tilting my lips at the thought of his shocked expression if he saw the four of us and knew that he couldn't even come close to comparing to any of my new loves.

Let him have his youthful home wrecker. She seemed like a consolation prize in retrospect, because I won the damned romance lottery, and I wouldn't have even bought the ticket if Michael hadn't dumped me for another woman. I couldn't believe I had those purple-eyed weirdos who'd abducted me to thank for me being in the right place at the right time to meet the three loves of my life.

I was happy in my thoughts as I made my way to the cockpit of the shuttle to check on Ilyan, who had a fold-out bunk there. When I entered and the sliding door closed behind me, shutting me into the small space, my greeting died on my lips in confusion as I didn't see him sitting in his chair or on the bunk that was currently tucked away in the wall.

I shrugged my shoulders and turned around to leave, only to yelp in surprise when I saw that he stood right behind me.

He caught me by my arms, his grip hard, and one look at his eyes told me that Evil Ilyan was back as he pushed me further away from the door and into the room.

"Where's Ilyan?" I asked, my voice quivering as a healthy dose of fear shot through my bloodstream.

Evil Ilyan still confused me. I'd gotten so comfortable with my mates that I'd almost forgotten about this one little detail.

"He didn't like the thought of you and Nirgal together," Evil Ilyan said with a mocking smile. "The coward retreated to the back of his mind rather than confront Nirgal and dispatch him the way he should have earlier."

I tried to jerk my arms out of his grasp, but his grip only tightened. "Ah, ah," he said in a menacing tone as I opened my mouth to protest his rough handling, "don't call out for your test subject." He jerked his chin towards the control panel, where a light was flashing. "I'll blow this shuttle to pieces before he can get through that locked door."

My eyes widened in horror as I stared at him, my mouth still gaping open. I hadn't even considered screaming for Subject 34 yet, not willing to admit that I was really in danger with Evil Ilyan. Despite my nickname for him, I had foolishly doubted that he was truly evil.

Until now.

"You would die too," I said in a harsh whisper, too afraid to speak much louder lest he decide I was trying to get Subject 34's attention.

He shrugged one shoulder, his hard gaze still fixed on my

face. "I should never have existed, and wouldn't have if Ilyan had the courage to blow his own brains out. I don't care if I live or die, but when I go, I will take as many of my enemies out with me as possible."

"We're not your enemies!" I lifted a hand to grasp his forearm, wincing as his grip tightened to a bruising degree. "I love Ilyan, and because you are a part of him, I...."

The smirk on his lips made me trail off before acknowledging any feelings for him, because I honestly didn't really know who "he" was. I knew Ilyan from my captivity, and his patience in trying to communicate with me. Sometimes, Evil Ilyan had been there instead, but he'd been far less patient, and far less interested in communicating with me.

He released one of my arms and caught the collar of the clean jumpsuit I'd put on after my trip to the cleansing closet. With a hard jerk, he unhooked it and pulled the top half of my suit open. I gasped as my breasts spilled through the wide gap in the front of the suit.

He crowded me backwards towards the control console, his hands lifting to the shoulders of my suit to yank it off my upper body. Before my shock retreated enough to return my voice to me, his head lowered, and his lips closed around my nipple.

His hands were rough on me as he tugged open the rest of my jumpsuit until it gaped to the juncture of my thighs. His mouth pulled hard on my sensitive nipple, his teeth nipping just enough to make me nervous. One hand cupped and massaged my breast as he tormented my nipple, shooting sparks of pleasure to my core. His other hand continued to drag the ill-fitted jumpsuit off my curvy hips and over my buttocks, leaving all but my legs bare.

"I like the sight of you naked and helpless," he said after releasing my tender nipple. "It was difficult to conceal how much it turned me on when we were in our cages."

He lifted his head, his eyes still hard and glittering like emeralds. "Unlike Ilyan, I won't lose myself to engorgement. I don't *need* you, Ronda." He grinned and even without sharp teeth, his smile looked menacing. "But I *will* have you."

Then his lips crashed down on mine, rough and punishing. His kiss seemed angry, his body tense and aggressive. Yet I still melted beneath the force of it as his hands stroked my naked flesh, running all over my body, while avoiding those places that ached the most for him to touch me.

He chuckled against my lips as my hips bucked when his palm stroked over my belly, his fingers barely teasing over my mound. "Not yet, human. You will wait until I allow you to feel pleasure. Just as I have patiently waited to take you."

I murmured a wordless protest against his lips that he cut off with his tongue delving into my mouth hungrily. I wasn't trying to make him stop. I wanted him to go faster because his roughness excited me. Had I the presence of mind to feel ashamed about how much it did, I probably would have. At the moment, I didn't care. I was in the arms of a madman, and I wanted him to take me, just like he planned to.

My body trembled beneath his touch, both aroused and nervous at his unpredictable nature. He pulled open his own jumpsuit, jerking it off his shoulders with one hand as the other continued to trail over my skin, moving closer and closer to the most sensitive parts of it without actually touching them.

His wings flared behind him after he pulled the jumpsuit off his shoulders and back. He left it hanging off his hips, his two appendages uncoiling from his spine. He then pushed me back until my butt bumped against the cold surface of the console. He continued to crowd me with his tall body until I was leaning on the surface of it.

"Spread your legs," he demanded, his hands moving to my inner thighs, one of them brushing teasingly over my folds.

My knees parted of their own volition, my legs shaking. He grabbed the fabric of the jumpsuit and pulled it off my thighs, over my calves, and then off my body entirely. He tossed it aside and returned his full attention to the juncture of my thighs.

"Spread them further." His tone brooked no argument, his hard gaze fixed on my seam.

My heart thudded in my chest as I braced myself against the console. My skin prickled with goosebumps and my muscles shivered with nerves and arousal. Still, I spread my legs wide, obeying him wordlessly. It wasn't just fear that he would follow through on his threat to all of us that had stolen my voice. I was turned on like crazy.

Right until the moment one of his appendages undulated towards my entrance.

I shied away from it, my knees instinctively trying to close as it stabbed unerringly towards my slick opening, but he caught my thighs, his fingers digging into my flesh as he held them still. He stared down at my slit rather than looking into my eyes, but his expression was intent and unforgiving as stone.

"Ilyan cannot bring himself to hurt you," he said coldly. "But I don't suffer that restriction. I may be a weaker fracture than one born of torment rather than only of deprivation, but I still don't need your approval or agreement for anything I do to you."

"Don't hurt me," I whispered, my throat going dry.

My words caused him to look up, his gaze pinning mine, a chilly grin on his lips. I gasped when his appendage impaled me, the clawed tip slipping inside me.

He pushed it further into me, my inner muscles stretching around the length of it as it began to vibrate. Despite the threat of that sharp point delving deep, the segmented girth of it felt good as it stretched me. He buried it so deep inside me that I felt the point of it poke my womb.

The vibration of it nearly brought me to climax all on its own, but then he used his fingers to rub my clit until I shuddered with a cry of orgasm.

As my inner muscles convulsed around him with my pleasure, the barbs that had laid flat on the last segment of his appendage extended. Without warning, he pulled his appendage free, rapidly dragging their sharp points along all my sensitive inner flesh.

His hand over my mouth muffled my scream as I clawed at his forearm with one hand. Despite the shock and pain, intense pleasure from my orgasm still fired through my brain and nervous system. The combination of sensations left me shaken, unsure whether I enjoyed it or feared it happening again.

My fear was well justified because he impaled my tender entrance with his other appendage, again vibrating as it delved deep, his fingers working over my throbbing clit as it sank inside me to bump my womb.

I tried to brace myself, knowing it would be pointless to protest. He'd already told me as much. Yet I shattered in a second orgasm right after the first, and he used that opportunity to once again scrape his barbs out of me.

My eyes watered with the confusing combination of pain and pleasure as he knelt between my thighs. His hands stroked my inner thighs, his fingers sliding over the throbbing, tender flesh of my seam.

"No other male's seed will be in you when I fill you." He slipped two fingers inside me, rubbing them along my tormented inner passage.

Despite the pain he'd caused me, he still had me moaning and writhing my hips as he fingered me, and when his lips closed around my clit I cried out with pleasure, clutching the edge of the console with both hands in a white-knuckled grip.

He brought me to another orgasm swiftly. My ravaged passage convulsed around his fingers as he thrust them into me.

After the last convulsions ended, he withdrew his fingers and rose to his feet. He freed his erection from his jumpsuit, pulling the fabric down beneath the jutting length of it. My aching inner muscles clenched in anticipation as he looked down at me, stroking one hand over his shaft.

"I intend to use you for my pleasure whenever Ilyan retreats, human. If you don't please him, you'll have no choice but to contend with me instead." He leaned over me, bracing his free hand on the console as he used the other to position the head of his shaft at my entrance. "I know you're thinking Subject 34 or Nirgal can stop me if you run crying to them." He grinned as he rammed his length into me in one hard thrust that stole my breath.

My inner muscles tightened around the invasion as he lowered his body over mine, his mouth moving close to my ear. "I will always find a way to outsmart them so that you end up at my mercy, Rhonda. The only way they can help you is if they kill Ilyan." He pumped his hips, dragging his length out of me, then driving it deep again.

He lifted his head and met my eyes, his own as hard and merciless as ever. "I know you won't allow them to do that, will you? You love him too much." He laughed wickedly as he began to pound into me, his gaze shifting from my face to my bouncing breasts. "You're as *weak* as he is."

Those words were too true for me to deny, not that I felt like I had the voice to do so, my breaths coming in hard gasps as he screwed me mercilessly. I had to remained braced on the console so I couldn't even clutch him to steady myself, my body rocking wildly as his rhythm picked up. His lips captured one aching nipple and the tug of them on it was as hard and punishing as his thrusts.

His two appendages that had ravaged my insides darted to my hips, the clawed tips impaling my flesh to hold my lower body steady as he reached his own climax, burying his length so deep inside me that I felt his seed gush against my womb.

Then he bit my breast as his shaft jerked inside me, his fingers finding my clit to rub it. It took just a few strokes of it for me to come, milking the last bit of his seed from his shaft, my entire body aching from both pain and pleasure in a way I'd never felt before. Even the blood trickling from his claw tips still embedded in my soft flesh didn't detract from the intensity of my climax and how much it shook me to the core.

I was most shaken by the fact that I'd liked what he did to me.

Evil Ilyan withdrew from my aching passage and tucked his shaft back inside his jumpsuit without a word, nor even a glance at my face. A satisfied smirk tilted his lips as some of his seed leaked from my swollen slit.

Then he pulled his jumpsuit back over his wings and onto his shoulders, turning his back to me to return to the blinking light on the console. As his fingers moved over the panel, he finally glanced in my direction, his eyes gleaming as a mocking grin showed his teeth.

"This is a simple notification light, not a self-destruct warning." He chuckled at my surprised expression. "You are too naïve to survive on the CivilRim." He straightened, running his fingers over the panel so the light disappeared. "So, I sent a message to the Akrellians instead. They have responded back, and I've passed on our coordinates."

I gasped, shooting up into a standing position, wincing as my sudden change in position reminded me of how tender I was inside. *"What?* We agreed that we would all be safest on the CivilRim!"

His expression hardened, the mocking smile disappearing into a tight line of his lips. *"I* agreed to nothing. I won't allow Ilyan's cowardice to drive us to the Rim. I have no desire to go there." He narrowed his eyes on me. "Nor should you."

"The Akrellians might kill you! And Nirgal!" I stepped closer to him to grab his bicep, but he shrugged off my grip as if it was nothing.

Despite being underweight still, he remained much stronger than me. I wasn't sure if it was a male thing, or an alien thing that made him so. I didn't suppose it mattered. He had the upper hand physically, but even if I could wrestle him away from the console, he knew how to control the shuttle so I wouldn't have any idea how to change our course to get away from the Akrellians.

"They might even hurt Subject 34! Or lock him up in some new research facility. We don't know what they'll do!"

He turned to face me, raking my body with an assessing glance, which reminded me I stood naked before him, his seed slipping down my inner thighs now. His eyes grew hooded, and his expression took on a more predatory look as he caught me by the waist, tugging me closer.

I foolishly thought he would kiss me when he lowered his head, but he moved his lips closer to my ear, his silky hair brushing over my naked skin. "Are you really afraid the Akrellians will kill Ilyan? Or are you more afraid that he will find Claire again?"

I sucked in a breath to protest, lifting my hands to shove on his chest. This time, I was able to muster enough strength to break his hold on me, and I backed away from him, my chest heaving with my anger.

I pointed an accusing finger at him. "How dare you

suggest I wouldn't take the best option for all of us out of jealousy?" I poked my own chest. "I know the CivilRim is dangerous for me, but the four of us would have a chance there and at least we won't be at anyone's mercy when we get there! The Akrellians will take us into custody as soon as they reach us and will likely separate us. Who knows if they'll ever let us be together again? And they could still see Ilyan as their enemy and kill him outright without even letting him plead his case!"

He regarded me without a change in his expression, his lips still tight and his eyes cast in the shadow of his lowered brow.

"If they kill Ilyan," I stared at him with tears filling my eyes, "then *you* will die too! Are you really that unconcerned with your own survival?"

"Yes." He turned back towards the console, his wings flicking in what I took to be a sign of annoyance.

I stared at him in shock, noting the hard lines and angles of his face and how different he looked when this part of him took over. "Do you really hate Ilyan so much?"

He glanced at me, and once again his gaze trailed down my body. Fortunately, I'd grown so accustomed to being naked in front of him that I didn't feel self-conscious. Well, I felt a little self-conscious with the remnants of his seed spilling out of me still and my own blood staining my thighs from where his claws had impaled me.

"*We* should not exist in this condition," he said with a scowl.

"If you really hate him that much, why haven't you already tried to kill him?"

Not that I wanted to give him any suggestions, but I needed to understand how Evil Ilyan's mind worked, because he was a part of my beloved mate. That meant I had to live with him occasionally showing up and ravaging our lives—and my body

—at his will. I needed to know what that will was and how I could keep it from destroying my loved ones.

His upper lip curled in disgust as he looked down at the console. "Because I suffer from Ilyan's cowardice, apparently. I'm unable to take my own life, just as he could not bring himself to take his when he should have."

I sagged in relief, closing my eyes as I released the breath I'd been holding while waiting for his answer. He was still in bad shape, but he wasn't an immediate threat to himself, nor to my Ilyan.

"Maybe you both realize that remaining alive to face the challenges life throws at you is actually the most courageous thing you could do."

I wanted to go to him and hug him, despite the tension that made his body as hard and unyielding as a steel girder. Somewhere inside him, my Ilyan still existed, and I wanted to draw him out, but first I needed to reason with his fracture.

"You have no idea what we've been through, human," he said in a harsh tone, still staring down at the console. "No idea what we've *done*."

"I know you've done some bad things." This time I did go to him and put a hand on his arm, but he didn't look up at me. "But you've been given a second chance. You can live a better life now and maybe redeem yourself for your past actions."

His bark of laughter was harsh with bitterness as he shot a glare at me. "When I say what *we've* done, I mean it, Rhonda. You think I'm the evil one, but there is no *good* Ilyan."

I shook my head, stroking my hand down his arm until I reached his hand. To my relief, he didn't pull away when I linked our fingers. "I don't believe that, and I don't think you do either. I believe in redemption, and I think both of you can find it."

He didn't resist when I wrapped my free arm around his

waist. Instead, he pulled me against his body again, but this time more gently. "Like I said, Rhonda," he murmured, his hand lifting to my nape to cradle it. "You are naïve."

I felt the tightening of his fingers on my neck, over my carotid, and my brain didn't register the meaning behind his actions before blackness overtook my consciousness.

THIRTY-TWO

I woke up in a cell, though it was a fairly nice one, all things considered. The bed was spacious enough that I didn't feel cramped on it. There was a small alcove with what appeared to be a toilet that had a fancy sprayer to clean up instead of a roll of toilet paper. Next to the toilet alcove was another closet-sized space that I assumed was a shower, given the drain in the floor and the showerhead on the low hanging ceiling.

In the bed portion of the cell was a little nightstand and a dresser with a pile of stretchy jumpsuits inside it similar to the one I currently wore. This one was actually fitted to my body and didn't have the two slits in the back for wings.

The room was fairly austere, though comfortably furnished, but that wasn't what told me it was a cell. The locked door was the real indication of my status as a prisoner.

I pounded on it in frustration, screaming at the top of my lungs for Subject 34, Nirgal, and Ilyan. My voice had gone hoarse by the time I got a response that came from an intercom apparently hidden behind a panel by the locked door.

"It is important that you remain relaxed, human," a sibilant voice said in a mellow tone, "we mean you no harm and do not wish for you to hurt yourself in your fear or agitation."

"Where are my mates?" I demanded, gritting my teeth as I glared at the panel. "You better not have hurt them either!"

"Be at ease. The males are unharmed."

I paced in front of the door, fuming at my imprisonment and at Evil Ilyan for betraying me. Betraying all of us apparently. I didn't know what he'd done to keep Subject 34 and Nirgal from fighting against the Akrellians when they arrived at our shuttle's location, but I was willing to bet he'd done something nefarious.

"They better *remain* unharmed," I growled, feeling helpless and impotent even as I plotted all kinds of vengeance scenarios if anyone hurt my mates.

"The Iriduans are currently undergoing interrogation and the engineered hybrid remains in stasis due to security concerns."

"Interrogation!" My eyes wide with panic, I pounded on the door again. "Stop torturing them! They've been through enough of that, you bastards!"

I knew it was fruitless, but they were torturing my guys and I couldn't bear it. I would beat myself to death trying to get through this damned door before I'd sit back and accept defeat.

"Forgive me for causing you more distress with my poor choice of words. Something might have been lost in the translation. The Iriduans are undergoing extensive questioning, but we do not use torture to acquire information. The Dancer forbids such measures, and with good reason. The information gained under such methods is often unreliable."

I eyed the panel suspiciously, my fists stinging from my desperate pounding. My heart still thudded in my chest and my head felt light with fear for my mates. "Please let me see them! I need to know that they're safe. I need to see it for myself."

"We can arrange that in time. For now, it would be best if you calm yourself because your heart rate is dangerously high. We would prefer not to sedate you any further than the healing tank on the Iriduan shuttle did. You are likely to feel ill from the sedative's effects, but we have given you an anti-nausea injection that should help. Do not worry, it is designed for your human physiology."

That was all the reminder I needed to recall Nirgal's words about the Akrellians controlling Earth. I had almost forgotten that fact in all the chaos my life had taken on recently.

"So, now that you've captured us, are you going to put me in the slave mines with the rest of the humans you've conquered? Are you delivering me to my new alien overlords?"

My tone was bitter and sarcastic, but the voice on the other end of the intercom didn't sound the least bit fazed by my attitude.

"It is clear you have not been properly informed of our role as a sponsor of the Earthlings in the Cosmic Syndicate. Earth is a protectorate of Akrellia. We guide and counsel your people in the hopes that they will someday reach the necessary level of technology and wealth to become a member species of the Syndicate. We are far from conquerors. We consider humans our cousins and treat them as fellow citizens, never as slaves. We do not abide slavery in any Akrellian-controlled space."

I sighed, my chest palpitating from my anxiety over my mates even as those words gave me a small measure of calm. I still wasn't certain I should believe these Akrellians, but I couldn't see any reason why they'd bother to lie to me. They had the upper hand over one human woman who couldn't even get past a cell door, much less pose any real threat to them.

"A human liaison is on their way to our location to meet

with you. She will assist you with reacclimating and aide you in recovering your past identity and any assets that may have been lost to you due to your illegal abduction from Earth. Until then, we have been informed by the Iriduans in custody that your name is Rhonda, though we have no family name for you. We would prefer to speak in person rather than through an intercom. However, the ambassador has explained that this isn't always ideal for humans who have been in stasis and had limited exposure to extraterrestrials prior to encountering us. We don't want you to be frightened by the sight of us."

"I have a mate who's genetically engineered from a giant alien scorpion," I said wryly, crossing my arms over my chest, "You aren't going to scare me, no matter how strange you look to a human."

"We are pleased to hear that," the voice said. "Someone will be with you shortly to escort you from your cell into an interrogat—a questioning chamber. It will be easier to assure you of our good intentions when you are not trapped behind a locked door."

"No kidding. But before I answer any questions, I want to see my mates." I sighed and returned to the bed to sink onto the foam-like mattress, watching the door, waiting for my new captors to let me out.

I was really getting sick and tired of being imprisoned by aliens. I could only hope that this time, the aliens weren't planning on experimenting on me—or my mates.

It didn't take long for the door of my cell to slide open. I tensed up as it did, not sure what I'd see on the other side. The slender form of a scaled female with delicate feminine features, flanked by two burly males with what looked like quills on their heads, was almost too normal to meet my expectations.

The lizard-like female smiled warmly at me, which allowed me to somewhat ignore the sharp points of her teeth as she gestured with one graceful hand for me to exit the cell and join her.

As I stood and made my way to the door, she touched her chest. "My name is unpronounceable for most humans, but I have chosen the human name Grace to make things easier for my human contacts. We welcome you on our ship, Light Step Across the Stars." She gestured to the cell beyond me. "We apologize for the meager accommodations. Our ship was diverted to your shuttle because we were the closest to your coordinates. Unfortunately, we weren't prepared for additional passengers."

"Please, Grace," I said without standing on ceremony, "let me see my mates. Their safety and well-being are all I care about right now."

Grace remained silent for a long beat, glancing over her shoulder at one of the males. His head quills stood on end, making him an intimidating spectacle but at this point, I didn't give a damn. All I wanted was to see for myself that they hadn't harmed my loved ones.

Finally, the alien female relented, her stiff expression softening as she gave me another sharp-toothed smile that still managed to look empathetic.

"I will take you to the brig where they're currently being held. The engineered hybrid must remain in cryo stasis until your relocation, per orders from our commander, but I assure you, he is as safe as he can be in that state. Safer than if he were able to attack us, because in that case, we would have no choice but to use lethal force. I'm sure you understand."

I nodded slowly, not liking the fact that Subject 34 would have to remain frozen, but also agreeing that he would be in even greater danger if he were free and attacked someone.

"What about Nirgal and Ilyan?" I knew the Akrellians were enemies of the Iriduans, so I really worried about what they might be doing to them to get whatever information they wanted out of them.

Grace stepped to the side and gestured for me to join her at her side, rather than leading me. I found the companionable gesture comforting as I fell into step beside her, the two males closing in at my back. Their presence sent a clear message if I held any thoughts of hurting Grace or anyone or thing on the ship, but they held back enough that I didn't feel crowded or menaced.

"Though the Iriduan Empire is an enemy of both Akrellians and humans, your," she shot a curious glance at me, "*mates* are being well treated. They are cooperating with us and willingly answering all our questions. We respect any Iriduan who breaks their lifelong programming to join the rebellion against the empire." She slowly shook her head, the ship's mellow lighting bouncing off the colorful scales that covered her skull. She didn't have the same quills as the males.

"So they're rebels now." I chewed my lip, still worried for them. "That's probably a label they will like more than 'traitors'."

She shot me another curious glance. "The Akrellian government has worked with the one called Ilyan in the past, though from my understanding, our people lost contact with him for some time, until he sent us your coordinates and a request for asylum."

This surprised me enough to freeze me in mid-step. Fortunately, the males stopped instantly as well rather than barreling into my back. Grace took one more step before turning to face me with a questioning expression that was remarkably human even on such an alien face.

"*Ilyan* worked with the Akrellians in the past?"

"You did not know this?" I didn't like the sympathetic tone

she took, as if she felt like I should be hurt by the fact that I wasn't aware of this.

Okay, I *was* hurt, but not as much as she might think. I didn't believe for one moment that *Ilyan* was the rebel, but it occurred to me that the Akrellians might not know that he was fractured. In that case, I had no intention of giving him away.

I still wasn't sure what I would do about Evil Ilyan, and unfortunately, it was a decision I would need to make alone, because I feared that if I told Subject 34 or Nirgal about his recent actions, they would want to kill him, or at the very least, keep him away from me.

"He hasn't mentioned it to me, but things have been very crazy for the four of us since we met." I smiled weakly, shrugging my shoulders like I was overwhelmed.

Her smile was as sympathetic as her tone. "I can only imagine what you've been through, and I'm sorry you had to endure such a horrible experience. Our human liaison will be able to provide the most effective therapy for you, but we have an emotional healer on board if you need to speak with someone about your trauma before she arrives."

I shook my head firmly. There was nothing a therapist could do for me that seeing my mates safe and healthy couldn't do. As for the trauma I'd suffered up to this point, it could wait. Maybe forever. My mates fulfilled me in a way I'd never been on Earth. They made me feel whole, even though my experiences should have left me broken. I hadn't even had nightmares with Subject 34 right there beside me to protect me.

Some rewards were worth the sacrifice, and I felt that my mates were more than enough compensation for what I'd endured. Just being with them again would heal me in a way years of counseling couldn't.

"Once I can talk to my mates, I'll feel a whole lot better."

Grace nodded, then gestured to the corridor. "Then we should continue to the brig. This way, please."

When we reached the brig, I noted that the cells there weren't nearly as nice as the cabin I'd been locked inside. These were much more like prison cells. Ilyan and Nirgal were sitting on the cots in their tight confines on either side of a central aisle, eyeing each other with clear hostility.

I exhaled a huge breath that I'd been holding on our way here when I saw that they both looked healthy and unmarked by the Akrellian interrogations. Then I sighed when I noted their tight expressions as they stared each other down, unaware of our entrance.

"When are you two going to get along?" I asked in exasperation as I rushed down the aisle towards them, forgetting about the three Akrellians watching me.

Both males jumped to their feet and their wings flared open as they stepped closer to the bars. They stopped just short of touching them as Grace warned me sharply that they were energized to shock if touched.

I looked from Nirgal's icy blue eyes to Ilyan's bottle green gaze, stiffening when I noticed how cold his eyes were. They made Nirgal's gaze at its worst seem warm and comforting. Understanding passed between us, and I shot a quick glance at Grace, who was politely giving us some space, though I doubted we were getting any real privacy.

"Are you two okay?" I asked in a low volume. "They didn't hurt you, did they?"

"We're fine," Nirgal said abruptly, cutting off any response Evil Ilyan might make. "I was worried about you. They swore you were unharmed, but it relieves me to see you looking as beautiful and healthy as ever."

"Pathetic," Evil Ilyan muttered just loud enough for me to

hear him, though I suspected Nirgal was well aware of his comment as his eyes narrowed into a glare at Evil Ilyan.

"So, you're a rebel," I murmured to Evil Ilyan after giving Nirgal my warmest smile.

I wanted to touch them both, to run my hands over their bodies to check that they had not been mistreated, but the bars kept us apart. I had to resort to turning my head back and forth between them like I was watching a tennis match.

Evil Ilyan regarded me with a long look that told me nothing about what was going on in that fractured mind of his. "I've been known to assist the rebels in the past."

"Did the asteroid have anything to do with that?" Now I needed to know his real story as much as I needed to know that my Ilyan was still okay behind the enigmatic eyes of his fracture.

For whatever reason, my Ilyan remained submerged. I wasn't sure how it all worked between them, and how Ilyan retook control. Evil Ilyan had implied that it was Ilyan's choice. That he had the stronger will. But surely Ilyan would not remind under this long if that was true.

Unless he didn't want to be with me, or he'd decided that he couldn't handle sharing me with Nirgal. I wasn't sure what to do about that, and now wasn't the time to discuss it, lest I give anything away to our current captors.

"I told you, I have my own reasons for every action I take. Those reasons aren't your business, human" His eyes glittered with their hardness.

Well, at the moment, it was probably best that he didn't elaborate on his past. I couldn't allow myself to be too caught up in those questions to forget that we were all being monitored.

"Did they treat you properly, my queen?" Nirgal asked,

shooting a pointed glance at Evil Ilyan that condemned him for not inquiring about my treatment.

I gestured to Grace and her guards, discreetly watching us from a short distance away without appearing to stare at us. "They've been kind enough to me since I regained consciousness." I narrowed my eyes at Evil Ilyan, then turned my back on him to face Nirgal. "But all I could think about was my mates. I feared they might have hurt you."

Nirgal huffed, switching his glare from Evil Ilyan to the Akrellians. "I imagine they would have preferred to, but we offered plenty of information to buy ourselves sanctuary." He scowled at Evil Ilyan. "And they have reluctantly offered it thanks to a deal Ilyan worked out without our input, though we will be under guard for an indeterminate amount of time after we reach Earth." His wings vibrated with outrage as he shot another glare at Grace and her guards. "Until we prove ourselves *trustworthy*." He said the last word as if it was a grave insult.

My eyes widened as his words sank in. "We're going to *Earth*?"

I wasn't sure how to feel about that. I had never planned on returning to my home world once Nirgal told me the Akrellians had taken it over. I was shocked that they were returning me to it, along with my mates.

I turned to face Grace, my question still hanging in the air, spoken loud enough for her to overhear it easily.

She nodded, a smile spreading her lips. "We have a sanctuary on Earth for political dissidents seeking asylum. It is isolated from the majority of the human population, but there are humans living there in harmony with the other residents."

"Humans in harmony, huh? Sounds like utopia to me." Despite my sarcasm, I felt a knotting in my stomach as new concerns flooded in. "What about Subject 34? He has to go with us to Earth. There's no way in hell I'm leaving him!"

Grace raised her hands in a defensive gesture that made me realize I had taken several steps closer to her, my voice raised. Her guards also moved closer, their eyes fixed on me as their head quills rose.

"Of course, he will be permitted to settle with you, though even in the sanctuary, he will need to remain isolated from the other residents until we can be assured he will remain peaceful. We understand how dangerous he could be if he feels threatened."

Grace glanced from me to Evil Ilyan, then returned her gaze to me. "Our commander has agreed to the terms your mate has set out in return for his full cooperation, and we won't inform the other test subject hybridized from the athraxius specimen of Subject 34's existence, or Ilyan's. At this time," she added in a murmur that I didn't miss because I was standing closer to her than my two mates.

I crossed my arms, eyeing her suspiciously. "The health and well-being of my mates is my number one concern. You find us a safe place where they won't be hunted down by the Iriduan Empire, and I don't give a damn if it's in the middle of the Mojave Desert."

Grace's eyes widened. "How did you know where the sanctuary was?"

Well, it could be worse. It could be in the sand dunes of the Saharan Desert.

THIRTY-THREE

Human bureaucracy never changed, even when aliens rolled in to help our species advance. The liaison was polite enough, but it was strange to try to describe my unconventional relationship with three alien males with another human woman. Fortunately, she didn't bat an eyelash, nor judge me as I thought she might, even though her accent placed her as firmly North American, so polyamory wasn't a particularly common occurrence in the culture she'd probably grown up in.

At least, it hadn't been in mine.

Upon inquiry, I learned that it still wasn't all that common in North America, but human minds had grown more open in recent years. I also learned the terrible truth about the Akrellian "occupation" and the Menops invasion that had necessitated their intervention.

There was so much paperwork to fill out, so many boxes to check, so many plans to make that I got zero time to spend with my mates, even though the Akrellians transferred us to a larger ship with better accommodations for all of us in adjoining cabins.

Ilyan remained submerged, and Evil Ilyan implied that he was keeping him that way until it was safe, because my green guy would have no idea what was going on, and his confusion might give away the truth about Ilyan's condition.

It was that confession that told me that Evil Ilyan's will wasn't as weak as he'd first implied. He *could* hold Ilyan back if he wanted to once Ilyan went dormant. He just couldn't take over when Ilyan was in control.

I worried about what Ilyan would think when all was said and done, and I felt desperate to have a frank discussion with all my mates, including my poor Subject 34, who was still a popsicle, much to my frustration. He would also be confused about what had happened and where we were when they finally thawed him out. No matter how much I reassured the Akrellians that he would listen to me and not hurt anyone, they were determined not to take any chances with him.

Whoever this Thrax was that shared his genes with 34, he'd given them a healthy respect—and definite fear—of Subject 34.

The story of Thrax and the other test subjects the Akrellians had also provided sanctuary for was one my liaison passed on to me through a documentary, of all things. It was bizarre to watch an alien-made video lauding those genetically engineered beings and their human partners as heroes who had aided in ending the invasion of Earth.

I finally got to see the face of Claire with her mate in a rare photo, him looking much like Subject 34, but not quite the same. She appeared madly in love with him as she stared up at him rather than looking at the camera, which relieved me, though I hadn't really thought she would try to steal Ilyan away from me even if she did ever learn he'd survived.

She looked like an interesting person. Probably more interesting than me. That still worried me, but at least we wouldn't be forced into the awkward position of meeting them. Hopefully, the Akrellians kept their word and never let Thrax and Claire know that Subject 34 existed and Ilyan was alive.

All the things I needed to learn to catch up on what had taken place while I was a peopsicle for a decade nearly overwhelmed me, and both Nirgal and Evil Ilyan also had to deal with an extensive info-dump about Earth, humanity, the Akrellian role in our people's lives, and a shit ton of other things that I felt were a bit much to take in all at once. Things were moving so fast, our time so stuffed full of crap to do that I felt like I had seen more of my mates when they were locked behind bars on the Light Step.

There was no time for making love, even if we felt comfortable enough on the transport ship to do so. I personally didn't, still fearing that I was being monitored, despite being in the privacy of my own cabin. I hoped the sanctuary on Earth didn't have such monitoring, or at least not in the homes.

Our liaison provided videos of our destination as we made our way to Earth, and I was surprised that the Nevada desert area we were relocating to looked inviting. The Akrellians had done extensive construction and terraforming to transform the desolate desert landscape into something beautiful while still retaining the xeric nature and almost extraterrestrial vibe of the Mojave Desert. When my liaison told me, with a wide grin, that the sanctuary was built on the former site of Area 51 I didn't believe her at first.

Then I had a good laugh that she joined in on. It was nice to know they had a sense of humor, and clearly, so did my fellow humans, since they'd ceded the land and facilities to their new allies.

I wasn't feeling amused when we finally landed, and I got the chance to take my first step back on home soil in over a decade. That step was taken towards a shielded housing unit that would be my new home. One that was set apart from the rest of the little settlement. The shield dome looked pretty, glittering in the good ol' Sol light, but it reminded me that we were still on probation.

Several Akrellians wheeled Subject 34's cryo unit in our wake as we made our way to our housing unit. I kept turning to check on it, worried that something might happen to it that could interfere with 34's safe reawakening.

This wasn't quite the homecoming I could hope for. We were still basically prisoners, though our prison turned out to be much nicer than the ones we'd left behind. Granted, we had the chance to earn our parole, and I couldn't entirely blame the Akrellians for showing caution with Subject 34. As we left the airfield and took the path to our shielded house, I saw some of the other citizens of the settlement stopping in their tracks to watch us go by.

I'd seen many strange creatures while in captivity but some of these extraterrestrials standing here in the desert on Earth seemed surreal. Fortunately, they appeared more curious than hostile, even when they glanced at my Iriduans. My liaison had explained that the asylum seekers understood the enormous cost Iriduans paid to betray the empire, so tended to regard them with respect in this settlement.

There were also more Iriduans than just my two guys here, and perhaps at some point, we would meet them and their families. Maybe we could all become friends. Or at least, friendly neighbors. I would love to host a backyard BBQ for my family and friends, and I could almost picture the four of us sitting at a picnic bench in our new backyard as we neared our residence. The house itself was isolated physically from the rest of the settlement past a cactus garden that surrounded the place like a spike-filled moat.

The home had a spacious front lawn and was larger than the tract home I'd left after my divorce from Michael. In fact, it was a five-bedroom home built in a style that my liaison explained was a combination of extraterrestrial architectural design elements, giving it a somewhat different appearance from my last home on Earth.

It was lovely, in its way, but the shield kept me from fully appreciating the property as much as I might have. The fact that it was really just a temporary quarter for "guests" who might pose some threat or be threatened by other residents also didn't make me see it as home.

A flurry of activities took place once the liaison keyed us through the shield and we entered our new—though temporary—housing.

Subject 34's unit was set up in the front living area and the process of thawing him out began while me, Nirgal, and Evil Ilyan wandered around the house in the trail of the liaison as she showed off all the amenities and answered all my questions.

My mates didn't ask anything, and I thought that strange at first, because Michael would have dominated the conversation with the liaison like he had with our realtor when we'd bought our house, cutting me off whenever I had a question to ask to interject his own or condescendingly brush my concerns aside.

Then I realized that they deferred to me out of respect for me, choosing to follow my lead and let me air any concerns I might have. Probably because I was their "queen" but also because I was human, and we were on my home turf. In fact, neither of them even spoke until the liaison asked if we had any other questions and I gestured for them to ask anything they felt they needed to.

They had a few, but not many. They'd done their research with all the info the Akrellians and the liaison had thrown at us on our way here.

My most pressing concern now that I'd toured the

furnished housing quarters and had been shown where all the basic supplies were was to check on 34.

We returned to the living area to find that his cryo unit was in the last stages of thawing him, and the Akrellians were packing up their instruments while shooting nervous glances at the unit.

"We will leave the cryo tank here until it is safe to retrieve it," the liaison said as they all headed towards the door. She turned to face me as it slid open behind her. "Are you certain it is safe for you to be here when he awakens? He will likely be disoriented and could be hostile because of it."

"It will be safer for *everyone* if she's here when he awakens," Nirgal answered for me, for the first time since we'd started this tour.

I nodded, not worried that Subject 34 would hurt me, even when he was disoriented. He hadn't hurt me when he'd first met me, his killer instincts in full gear. "I'll be fine but thank you for asking."

The liaison smiled brightly, waving. "Well then, I'm sure you're all tired and would like to rest up. Don't forget your orientation appointments tomorrow. We'll host the first of them at the welcome facility, but once all of you are acclimated," she shot a nervous glance at the cryo unit, "we have in-home volunteers who can help you with whatever you need during this difficult time."

Then she left and we were finally alone. I wanted to sag in relief, but I also feared we were still being watched. Apparently so did my mates, because they left my side to do their own sweep of the house, examining everything carefully.

I wasn't sure whether the Akrellians knew my Iriduans had circuit scanners in their optic implants. If there were surveillance electronics within the house, my mates would be able to figure that out. The ship cabins had been more difficult because of all the climate control electronics buried within the walls, though they'd told me they didn't think the cabins themselves were monitored.

You would think I would have grown accustomed to being watched all the time, but the exact opposite was true. After being observed in a research facility for what seemed like a lifetime, I now felt paranoid about having unseen eyes on me. That was probably something I would have to deal with in the therapy the liaison had promised.

My Iriduans returned as I was checking on the status of the thawing process, irritated that it took so damned long. I needed to talk to 34. I needed to hold him and reassure myself that he was safe and well. I could barely make out his form behind the foggy shield of his cryo tank.

Arms slipped around my waist as Nirgal's scent enveloped me while I stood in front of the tank. He rested his chin on my head, pulling my back against his chest.

"All his vitals look good. He'll recover quickly, my queen."

THIRTY-FOUR

I sagged against Nirgal's body, lifting my hands to close around the nape of his neck. I shifted to the side so I could look over my shoulder at him. He lowered his head and kissed me, and it was far more than the short, perfunctory kisses that were all I'd felt comfortable sharing with my mates while on the Akrellian ships.

I turned in his arms, one of my hands sliding up the back of his head, feeling the softness of the hair that darkened his scalp. It would be a while before it grew out to anywhere near the length it had been when I'd met him, but he already looked almost as healthy and strong as he had been when he'd held me captive.

We'd come a long way since then. Much farther than I could have ever imagined the day I woke up to find myself at his mercy. Now, his kiss made me want to submit to him and beg him to put me back at his mercy. His hands clutched at the back of my jumpsuit, pulling me hard against his lean body. The ridge of his erection already pressed against my soft belly as his lips claimed mine.

My eyes closed as I inhaled his delicious, subtle scent, alien but undeniably masculine. His lips felt warm and yielding as they caressed mine. His tongue tasted of chocolate as it delved into my mouth to tangle with mine. I smiled inwardly at that flavor because it told me he'd been snacking on the candy our liaison had given us as part of a welcome gift. Nirgal had become a huge fan of chocolate ever since cautiously tasting a chocolate bar.

I moaned as his kiss deepened, his hands sliding down my waist to grip my buttocks, grinding his erection against my body.

"I want you naked," he said in a ragged voice as he broke our kiss. "Strip for me."

I glanced around before returning my eyes to his face, noting how dark his beautiful blues were with his dilated pupils. "Here? In the living room?"

Evil Ilyan was nowhere to be seen, and I worried about that, but also understood it. I would check on him soon, because we needed to have a frank talk, but it was about things I couldn't discuss in front of Nirgal.

For now, I had my evil scientist in front of me, demanding I strip naked for him and damned if I didn't want to, but having sex in the living room felt scandalous to me. It was such a public part of the house, and I'd never felt comfortable doing such a thing with Michael. Not that he'd ever wanted me so badly that we couldn't make it to the bedroom.

"Rhonda," he said in a warning growl, his dilated gaze dropping to the collar of my jumpsuit like he debated pulling it open himself.

Fuck it! I wanted him so badly I was practically shaking with need. I lifted my hands to unhook my jumpsuit, then peeled it down my body, eyeing him with hunger. "I want you naked too, Nirgie."

He didn't even flinch at the nickname, nor did he hesitate to pull off his jumpsuit, shrugging out of the form-fitting garment that had already left little to the imagination with such eagerness that I worried he'd harm his wings. That was a silly concern, because those beauties were strong as hell, despite their delicate, glasslike appearance.

I admired his lean body, noting with relief that it had filled out with his recovery, his belly no longer concave, his ribs no longer pushing against his skin. I loved the striping that crossed his iridescent orange flesh. It wasn't exactly like a tiger's stripes, but the black on orange still reminded me of that beautiful predator.

Besides, now that Nirgal had seen videos of tigers during his Earth research, he loved the comparison.

My gaze lowered from his firm belly to the huge erection that jutted from his groin, the black stripes circling it the way my fingers itched to. His cerci uncoiled from his back, already vibrating with his excitement as we gazed at each other's naked bodies.

The look of hunger in his eyes made me feel like a goddess, even though I had access to a mirror, and I knew what I truly looked like. By human standards, I wouldn't even rate a second glance, and no doubt someone would be sure to suggest I should hit the gym more often. By Iriduan standards, I would probably be considered a troll, given how stunning they and their females were and how narrow their beauty standards were.

Yet Nirgal looked at me like he desired nothing more in life than to touch me, and whenever he did touch me, I felt his need in the way his hands caressed me. It turned me on so much that he actually wanted to look at my naked body before making love to me, especially since Michael had insisted on light's off during our last years together and had neglected to caress my body, even encouraging me to keep my night gown on so I wouldn't have to bother redressing afterwards.

No wonder we were both so damned miserable in our marriage! I couldn't believe I'd put up with that shit for so long. Had I really convinced myself that I was happy—or had I feared I couldn't do better?

Now, my handsome alien mate stared at me with his erection jutting and his cerci vibrating and his eyes dilated until they were almost completely black. When I stepped closer to him, he snatched me up like I was a precious prize he fully intended to claim as his own.

His hands roved all over me, warm palms sliding over my soft flesh, gripping handfuls of it as he kissed a path from my lips down my neck towards my stiff nipple. His cerci also rubbed over my skin, the vibration causing it to tingle as the barbs rippled on the ends of them, occasionally scraping my skin far more gently than Evil Ilyan's barbs had scraped my inner passage.

I clutched Nirgal's head as he caught my nipple between his lips, my fingers playing in the short, silky hair that capped his skull. It was growing in black rather than orange, which I found intriguing. Nirgal had mentioned off-handedly that he'd dyed his hair to match his skin color because it was considered more attractive to be color-coordinated.

Despite being trained as a scientist rather than a candidate for a mate, my Nirgal was as vain as any other Iriduan male. I found that oddly endearing about him, even as he defiantly flaunted his "juvenile" stripes. When I'd told him I liked his hair black, he'd vowed never to dye it again.

Now, I moaned in pleasure, my core heating as he suckled my nipple. One hand caressed my other breast as his lips ravished the tender bead. His other hand stroked down my body, slipping to my mound. He made an appreciative sound that vibrated around my nipple when his fingers encountered the wetness of my arousal as he rubbed his fingers along my seam.

My hips rocked as he slipped his fingers inside my aching entrance, fingering me in slow thrusts. Encircling his shaft with my hand, I stroked gently along the impressive length of it, my inner muscles clenching at the thought of taking all of that inside me. I was both eager and hesitant.

He suddenly lifted his head from my nipple, glancing around the living room as if something had just occurred to him. "You said you wanted to do this in a bed the last time we were together."

My fingers tightened on his shaft as he made to pull away. "Don't you dare stop! I need you, right now! I don't think I'll make it to one of the bedrooms."

He buried his face in the crook of my neck, inhaling deeply. Then he said some Iriduan curse about rotten silk or some shit before he crowded me back against the side of 34's tank. Lifting one of my legs up, he fitted the head of his erection at my entrance.

I released his length as he began to slide it in, both of us moaning in pleasure.

"By the Spinner, Rhonda," he said in a guttural groan, "you squeeze me so tight and yet it feels so *incredible!*"

"You're huge, Nirgie," I said breathlessly, willing my inner muscles not to tighten further so that I didn't feel any discomfort as he impaled me on his massive shaft. "And you feel so damned good too that I'm already close to coming."

He stared down at me with his dark eyes, a smirk tilting his lips. "Close, are you?"

I felt one of his cerci stroke over my clit, the barbs thankfully flattened to the side of it. The vibration of it brought me closer to my peak.

"You're cruel, teasing me like this," I gasped as he drove his shaft deeper inside me, his cercus caressing my clit while the other moved to play around my entrance, vibrating against the sensitive skin that surrounded his huge girth impaling me.

"Come for me, Rhonda," he said in a commanding tone, but he really didn't have to give that order.

My back arched against the cold metal of the cryo tank as I climaxed, and he chose that moment to thrust fully into me, groaning as my inner muscles convulsed around him.

I didn't get a chance to recover before he begun to pound into me, moving frantically like his control had snapped. His body pinned mine to the cryo tank as he screwed me mercilessly, his knuckles paling to peach as he clutched the tank on either side of my head to give himself more leverage. He buried his length to the hilt over and over again, shoving my body against the tank with almost bruising force as he chased his own climax. His cerci continued to tease my throbbing flesh until I came again, just as his shaft jerked inside me to shoot the first ropes of his seed against my womb.

He leaned his forehead against mine as he slowly withdrew from me, lowering my leg, which trembled in the aftermath. Both of us were panting as I clutched his shoulders.

"You drive me so crazy, Rhonda," he said, nuzzling my hair and inhaling deep. "I never dreamed being mated was like this! When I think of what I might have missed if you'd never come into my life, I hate the empire for choosing my lonely future for me."

I lifted my head to kiss him, and he pulled me against his chest, deepening the kiss for a long moment before we had to break apart to suck in breaths.

"I love you, Nirgal." I caressed his jaw with a fingertip. "I want to make you happy."

"You already do." He cupped my face between his hands,

and I gazed into his eyes, watching with interest the slow constriction of his pupils as the beautiful blue returned. "Even when you were infuriating me in the very beginning, deliberately needling me to anger me, I felt more alive than I ever have before. More," he paused as he searched for the right word, "emotional—more *passionate* about something other than my work."

I grinned at his words, ignoring the wet slide of his seed down my inner thighs. There would be time to clean up later. Right now, all I could focus on was him. "Are you saying I really got to you, Nirgie?"

He chuckled. "If you don't wipe that wicked smile off your face, I'll prove to you again how much you *get* to me, my queen."

I was about to goad him into doing just that when the tank at my back released a startling klaxon that had both of us jumping.

THIRTY-FIVE

My heart leapt to my throat as Nirgal pulled me away from the tank, just in time for the front shield of it to slide upwards, emitting a cloud of vapor.

"Perhaps we should clean up before greeting Subject 34," Nirgal whispered in my ear, cradling my back against his chest as his arms encircled my shoulders. "It will take some time for him to reorient himself, and you can make it back here by the time he returns to full awareness."

"Are you sure he's okay?" I stared at the tank in concern, disliking the sound the initial klaxon had made, though it had only been a brief alert before falling silent.

Still, lights were flashing on the tank, and I willed the vapor cloud to part further so I could see my beautiful monster more clearly, rather than just the dark, hulking shadow of his form in the misty confines of the tank.

"All his vitals remain in normal range. Trust me, Rhonda, I know Subject 34's health status better than anyone. I would recognize if he were in distress. He will recover just fine, but it will take a bit longer."

Reluctantly, I retreated from the living space, rushing to the closest bathroom, outfitted with state-of-the-art hygiene technology that cleaned me up in no time, though each passing moment felt like an eternity as I wanted to return to Subject 34. I needed to be there for him when he regained consciousness.

Refreshed and redressed in a fresh jumpsuit, a brief thought of clothes shopping in my head, I rushed out of the bathroom and collided with my green guy.

And he was *my* green guy this time. He caught me by my shoulders as I looked up into his eyes, noting that my Ilyan had returned.

"How does it feel to be back on Earth?" he said with a slight smile, dropping a quick kiss on my lips.

"How did you know where we were?" I had missed him more than I realized. I felt a wave of relief to see his softer, less hardened demeanor.

Like Nirgal, my Ilyan was arrogant, vain, and stuffy at times. But he was also capable of being charming, sexy, and affectionate. That last really meant a lot to me, especially with Ilyan, because it differentiated him greatly from his fracture, who had maintained a vast emotional distance during our journey, refusing to answer any personal questions I asked him.

"I left myself a message, apparently," he said, his brows pulling together in a disconcerted frown. "I don't like not remembering what I've done or where I've been. I suppose a message is better than leaving me in complete confusion."

I touched the lines between his brows, and his lips tilted in amusement as it smoothed out beneath my fingertips. "I am happy to see that he has not made you despise me, my queen." His smile faded as he studied my face, lifting a hand to brush my hair away from it. "I should not have retreated and let him gain control. The thought of you with Nirgal... it bothered me too much and I took a cowardly way out. I'm not accustomed to dealing with strong emotions. Especially the unpleasant ones. Can you ever forgive me for abandoning you when you needed me most?"

I embraced him, hugging him around his narrow waist with both arms as I laid my cheek against his chest. "I love you, Ilyan, and I really missed you. I'm so sorry that my being with Nirgal upset you so much. I don't want you to be hurt by our relationship."

I feared what the future would hold for all of us if Ilyan had such a difficult time with jealousy towards Nirgal. This was exactly the kind of issue I'd expect with our relationship, and I'd been afraid there would be fallout from it.

"No, you don't have to apologize to me, Rhonda." He pulled out of my embrace so he could meet my eyes, his inhumanly vivid green eyes warm and filled with regret. "Nirgal and I have history that has nothing to do with our relationship to you. You're right that we need to deal with our past and get rid of the antagonism that keeps us from being the friends we once were. To be harem brothers, we can't do anything less without bringing unnecessary distress to our mate. He knows this as well as I do."

He kissed me again, and I protested when it was far too short to satisfy my hunger for him. "We *will* fix this, Rhonda, and I swear to you, I will never leave you like that again. I won't hide from my problems any longer. You deserve better than having a coward in your harem."

I put a finger over his lips, silencing any more self-denigrating things he might say. Clearly, I wasn't the only one who might need therapy after all that we've been through.

I knew that I could never tell Ilyan what his fracture had said and done to me. He was already beating himself up over going dormant and letting Evil Ilyan take control. In the long run, it might have been the best decision because Evil Ilyan's betrayal led to us returning to Earth. We had a home now, and a promise of safety, and possibly even the chance at making friends outside of our own little family, though I didn't feel like I needed them.

"Rhonda!" Nirgal shouted from the living room. "Perhaps you'd like to join us now."

The strained sound of his voice raised my eyebrows as I broke away from Ilyan and rushed down the hall to the living room.

"34, no!" I shouted in panic as I saw him holding Nirgal by the throat with one lower hand, both his pincers extended as my evil scientist dangled from his grip, his own hands clutching around Subject 34's hand on his neck.

34 dropped Nirgal and turned to me, his eye shields parting to reveal his beautiful black eyes, even as his mandibles parted to show his beloved face.

I switched my attention from 34's face, which was already shifting from a scowl to a more relaxed look of contentment to Nirgal, who had collapsed in a heap, coughing as he clutched his throat.

"Didn't kill him," my beloved monster said defensively.

I ran to him and hugged him tight around his waist, so accustomed to being cautious about his stinger markings that I avoided brushing against them out of habit.

His lower arms wrapped around my shoulders, his pincers retracting so his upper hands could touch my face as he looked down at me.

"I missed you so much!" I said fervently as I blinked back tears. "Are you okay? Are there any side effects of the stasis? Nausea? Headache? Disoriented vision?"

34 made his amused chittering sound as he lowered his head to claim my lips in a passionate kiss that I returned

eagerly. My hands moved to slide up the chitin plates that covered his chest to his broad shoulders, then I caught the ridged back of his neck, pulling him closer to me. Our kiss deepened and his scent filled my head, driving me wild with arousal that soaked the crotch of my new jumpsuit.

His lower hands left my shoulders to part my jumpsuit, jerking it open so his hands could slip inside it to cup my breasts.

It occurred to me that I might end up spending a good portion of my life naked with three passionate alien lovers in my home. I had no problem with that. None whatsoever. I could save a fortune on clothes.

Subject 34 seemed in a hurry to remove mine, and that was something else I had no problem with. In fact, I even tried to help, shimmying my shoulders to pull the jumpsuit off them. He took it from there, his lower hands dragging the fabric down my body, unpeeling it from me like I was a banana. His mouth switched to my neck, then trailed lower as he exposed my naked flesh.

I moaned in pleasure at the feeling of his lips on me again, his hard, cool hands covered in their chitinous plates so different in feel from the warm hands of my other mates. *He* was so different from my Iriduans, his scent so delicious that it made me lose my head in a way that nothing else could.

He teased my nipple with his lips, then lifted his head to meet my eyes with his. "Are you hungry?"

I released a hard breath, nodding my head wordlessly. I know he meant literally, and I was fine in that regard, but yes, I was so hungry for his body that my stomach ached with anticipation to taste him and then feel him vibrating inside me.

His smile was slight. He rarely smiled widely because it threatened to split his bisected lips and he tried to keep that from me, as if I didn't already know what his real mouth looked like.

As if he could ever repulse me.

I dropped to my knees before he fully released me. His lower hands cupped my breasts, continuing to tease my nipples as my knees hit the tile floor. My lower legs were still tangled in the jumpsuit, but I didn't care, too caught up in my excitement and need for him.

Although I did spare a thought for becoming a nudist within my home, because it seemed more efficient at this point.

His erection already jutted from his armored body, and my lips closed hungrily around the head of it, my moan of pleasure bringing an answering one from him.

I still had so much to say to him. I wanted to discuss where we were, and what had happened while he'd been in stasis. Instead, his pheromones were too strong for me to think. All I could do was feel this powerful need for him as my lips coaxed fluid from his shaft.

He seemed more impatient and driven with a need to be inside me, flooding my mouth with his ejaculate with far less sucking than I would normally do for him. As soon as I'd swallowed, licking my lips as he pulled away, he pounced on me. He dragged me off the ground, then off my feet, his lower hands yanking the jumpsuit fully off my legs.

Before I could even suck in enough breath to protest—not that I would have—he parted my thighs and caught my hips in his lower hands, his upper hands firm around my waist to hold me up. The strength he possessed never ceased to amaze me and should terrify anyone who got on his bad side.

Which probably explained the abundance of caution the Akrellians took regarding Subject 34.

His entire body vibrated as he pulled my hips towards him, the head of his shaft slipping past my wet entrance. He impaled me in one swift thrust that had us both making guttural sounds of pleasure. My excitement left his shaft dripping from my slick as he began to move.

His hard hands kept me pinned as he thrust at a pace he knew I liked the most, the vibration over my g-spot bringing me quickly to orgasm. As I cried out with my release, I felt the flush of his ejaculate filling me. Even in my lust-addled brain, I recognized what that meant.

For the first time since I'd met him, Subject 34 had given me his seed.

THIRTY-SIX

My Iriduans had left the living room not long after 34 freed Nirgal, and I could only hope they were finding a way to get along and get over their antagonism. I worried about them even as I snuggled against Subject 34, feeling safe in his arms as he held me in the aftermath of our lovemaking.

As much as I wanted to check on them, I felt like I owed it to 34 to spend this blissful time with him and explain where we were and what was happening.

Though I did keep out some of Evil Ilyan's actions that I still feared would end up getting my green guy killed.

"So, now we're here on Earth, and according to the Akrellians, we can stay here as long as none of us hurt someone."

I tilted my head to look up at his face. I sat on his bent thigh as he sat on the hard tile. He hadn't liked the soft couch any more than he'd liked my bed on the shuttle. His lower arms rested on my thighs and his upper arms wrapped around my shoulders, holding me close against his chest. Like always, he seemed to envelope me with his own body as if to shield me from danger.

"I know it isn't the option we all agreed to." I traced my hand over the joints of the plating on his fingers. "But I think, in the long run, Evil Ilyan's decision to ally with the Akrellians might have been the best one for us."

"Rhonda is here. Here is Rhonda's home." He lowered his head to nuzzle my hair. "Rhonda is 34's home. 34 happy."

My monster was one of few words, but he was a philosopher in his own way, boiling down the complexity of our situation into a simple, profound statement that made me feel like the most loved woman in the universe.

"You really don't mind staying here on Earth?" I worried that he would feel out of place if people stared too much at him, and on Earth, even surrounded by other extraterrestrials, he was likely to get some odd looks. Not everyone would appreciate his beauty the way I did.

"Before Rhonda, 34 restless. Hunt, kill, eat—no longer satisfy. Struggle to find reason to leave crevice. 34 not care about surviving anymore. Need something more. Not know what, until 34 catch Rhonda's scent. Then know. Need Rhonda." He tucked me closer against him. "Only need Rhonda. Nothing else important to 34."

I'll admit. I teared up at those words. Ilyan and Nirgal could wax poetic as they promised me the universe, and I felt the flutter of my heart and soul at their pretty words, but the simplistic declarations of love that Subject 34 made to me were as primal and visceral as my love for him.

I realized that each of my mates satisfied a need inside me, each of them bringing something different and exciting in its own way to my life. Though I never would have said that I needed more than one man to make me happy, and I still wouldn't claim that, together they made me so blissfully happy that I didn't believe any one man could have ever done the same for me.

That reminded me that all wasn't perfect in my own sexy version of a fairy tale. I really needed to make sure that Ilyan and Nirgal weren't killing each other, though I doubted either of them would actually hurt each other, if only because they knew it would hurt me.

Still, their divisiveness hurt me.

When I told Subject 34 about my concerns, he shrugged and told me he didn't smell blood in the air. That didn't reassure me as much as I'd hoped, and I bade him to let me up to go check on them. It felt good to have him with me as I made my way around the house in search of my other mates, my heart thudding harder as I checked each empty room.

I was near panic when I went through the entire house finding no sign of my mates. I rushed to the back door, and it slid open at my approach, the house informing me of the external temperature, humidity level, and UV intensity as I stepped outside.

I spotted color moving among the cactus garden—a bright splash of orange, and nearby, a more vivid green than the cacti themselves.

Relief washed over me as I made my way to the garden path, wending through the clusters and patches of exotic looking plants, all of which came from Earth herself, each as strange and bizarre as any alien life form.

As beautiful and intriguing as the garden was, my eyes fixed on my mates, my brows lifting in surprise as I grew closer to them.

Nirgal stood on the path near a cactus patch with a tablet in hand, the sight of it making me grin even through my worry. His fingers moved rapidly over it, entering in data as Ilyan knelt dangerously close to a whole pack of sharp spines, prodding a scanning probe into the mass of spiky plants.

He withdrew the probe and glanced at the readout that he

apparently saw on the side of it, before reciting a series of data points to Nirgal, who dutifully recorded them.

They both looked up from their work when I laughed aloud. "*What* are you two doing?"

They glanced at each other, then returned their beautiful gazes to me. "Examining these intriguing specimens," they said in unison.

I wanted to clap for joy just to see them working together, intrigued by something science-related, because I could tell that their love of knowledge and research was what had brought them together as friends in the first place.

I hoped that their love of me wouldn't tear apart the fragile bond they appeared to be reforming, and I almost wanted to retreat just to avoid that happening. Still, now I was intrigued, stepping a little closer to Nirgal as I studied Ilyan and the cactus he knelt beside.

"Be careful, honey," I said reflexively, as if he wasn't aware of the sharp spines right by his head.

He grinned at me, seeming pleased at my concern for his welfare. "If I end up wounded, would you take care of me, my queen."

Nirgal grunted and shook his head. I took that as his version of rolling his eyes. Still, he didn't respond with any negative remarks, so I considered that progress.

I crossed my arms over my chest as I mock-glared at him. "Not if you get hurt on purpose, my darling green guy. In that case, you'd have to pick all the stickies out by yourself."

"Green guy," Nirgal murmured in an amused tone.

Ilyan lifted his chin as he rose to his feet, his wings flaring with irritation. "I like the nickname my mate has given me."

"Better than Evil Ilyan, I suppose." Nirgal's wings flickered just once before returning to being tightly folded against his back.

"Oh, pumpkin, don't tease my green guy!" I smirked at Nirgal, wondering if he'd remember the nickname.

I was pretty sure I'd called him that in the past, so he was bound to have looked it up.

"Better than douche," he said to me with his own smirk.

"I personally think douche is a *perfect* nickname for you, Nirgal Mashda." Ilyan tucked his scanning probe into the pocket of his jumpsuit, then brushed his hands together even though not a speck of dirt marked his iridescent green skin.

Nirgal snorted in outrage, casting a glare at Ilyan. "And I think she gave the nickname 'Evil Ilyan' to the wrong part of you."

I held up both hands. "Please, stop being mean to each other!"

They turned to face me, grins spreading on both their faces.

"We were always mean to each other," Ilyan said, shrugging one shoulder.

Nirgal narrowed a glare at him, then returned his attention to me, nodding slowly. "Even when we *were* friends."

Oh, so it was that type of friendship. The shit-talking kind of relationship. That I could handle. I could work with that, though it would be strange and sometimes disconcerting to hear them sniping at each other all the time.

"But," I looked from one to the other, "are the two of you friends *now*?"

They looked at each other again, both flicking their wings in a way that I couldn't entirely interpret.

"I think we can get there again," Ilyan said. "I forgive you, Nirgal, for urging me to remain out of stasis until I fractured."

Nirgal's smile had completely disappeared, but a solemn expression replaced it rather than a defensive scowl. "I will find a way to make it up to you, my old friend."

"Keeping my fracture from causing any damage to our harem or our queen will go a long way towards doing that."

As Nirgal swore he would make certain of that, I swore to myself that none of them would ever find out about Evil Ilyan's treatment towards me.

Even though I'd ended up liking it to the point that I wanted him to be rough with me again—if he so happened to show up—I doubted my mates would understand or accept my reassurances as anything more than a cope.

It was probably for the best that Ilyan vowed never to retreat to the back of his mind again, so that his fracture couldn't retake control. Though I regretted not being able to truly talk to Evil Ilyan about anything involving his rebel actions, or his prior connections to the Akrellians, I most regretted that I'd ended up falling in love with him despite the emotional distance he'd kept between us. Thinking that I'd never see him again made me sad and regretful that I didn't make the most of my time with him.

I determined to not make that same mistake with my other mates. Now that we had a home of our own and plenty of privacy, we had a lot of lost time to make up for.

THIRTY-SEVEN

Our sleeping arrangement wasn't ideal, but it was the only one I could feel comfortable with, at least until Ilyan and Nirgal got along better. Perhaps they would never be okay with sleeping in the same bed with me at the same time. Honestly, it wasn't a terrible idea for all of us to have our own personal space anyway, so each of us had a room to ourselves.

Subject 34 didn't bother with his, choosing instead to sleep on the floor beside my bed in my room because he preferred the hard tile to the soft foam mattress where he felt like he was sinking. If, for whatever reason, he couldn't be in my room when he slept, he would sleep in the hallway outside my door. He didn't like being far from me, especially after being tricked by Evil Ilyan. He confessed that he was afraid I would be taken from him again.

I could cuddle with him and even fall asleep in his arms, but only if I joined him on the floor, which I didn't mind doing. He really didn't like soft furniture at all.

Nirgal and Ilyan planned to alternate their nights spent in my bed for sleep, though all three of my mates wanted to have sex with me every day, and I figured we would definitely need to set some kind of schedule after I made up for lost time with them. They would wear me out quickly otherwise.

On our first night in our new home, Nirgal, Ilyan, and I explored the kitchen, then they figured out how all the fancy appliances worked for me so that I could make them all dinner from the food that had been supplied to us by our hosts.

They watched me prepare the roast and potatoes curiously, and I even caught Nirgal making some notes on his new tablet, which made me grin.

The conversation between the three of us flowed surprisingly easily, with Subject 34 occasionally adding some short remark that demonstrated not only that he was following the conversation, but he had his own thoughts about the topics in discussion.

Nirgal and Ilyan continued to snipe at each other, obviously competing when it came to everything they did, and I had to wrestle the potato peeler appliance away from them as they fought over which one got to help me.

Despite their apparent antagonism, their constant ragging on each other took on a more playful and teasing tone as we all grew more relaxed in our new home. Subject 34 occasionally spoke up to let them know he thought they were both idiots.

As we sat down for dinner, the roast cooking phenomenally fast in the fancy high-tech oven, I looked at my little family seated around a dinner table, right here on my home soil of Earth. Each one of them was dear to me, and each of them had made my life so much better than I could have ever dreamed of. Everything that I'd been through to get to this point was so worth the end result.

Then Subject 34 scarfed down the entire roast in a few alarming bites and my Iriduans yelled at him and threw potatoes at him, and Nirgal said that it was time to move on to Subject 35, which made 34 toss the table, sending dishes flying.

Next thing I knew, all three of them were flying around the living room in a free-for-all melee. Obviously, 34 dominated the fight, but Nirgal and Ilyan were working together to flank him and gain an edge, eventually managing to drag him back to the floor where all three of them crashed with a loud thud.

I would have been screaming for them to stop, worried about their safety, if I couldn't tell that Subject 34 was only playing around. His stingers remained sheathed, his pincers never extended, and he took care not to toss my Iriduans around too hard.

Sure, they made an absolute mess in our dining room, but the cleaner robot was already mopping up potatoes and gravy as I watched my mates roughhousing.

The battle ended in a draw, mostly because 34 wasn't using his full strength or speed. If I ever needed any reassurance that he wouldn't hurt my other mates, this little fight was it. Despite the violence of their unexpected combat, my heart soared, because they were bonding in a way I hadn't hoped for so soon after settling here.

34 toppling the table had left Ilyan covered in gravy, so he made his way to the bathroom after they all picked themselves up and dusted off. I rushed to check on Nirgal, who was brushing off his suit and checking his wings. After a quick kiss that lasted far longer than I intended, I went to make sure that Ilyan wasn't too bruised up as Nirgal headed back to the refrigerator to seek an alternate meal.

I heard the shower running in the master bathroom that adjoined my room and I knocked on the door, asking him if he was alright.

"I'm not sure, Rhonda," he said, his voice sounding

strained. "I think I might be injured. Perhaps you can come in here and examine me."

Okay, I fell for it. I'm not gonna lie. I rushed into the bathroom, my heart in my throat, worried that I'd been too casual about the fight when maybe it had been more serious. Or at least had more serious consequences. Obviously 34 wasn't trying to hurt my Iriduans, but he was so much stronger than they were.

Inside the steam-filled bathroom, Ilyan stood under the shower head, water sluicing over his body, now filling out to look much healthier, lean muscle tone rippling beneath his iridescent skin as he lifted both arms to rinse out his hair.

"Where are you hurt?" I said, barely pausing to take in the gorgeous view of my handsome mate standing there wet and naked behind the foggy glass doors.

He moaned pitifully. "Everywhere. I think you need to check every inch of my body to assess my injuries."

Then he turned his face away from the showerhead, meeting my eyes with a sly grin on his lips.

Clarity struck, though some would probably say I should have seen through his ploy sooner. I thought about being mad that he worried me unnecessarily, but then he gestured with one hand for me to join him, and I threw all thoughts of punishing him for teasing me out the window.

Then I threw off my jumpsuit and pulled aside the glass door.

His skin was slippery and hot from the water temperature that made me hiss as it struck me. With a word he commanded the shower to lower the temperature to my preferred level as he pulled me against his naked body.

His erection already jutted from his groin, and my belly pinned it between us. He took advantage of this to rub it against my mound, the pressure of that hard ridge stroking over my clit. His hands roved over my skin as his lips closed over mine, cutting off my moan of pleasure.

"I want to taste you," he said when we broke the kiss long enough to catch our breaths.

Little gasps escaped me as he continued to rub his shaft between my folds to tease my swollen nub.

I clung to his slippery shoulders as he kissed his way down my body. He paused at my chest to suckle each of my breasts in turn, his tongue flicking over my nipples as my hips writhed against his lower body, driving my clit harder against his stiff erection.

"Oh yes," I said breathlessly while the water continued to rain down on us as he knelt in front of me.

His lips found my clit, sucking on it as they had on my nipples, his tongue teasing over the sensitive pearl until I was crying out with pleasure. My fingers clenched in his wet hair as his mouth worked over my clit. By the time he slipped two fingers inside my slit, I was far more slippery inside than the water had made my body.

My orgasm came swiftly, and I braced myself against the cool tile with one hand while my other shifted to grip Ilyan's shoulder. His muscles rippled under my palm as he grabbed my thigh with his free hand and pulled it over his shoulder. His mouth still on me, he pushed me back against the wall to further brace me.

His tongue replaced his fingers, licking my soaking slit, then delving inside my still convulsing passage. The fingers he'd been thrusting inside me moved to my throbbing clit to rub it in teasing circles until I came a second time, my body jerking against the wall, pinned to it by his head between my legs.

His wings battered my calf with his own excitement, flinging water droplets everywhere, but my eyes were closed with ecstasy, so I barely noticed as they spattered over me, competing with the downward fall of the shower spray.

He ate his fill, leaving me begging for mercy, before finally releasing my leg. He rose gracefully to his feet, his eyes nearly black as he caught me by the shoulders. I leaned in to kiss him, but he spun me to face the wall before our lips met.

His hands slipped around my waist as he nipped and kissed my shoulder and neck. He slid them upwards to cup and massage my breasts as he rubbed his erection against my lower back and buttocks. His cerci came into play then, vibrating as one stroked over my clit and the other slipped between my legs.

I gasped as the clawed tip of it parted my folds, recalling what his fracture had done to me. More of my slick dampened my entrance at the memory.

He nipped the delicate skin at my neck as his hands moved to my arms, sliding down them to capture my wrists. He lifted my hands and pressed them against the tile, his body crowding me against the hard surface of the wall.

His cercus pushed further inside me, vibrating against my sensitive inner flesh as it sank deeper.

"The things I want to do to you," he said in a guttural growl as he nipped my shoulder hard enough to get a yelp from me. "I should not even think them." His hands pinned mine to the tile as I shivered at the rough sound of his voice. "But if I had you at my mercy, my queen... ah, the *things* I would do to your sweet body."

As if to punctuate his point, his cercus thrust deeper, the sharp tip dangerously close to scraping my inner walls. But it wasn't that risk that made my inner muscles tighten around it. I recalled very well what the barbs currently rippling within me felt like when fully extended.

To my relief—or perhaps disappointment, since I still felt confused about the pleasure-pain experience of them scraping me—he withdrew his cercus without extending his barbs. His feet pushed mine further apart as he shifted his hips against my buttocks so that his erection traced my crack downwards until it slipped between my legs.

His hands pushed harder against mine as he buried his length inside me in one hard thrust. We both moaned loud enough to compete against the sound of the shower running.

"Ah, Rhonda," he said, peppering my neck with kisses. "You feel so good. The way I want to claim you, the way I want to play with your beautiful body, makes me think Nirgal is right." He thrust hard into me, rocking my hips forward until my mound bumped against the tile. His cercus still toyed with my clit, the other now sliding around my waist towards my back entrance.

"Right about what?" I managed to gasp as he pumped into me again.

My nipples tightened further as his weight settled against my back, bringing him closer and giving him more leverage to drive deep.

"Maybe you gave the nickname Evil Ilyan to the wrong part of me." He bit my shoulder, causing me to cry out in surprise more than pain at the unexpected sting of his teeth.

At the same time, he began to pound into me from behind, his hands leaving mine to stroke down my body, rubbing all over my water-slicked naked flesh as he screwed me hard. All the while, one cercus teased my clit and the other poked exploringly at my back hole.

The clawed tip delved inside that tight entrance just as I climaxed, and my orgasm seemed to trigger his. His seed shot into me with strong movements of his shaft against my convulsing inner walls.

"I hope you can forgive me, my queen." His voice was muffled as he pressed his lips to the tender spot on my neck.

"Tell me to stop if I ever make you uncomfortable, and I will. I swear it. I can never hurt you, Rhonda. Not unless you want me to."

I shivered at the promise in the tone of his voice as he said those last words. Then I grinned against the tile, my heart still pounding and my breath still panting out of me. "I don't recall saying anything about stopping."

He moaned against my neck, then inhaled deeply before pressing a kiss to my throbbing pulse. His cercus probed a little deeper into my rosette. "I researched human sexuality after... some time ago. I learned about the things your people do to each other for pleasure. There are so many I want to experiment with, so many I want to try, and you are the only subject that I desire, my queen. Will you let me experiment on you?"

I tilted my hips backwards, spreading my cheeks wider in the process even as my buttocks pushed against his lower body.

"*Hell* yes!" I said with conviction, then a long moan left me as his cercus delved deeper into my back hole. His shaft remained stiff inside me even though I could feel the wet slide of his seed down my inner thighs.

"I'm so glad you said that," he purred in my ear as he pushed deeper into my rosette—a place I'd only let Michael enter on the rare occasions where I was drunk enough to be relaxed so it didn't hurt as much.

Right now, the discomfort was negligible compared to my excitement and the pleasure I felt as he began to thrust inside my tender inner passage again.

I would be walking funny in the morning, I suspected, but I didn't give a damn. I'd let Ilyan experiment on my body all night long.

THIRTY-EIGHT

As pleasurable as our time together was, my mates and I weren't allowed to simply bask in our happiness. We had so much to do to assimilate into the community in order to leave the shielded portion of the settlement. Not only were there tons of digital paperwork to fill out, counseling to attend, educational seminars to endure, but we were also offered job training for potential future employment.

My Iriduans were initially offended at the idea that they needed any more training, least of all coming from a species they considered inferior—yes, they remained arrogant, and I doubted I'd ever change that and wasn't even sure I wanted to. However, their desire for more knowledge overrode their initial feelings of superiority, and they ended up diving wholeheartedly into various studies regarding Earth and humanity.

That they would become research scientists seemed a given, and they already had employers lining up to hire them, even in this isolated settlement. Because of the diverse knowledgebase and skill set of this asylum settlement, the results of the work performed here was used all over the world as well as in other places in the galaxy. The same held true whether it was within the agricultural domes, the medical centers—where geneticists were eager to hire my mates, the educational centers—where many of the asylum seekers shared knowledge of their people and worlds, the food production centers, and even the art and media center—where I was offered a dream job, and I would finally be able to support myself with my creativity.

I was intimidated at first, especially since the only real evidence my new employers had of my skill was a handful of sketches that I'd made while a captive. Subject 34 had managed to save all the ones he'd taken from my sketchbook, stowing them somewhere under his plates during all the crap we'd been through since then.

It had been 34 who shared the sketches when one of the directors of the art center had dared to approach him in the intake center and asked if he would consent to modeling for some of their projects. I didn't even know he still had them until he returned home from the intake center and told me that the people who smelled like my art stuff wanted me to "do art" for them.

My initial project was to paint some murals around the settlement to aid with morale and improve the aestheticism of the various structures, and I leapt into the challenge whole-heartedly. My mates admired my sketches and the digital canvasses I created for references.

But what they really found intriguing was a canvas I felt inspired to do for our own home.

It was a gritty alien landscape. One I'd never seen before in person, but still very familiar to me. Once, I'd tried to paint this vision from one of my most surreal dreams, and I'd failed.

Now, the paint flowed from my brush onto the canvas as if it were doing all the work for me. I knew exactly why I'd failed before. I'd tried to create something I didn't have yet in my life.

I'd tried to create a vision of hope and anticipation, even in my darkest dream, when I had lost both and had yet to find them again.

Now, mixing the colors was easy—all the shades of orange and beautiful blue, the different shades of black, the vivid spot of green. I knew the colors I wanted to see on that canvas well now and could mix them in my sleep.

I had almost finished the canvas when I heard my mates return home from the medical research center. All three of them spent much of their time there now since Subject 34 was also convinced to help out humanity and the Akrellians in return for our sanctuary here. His ability to create beneficial compounds not found in nature was priceless to the researchers.

I left the porch where I'd found the best light to paint when the house informed me that they'd returned. When I entered the living room, my Iriduans were fighting over a large shipping box. As I sighed and crossed my arms over my chest, they dropped the box and came to me at the same time. I considered it progress that they didn't fight over who got to kiss me first.

Once all our greetings were complete, my two Iriduans returned to the box while Subject 34 and I looked on in bemusement. They got the package open, crowing in victory as they pulled out bags filled with colorful fabrics and several mystery boxes.

Another fight ensued over one of the bags, and Nirgal ended up successfully wrestling it away from Ilyan. Then they grabbed all their prizes—which they refused to explain to me, despite my repeated questions—and raced to their respective rooms.

Ilyan was the first to return, and he had changed from his jumpsuit into khaki slacks and a custom-made, button-down shirt that had slits for his wings. He wore loafers on his feet with no visible socks.

He was adorable as he strutted back and forth, showing off his new clothes, and I had to hide my grin at the fact that the outfit was remarkably similar to one his favorite character—a human, no less—wore on the old detective show we watched together in the evenings.

I understood now why they'd been so excited about the package. We'd been wearing jumpsuits for a lifetime, it seemed, and my Iriduans didn't like that style of outfit much, though many of the residents of this settlement preferred the simplicity of the uniform-like one piece. We'd all placed orders through the shopping app provided by the house. It even showed us on a full length mirror an overlay of the outfit over our reflections to help with our selection. I suspected some of my clothing was in that shipping box, but since they'd taken it all, I'd retrieve it later.

Both Ilyan and Nirgal hadn't wanted me around when they'd picked out their new clothes because they wanted to "surprise" me.

I was vocally admiring Ilyan's new outfit when Nirgal strolled into the living room, wearing skinny jeans that clung very nicely to his leanly muscled legs and small but shapely ass. My mouth went dry as I stared at him, noting the leather biker jacket over white tee-shirt and the heavy boots on his feet. His black hair had grown enough to curve over his brow and cast appealing shadows there. He still felt self-conscious about how short it was though. The black striping on his visible skin looked like edgy tattoos.

As much as they ragged on each other, Ilyan never, ever made fun of Nirgal for his hair or his stripes. That was one of the best indicators that they were friends. As wicked as my green guy could get, he wouldn't be downright cruel on purpose to those close to him. He knew Nirgal's feelings about these topics and so avoided them.

He did, however, have no problem mocking Nirgal's new clothes.

"What are those trousers?" Ilyan asked, eyeing Nirgal's jeans with an expression of disgust that was completely transparent.

He was totally going to buy himself a pair. I could already tell.

Nirgal swept his hand down his body like a game show hostess. "They are called 'jeans,' and they are a marvelous human invention. They show off my superior body very nicely for my mate."

Ilyan huffed, but I could see that he felt a bit deflated since his khaki pants were on the baggier side. His wings sagged as he glared at Nirgal. "I suppose it's appropriate they're called genes, since they make it clear you need new ones. Did you inherit those scrawny legs from your mother or the srenrikas she mated with to spawn you?"

Subject 34 made his amused chittering sound even as I choked back laughter, swallowing it to shake my head at Ilyan.

Once I managed to speak without laughter in my tone, I chided him. "Now, Ilyan, don't make fun of Nirgal's body! He has *very* sexy legs."

Nirgal's chin lifted as he glared at Ilyan. "You hear that, pond-skimmer? I have *sexy* legs." He struck a little pose that had me giggling, though I covered my mouth to muffle the sound.

"My legs are far nicer than yours," Ilyan said with a huff, crossing his arms over his chest. "But I don't need to flaunt them like a mate-baiter."

Nirgal's glower told me Ilyan had dropped a stinging insult, though I didn't always understand their cutting remarks to each other. Their reactions gave me context.

I held up both hands before Nirgal could reply, because even though their sniping was the norm, they were both looking less excited about their new clothing than they had been when they'd come out to show it off.

I didn't want that at all!

"All right, no more insults from either of you! You both look extremely handsome, especially with your new outfits. I love them, and the styles definitely flatter your beautiful bodies, though you both will always look best when you are naked in my bed."

I wanted them both to be happy, and I especially cherished the moments when my mates—displaced from their lives and careers and their entire world and culture—found things to love about their new home and family and adopted culture.

My words definitely had the desired effect of heading off their insults, but it also got their attention focused in a very different direction and both sets of eyes dilated as they switched their focus from glaring at each other to staring hungrily at me.

"34 look best," my monster mate said with conviction, waving a lower hand as if brushing aside the other two. "Not need clothes like fancy soft meats." He tapped his chitin-plated chest with his upper hand as he crossed his lower arms. "Already handsome."

Before any of us could respond, 34 followed this up with sweeping me up in his arms and racing away from the other two, carrying me to my room as I laughingly protested.

My Iriduans were not as amused.

"Hey! Bring our mate back, you poacher!" Ilyan shouted.

"I *knew* I should have dumped your test tube, you queen

snatcher!" Nirgal yelled, his voice closer as both males followed on our heels.

34 slammed my bedroom door in their faces, ignoring their angry pounding as he locked it and then tossed me on the bed.

As 34 caught my ankles and tugged me to the edge of the bed, his facial plates open so I could see the predatory look in his eyes as they fixed on me, the door panel vibrated from my Iriduans trying to break in.

"34 hungry, Rhonda." He grinned wickedly. "Time to eat."

I would have to return to admiring my Iriduans' outfits soon, but there was no reason we couldn't take a snack break. I would make it up to them.

I looked forward to it!

THIRTY-NINE

I lay in bed one night, a handful of weeks later, cradled in Nirgal's arms in post-coital bliss. My breaths were only just growing even again as I traced the markings on his chest with a fingertip. His seed slicked my inner thighs as it slowly leaked from me in the wake of him withdrawing his shaft.

"It's a good thing I can't get pregnant," I said with a sleepy grin as I dropped a kiss on one orange pec that twitched beneath the brush of my lips.

Suddenly, Nirgal stiffened, then shot up in the bed. He stared down at me with an alarmed expression widening his eyes that raised my own alarms.

"Blighted silk!" His eyes shifted like he was making calculations in his head as he looked at the comforter covering our lower bodies. "How could I forget?"

His gaze rose to meet mine, his eyes no longer dilated but still a darker sapphire blue that showed more of his emotion, rather than his usual icy blue.

"Nirgal," I said in a worried tone that did nothing to convey how much my heart was pounding as I sat up and clutched the comforter to my chest. "I *can't* get pregnant, right? I mean, you guys did all kinds of invasive things to my body, so surely, you made sure I couldn't accidentally get pregnant... *didn't* you?"

He didn't like it when I brought up our sordid past, and since I knew he regretted it, I tried not to, but sometimes, like right now, we needed to discuss what had happened. Especially since his current panicked demeanor was giving me a very bad feeling.

"The sterilization was only temporary. We didn't plan on breeding you because of your... because it wouldn't be ideal, as per protocol, but we decided to keep the option open, so did not permanently sterilize you. It's been...."

He ran his hand over his short hair, turning his face away from me, though I could tell by the twitching of his wings, one of them still bent beneath his body, that he was agitated.

"It's been too long since you've been given birth control!"

I closed my eyes, swallowing thickly as I fell back on the bed. I covered my face with both hands, my mind racing as I ran some of my own calculations.

My last physical exam was at the intake center, not long after we first arrived here. I should have had a period since then but hadn't yet. I hadn't thought much of it because I hadn't had periods while in captivity, probably because of the birth control method the Iriduans had used on me.

In fact, the thought of having a child had been so far from my mind with all the chaos of my life lately that this was the first time I'd really spent longer than a brief moment to consider it.

Shit.

"Do you think I could be pregnant, Nirgal?" I lowered my hands from my face, opening my eyes to meet his, now that he'd turned towards me, staring down at me with stark guilt in his expression.

"It is possible." I wasn't sure from the tone of his voice whether this bothered him or not. Despite his expression, he sounded neutral. "Rhonda, if you are… I swear to you, I'll make sure your health isn't put in jeopardy! No matter what you decide to do, I will support your decision, as long as you are safe."

I had to swallow through a dry throat several times before I could speak again. "Whose do you think it would be?"

His expression blanked, his eyes lightening to a cooler blue. It was his defensive mode. Whatever he felt about the topic in discussion, he didn't want me to read it in his expression.

"Is that important to you, my queen?"

Again, his tone remained neutral, not giving away how he felt about any of this.

I sat up again, not even bothering to pull the cover up to conceal my naked breasts, my nipples still tender and tingling from his earlier attentions.

"If you're asking whether I would prefer a child from one of you over the other, then no, that would never be important to me. I'd love any child I created with my mates."

The fervency of my own words surprised me. It wasn't like there wasn't another option than having an alien hybrid child at my age, even if I was pregnant. Yet the thought of a life growing inside me that reflected the love and commitment I had with my mates suddenly sparked the maternal instinct I'd denied in myself for so long while I'd been married to Michael.

The more I thought about it, the more I realized that I wasn't worried that I might be pregnant. My concern became a hope that I feared would be dashed in the morning after a trip to the medical center for another full scan.

Nirgal watched my face with a tenseness in his lean frame that told me he remained uncertain about my feelings or what direction they might take. His tension also told me he was likely blaming himself again for what he'd done to me in that research facility.

I'd awakened his conscience in that place, and now it never seemed to leave him alone. He dealt with a lot of guilt that I wished I could alleviate, but no matter how happy he made me, how content I was in our life, he still held his own actions against himself. Someday, I hoped he could forgive himself the way I already forgave him.

"What if it's Subject 34's child?" he asked in a careful tone. "Has he given you his seed at any point?"

"Can he really impregnate me? Despite how different we are?" I was grateful that Subject 34 wasn't sleeping in my room tonight, and we were talking low enough that I didn't think he could hear it through our door.

He nodded, his eyes never leaving my face. "He can. He was designed to hybridize with Iriduan females and likely human females as well. That was Ilyan's decision, by the way. I considered removing the athraxius hybrid's ability to reproduce sexually, but my directors said to leave it alone." He shrugged one shoulder. "They wanted it to be an option to breed a better iteration if we couldn't design one. Obviously, my 33 previous failures did not impress my leadership enough for them to have faith that I could capture the wind in a bottle more than once."

I barely heard the rest of his explanation, too focused on the words, "he can." I wasn't horrified at the thought of having a little scorpion hybrid baby like I probably should be. I loved my monster man so much that I didn't shy away from the thought of giving him an adorable little monster baby. We would just have to make sure we could control its appetite, because my man was a voracious eater, and our grocery bills were ridiculous because of it. We'd go bankrupt trying to feed two of them.

The slow smile that crossed my face appeared to reassure Nirgal and his shoulders relaxed, his wings settling at his back.

"I would gladly have any of your children." I pushed down the hope that swelled inside me.

I knew the statistics. I knew my odds of having healthy children decreased significantly at my age—or they did, back before advanced alien medical technology had been shared with humans. Now, we all benefited from "rejuv" treatments that turned back the clock on our biology, repairing damaged cells and DNA and replacing all those biological factors that time and age stole from us, vastly extending our lifespans.

Maybe those treatments even returned our fertility. In fact, Nirgal had mentioned something about my fertility in the very beginning. Something about my "ovaries" and "breeding" that I had forgotten until now.

Hope was a dangerous emotion, especially when it dug up old dreams out of the graveyard of your mind where you thought they were safely buried. It had taken a lot to bury my dreams of having children of my own, but I'd prioritized Michael's wishes over those dreams, allowing him to convince me that children would just be a nuisance in our lives, and that we weren't the kind of people who would be a good fit for parenthood.

"Rhonda?" Nirgal stroked my hair away from my face. "Are you okay?"

I turned towards him, throwing my arms around him to squeeze him in a tight hug. My eyes teared up as I thought about what I might—or might not—learn tomorrow. I almost wished I didn't have this conversation, because now, the idea was in my head, the zombie dream resurrected to shamble around my brain until someone either shot it in the head or brought it back to full life.

God, I hoped it was the latter!

FORTY

All three of my mates sat with me, crowding the examining room, as I waited for the results of my scan and blood tests.

Nirgal and Ilyan looked very sexy in their uniform biosuits, though their expressions were as nervous as mine probably was. Subject 34 kept his facial plating closed, which was not typical when he didn't feel threatened.

Ilyan and Nirgal had been cautiously excited when we discussed the possibility of me being pregnant this morning. Subject 34 had closed up—literally—at the suggestion that any child I might be carrying could be his.

The Akrellian physician walked into the room, nodding at my mates in greeting, familiar with them now, since they came into contact during their time working at the center. Then he turned to face me, and I struggled to read his expression. My stomach dropped as I noted that he wasn't smiling. Perhaps he was gearing himself up to disappoint me.

He skirted around my mates to stand in front of me, asking me a few questions that I answered in a shaking voice, too nervous now to hide it.

Then he did smile toothily, but it was too cautious for my comfort. "You *are* pregnant, Rhonda, though it is still very early."

I exhaled the breath I'd been holding, feeling lightheaded as I dropped my head back on my chair, my eyes closing.

"I'm sorry if this isn't the news you wanted to hear," the doctor said, laying a compassionate hand on my shoulder.

I lifted my head and opened my eyes, sucking in a deep breath before answering. "No, it is." I glanced from one of my mates to the other. "It really is!"

His smile widened as he nodded. "That's good then, because your test results look promising, and the scan showed two healthy implantations that are developing normally—for hybrids."

My brows lifted and my eyes widened with my shock as all my mates froze.

"Two?" Ilyan asked, raising a hand to run it through his verdant hair, mussing the usual smooth length of it with his agitation.

"Fraternal twins, as the humans say," the doctor answered him with a glance towards me. "It's still very early in the pregnancy, so we can't be entirely certain, but we believe from initial scans that one of them is the offspring of Subject 34 and the other an Iriduan-human hybrid."

The doctor wasn't a fan of referring to my mate as a "subject" but my monster had taken that name quite proudly, and had no intention of changing it for a less "objectifying" moniker.

Believe me, we'd tried to convince him to take on a different name, and we even made several good suggestions, but he wasn't having it. As far as he was concerned, he was Subject 34. 34 for short. Whenever he dug in his heels, the discussion was over.

Right now, he twitched at the news as if someone had hit him with a cattle prod, making a chitter-growl sound that I hadn't heard him utter since we left the research facility.

My happiness at this incredible news dimmed a bit at 34's unexpectedly negative response to the idea of me having his child. I still couldn't see his face, and all his defenses were up as he moved to stand as far from the rest of us as possible in the tight confines of the exam room.

The doctor shot several nervous glances at him before returning his attention to me. "I'd like to discuss this further with you, but I can see that the news has come as... some surprise. Would you like me to give you and your mates some time to talk alone before we continue?"

I nodded quickly, though I was eager to hear the rest of the doctor's information. Something was up with Subject 34. He'd given me his seed, so why was he so freaked out at the thought of me having his child?

I was crushed at the thought that he might not want it. He certainly hadn't seemed happy about it this morning, and now his response was even more pronounced.

The doctor left the room and Nirgal and Ilyan flanked me, each placing a hand on my shoulders as we all looked at Subject 34.

"You're not happy about this, are you, 34?" I couldn't hide the hurt in my voice, and both my Iriduans squeezed my shoulder reassuringly as they glowered at 34.

"34 seed hurt family." All four of his fists clenched, the tips of his stingers poking out from behind him as if he felt threatened.

"Giving me your seed didn't hurt us." I shook my head as I looked from Ilyan to Nirgal, then back to 34. "I'm happy that I'm finally going to get to be a mom! And Ilyan and Nirgal have already told you that they want to be dads. Why would you think getting me pregnant would be a bad thing?"

He shifted his attention between the three of us, his defensive stance not relaxing. "Rhonda not swell with seed from fancy mates. 34 think safe to give seed too."

My mouth gaped as I stared at him, finally comprehending his words. "You didn't think you could get me pregnant? You thought I was still sterile?"

He crossed his upper arms over his chest, his lower arms still clenched into fists. He nodded once, short and abrupt.

I blinked back tears, my lashes fluttering madly to keep them from breaking loose. Still, I already felt that I wouldn't be able to hold back the waterworks for long. "Why did you...," I struggled to speak, feeling the sob building in my throat as I lifted a hand to my mouth, "why give me your seed at all, 34, if you didn't want a baby with me?"

His wings flicked with distress he rarely showed as he saw my reaction and realized that he was hurting me. My Iriduans weren't happy about it either. Ilyan stroked his hand over my back and Nirgal brushed my hair away from my face that was growing damp despite my best efforts to keep the tears at bay.

"34 give seed because fancy mates give. Not want to be left out."

I couldn't hold back the sob anymore, shaking my head as I turned my face away from him. I tried to hide it with my hands as Ilyan pulled me close and Nirgal snapped something at Subject 34 that I didn't hear in my own distress. Only the coldness of his voice registered. I hadn't heard him speak to 34 like that since the control chip was in 34's brain.

"Tell her why you fear your own offspring," Ilyan said with a lot more calm than Nirgal was displaying.

I lifted my head from his chest in surprise, sniffling as I

rubbed the tears from my eyes. Nirgal had Subject 34 uncharacteristically cornered and cowering away from the smaller male as he lashed him with cold words about hurting his mate. The accusation seemed to injure 34 more than the control chip ever had.

34 looked at me, his facial plates still closed. "34 seed kill. Like 34. Kill everyone. Maybe even family."

FORTY-ONE

My stomach knotted with nerves as I sat waiting at the air center. The blast of desert heat that filtered through the climate control shield whenever a shuttle landed or departed wasn't what left me sweating. The babies growing inside me weren't the cause of my nausea today, though they had given me plenty of it in the last month since I'd learned I was pregnant.

Subject 34 paced beside me, an uncomfortable distance between us that wasn't physical. We had yet to resolve the primary issue that was driving a wedge between us when I'd always believed we were inseparable.

He still feared that me having his baby put us all at risk. Most of all me, since I was his primary concern. I still insisted that we would find a way to make things work, even if our baby was a little on the dangerous side. I refused to believe that the child would be malicious. Even as an adult, Subject 34 didn't kill out of malice. There would be no reason for his child to do so.

My doctor had also expressed similar concerns to Subject 34, even going so far as to worry that the fetus might end up harming its twin during gestation, purely out of reflex. He'd offered an injection that would abort that pregnancy while leaving the other intact.

I'd screamed at him and threw a few things after that suggestion. I'm not sure what, but they had been heavy enough to leave dents in the walls of the exam room as my doctor fled. My Iriduans hustled me out of the medical center and stuffed me full of food so that I was a little less emotional and infuriated, because I was fricking starving all the time now, and no matter how much I ate, this pregnancy and the resulting nausea were causing me to lose weight rather than gain it.

My weight loss made 34 upset enough to insist on feeding me, despite my anger at him for the hurt his rejection of our child made me feel. Even though he didn't want our child, he wouldn't allow me to waste away as it grew inside me. Still, the intimacy of the process had completely disappeared, and I mourned its loss as he gave me his fluid as soon as my lips closed around his shaft and made no move to take things any further than that.

It was almost like he was angry at *me* for insisting on having this child, and I feared that our mutual hurt and anger was destroying our relationship.

That was how we came to be here in the air center on this sweltering day.

I was deep in my thoughts, sitting so close to my precious mate, smelling his heady scent, though fortunately not the aroused version that left me shaking with need. If he was affected by my nearness, he didn't show it, but that wasn't necessarily unusual. His body language was often subtle. The fact that he kept his face covered more often than not told me plenty about his feelings lately.

Then he suddenly stiffened, a growl emanating from him as he froze, facing the air center arrival terminal.

He'd sensed them before I saw them, but they weren't easy to miss as they made their way towards us.

Subject 34's stingers ejected, coiling on either side of him as his wings flared. His pincers extended and spread open as his body sank into a fighting stance.

I jumped to my feet and put a staying hand on his shoulder as I saw the little girl at her mother's side, the fingers of one of her four arms in her mouth as she eyed us nervously.

Subject 34 barely relaxed beneath my touch as the small family approached us, the hulking male—looking similar to my monster, but not the same—stepped between his mate and her two children and my mate, his own wings flaring as his stingers extended. His pincers were larger than 34's as they extended and spread but 34 was just as tall and big as he was.

"Daddy!" the little girl said, trying to peer around her father's chitin-covered leg even though his lower arm pushed her back behind him. "I wanna see! He has stingers too! I wanna see, Daddy!"

"Thrax," Claire said from behind her mate, catching the girl's upper hand as she juggled her sleeping toddler in her other arm, "I'm gonna take Ava to get a fruit juice at the bar." She smiled at me, her facial piercings catching the light with the change in her expression. "Would you like to join us, Rhonda? We can let the boys," she glanced wryly at her mate, then mine, "get better acquainted."

Then she scanned the surrounding area, which had emptied out of all travelers save us. "There's plenty of room here for it."

I instantly felt a kinship with this woman, even though she'd been a rival in my head since I'd learned about her connection to Ilyan. As long as she didn't ask to see him—or demand retribution for what he'd done to her and Thrax—we would get along really well. I sensed in her the same kind of creative fire that I felt within myself, though she chose to wear her creativity openly in her style. I loved the confidence of her self-expression, and wished I possessed it myself.

Perhaps then I would wear my hair in neon colors, pierce my face and body, wear large gauges in my ears and dress like a goth princess. I certainly could appreciate the aesthetic as she brought the look together expertly.

I felt rather dowdy and mundane in my simple sundress with the splash of colorful desert flowers and succulents. Still, she complimented me on the design and seemed impressed when I told her I'd painted the pattern and uploaded the image to our clothing app to be printed on my dress.

We made our way to the refreshment bar in the air center with me casting worried glances back at the two males who still faced each other off, their stances defensive and threatening.

"They'll work it out," Claire reassured me with a broad grin. "Thrax is way too thrilled to meet someone like himself to put your mate in the hospital. I promise!"

"I'm worried that Subject 34 won't be as welcoming," I confessed as we stopped at the bar.

Claire bent to ask Ava what she wanted to drink.

"I want to order for myself!" the adorable little girl insisted, her chubby lower hands planted on her hips while her upper hands extended, her fingers grasping for the menu tablet.

Claire laughed and shook her head. "She's so independent! Won't let me do anything for her!"

"Well," I gestured to the sleeping toddler held against her in her other arm, all four of his arms clutching his mother's billowy black shirt in his sleep. "You do have your hands full."

Claire smiled beatifically as she stroked her free hand over her son's silky hair. "He wore himself out on the shuttle ride here, trying to look out all the windows simultaneously." She chuckled, then kissed her son's head.

Then she turned her attention back to me. "Thrax is tough," Claire said reassuringly after handing Ava the tablet. "It takes a lot to hurt him, though I don't doubt your mate is capable of making him sting."

She studied the two males as I did, my attention shifting between them and little Ava, whose tongue stuck out with concentration as she swiped on the tablet.

To my relief, both the males seemed to relax, their pincers snapping closed and retracting almost simultaneously as 34 straightened out of his fighting stance.

Whatever Thrax was saying to him seemed to be working to calm Subject 34 down.

I breathed a heavy sigh of relief, then glanced at Claire and saw her watching me, a thoughtful expression on her face.

"I don't hold any ill will towards your mate. Neither of us do."

Her words caught me off guard as I quickly glanced at Subject 34 and Thrax who were now slowly circling each other, but more in an examining kind of way than an "about to kill each other" way.

Then I realized she wasn't talking about 34, my gaze snapping back to her face. "I... thank you for saying that. I'll admit I was worried you'd want vengeance."

She shook her head slowly. "I've come to realize that some people aren't necessarily evil but are an unfortunate product of their upbringing. The Iriduans have a *terrible* upbringing! It gives me a lot of sympathy for them, despite the bad things they often do. It also gives me even more respect for those who can break free from the programming."

She regarded me with a wisdom in her eyes that seemed unusual for someone so young. "Ilyan never thought he was a monster. He believed that his actions were justified, perhaps even heroic, as long as he was working towards the 'greater good'. Understanding that puts things into perspective, I think. Sometimes I ask myself how far I would go, how much I'd be willing to do, if my own family and way of life was at stake. I still haven't been able to answer that, and I hope I never have to find out."

I swallowed the lump of emotion in my throat, struggling to form the words to express my gratitude for her understanding. "I know exactly what you mean, and I appreciate your under-standing. I really do!" I watched Ava finish her order, then hand the tablet back to her mom, seeming so mature for a child who couldn't be more than seven or so. "I also really appreciate you making the trip here to talk some sense into my mate and introduce him to your precious children so he can see that they're not...."

I trailed off as I met Ava's curious dark eyes as she listened avidly to my words. I didn't want to say the word "killers" in front of this clearly innocent child.

Claire shrugged off my words with a bright smile. "I have to admit that coming here was definitely Thrax's idea first. When he found out there was another hybrid like himself, nothing would stop him from making this trip to meet your 34."

My stomach chose that moment to growl in demand, even though I'd stuffed myself for breakfast and 34 had also sated my hunger hours before breakfast, when I woke in the middle of the night in search of a snack to fill the gaping emptiness in my belly.

I covered my stomach with both hands, my cheeks burning with embarrassment.

Claire smiled ruefully as she glanced down at my stomach. "I hear you're carrying twins. I imagine you'll spend most of your pregnancy eating non-stop. I recommend high calorie, high fat foods. You can't treat this like a regular, human preg-nancy. I also had to get vitamin injections because even fortifying my meals wasn't enough to provide all the nutrition I needed during my pregnancies. I can give your doctor all the information from my own physician that will be useful for you."

"I have to find a new doctor, I think." I took the menu tablet that she handed me, as Ava's fruit juice rolled out of the kitchen on the conveyor belt of the bar, the cylindrical glass sealed to prevent spills. "I'm pretty sure I threatened the life of my current one. I can't remember exactly what I said, but I was angry. Ever since then, he's been very formal and uncomfortable with me."

Claire shook her head with a commiserating expression. "Your emotions are going to be a complete mess during your pregnancy, though they should stabilize in the last trimester, although you'll feel," she glanced down at Ava, who still watched us curiously as she collected her juice from the conveyor, then she turned slightly away from her daughter as if to impart some secret she didn't want little ears to overhear, "in *need* all the time, if you know what I mean." Her voice was lowered so that I had to lean forward to hear her words.

I nodded in understanding. That part of my pregnancy already seemed to be happening. I'd worried that my mates would end up wearing me out, but during this hormonal chaos of my pregnancy, I had more than enough desire for them to keep them busy.

Claire helpfully pointed out some of the best foods to satisfy the gnawing hunger in my belly and recommended I order all of them, even though it was a ton of food.

"Has Ilyan explained the athraxius biology?" she asked curiously once I'd entered my order and set the menu back on its stand on the bar. "About how they only reproduce once, through parthogenesis, and the parent is left weakened so the offspring often will kill and consume them."

I sighed heavily as I leaned on the bar. "He did. In extensive detail. *Minute*, extensive detail."

I swear, Ilyan was getting almost as bad as Subject 34 when it came to worrying about this baby's impact on my body. He trotted out horror story after horror story about the parent species that Subject 34's DNA came from. I think he'd almost convinced himself that my doctor was right about things.

Only Nirgal remained optimistic, but I think that was only because he knew how important this was to me. If my determination wavered at all, I feared he'd stand with my other two mates.

"He's scared," I added, defending him as I always would, even when I disagreed with him. "I think they all are. He worries that the toll on my body will end up being too much for me to recover from, even with the rejuv treatments."

"Mama," Ava piped up, her lips pink from the juice she was drinking through a spout that popped up from the lid of the cylinder, "can I go see the pretty picture?"

Her lower hand pointed to a mural that I'd been painting behind the welcome desk. It was still unfinished, but I'd made significant progress, despite the challenges of my pregnancy.

Claire noticed the mural and made an admiring sound. "That's gorgeous! I don't remember seeing that painting the last time I visited Area 51."

"I haven't finished it yet," I said with a flattered smile, "but I appreciate the compliment. It's funny you still call it Area 51. Most of the residents call it Groom Lake Settlement now."

Claire looked at me with surprise. "You painted that? You really do have talent! I love the way you play with colors and patterns while maintaining the realism of the subject." She eyed my dress again. "If you are ever looking for a job, I would love to have you design some fabric patterns for my clothing line!"

"You paint good," Ava agreed, staring up at me with wide black eyes. "Can you teach me to paint?"

"Ava," Claire said in a patient tone, "why don't you go over to the desk and ask the attendant bot if you can look at the painting closer?" As Ava's expression brightened, Claire added a warning. "No touching though, okay. Miss Rhonda has worked very hard to create that lovely picture, so you don't want your dirty fingers to mess it up."

Ava agreed solemnly, then broke from us to rush to the welcome desk with flattering excitement to get a better look at my mural. I grinned as I watched the little girl address the welcome bot with all four arms behind her back in a very formal pose. She was so much like any other innocent little child that even with four arms, she didn't appear to be the monster my mate feared his child would be.

My gaze returned to the boy still conked out on Claire's shoulder. He looked as sweet and innocent as her daughter.

"How do I convince Subject 34 that his baby won't hurt me, or anyone else?"

Claire pressed a kiss to her son's head, then glanced over at Thrax and 34, who now appeared to be talking, their movements eerily staccato—more insect-like than humanoid—but they seemed companionable at this point. Neither looked as defensive.

"Maybe *you* won't be the one to convince him," Claire said thoughtfully, stroking a hand over her son's hair.

FORTY-TWO

Claire and Thrax's visit marked a shift in Subject 34's attitude towards my pregnancy, which in turn brought us closer together again. Now, he was excited, anticipating the thought of being a dad and no longer spouting doom and gloom about how dangerous his offspring would be.

Sure, both Thrax's children possessed lethal venom and stingers, but they had learned not to use them to harm anyone unless they had to defend themselves. Claire and Thrax gave us tons of advice and even some instructional videos on how to deal with our newborn if he reflexively stung.

My new doctor was also more positive about the pregnancy and even showed eagerness to oversee the birth of such an unusual hybrid. With Claire's medical information, she was better able to design a meal plan for me to keep me from being too drained for both my own health and my other baby's growth. Of course, Subject 34 was a big part of that plan, and to my relief, his new attitude about this pregnancy brought back his desire to make the most of feeding me.

That was a relief because I felt that "need" Claire had

mentioned all the time. I pounced on my mates at every opportunity, and they alternated their days off so that at least one of them was always home to attend to me. They really were treating me like a queen, even though I insisted on returning the favor, uncomfortable with the experience of being given anything I wanted with nothing expected in return. Michael had never done that for me. Every gift, every nice gesture, every dime spent on me came with strings attached.

Life went far more smoothly after Subject 34 and I bid farewell to Claire and Thrax, who couldn't visit for very long since Claire had a major fashion event to attend in New York. I didn't pay much attention to the world beyond our little settlement, but I did consider her offer to design fabrics for her clothing label. It would be an honor to know that my art decorated one of the most popular up-and-coming designers to hit Earth's fashion scene. A designer who was already a household name on Akrellia.

Ilyan and Nirgal avoided Claire and Thrax while they were in Groom Lake, but me and Subject 34 spent all the time we could with them in their temporary housing facility, allowing us both to get well acquainted with them, their precious babies, and the details of their own unusual stories and life on Hierabodos V.

I hoped my family could visit them one day on their home world. Perhaps I might even feel comfortable enough to bring Ilyan along, though *he* might not feel that degree of comfort. If not, I would never force him to accompany me. It was enough that Subject 34 and Thrax were now as close as their kind could be to each other. Neither was very social, but Thrax had learned to be more comfortable around people and even had an extensive list of true friends and allies now, and my 34 had made me and my mates his family and had even managed to form tentative friendships with some of the workers in the medical center.

Everything was going wonderfully in our lives as my due date neared, and we all anticipated the birth of my two sons. There remained only one dark cloud over our happy little family, and that was the uncertainty of Ilyan's fracture.

One day, when Ilyan was the one home with me, he cornered me as I was leaving the shower. Though I felt like a blimp, hauling around a lot of extra belly without much extra anywhere else on my body, despite my high calorie diet, he still looked at my naked form with hunger in his eyes.

My mates' desire for me would never cease to amaze me, yet I'd looked at myself in the mirror lately and I didn't recognize the woman looking back. She looked more beautiful than I could ever recall being before I was abducted. My skin glowed, my hair had a luscious shine and fullness to it despite the sprinkling of gray, my eyes sparkled, even though crow's feet crinkled at the corners of them. My body felt firmer and more toned from all the bedroom activity, even when I had been a little fluffier before my pregnancy.

Most importantly, I wore an expression of true joy that made my smile bright and lifted all my features, changing what had once been a rather average appearance into something beautiful. I had blossomed from the love of my mates, and they had helped me to fall in love with myself as I got to see myself the way they saw me.

Ilyan's hunger matched my own as he caught me by the hips, yanking my towel away from me to toss it on the floor. He pushed me towards the bedroom, and I didn't hesitate to bend over the edge of the bed, groaning a little as the position relieved the pressure on my lower back.

Then I was groaning for another reason as he buried his length inside me without ceremony. His hands rubbed over my naked body, unconcerned with the drops of water left behind from my shower as he thrust into me from behind.

Then he suddenly froze, only his shaft twitching as he stood behind me.

"Why didn't you tell me, Rhonda?" he said in an odd tone.

Alarmed by his behavior, I pulled away from him, his erection slipping out of me as I crawled onto the bed and turned around to face him.

He stared at me with a betrayed look in his eyes, the dilation of his arousal constricting until his eyes were green, but not the warm green I was used to. They had hardened as he regarded me, as much as his expression did.

"Tell you?" I asked breathlessly, shaking my head in confusion.

"Why didn't you tell me what my fracture did to you?" he said, this time in an outraged tone. "What he used *my* body to do to my queen?" He pointed at his chest, still wearing a shirt, though he'd pulled his pants down to free his erection and now they crumpled around his ankles, seemingly forgotten by him, even though his shaft had gone flaccid in his obvious distress.

"Why would you keep such a thing from me?"

I climbed to my knees, moving towards him with my hands reaching for him, but he took several steps away from the bed. "I'm so sorry, Ilyan! I didn't want to hurt you or upset you."

"*Upset* me?" His tone remained outraged, but I detected his feeling of betrayal beneath it. "You kept something this huge from me because you think I'm too weak to handle being 'upset' by it?"

My eyes widened with my shock. "What? No! Ilyan, it's not like that!"

He bent to grab his pants and jerk them back up to fasten them around his lean waist. "Do you know, I'm being flooded with memories now from my fracture. Some of them are true nightmares, and some are... enlightening. But nothing I'm recalling comes close to the painful realization that you let him hurt you using my body and never once told me about it. You never even hinted that he'd done something like that to you!"

"Ilyan," I whispered, even more shocked by his revelation that he was recalling more of what his fracture had done, "I didn't tell you at first because I knew you would be angry at yourself, because he *is* a part of you. Besides, there was nothing you could do about what happened. Nothing that could change it. And, besides, I ended up...," I bit my lip, not sure how he would take my confession, "liking it."

I watched him warily, feeling very vulnerable kneeling on the bed naked, my belly bulging in front of me, my breasts heavy and sore, my stretchmarks adding to the map of life experiences that marked my skin as clearly as Nirgal's stripes marked his.

He turned his face away from me, his jaw ticking. His fists clenched at his sides as his wings tucked tightly against his back in a defensive posture.

"You *liked* it?" he ground out. "When he scraped you without your consent?"

I shrugged helplessly. "I mean, it was without warning, but I wouldn't say it was without my consent. Honestly, I was excited enough that I would have told him yes, even if he explained what he was about to do first. It was uncomfortable—maybe even painful, yes, but the overall experience was... exhilarating, and I wanted more." I cocked my head as I studied him, trying to gauge his reaction to what I was saying. "Do you not recall how excited I was during that encounter?"

He gave nothing away in his expression, but his defensive posture didn't relax. "You were frightened. That's what I recall."

I shrugged my shoulders, trying for a nonchalance I definitely didn't feel. "I've been frightened before and still greatly enjoyed myself, Ilyan. I don't want my mates to be too hesitant to chase their own pleasure with my body, for fear that I won't enjoy it too."

"You are our queen, Rhonda!" Ilyan finally turned to look at me, his eyes pinning mine. "We can never hurt you."

I crawled closer to him, until I balanced on the edge of the bed. "Ilyan, you said you would never hurt me, unless I *wanted* you to." I reached for his shirt and caught a fistful of fabric.

He let me tug him closer, his arms sliding around my waist, my belly keeping me from pulling him against my naked body.

"I liked what your fracture did to me, Ilyan," I whispered against his lips. "I wouldn't mind if he did it again."

He pulled his head back, staring down at my face as his eyes began to dilate again. "I don't think he and I are separated anymore, Rhonda. This flood of memories... I think they've come because I am healing. Being with you, being accepted by my mate, it's cured me of my fracture." He slowly shook his head. "I wasn't even sure that was possible until now."

"So," I said, my heart leaping with happiness at this news, and hope that he was correct, "does that mean Evil Ilyan is now a part of you again?"

His mocking grin was answer enough before his lips claimed mine.

FORTY-THREE

I do not want to ever relive that childbirth! It wasn't the pain of my contractions, or the complications caused by the distress my precious little monster felt during labor that caused his stingers to eject. Fortunately, his venom glands weren't fully developed yet so no one got hurt, including his twin brother.

Yes, those things were stressful, as was the C-section I ended up having due to the difficulty giving birth to the two hybrids. But what caused the greatest problem was dealing with my three spastic mates, all of whom panicked almost the entire time I was in labor until I wanted to ban them from the room. Going into surgery for the C-section ended up being a relief since the three of them weren't all allowed in there.

Instead, my mother sat beside me, holding my hand.

Yep. My mama.

If you had asked me before I was abducted whether my mother would be with me during the birth of her two alien hybrid grandbabies, I would have called you crazy, or asked if I could have some of what you were smoking.

Ten years after I disappeared from the face of the Earth, I

reunited with my parents, who were getting on in years, but you could hardly tell since they had also undergone rejuv treatments. Their reaction to seeing me again, heavily pregnant, near bursting, and a little sheepish and uncertain as I met them at the arrival terminal, told me that I'd never been fair to them in my complicated feelings towards them, and it was time to make up for that.

We cried as we hugged, and they were remarkably unjudgmental when they met my mates, including Subject 34, who seemed more nervous about their reaction to him than I was. I should have realized that they would embrace the strangeness of my new life with enthusiasm. After all, they'd always believed that I was unique and special and had a destiny that would be far from ordinary and mundane.

I realized now that they'd never meant to put pressure on me to live up to that belief and that their words to me had always been intended to encourage me and guide me, not push me to be someone they could brag about.

Knowing how I felt about the lives growing inside me was what finally convinced me to contact them. They'd already been contacted by the liaison to inform them I was alive and safe, but I'd requested not to be connected to them until I could settle into my new home with my new family. At the time, a reunion with my parents seemed like too much to deal with after just arriving on Earth with ten years gone, after being through what we'd endured, and while trying to adjust to my new family life.

My decision had hurt them, but they didn't bring up that pain or try to make me feel guilty for it when I finally saw them again.

My parents had lived through not only the mysterious abduction of their only child by a strange man at the hardware store, never to have closure during the ten years that passed, but also through a Menops invasion that had devastated our planet and decimated a good portion of the population, followed not long after by a terrible plague that had claimed more lives.

They had suffered greatly since I'd been taken, and I could see the roadmap of that suffering in the lines on their faces. Yet now they were all smiles to be reunited with me and discover that they had two unique and unusual grandbabies on the way.

The C-section went smoothly, and the first squalls from my sons were music to my ears. My mom cried tears of joy and relief as they sealed me back up, using tech far more advanced than I would have had ten years ago, so my healing time would be far less.

Which turned out to be good, because even with the help of three mates and my parents, my babies were a handful, even in their first few weeks of life!

Still, every once in a while, we all found the time to have a nice family dinner together while my sons slept peacefully in their nursery. Little Eshkar, who DNA tests revealed to be Ilyan's biological child though he looked human save for the pointed ears, and Oro, who had four arms like Thrax's sons and his own pair of stingers, didn't share the same crib for safety reasons, but when they were awake, they always wanted to be together, seeming to find comfort in each other's company. Their closeness was a relief for me, as I didn't want to have to separate my sons too often. I wanted them to be close like the rest of our family.

"I saw Michael before we came here," my mother said in a low voice to me after a well-deserved peaceful family meal. "Did you know that he visited us many times throughout the years, hoping that we'd learned something about your whereabouts?"

I raised my eyebrows in surprise, glancing at my mates in the kitchen, demonstrating the fancy food processor to my dad, who looked suitably impressed. Impressed enough that my mom would probably get one for him for Christmas, which was coming up in a few months.

Our new home, which was still under construction, would also have a top-of-the-line kitchen, just like this temporary housing.

Honestly, it had turned out to be a lot longer than temporary, but by now, we'd made many friends and the community we lived in would be a lot more comfortable with Subject 34 living among them unfettered since they'd had plenty of time to get to know him.

"I guess he did care about you, Ronnie," my mom said, bringing my thoughts back to the conversation at hand, "though I honestly never forgave him for what he did to you. I hated him for hurting you, especially after you disappeared. I blamed him because I believed you never would have talked to that strange man if you hadn't had your heart broken by Michael."

My mouth dropped open as I stared at my usually very calm and upbeat mother using an almost vitriolic tone. Then her expression softened as she also glanced at my mates, her gaze following Subject 34 as he made his way to the nursery to check on our sons.

"Michael was never good enough for you," she said, returning her gaze to me. "He didn't deserve you, but I didn't want to chase you away by telling you that you could do so much better. Instead, I chased you away for a different reason. I'm so sorry you believed that all we cared about was appearances. We never wanted to squeeze you into a box. We tried too hard to keep that from happening to you because we thought we were being supportive. In the end, we only ended up putting pressure on you, and your father and I regret that more than anything. Then Michael came along and shoved you into a box to please him, and we couldn't say anything about it, because it was your choice and we wanted to respect that."

"I'm sorry too, Mom. I should have realized that you only wanted the best for me, instead of thinking I wasn't living up to your expectations."

My mother shook her head, lifting a hand to brush my hair away from my face, a gentle smile on hers. "Wisdom sometimes comes at a high price, Ronnie. Regrets, on the other hand, are free and still aren't worth it. I don't want to waste another moment of our lives wishing I could go back and fix the past. Your father and I have decided that we want to live for the future." Her smile broadened into a grin. "And what an exciting future it is!"

I nodded, taking her hand and squeezing it with all the love and affection I was now freely able to feel for my parents. "I do too, Mom. I want to live for tomorrow. But I also won't let today pass without appreciating every moment of it. I spent too much time waiting for something I could never quite define before. Now I've found it, and I'm going to cherish it for as long as I live!"

My gaze shifted from my mom's face to Subject 34, who reentered the living room, carrying one of my sons in each set of arms, his facial plates open and an expression of awe on his face that I knew I would have to add to my many sketches of my mates. I grinned as my Iriduans stopped speaking to my father in mid-sentence to rush to 34's side to coo over their sons.

My guys sometimes fought over who got to hold the boys, which meant I also had to put my foot down at times, just to cradle my babies in my own arms. Ilyan had told me in an aside that the solution to the problem was to make more babies, so we all had one to cuddle at the same time.

I'd threatened to slap him upside the head, much to his

amusement, but then he'd cornered me in my room and preceded to work on making his suggestion a reality.

I was so happy that sometimes I wondered how I made it through each day before I was abducted and met my mates. I wondered how I could have ever believed I was content, when a part of me hadn't even been awakened yet.

Now, I truly felt alive, surrounded by love and companion-ship that my introverted self never would have dared to imagine before.

I had my family, a career that fulfilled me, and friends both near and far, and all of it gave me the inspiration that made my art vivid and compelling, when it had always been lifeless before.

EPILOGUE

The hardware store had been demolished even before the Menops invasion, but I still decided to visit the spot where it had once stood. I thought about the two young women who had been taken with me that day when I was abducted and felt a great sadness that they'd yet to be found by any of the organizations out there in the wider galaxy that worked to find and free slaves.

Even the creepy Iriduan pirate bitch and her equally creepy mates were never found, though Nirgal had given as much information as he could about them. They'd worked for the Iriduan government, a job that was apparently compulsory after the pirate woman was taken prisoner for crimes she'd committed previously. The empire had no intention of aiding the Akrellians or humans in locating their own agents.

I hoped those women had found the same kind of happiness I had, or at least some situation where they were content and safe. I feared that they hadn't, but there wasn't much I could do about it, other than continue to donate paintings to Akrellian organizations for their fundraisers in the hopes that the money they earned would someday go towards the operation that brought those women home.

The entire block where the hardware store had once stood had been demolished as well, so it was now little more than an empty debris field. A lot of places on Earth looked like this now, but humanity was slowly rebuilding, with help from the Akrellians and even the Bigfoot-looking aliens called Ultimen. We didn't have those in our settlement, since their governments didn't typically persecute political dissidents.

Despite the condition of the buildings, vehicles still skimmed past above the road at my back as I walked from one end of the hardware store's old foundation to the other. The road condition was terrible, but the flying cars were now a thing, so it didn't matter anymore.

One of those cars turned around after zooming past me, then sped back in my direction. I looked up in concern as it came closer, but it didn't leave the boundaries of the road. It came to a standstill, hovering several feet off the ground, and the top of the vehicle lifted.

"Ronnie?" Michael said, his mouth an O of surprise, his eyes nearly as round and wide open. "Is that really you?"

He looked his age, though he had probably had at least one rejuv treatment, and I didn't think the past years had been all that kind to him. Like my parents, he had been through a lot while living on Earth during the dark times. I supposed I had some sympathy for him on that. His family had survived, and I was thankful for that. I didn't want anyone to lose a loved one, not even someone who'd hurt me so deeply in the past. Far too many people on Earth had endured that already.

I waved. "Hey, Mike. How you been?"

"How...?" He blinked stupidly at me. "Is that all you can say, Ronnie? After all this time?"

It was my turn to look surprised. "Excuse me?"

He climbed out of his vehicle and approached me, and I noted with some satisfaction that his body had grown far fluffier than mine had been when he'd bitched about it during our marriage. Stress was a bitch, and so was karma.

"You just disappear on us, you're gone for ten years, while all hell breaks loose on Earth. Only after things calm down, do you show up again, out of the blue, happy as a clam, looking like you've gone back in time ten years instead of getting older, and all you can say when you see me is, 'how you been?'"

I regarded him speechlessly as he poked his own chest. "I worried about you every day, Ronnie. I wondered where you'd been taken. What had happened to you? My guilt ate at me, and it caused a rift in my marriage. My wife even left me and took the girls. All because I couldn't stop thinking about what had happened to you!" He gestured to me. "And now you're here, looking better than you've ever looked before, and you act like nothing ever happened."

I pursed my lips tightly, my gaze raking from his feet to his thinning hair. "Oh, something definitely happened, Michael. You dumped me after I spent twenty years taking care of you as a loyal and devoted wife so that you could move in with your side chick who didn't have to put up with your dirty socks and skid-marked underwear and lackluster bedroom performance. Then, I got *abducted* and tortured and held captive, and you have the nerve to act like I've been away on a freakin' vacation this whole time?"

I lifted my chin, feeling like I was channeling my Iriduans with all their arrogance as I looked down my nose at Michael, even though he was taller than me. "Don't you *dare* put the blame for your life falling to shit at my feet, Mike. I've been your excuse for far too long. It's time to start blaming yourself for your life's failures."

"Ronnie!" Mike cried as I turned my back on him to make

my way towards the pile of debris where my vehicle was parked out of sight of the road. "Wait!"

He grabbed my shoulder to spin me back around, and I quickly jerked out of his grasp, my heart pounding as I shook my head. "Don't touch me, Mike." I glanced towards where my vehicle was hidden, studying the shadows formed by debris and toppled walls. "For your *own* sake."

Then I smiled grimly at Michael. "I didn't come here alone. I suggest you leave now. My mate doesn't usually give a warning before he strikes."

I know it's petty, but I enjoyed the way his face paled as he glanced around quickly, then he shot one last look at me before rushing to his vehicle, his belly jiggling as he clumsily ran.

"Rhonda sure I can't kill him?" 34 asked as the vehicle sped away.

My heart lifted as I turned to see my mate appear from a cluster of shadows nearby, his hard black eyes regarding the vehicle as if he considered giving chase.

"I would rather you didn't." I met him midway to stroke my hand over the chitin plates covering his chest. "He's not worth the paperwork we'd have to fill out in the event of an 'incident'."

He shifted his gaze to me, his forbidding expression lightening. "Nirgal and Ilyan can track him. 34 can kill him quietly. No one will know."

I laughed, shaking my head firmly. "What am I going to do with you, 34?"

His eyes took on a different look as his gaze trailed down my body. "34 has suggestions."

AUTHOR'S NOTE

If you made it this far, thank you SO much for reading the latest book in my Iriduan Test Subjects series! You have no idea how much it means to me to share my worlds and stories with such awesome readers.

I really hope you enjoyed this story. I know that the reverse harem trope is a departure for the series, and I understand that it isn't everyone's cup of tea. I try to remain consistent with a series when it comes to MF versus RH, but some characters have a story that involves multiple partners, and this story just so happened to be one of them. At this time, the only other RH I plan for this series will be Ava's story, which I have already made clear will be RH, so for those fans who prefer only MF romance, don't worry, the series isn't changing permanently! This book was a one-off in that respect (other than Ava's ;) It's coming, it's coming! I swear! :D)

Because this story was a bit of a departure from the series, I am really nervous about how it will be received. The idea for this story came to me when I wanted to do some things in the first book of this series that I ultimately didn't do, because I wasn't sure how it would be received. One of those things was to address the fate of the villain, Ilyan. I'm a sucker for a villain redemption story, though I suppose this one isn't necessarily a redemption, but I felt like it would be fun to give him his own HEA. I've had plans to bring him back into the series since I "killed him off" in the first book.

Another motivation for this story was that I really loved Thrax's character design, and I wanted to write another character with many of the same traits and characteristics as him. I loved writing his character and his transformation from heartless killer to empathetic lover. This time, I don't give Subject 34's perspective in order to keep my readers guessing throughout the story. I chose this very narrow point of view (only Rhonda's) as a way to immerse my readers and leave them as uncertain and off balance as the heroine during her story. I know that many readers of romance love to look inside the heads of the heroes to see what they think about the heroine, but in this case, I wanted to show that through their actions, dialogue, and body language instead of simply telling it by exposing the thoughts of Subject 34, Nirgal, and Ilyan.

I hadn't planned on writing this story when I did, though I always had plans to return to the Iriduan experiments on the athraxius. While I was working on Shulgi's story, I got this intense desire to write another athraxius story, and I ended up writing both books simultaneously. I felt inspired by this story, just as I did by Shulgi's. I can't always explain why this happens—why stories take hold of me like they do and push every other work in progress aside. I know it is probably frustrating for my fans who are waiting patiently for other books. I appreciate you all for your patience and understanding!

I do have other books in the works. I don't want to mention any details at this point. I like to wait until my projects are close to completion before dropping details. I will say, yes, I definitely DO want to write Ava's story and soon. I just can't make promises yet because I don't want to disappoint anyone by failing to meet them on time.

I have some things going on in my personal life in regards to health that are throwing me a bit for a loop, but I'm still making an effort to get to the keyboard every day and work on something. I expect that this disruption will only be temporary, and I'm looking forward to being able to focus fully on my stories again.

I love to create these worlds, characters, and stories, and I am immensely grateful for all your support that allows me to do this for a living! Thank you a thousand times over!

Stay tuned to my social media (I know I'm really slow to post, sorry!) and be sure to follow my newsletter for exclusive sneak peeks and updates.

http://eepurl.com/gudYOT

Thank you all again for taking the time to read my book.

You can also follow me on my Facebook page:

https://www.facebook.com/The-Princesss-Dragon-343739932858

Or you can check out my blog:

https://susantrombleyblog.wordpress.com/

You can also drop me a line at my email addy:

susantrombley06@gmail.com

Bookbub: https://www.bookbub.com/authors/susan-trombley

Goodreads: https://www.goodreads.com/author/show/3407490.Susan_Trombley

Amazon author page: https://www.amazon.com/Susan-Trombley/e/B003A0FBYM

Book Links:

Iriduan Test Subjects series

The Iriduans are up to no good, determined to rule the galaxy by creating unstoppable warriors using monstrous creatures found on their colony worlds. Can the courageous heroines captured by the Iriduans to be breeders to these monsters end up taming them and turning the tables on the Iriduans themselves? This is an action-packed science fiction romance series where each book features a new couple, though there is an overarching storyline in addition to each individual happily-ever-after.

The Scorpion's Mate
The Kraken's Mate
The Serpent's Mate
The Warrior's Mate
The Hunter's Mate
The Fractured Mate
The Iriduan's Mate
Into the Dead Fall series

Ordinary human women are abducted by an enigmatic force that pulls them into a parallel universe. They end up on a world that is in the aftermath of a devastating apocalypse and is now just a vast, inter-dimensional junkyard. There they will encounter alien beings from many different dimensions and discover the kind of love they never imagined, forming a life for themselves out of the ashes of a lost civilization. This series is an exciting reverse-harem, post-apocalyptic alien romance that introduces beings from many different worlds and includes a mystery that spans the entire series, though each book ends on a happy note.

Into the Dead Fall
Key to the Dead Fall

Minotaur's Curse

Chimera's Gift

Veraza's Choice

Shadows in Sanctuary series

The humans of Dome City have been raised to view the horned and winged umbrose as demons, but when their separate worlds collide, these brave heroines must face the truth that nothing is ever what it seems. Can love alone bridge the divide between human and umbrose and put a stop to the tyranny of the adurians, who are the enemies of both? This futuristic science fiction romance series features a new take on the demon/angel paradigm on a world where humans have forgotten their origin, but still cling to their humanity. Each book features a new couple and can be read as a standalone with an HEA, though there is an overarching story throughout the series.

Lilith's Fall

Balfor's Salvation

Jessabelle's Beast

Fantasy series—Breath of the Divine

When a princess is cursed and transforms into a dragon, she falls in love with a dragon god and sparks a series of events that plunge the world of Altraya into grave danger. Myth and magic collide with the cold ambitions of mankind as those who seek power will do anything to get it. The dragon gods work to stop the coming danger, but it might be the love of a human woman that holds the key to the salvation of the world. This fantasy series features a different couple in each book and a satisfying ending to each story, but there is also an overarching story throughout the series.

The Princess Dragon
> The Child of the Dragon Gods
> Light of the Dragon

Standalones or Collaborations

The well-known story of Rapunzel gets a science-fiction twist in this fairytale retelling featuring an artificial intelligence and a plucky princess determined to prove herself to be much more than a pretty face. This is a futuristic science fiction romance that introduces a new universe where humans live on colony worlds after being forced to flee a deadly AI on Earth centuries prior to the story.

Rampion

Children of the Ajda

Guardian of the Dark Paths

Made in the USA
Monee, IL
05 October 2022